182

Their Story Grows...

The Brands. Each is a descendant of Zebulon or Jeremy, brothers and bitter rivals. With their deaths, a new epoch unfolds, and Rebecca Brand—once the reigning belle of Washington society, now a mother and grandmother—sees the family tree spread its branches across a continent, as the borders of America itself expand westward.

They will be in Texas when the Alamo falls...serve as confidants and friends to President Jackson...fight against the silver-tongued politicians in the marble halls of the American Palace. And always, as the Brand legacy commands, they will heed no other voice but the calling of their hearts...

VALIANT HEARTS is their story, it is our story, and it is one of the most magnificent stories ever told...

"Superbly researched . . . as informative as it is entertaining . . . *marvelously readable fare.*"
                    Jennifer Wilde, author of
                    Once More, Miranda

By *Evan H. Rhodes* from Berkley
THE AMERICAN PALACE series

BOOK 1: *Bless This House*
BOOK 2: *Forged in Fury*
BOOK 3: *Valiant Hearts*

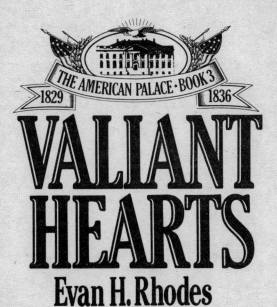

THE AMERICAN PALACE · BOOK 3

1829 1836

VALIANT HEARTS

Evan H. Rhodes

BERKLEY BOOKS, NEW YORK

VALIANT HEARTS

A Berkley Book/published by arrangement with
the author

PRINTING HISTORY
Berkley edition/July 1983

ISBN: 0-425-05969-3

For Rena Wolner

Preface

THE WHITE HOUSE ... nowhere in all the world is there a
more dynamic symbol of man's unending struggle to achieve
freedom.

When the cornerstone of the building was first laid in October, 1792, the mansion was called the American Palace. In
1810, the name, the White House, first came into popular use.
But no matter what the name, the mansion has always been
imbued with an almost mystical significance, for in this house
that belongs to *all* the people, lives the *one* man they've chosen
to lead them.

Even as the blocks of Aquia sandstone were being fitted
into place, fortune decreed that one American family would be
forever involved with the White House, and with its occupants:
Jeremy Brand, the dreamer, the builder, who gives his life for
the mansion; Zebulon Brand, his brother, the adventurer, the
opportunist, his life and lusts figured with violence; and the
beautiful, ambitious Rebecca, beloved by both men, a woman
whose intelligence and patriotic passion serve as conscience to
the new nation. Together, they found the Brand dynasty.

Swept along with the Brands, we're plunged into the tur-
bulent history of this country, all seen from the vantage point
of the most powerful office on the face of the earth—for decisions made in the White House affect all our lives.

Working in and for the government, or ministering to the
Presidents, the Brands have a perfect opportunity to experience
not only the greatness of our leaders, but also to discover their
secret human side. We learn the answers to these questions:

Which President defended a known adulteress, an action
which almost brought down his administration?

Which President, after being defeated for a second term,
was elected to Congress and served his district for more than
fifteen years, winning such admiration from his fellow legis-

lators that he was called "Old Man Eloquent"?

When was the first attempt made to assassinate a President, and who was that President?

Which President threatened to hang a senator?

Which President, in an effort to keep everybody happy, refused to commit himself on most issues, and because of his political acumen was known as "The Little Magician"?

As the generations of the Brands multiply and prosper, and as their involvement with the nation and the White House grows ever more complex, more questions will be asked and more answers revealed.

Which President had the most children—fifteen in all?

Which President had a dream that prophesied his murder only three days before it happened?

Which First Lady taught her husband to read and write?

Which President admitted that he sired a child out of wedlock, yet nevertheless was elected to the highest office in the land?

Which President was so in love with his wife that he wrote passionate letters to her every day of his life?

Which First Lady acted with such a strong hand during her husband's debilitating illness that she was called Madam President?

Which President and his wife had a love relationship so passionate that they were always breaking their bed in the White House?

Which First Lady ran the White House as though it were a military camp and furnished the rooms in a style that became known as "early Holiday Inn"?

Which President was reputed to have the strongest libido of all forty Presidents?

Which President was first to fall victim to the dread curse leveled against the White House? What was that curse, and will its evil portents be visited on the current occupant in the White House?

All this, and more, will be revealed in this book and in the subsequent books of the continuing saga, *The American Palace*.

And now Book Three, *Valiant Hearts*, continues where Book Two ended, with Andrew Jackson's election, his adoring mob wrecking the White House, and Rebecca Brand, seeing her daughter Suzannah elope with a frontiersman Rebecca loathes, suffering a stroke that could prove fatal.

"There are two things I regret most not having done while I was President . . . I should have hung John Calhoun and shot Henry Clay!"

ANDREW JACKSON

THE BREECH-BRAND FAMILY TREE

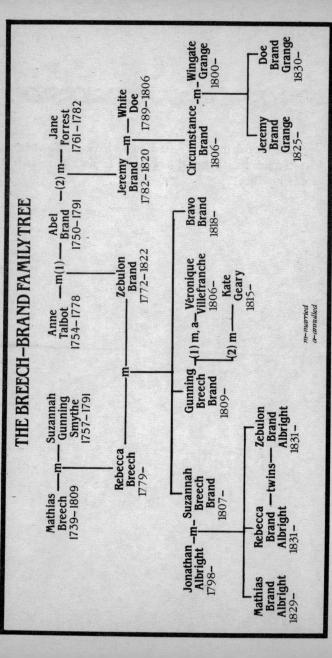

PART ONE

Chapter 1

SUZANNAH BRAND'S hand trembled as she dipped her handkerchief into a pitcher of cold water and applied the compress to her aching eyes.

Letitia clucked sympathetically when she entered Suzannah's bedroom. "You been crying again, ain't you?" she said. "Look at them eyes. All red-rimmed. A body'd think you was a hundred 'stead of nigh onto twenty-one."

"Oh, Letitia, what am I going to do?" Suzannah whispered to the maid.

Letitia took Suzannah in her arms and stroked her hair. "That ain't nothing I can tell you. No ma'am, that's only for you to decide. But I can tell you what I been saying since you was a little girl: Listen to your own heart. And not your mother's neither. That Devroe Connaught, maybe he is the richest man in these here parts, and maybe he is the biggest catch, like your mother says, but I never trusted nobody with weasel eyes and them thin lips. Looks just like his father, Sean Connaught, and you knows how much trouble our family had with *him*. But you got to make up your own mind, and that's all I've got to say about that."

Rebecca Brand called up the stairwell of the Federal-style house. "Suzannah, will you hurry? We don't want to keep Devroe waiting when he gets here."

Letitia screwed up her face and shook her ample frame. "Cold wind passes over my heart every time I hears his name. You mother fusses and frets over him like he was some kind of prince."

"Well, in England, his family is considered nobility," Suzannah said, sighing.

"Well, this ain't England. This here's the United States of America, and we beat them British in the Revolutionary War

3

and beat them again in that there War of 1812. So why don't
that Devroe just go home?"

Suzannah stood up and straightened the long skirt of her
pink cambric dress. Usually the soft pastel shade heightened
the color of her lustrous dark brown hair and her wide-set brown
eyes, but this morning, the drabness she felt deep in her soul
clouded her innocent beauty. She opened the doors of her
armoire and reached for a woolen cloak.

"Take this one here," Letitia said, handing her a heavier,
fur-lined cape. "Apt to be cold today."

Suzannah felt a wave of fear at the sight of her trousseau—
dresses, and gowns, and riding outfits, and nightclothes that
had kept the seamstresses of Washington sewing for months.

"I can't believe the wedding is this Saturday," she murmured. "Oh, if only I had more time to think, to decide."

"I know it," Letitia said. "Six months ago, why I thought
this day would never come. Now here it is Wednesday, and
March the seventh's creeping up on us and no way of stopping
it."

Suzannah pressed her fingertips to her temples. "If only
Jonathan had written! Just one letter. Then maybe..."

Jonathan Albright, a young aide to General Andrew Jackson, had been a suitor for Suzannah's hand. Two years before,
in 1827, Suzannah had been ready to marry this tall, gangly,
volatile young frontiersman, to go off to Nashville with him.
But Rebecca, who'd always had a strong aversion to Jonathan,
collapsed when she discovered Suzannah's plan. Fearing to
aggravate her mother's condition, Suzannah had agreed to wait—
over Jonathan's strenuous objections. Though Jonathan promised to write, she never received any communication from him,
nor had he answered any of her own letters. Then through
Devroe Connaught, Suzannah heard a rumor that Jonathan had
gotten married in Tennessee. The news cast her into a terrible
despondency, and only Devroe's constant attention had eased
her anguish. When Devroe pressed his suit, Suzannah managed
to keep him at bay for a year. But then Rebecca had lent her
formidable pressures to the match, and finally Suzannah had
agreed to marry the austere Englishman.

"I wish I could be sure that Devroe truly cared for me,"
Suzannah said. "Oh, he couldn't be more attentive, but that
isn't *love*. He could have his pick of any of the heiresses in
Washington, so why me?"

Letitia rubbed her worn hands together. "Lot of bad blood

once flowed between the Connaughts and the Brands. Sometimes I think . . ." She broke off, not wanting to worry Suzannah unnecessarily.

Letitia had been in the Breech-Brand family for more than sixty years, as far back as she could remember. She'd first been a slave to Mathias Breech, then had become maid to his daughter, Rebecca. Some seven years ago, Rebecca had freed Letitia. But knowing no other kind of life, Letitia had chosen to stay on with her mistress.

Letitia clasped Suzannah's hands and her eyes grew moist. "I loves your mother, you knows I do. Set me free she did. But it ain't fittin' for her to make you marry that Devroe." She leaned forward conspiratorially. "You listen to me, Miss Suzannah. This afternoon, after the inauguration of this here Andrew Jackson, you be going to the White House, won't you?"

Suzannah looked at Letitia, not quite understanding what she was getting at. "Every newly inaugurated President has an open house at the White House."

Letitia nodded. "Right, and when you gets there, I want you to—"

"Suzannah, where are you?" Rebecca called up the stairs. "Devroe's carriage is here."

Gunning Brand, Suzannah's nineteen-year-old brother shouted, "If you don't hurry, we're going to forfeit our place at the ceremonies."

As Suzannah flung her cloak lined with stone marten over her shoulders, she said to Letitia, "You want me to what?"

"No time for that now," Letitia said. "Just keep your eyes open when you gets to the White House. Now not another word, or your mother will skin me alive."

Downstairs, Rebecca Breech Brand paced the spacious entrance hall of her substantial brick house. When she married Zebulon Brand twenty-two years before, she had insisted that they build their town house in the best area in Washington— not that there was much of anything in Washington in those years save the fetid, miasmic swamps of the Potomac, and forests teeming with game. But she'd studied Major Pierre L'Enfant's plan for the capital, and had astutely chosen a large lot on New York Avenue and Eighteenth Street. The Brand house stood nearly opposite the Tayloes' mansion, known as the Octagon House, and was also within sight of the White House. Rebecca believed fervently in the new nation, believed that it would grow beyond anybody's wildest dreams—and when it did, she wanted to be close to the seat of power. And the seat of power was the American Palace, the White House.

As she waited impatiently for her daughter, Rebecca's face and figure belied the fact that she was about to be fifty years old. Her figure was still trim, her waist nipped, her bust high. Her skin had lost little of its radiant luster, her hazel eyes had grown even more intelligent-looking with years of experience, and only her titian hair, now streaked with strands of gray, gave evidence of a half-century of vibrant living. In her youth, she'd been the acknowledged beauty of the District of Columbia, a beauty who had inflamed, among others, the Brand brothers, Jeremy and Zebulon. But Rebecca had also been afflicted with a keen, discerning mind. When neither her father nor her husband allowed her to use that mind in aiding them with their business or financial affairs, Rebecca had found secret release by writing political tracts under the presumably masculine pseudonym, Rebel Thorne. Except for her maid Letitia and Joseph Gales, the editor of the *National Intelligencer*, nobody knew Rebel Thorne's identity. Which was fortunate, for in the last election campaign, Rebecca had written scathing articles against Andrew Jackson. When Jackson was elected over John Quincy Adams, he'd sworn revenge against those who'd so bitterly opposed him, and the name Rebel Thorne was high on his list.

"There you are at last," Rebecca said, as Suzannah came down the stairs. She regarded her daughter appraisingly. It's extraordinary, she thought, how much like her father Suzannah looked. In Zebulon, however, the winged brows and the sensual mouth had taken a hedonistic, brutish turn. But Suzannah's beauty was something at once naive and mysterious.

"You look lovely," Rebecca said. Then she looked more closely at Suzannah's eyes, and knew that she'd been crying again. But she made no mention of it. Come Saturday, her daughter would be safely married to Devroe Connaught, and Rebecca would breathe easier about Suzannah's future.

Gunning bounded in from the dining room, munching a strip of bacon. In his navy velvet longcoat, ruffled white shirt, and fawn-colored trousers, he cut a dashing figure. He wore his thick thatch of red-blond hair fashionably long, and his sideburns reached down to his jawline. He favored Rebecca in coloring and appearance, and was handsome enough to be in constant trouble with the wenches in every tavern in Washington, Alexandria, and Georgetown.

Ten-year-old Bravo Brand scampered up from the basement, where he'd been tinkering with one of his devices. He didn't look much like Rebecca's other children. His hair was almost white, and his startlingly blue eyes were inquisitive, yet somehow remote. His boundless energy kept him busy from morning till night. Already, he'd dismantled every mechanical object in the house and put them back together again—most of them, anyway.

"I'm ready," Bravo said, his engaging face wreathed in a broad smile.

"I told you that you couldn't go with us," Rebecca said to him. "There isn't enough room in Devroe's carriage."

"Besides, Devroe doesn't believe that children should accompany adults," Gunning said, as he cuffed his brother. The blow landed a bit too hard, and Bravo reeled away. Then he came at Gunning, but Gunning held him at arms' length.

"Will you two stop that?" Rebecca said. "I've never seen two people fight the way you do."

Gunning gave Bravo a final punch on the arm that brought tears to the boy's eyes, but he fought them back. The moment Gunning saw the pain on Bravo's face, he felt sorry. For the most part he liked his brother, yet there were times when his old, pent-up anger surfaced . . . Tanzy's pruning shears might have been the weapon that killed his father, but Bravo had really been the root cause of his death, and Gunning had never forgiven him for that.

Bravo slipped his hand into Suzannah's. "I wish you weren't going to marry Devroe."

Suzannah hugged Bravo—she had almost the same wish herself.

Rebecca herded Suzannah and Gunning outside, where the black-and-gold Connaught coach stood waiting. Sisley Urquhart, Devroe's liveried footman, helped them into the gold-velvet interior, where Devroe Connaught sat waiting impatiently.

"Do hurry," he said. "I've sent my slave Ebon ahead to the Capitol to secure our place, but I don't know how long he can hold it. There's quite a mob in Washington."

Rebecca sank back into the plush, upholstered seat. Her heart was palpitating at an alarming rate, and she tried to control her uneasiness. "I think it's somehow appropriate that this inauguration falls on Ash Wednesday," she said with a tight smile. "Mark my words, we'll live to rue the day that Andrew Jackson was elected."

"It is indeed a day for sackcloth and ashes," Devroe said, as the carriage proceeded toward Pennsylvania Avenue. "I hear rumors that Jackson intends to destroy the Bank of the United States. If he does, we'll have nothing but financial ruin."

Devroe Connaught smiled at Suzannah, and she smiled back. For the moment her fears were calmed—he was such a perfect gentleman, with superb manners, and always so impeccably dressed that he put every other man to shame. He had a high forehead, thinning hair of a color somewhere between blond and brown, and watery blue eyes. He'd been educated at the finest schools in England, and his clipped, precise speech was a beautiful thing to hear. He couldn't have been more attentive to Suzannah, yet she could never get over the feeling that she didn't know him, that no matter how much time they spent together, she would never get to the heart of the man. Suzannah tore herself away from these melancholy thoughts as she heard her mother warm to the subject of Jackson's character.

"Can you imagine a man living in the White House who's fought upwards of fourteen duels, and murdered two men?"

"But mother, they *were* duels," Suzannah said, feeling somehow that in defending Jackson she was also defending Jonathan Albright. "Duels that were fairly fought."

"Murder is murder," Rebecca responded. "When Aaron Burr killed Alexander Hamilton in a duel, that forever ended Burr's hope of becoming President. The same thing should have happened to Jackson, but instead, the rabble elected their hero."

"My sentiments exactly," Devroe cut in. "When the reins of government are indiscriminately given over to the common man—to the lowest common denominator of society, as it were—then a government is well on its way to decay. Surely you agree with that, Suzannah."

Suzannah clutched her hands together. "No, I don't. And Mother, I remember when you didn't think that way either. If we're to be a true democracy, then everybody's voice should be heard. Doesn't Andrew Jackson, who's received the highest number of votes ever tallied, really represent the will of the people?"

"Only because the voting franchise has been broadened to include all the riffraff," Rebecca said.

"Yet for most of your life you've fought to have the franchise broadened to include women," Suzannah said softly. "Are we to embrace democracy only when it suits our own ends?"

Devroe's lips thinned into a bloodless line, and Rebecca, sensing his annoyance, quickly changed the subject. "Gunning, why is it that you're not in uniform?"

"Because General Jackson insisted that he didn't want an honor squad to accompany him to the Capitol or to the White House." Gunning had recently joined the President's Honor Guard, an army unit formed originally by General George Washington to serve the President. Gunning had been looking forward to participating in the pomp and ceremony of the day and felt extremely put out that his privileged position had been taken from him.

Gunning slapped Devroe on the thigh. "How I envy you the trip to the Continent, you lucky dog! Are all the arrangements made?"

Devroe tensed against the familiarity. "To be sure," he said, masking his annoyance behind a smile. "We've the best cabin aboard the *Magnificent*, sailing from Baltimore. The moment the services are completed at St. John's Church, we drive posthaste for Baltimore, then set sail with the tide. They say the *Magnificent* is the fastest ship afloat and can cross the Atlantic in less than five weeks."

"Extraordinary how everything is speeding up these days," Rebecca commented.

"A little too fast for my tastes," Devroe said. "But Suzannah, when you see the Connaught estates, I know you'll experience the true meaning of a family history that stretches back almost a thousand years."

Suzannah smiled wanly, but could think of nothing to say.

"From there you go to Paris?" Gunning asked.

"What would any honeymoon be without Paris?" Devroe responded. "I can scarcely wait to show the city to you, my dear." He patted Suzannah's hand.

A pity you'll never see it, Devroe thought, as the carriage turned onto Pennsylvania Avenue and headed toward the Capitol. The damp March air was still edged with winter, and patches of snow lay in the fields. The people heading toward the inauguration were dressed warmly. But Devroe saw little of that; his mind was on the honeymoon voyage. Once Suzannah was his, the blood feud that had existed between the Connaughts and the Brands would be balanced once and for all. If only these fools realized it, he thought. Even the redoubtable Rebecca had been taken in. But then, what could one expect from a stone merchant's daughter with pretentions to rising in society? No matter how fine a table she set, no matter how often she was invited to the White House, no matter what position she claimed in Washington society, in England, among the aristocracy, *his* aristocracy, Rebecca would be considered nothing more than a member of the merchant class, a small step above a servant.

But to gain his end, Devroe had worked his charms with caution and skill. Zebulon Brand had been responsible for the death of Devroe's uncle, after whom he'd been named, and for the consequent madness of his uncle's wife, Elizabeth. Seduced by Zebulon, cast aside, then witness to the horrifying murder cf her husband, that poor woman still haunted the halls of the Connaught plantation in the hills above Washington. As if those outrages against civilized society were not enough for one family, the younger Brand brother, Jeremy, had had an affair with Marianne, Elizabeth's daughter; and on the battlefield at New Orleans, through cowardice and deceit, he had killed Devroe's own father, Sean Connaught.

Though both Brand brothers were now dead—damn their souls!—surely their crimes against the Connaughts cried out to heaven for vengeance. And the gods had seen fit to place Devroe in a position to exact that vengeance. In his mind's eye, he saw what would transpire while he and Suzannah were crossing the Channel from Dover to Calais. A moonlight walk on the deck, a sudden push over the rail, and Suzannah would be swallowed by the dark waters. A pity it had to be this way, for he'd even grown a bit fond of the simple girl. But as always with the Connaught clan, family and honor came before all else. And honor demanded retribution against these murderers, these criminals, these rejects of Europe, these Americans, these Brands.

With Suzannah gone, he would return to America the grieving widower, allow a year or so to pass, and then complete the ruin of Gunning. As for Rebecca's younger son, Bravo, there would be time enough to plan something for him—a crippling accident, maiming, or possibly blindness . . . yes, Devroe liked those possibilities. Such plans gave focus and shape to his life. He would mete out justice, and the Connaught honor would be avenged. Only when all the Brand children were either dead or crippled would Devroe reveal his true purpose to Rebecca. But he would allow her to live, so that every moment for the rest of her life she would suffer the agony visited upon her children, regret the day that she'd ever crossed the Connaughts.

Gunning's voice interrupted Devroe's reverie. "I say, Dev, have you ever seen such a mob? Look at them! I understand that more than thirty thousand people have jammed into Washington. There isn't a hotel room to be had anywhere, all the taverns have run out of liquor, and people have set up tents and blanket rolls in the open fields."

"All to pay homage to their hero," Rebecca said, a note of derision in her voice. "If only they realized the truth."

"What is the truth, Mother?" Suzannah asked quietly.

"Don't you know that Jackson's wife Rachel was a bigamist?" Gunning said. "She ran off and married Jackson, even though she hadn't yet been divorced by her first husband, Lewis Robards."

Rebecca shook her head with annoyance. "I care nothing about those charges. Rachel was convicted, true, but she and Andrew had made an honest mistake. They did remarry when Robards finally secured a divorce. What better testimonial to their love than that they've lived together happily for more than thirty years? No, I'm talking about Jackson's response to anybody who disagrees with him. Why, the man has fought fourteen duels, cut, maimed, and wounded twelve opponents, killed two. What if a legislator disagrees with such a hothead? Will he suffer the same fate as Jackson's other victims?"

Gunning half-rose out of his seat. "Look, isn't that Jackson walking up ahead?"

They leaned out the carriage windows, straining to see. Sure enough, Rebecca caught a glimpse of Jackson; that shock of unruly white hair could belong to no other. He wore a tall hat with a ten-inch mourning band around it. Rachel had died two months before—a victim, Jackson claimed, of the vicious, slanderous presidential campaign.

Rebecca studied Jackson. Though he was sixty-one and in poor health, as he marched along Pennsylvania Avenue in military cadence, his posture remained ramrod straight, and his attitude one of total command. Seeing his long face, craggy features and piercing blue eyes, Rebecca couldn't deny the President-elect's appeal, and she regretted the circumstances that had pitted them against each other.

"Why is he walking in all this mud and snow?" Devroe sniffed.

"Something of a conceit," Rebecca said. "Jackson wanted to emulate Thomas Jefferson, a man of the people. And Jefferson walked to his inauguration."

"Who are those derelict old men marching alongside Jackson?" Devroe asked. "I've never seen more disreputable uniforms."

"Those fifteen men are the surviving heroes of our revolution," Gunning said.

"But you said that Jackson didn't want an honor guard," Devroe recalled.

Gunning nodded. "Those men presented themselves to him with the claim that since they were too old to fight, they really didn't represent a guard. Jackson didn't have the heart to refuse them."

When Devroe's carriage finally arrived at the Capitol they found that his slave Ebon, a giant black, had managed to save a space for them. An impenetrable crowd jammed the grand steps, preventing Jackson from fighting his way to the inaugural platform that had been built at the top of the steps. He ducked into a doorway on the lower level of the building, and finally appeared on the platform above. At the sight of him, the mob broke into a rousing cheer that lasted for several minutes. Jackson bowed to the crowd and then raised his hand to still them.

For an instant, Suzannah thought that she recognized a familiar face among the aides that surrounded Jackson, but then she lost the face in the crowd. It's only your imagination, she thought wistfully. You're too old for such romantic fancies; reality is this man standing beside you, and the wedding on Saturday.

Andrew Jackson began his inaugural address, and to Rebecca's surprise it was marked chiefly by its blandness. He mentioned the problems of patronage, promising to overhaul the system. In regard to federal power versus states' rights, he advocated a just respect for the rights of the individual states— a conciliatory gesture to his Vice-President, John Calhoun, the leading spokesman for the South.

If ever a man had been favored by the gods, it was John C. Calhoun of South Carolina. He was tall and imposing, with dark hair, piercing dark eyes, and a magnetic personality that at once inspired fear and awe. Considered the most intelligent politician in government, he was expected by everybody, including John C. Calhoun, to be President one day.

Then Andrew Jackson's address was over.

Chief Justice John Marshall, dressed in a black robe and carrying a Bible in his hand, stepped forward. Though Marshall was seventy-four years old and somewhat feeble, his mind was still vigorous.

Rebecca's admiration of the Chief Justice of the Supreme Court was unalloyed. He'd been a friend for most of her life, had married her and Zebulon, and had instructed her on how to proceed with her divorce from him. "What an extraordinary effect Marshall's had on our government," she said. "He's officiated at the inaugurations of Thomas Jefferson, James Madison, James Monroe, John Quincy Adams, and now Andrew Jackson."

"I think it's time he retired and made way for a younger man," Gunning said.

Rebecca shot her son a baleful look. "You should thank God for Marshall." She cast her mind back through the years. In 1807, at Aaron Burr's trial for treason, Marshall had established the supremacy of the Supreme Court over the legislative and executive branches of the government in interpreting the Constitution: He ruled that no man, not even the President of the United States, was above the law, and forced President Jefferson to submit evidence that the court had subpoenaed. Without Marshall, the government might have been saddled with an ineffectual court, which could have easily given way to a despotic chief executive—the very thing she feared most in Jackson's ascent to the presidency.

A hush fell over the crowd as Jackson prepared to take the oath of office.

Chapter 2

JACKSON'S VOICE rang out as he repeated after Chief Justice John Marshall: "I do solemnly swear that I will faithfully execute the office of President of the United States, and will, to the best of my ability, preserve, protect, and defend the Constitution of the United States."

Jackson then raised the Bible to his lips and kissed it.

Suzannah winced as an old soldier shouted in her ear, "It's done! Old Hickory's President, by God!"

Then the crowd surged forward. They broke through the ship's cable that served as a barricade and rushed up the steps to the inaugural platform, eager to lay their hands on the President. They pulled and tore at him, snatching buttons off his jacket. Jackson fought his way down the long flight of steps to get to the horse his aides had waiting for him. It took him an interminable time, stopped as he was at every step by adoring well-wishers.

At last Jackson reached his horse; he mounted, and with the mob clutching at his stirrups, rode toward the White House. The crowd streamed after him, in carriages, wagons, carts, and on foot. The crush of people carried Devroe's carriage along with it. As she watched, Rebecca felt a pulse of fright at the uncontrollable power of these thousands upon thousands of people. On such a frenzied crest had Napoleon come to power, and with such support from the rabble, a President could easily become dictator. Jackson's admirers were wearing necklaces made of hickory nuts, carrying canes and brooms of hickory, were riding on horses with saddles of hickory bark.

"We might as well go to the White House and see how Andrew Jackson handles this mob," Gunning said gleefully; the tumult surrounding them was bringing out the wide wild streak in him.

"Jackson forever! Hurrah for Jackson!" came the shouts

14

from the crowd. "I'll never forget this day as long as I live!" yelled an octagenarian from Missouri who'd made his very first trip to Washington. The mob took up the chant. "Jackson's President! The White House is ours!"

"This is madness!" Rebecca cried, as the carriage was carried along like a piece of flotsam in the tide of humanity. Don't go to the White House, she thought, it's far too dangerous; someone is certain to get killed this day.

But she had other things to consider—her secret career as the pamphleteer Rebel Thorne. That career, which gave direction to her life, had prevented her from going mad over injustices that women had to suffer. Her writing also acted as a safety valve for her volatile and patriotic nature. When the British invaded Baltimore in 1815, in the Second War for Independence, Rebel Thorne's fiery newspaper articles had roused the lethargic, defeatist Baltimoreans, and they'd fought off the invaders. Thereafter, Rebel Thorne's voice was heard on every major issue confronting the new nation. Presidential elections particularly concerned her. And though she was frightened of this unruly mob, she still had enough of the reporter in her to want to see how the day's events would end. So she allowed herself to be swept along with Devroe and her children to the White House.

In the splendid and spacious East Room of the President's mansion, Circumstance Brand Grange was putting down the last trays of cakes, ice cream, and orange punch on the groaning serving table.

"There's enough food here to feed an army," she said to her husband, Doctor Wingate Grange.

The couple, in their midtwenties, smiled at each other. Though they'd been married nearly six years, they still acted like newlyweds. Circumstance, the daughter of Jeremy Brand and a Shoshone Indian named White Doe, had inherited the best traits of both her parents. She had the long sable hair, angular face, and high cheekbones of her mother. Her eyes were a legacy from her father—a startling aquamarine, they further accentuated her exotic looks.

People were automatically drawn to Wingate, a lean man of medium height, with curly brown hair and sparkling brown eyes; his smile made acquaintances and even patients want to smile back. Born in a part of Maine still hotly contested by

both the United States and Canada, Wingate had been impressed into the British navy at thirteen. His father had been
a physician, and since Wingate came to the calling naturally,
he served as assistant to the fleet's doctor. He was aboard the
British armada when it invaded the Chesapeake in the War of
1812, and tended Jeremy Brand when he was taken prisoner.
Wingate saved Jeremy's life, and later, having escaped the
British, the two fought side by side at the Battle of New Orleans. When the war was over, Wingate came to Washington
to visit Jeremy. He worked with him on the construction of the
White House, earning enough tuition money to attend Georgetown University. After Jeremy's death in a horrible fall from
a scaffold at the White House, Wingate persuaded Circumstance to marry him. They had one child, a son they named
Jeremy.

Circumstance and Wingate had been working since dawn
along with the rest of Andrew Jackson's family and staff to get
the mansion ready for the open house. Jackson, true to his
promise that his would be a government of the people, had
invited absolutely everybody to the reception.

When Jackson arrived in Washington three weeks before,
Wingate had gone to Gadsby's Inn to pay his respects to the
general. Jackson remembered Wingate and his healing hands
from the Battle of New Orleans, and greeted him warmly. But
when Wingate introduced Circumstance to him, Jackson's face
hardened. He had immediately spotted her Indian blood. Living
on the frontier, in constant danger from Indian massacres, he
had an eye for such things.

Wingate quickly told Jackson that Circumstance was Jeremy
Brand's daughter. That placated him.

"Your father was a brave and good man. At the battle for
New Orleans, we owed him a great deal. Any child of his is
welcome in my house, at any time."

"Thank you, General," Circumstance said. She knew about
Jackson's treatment of Indians, and realized that she had to
tread very carefully in order to attain her ends. She disliked
doing it, but in this case the goal was more important than false
pride. "General, as you know, my father helped build the White
House. Shortly before he died, he was compiling a record of
this mansion, a history that could be left as a legacy for the
people. Since his death, I've taken over that task."

"A legacy for the people?" Jackson repeated. "I like that

Vaughan said. "If Mexico retains Texas, it and the land we claim in the Oregon Territory will give us enough control to thwart America's expansionist dreams."

"I've already indicated to the Mexicans that Great Britain is ready to help her in any way she can."

"Good," Vaughan said. "I'd no idea you'd progressed so far with this situation."

"Something is going on in this country that may prove even more fertile for our interests," Devroe said. "It's a response to the heavy tariff bill Congress passed last year. The southerners call it the Tariff of Abominations, and threaten to secede unless the law is nullified."

Vaughan raised his eyebrows. "I'd heard such rumblings. Do you believe them?"

Devroe nodded. "The southern states find themselves in a very difficult economic position. Since they do very little manufacturing of their own, they must import most of their goods, primarily from England. The northern states, to protect their infant manufacturing industry, have forced this abominable tariff through Congress, thereby hiking up the price of everything that the South imports."

Vaughan stroked his jaw. "Then this tariff hurts England also, doesn't it?—since it makes northern goods artificially competitive with ours."

Devroe nodded. "It's in Great Britain's best interests to have this tariff repealed."

"And where does Andrew Jackson stand on all this?"

"One never knows with these unpredictable Americans, but he was born in the South, he owns slaves, and he's known to be sympathetic to the states-rights cause. If the South should secede, it's not inconceivable that Great Britain could once again establish her supremacy on this continent."

"Would that we could live to see that day."

"Well, we shall do what we can to sow the seeds of discontent among the states," Devroe said with a half-smile.

"Ah, the age-old adage: Divide and conquer," Vaughan said. "Do you have anything specific in mind?"

"I do, and I'll begin to implement my plans just as soon as I return from my honeymoon on the Continent," Devroe said. "Speaking of which, I do think that I'd better find my wife-to-be."

• • •

In the Grand Entrance Hall, the crowd pushed and shoved as they bunched up at the doors leading to the other rooms. A constant pressure was kept up as tens of thousands of people on the lawn pushed harder, determined to get inside "their" house.

A woman beside Suzannah fell in the crush and screamed. A child was nearly trampled underfoot, and Suzannah snatched her up and gave her back to her mother. Glasses and china were smashed to the floor, and one stately matron had her dress ripped off her back by a farmer's hickory rake.

To get a glimpse of President Jackson, people began to climb onto chairs and sofas. Two riverboatmen from Kentucky hopped onto Dolley Madison's pier table, which crashed under their weight. The elegant French furniture that the James Monroes had imported, including the crimson damask sofas and the masterpieces of Bellangé's chairs, were reduced to kindling. Muddy boots slipped on vanilla ice cream and orange punch. Some of the crowd found their way upstairs to Jackson's private quarters. A little girl jumped up and down on his horsehair sofa, shrieking, "Mamma, Mamma! Just think, this sofa is one millionth part mine!"

With faltering step, Suzannah fought her way into the East Room; she thought that in the large room she might find a safe corner. She caught sight of Andrew Jackson standing near one of the fireplaces, a cordon of his aides surrounding him.

John Eaton, the senator from Tennessee whom Jackson had just named his Secretary of War, stood at the President's side. Beside Eaton stood his wife of two months, the notorious Peggy O'Neale Timberlake Eaton, a woman surrounded by such scandalous gossip that most of the matrons of Washington society refused to acknowledge her, much less entertain her in their homes.

And then Suzannah saw him—almost at the same moment that he saw her. His face lit up and he started to fight his way toward her. She blinked, but there could be no mistake. Nobody else had those wide scarecrow shoulders, that tumble of unruly brown hair that wouldn't be tamed. "My God," she whispered, "it's Jonathan!"

Jonathan Albright reached for Suzannah, but a rollicking sailor stumbled between them, pressing a jug of whiskey at her. Jonathan pushed him aside, and when the sailor persisted, grabbed him by the scruff of the neck and propelled him away. Then he positioned Suzannah in a corner and stood with his back to the crowd, protecting her.

"I love you," he said.

"Don't say that, please don't," she begged. "Will you never cease breaking my heart?"

His dark eyes searched her face. "I love you," he repeated insistently. "Why didn't you ever answer my letters?"

"But I never got any letters!" she protested. She didn't dare believe him, yet she felt her pulse quicken as it did whenever she was in his presence. "I wrote to you, but I never got an answer."

"How can that be? I never received a one."

"But I did write! I gave them to our stableboy, Tad, and—" She broke off, then exclaimed with sudden recognition, "Mother! She must have intercepted them. But what of your wife?"

He looked at her blankly. "Wife? I'm as free a man as the day I left you in Washington. Who told you I was married?"

"Devroe Connaught."

"Oh, that slippery, lying bastard!"

"Devroe said that his lawyer met you in Nashville and you were with an attractive woman."

"Who?" Jonathan was puzzled. "Oh, I know! That must have been Emily Donelson. But she's happily married to Andrew Jackson's nephew. There they are, standing next to the general. Damn that Devroe for spreading such a lie! Listen to me, Suzannah. Do you love that man?"

"The wedding is set for this Saturday. All the arrangements are made."

"Do you love him?" he demanded.

"I don't know. When you didn't write, he was so kind, and I thought I might get to..." Her voice trailed off, then she shook her head firmly. "No! No, I don't love him."

He scooped her into his arms and tried to whirl her around, but they were bumped by the crush of people. "Come away with me," he said. "Right now."

Her hand flew to her mouth. "But I couldn't do that. What of my family? What of Devroe? What of Mother?"

"You saw what happened the last time you let her dictate to you. We'd have been married going on three years now, had a couple of children. Oh my darling Suzannah, I love you so much I feel as if the good Lord has opened my heart again."

He kissed her then and she gave herself up to his warm embrace, feeling the press of his hard, sensuous lips, his strong muscular arms around her. How different from Devroe's formal

embrace. Devroe had woven a silken web of manners and form
around her, but Jonathan, with his sheer physical presence,
had swept it all away. At that moment, she knew in her heart
that she would never love anybody but this tall, rangy, homespun frontiersman.

When he released her she whispered, "What are we going
to do? How can I go with you this instant? I don't have any
of my things with me."

"Letitia's packed a small bag for you. Everything you'll
need is in my saddlebags."

"Letitia?"

He grinned broadly. "She knows. What's more, she's been
planning this with me ever since I got back to Washington.
She said to tell you, 'Listen to your heart.'"

Suzannah shuddered in confusion and he gripped her hands.
"I've got two horses waiting for us just beyond the White House
grounds. It's your choice. You can ride to your mother and to
Devroe Connaught, and the safe life that they offer, or you can
take your chances with me. I can't give you any of the things
he can—Paris, a fine house, jewels. But I swear I'll love you
like no other man on this earth. Love you every minute of my
life, and with my every heartbeat until the day I die. Will you
come?"

"But aren't you still on President Jackson's staff?"

He nodded. "And the general will have a fit when he finds
out that I've gone. But you're worth it. He did a few things
for love in his day."

"But mother and Devroe! They'll find us. I'm still not yet
twenty-one. She can force me to come back. Don't you see?
She has the law on her side."

"Thought of that already. That's why we're leaving the
United States. We're going to Texas to join up with a man
named Stephen Austin. He's founded a colony of Americans
there. Sam Houston's told me all about it and even thinks he's
going to settle there himself someday soon. Now they tell me
there's not much of anything where I've written in a claim for
some land—just a little Spanish mission called the Alamo. But
we're going to get away from the long arm of your mother."

"You mean go right this minute? Without telling her?"

Jonathan's jaw set. "I'm not taking any chances on losing
you again. She's a mighty strong woman, capable of doing
just about anything to hold you. Suzannah, you've got to decide. Is it your life or hers?"

"Suzannah?" Circumstance Brand Grange called out excitedly when she saw her cousin and the familiar figure of Jonathan Albright. She pushed her way to where they were standing. "Suzannah, what—"

"Oh, Circumstance, if only you knew—" Suzannah began.

Circumstance looked from Suzannah to Jonathan. "Don't say anything. Not another word. Just go. And don't tell me where, or I know your mother will force it out of me."

Circumstance and Suzannah had been friends since they were children. Several years before, Circumstance had urged Suzannah to go off with Jonathan, but Rebecca's illness had prevented that. Circumstance not only disliked Devroe Connaught, she distrusted his motives. The feud between the Connaughts and the Brands ran too deep for Devroe suddenly to have forgiven everything.

Circumstance kissed Suzannah on the cheek. "If you love Jonathan, then go. Right this very minute. What you decide now will set the course for the rest of your life. Your mother will survive. Hasn't she always survived?"

At that moment, Andrew Jackson cried out. The crowd had pressed so close around him that he was in danger of being crushed.

"Clear some space, give him air!" Wingate shouted. "Can't you see he's ill?"

But the mob had one thought only, to lay hands on its hero. They forced Jackson against the wall, and he started to breathe in heavy gasps.

"Over here, help!" Wingate shouted to Sam Houston and John Coffee. "Quick, before the general is smothered!"

A band of Jackson's aides, including Jackson's friend and portraitist, Ralph W. Earl, formed a ring around the President and fought their way to one of the tall windows in the East Room. Circumstance went to join them. With a sharp jab, Wingate shoved his elbow through the pane, then kicked out the entire sash. Wingate, Sam Houston, and Ralph Earl lowered the half-fainting President out the window and down to the grass.

"Quickly, get him back to Gadsby's Inn," Wingate ordered. "We can lock the doors at the inn and I can treat him there."

Jonathan and Suzannah made their way to the smashed window where Sam Houston was still standing. "The President's gotten away, thank God," Houston said. "This mob is maniacal!" Then Houston looked at Suzannah admiringly. "Jonathan told me you were beautiful, but I didn't expect anything like this."

Suzannah blushed furiously.

Jonathan took Suzannah's hand. "I'm waiting for your answer."

But Suzannah couldn't bring herself to speak.

Sam Houston said, "Jonathan, are you sure you know what you're doing? You know that Jackson will explode when he finds out that you've deserted him. If you stay with him in Washington, you could probably have any job you wanted."

"This is what I want," Jonathan said, drawing Suzannah close to him. "Sam, this is the only way I know how to make it work. I know you'll be able to smooth things out for me with Jackson."

Sam Houston barked with laughter. Then he shook his shaggy mane of hair. "If that's what you want, who am I to stand in the way of love? Miss Suzannah, I know you're far too good for this young lout, but let me say a few words in his defense. When we fought the Creeks at Horseshoe Bend, this man was my good right arm. During the Seminole Wars in Florida, the general and I came to depend on him like no other scout. He's the best I ever met, a sharpshooter that could rival Davy Crockett, and he doesn't know the meaning of the word fear. Pray God that I never have to fight in another war, but if I do, I'd want Jonathan Albright fighting alongside me. I know that may not sound like much of a recommendation for a husband—but then, marriage is a little like war!" he finished with a big grin.

Suzannah laughed also, warmed by the genuine honesty of these two men. Then she heard her name being called. She looked past Jonathan and her face turned pale.

Jonathan turned then and saw Rebecca and Devroe fighting their way toward them. Devroe, his face livid with anger, flailed his riding crop about him, beating a path.

Jonathan gripped Suzannah's arms. "You've got another second or two at the most. Your life, or hers?"

With a tiny cry, Suzannah took his arm and pulled him toward the window through which Jackson had escaped. Jonathan vaulted onto the ground, and reaching up, caught her as she dropped into his arms.

Rebecca screamed, "Stop that man! He's kidnapping my daughter!"

She and Devroe fought to get to the window. But by the

time they reached it they saw Suzannah and Jonathan galloping along Pennsylvania Avenue, heading west.

Rebecca clutched her throat, fighting off a dizzy spell. "He's nothing but a common criminal," she gasped. "He must be caught."

Devroe's lips compressed into a tight, bloodless line. "Consider it done, Mrs. Brand. My men will start after them immediately. They won't get far. My horses are the fastest in these parts, and my dogs are the best trackers."

"He kidnapped her," Rebecca repeated over and over.

"To be sure," Devroe said curtly.

"There's no reason that the wedding can't take place as scheduled—" Rebecca was grasping at anything to hold her crumbling world together.

"No reason at all," he responded. "Unless, of course, the blackguard has a chance to—well, you do remember that the Connaughts have always insisted that their brides be chaste." With a perfunctory nod at Rebecca, Devroe started to leave.

"I'll go with you," she said.

"Absolutely not. You would only slow us down." He didn't want her there when he captured Suzannah and her paramour. Their meeting might provide the perfect opportunity for him to exact his revenge. A stray bullet would be blamed for Suzannah's death. "No, Mrs. Brand, I must go alone, but I'll report to you the moment we bring Suzannah back."

When Devroe had gone, the press of people in the East Room became so unbearable that Rebecca moaned and struck out at them. Then a bright waiter had the idea of carrying out the food and the punch bowls, and the greedy crowd followed the waiters out onto the lawn.

With the room emptied somewhat, Rebecca stood in the center of the parquet floor. Her feet felt so leaden she could barely walk. She looked around her; the grandest room in the American Palace had been wrecked. As she surveyed the damage, it seemed that everything she'd ever worked for, every dream she'd ever had—of a secure family, a decent intelligent government—had been snatched from her.

Gunning, involved with Véronique Villefranche, a fortune-hunting trollop. Suzannah kidnapped. The White House wrecked by a lawless mob. Even the President had had to flee for his life! How could the country possibly survive?

The blood began pounding in Rebecca's head. She felt herself grow faint with the onslaught of another of her attacks, only this time it felt like an iron first closing around her heart. Does God mean me to die at this lowest ebb of my life? she wondered. Is this my punishment for everything I've caused to happen? And what will happen to my children? Alone ... defenseless ...

"No, I won't die!" she screamed inwardly. "I must save Suzannah!"

She saw Circumstance approaching her and lashed out, "You knew about this all the time! Tell me, where's Jonathan taking her?"

Circumstance shook her head. "I knew nothing about it, nor do I know where they're going." She wanted to say more, to tell Rebecca to leave her daughter alone, let her find her own happiness, but she saw how desperately ill she was. She reached out to steady her as Rebecca swayed on her feet.

Rebecca pressed her hands to her pounding temples, trying to contain the surging blood that threatened to overwhelm her. "I must live, I will!" she cried out as the darkness engulfed her.

Chapter 3

REBECCA REGAINED consciousness in intermittent stages that were figured with darkness and light. Slowly, she began to understand that an entire day had passed. Her own room, the luxury of her tall fourposter, the fresh white linens on the pillows and the featherbed, the sun filtering through the subtle floral chintz at the nine-paned windows, all made her feel safe, but vaguely confused.

She turned her head at the sound of shuffling feet and saw Letitia moving toward her, her dark face heavy with concern. Letitia sighed with relief when she saw that Rebecca's eyes were open.

"Oh Lord, how we prayed and prayed," Letitia said in a singsong. "And the good Lord, he must've listened, 'cause you come to yourself at last. Now you stay right there, cause I'm sending Tad to fetch the doctor back."

An hour later, Wingate Grange arrived. "This has turned into some inauguration," he said to Rebecca. "First Jackson collapses, and now you. Well, at least you're conscious; you weren't the last time I was here." He examined Rebecca, poking and pinching her feet and hands, and sometimes even hurting her. When that elicited her sharp response he nodded agreeably. "Good, good. Your temples aren't throbbing, your heartbeat is considerably slower and steadier, so you don't need to be bled. I can't find any paralysis anywhere—"

"Thank the Lord," Letitia interrupted.

"And so I don't think you've had a stroke," Wingate finished.

With that, Rebecca tried to raise herself on the bed, for the recollection of all that had happened overwhelmed her. "Suzannah! Where is she?"

"We haven't heard anything yet," Wingate said. "Circumstance told me all about it. Said that Devroe has collected some

27

of his men and has gone after Suzannah and Jonathan."

"I've got to..." Rebecca tried to get out of bed, but the effort proved too much for her, and she sank back. "Oh, my God, the wedding," she said weakly.

"Circumstance is taking care of it. She's talked to Reverend Hawley at St. John's and postponed everything."

Rebecca clutched the coverlet, feeling a sinking sensation in her chest. She said in a low voice, close to tears, "Thank her for me, Wingate, will you?"

He nodded, then placed a jar on the nighttable. "She sent you this calf's-foot jelly, and wants Letitia to brew some camomile tea—says it will calm you. Now I want you to rest easy; I'll be in to see you tomorrow." He turned to Letitia. "Don't let her get out of bed. And she's to have no excitement, do you hear?"

"No excitement is all right by me, but you'd best tell her that yourself."

As she lay abed the next day, Rebecca fretted. Not hearing news of Suzannah was driving her to distraction. By the end of the day, she'd forced herself to get up and walk about. When Gunning came home from duty at the White House, she said to him, "You must go after Suzannah."

"Mother, what good would that do? Devroe and his men have a two-day start on me."

"Then why haven't we heard anything?" she asked sharply.

"Jonathan Albright is as slippery as an Indian. But Devroe will get him." He saw the look of distress on his mother's face and sat down on the bed. "Mother, you know I'd go, but Jackson's refused to give anybody leave. Not until he has the capital in order again." He stood up.

"Where are you going?"

"No place in particular. Thought I'd join some of the men in my regiment down at Rhode's Tavern."

And then you'll be off to see that hoyden, Véronique Villefranche, she thought, but she didn't have the strength to take him to task about that. It would have to wait for another time.

Gunning, she thought. Of all of her children, surely he was the most complex, capable of making her laugh as no one else could, but also capable of a self-centeredness that could hurt her cruelly. Only Zebulon had been able to contain him, for both of them had tempers like summer storms; when Zebulon died, Gunning had been left adrift.

• • •

Some hours later, Rebecca, wandering around Suzannah's room, discovered that several of her personal possessions were missing—a silver hairbrush and mirror that Zebulon had brought back from one of his shipping ventures, and a cameo pendant that had belonged to Rebecca's mother. Rebecca became suspicious and confronted Letitia.

"It had to have been planned. Somebody must have helped her."

"Now don't go exciting yourself," Letitia stammered. "You heard what the doctor—"

"Never mind about that!" Rebecca rasped. "You knew, didn't you? Answer me!"

Letitia dropped her gaze and nodded slightly. "Yes, I helped that child." Then she looked up at Rebecca, a glimmer of rebellion in her eyes. "And I'd do it again, I would. Because that girl was dying before her time of a withered old heart. If she was happy with that Devroe, she wouldn't have gone. But she's *done* gone, and that's all I got to say about it."

Rebecca's slap caught Letitia across the face, and then she beat at her weakly with her fists. "How! How could you do this to me? Where has she gone? Tell me!"

Letitia stood her ground, trying to contain her mistress while she vented her rage.

"Where has she gone?" Rebecca kept screaming.

"Suppose it won't hurt none to tell now," Letitia said, trying to block Rebecca's windmilling arms. "Jonathan mentioned they's going first to Pittsburgh, then on to Nashville to pack up a wagon and things, then they're heading for Texas."

"What?" Rebecca cried. "And you let her go to that wilderness? What if she dies? Her blood will be on your head!"

Letitia's black eyes widened. She hadn't thought of that.

"Get out of my house, out of my sight, you—you Benedict Arnold! I never want to see your face in here again, never! Get out!"

Fearing that if she stayed she'd only aggravate Rebecca more, Letitia backed toward the door.

Rebecca picked up a small lazy Suzan that Thomas Jefferson had designed for her years ago and hurled it. Letitia ducked and ran.

Hearing the screaming, Bravo bounded up the stairs. When she saw her younger son, Rebecca fought to control herself. Bravo, tall and sturdy for his age, helped his mother to bed, then brewed her the camomile tea that Circumstance had pre-scribed.

Exhausted by her outburst, Rebecca cried herself to sleep. Even Letitia had turned against her. She slept until early the following morning, and got up feeling oddly alert and hungry. She'd always been an essentially healthy person with a magnificent constitution, and now her strength was reasserting itself. She pulled the bellcord for Letitia to bring her breakfast, then remembered that she'd ordered her out of the house. She put on a crisp cotton peignoir and slowly made her way downstairs.

When she got to the kitchen she was startled to see Letitia baking biscuits. Coffee was boiling on the new cast-iron stove, and smokehouse-cured bacon sizzled in the heavy iron frying pan.

"You looks a whole lot better," Letitia said. "Glad to see it. Knew you couldn't manage nothing yourself. You never was any good in the kitchen. If I didn't cook everything and hand it to you, you'd starve."

Rebecca tried to glare at her, but the glare dissolved into tears. She began to tremble and Letitia helped her to a chair.

"Hush now, my Rebecca," Letitia whispered, crooning to her the way she'd done when she was a child. She cradled Rebecca's head. "You know you're the mostest person I love in the whole world. Wasn't for you, I wouldn't have my Tad—he'd a been sold like my other children, to Georgia, to Mississippi, where I'll never see them again. Never meant to hurt you, God knows I'd lay down my life for you. But I couldn't let you do that to my Suzannah, I just couldn't. And you got to forgive me or I'll die."

The two women sat there for a long time, grieving for children lost, holding onto each other until they'd cried themselves out.

Later that morning, despite Letitia's strenuous objections, Rebecca rode out to the Connaught estate in the hills above Washington. She was determined to find out if there had been any news from Devroe. The weather was still brisk, the March winds sang through the pine branches, and pockets of pale blue snow still lay in shaded spots. The air felt sharp in her nostrils, clean and crystal clear, and the view of Washington from this height was nothing short of magnificent.

The Capitol and the White House stood on their respective

rises, joined by poplar-lined Pennsylvania Avenue. Some fine residential houses were built on the grand radial avenues, which were intersected by the grid of streets. Many areas were still forested, but there could be no doubt about it, the capital was firmly entrenched in the District of Columbia, and here it would stay. Across the Potomac, Alexandria was also growing, though the silting of the Potomac had lessened its importance as a port. If the capital had one business, it was government.

When Rebecca reached the Connaught estate, she found to her disappointment that the servants hadn't received any word from Devroe. As she was leaving, a door on the side of the pillared house opened and a quaint doll-like figure, its face carefully made up, beckoned to her.

Rebecca could hardly believe that she was looking at Elizabeth Connaught. Though she ws fully sixty years old, she still comported herself as if she were in her twenties, the same passionate young woman who'd intrigued and seduced Zebulon Brand in his youth.

Rebecca hurried to her, at once drawn and repelled by the painted face. "Have you heard from Devroe?" she asked anxiously.

Elizabeth's forehead creased as she tried to think. "Devroe? Oh, my husband's dead. Zebulon—"

"No, no," Rebecca interrupted. "Not your husband; your great-nephew—Sean Connaught's son, who came from England to live with you. Have you any idea where he is?"

Elizabeth nodded.

"You do? Where?"

Elizabeth drew her into a small sewing room. Ranged around the walls were long panels of petit-point tapestry, all done in the years since Elizabeth had lost her reason. Strange though they were, the embroidered scenes were masterpieces of patience and precision.

The history of Washington paraded before Rebecca's eyes and she stared, fascinated, at the variegated greens of the wilderness it had been in 1792, when they'd first laid the cornerstone of the American Palace. Then she saw a scene on the Potomac River, with two men fighting while snakes struck at one of them—exactly what had happened between Devroe and Zebulon—while a fiery sunset flamed the waters.

"You see here," Elizabeth whispered, "the fire has eaten tomorrow."

"You said you knew where Devroe was," Rebecca said,

trying to pull herself away from the fascination of the tapestry.

"In a moment," Elizabeth said. Her hand clamped on Rebecca's wrist and she drew her along the wall.

Rebecca saw a panel of burning orange and gold flames that engulfed everything.

"That was when the British burned the city. I had to work ever so hard that night, sketching the flames from up here while they turned night into day," Elizabeth said.

Rebecca's heart contracted when she saw the quaint figures on the next panel, but there was no mistaking them. The towhaired man had to be Jeremy, and the dark-haired beauty was Marianne Connaught, Elizabeth's daughter. Lurking in the background, against a forest of masts of the British armada, stood the haughty figure of Sean Connaught. Rebecca remembered the torment that she'd gone through when Jeremy and Marianne had their long love affair, while she suffered in the arms of a husband she no longer loved.

They came to the last, unfinished section of the canvas, with purple and black threads hanging from the incomplete human figures.

"When I'm finished, this will be Sean Connaught," Elizabeth whispered. "And this will be Jeremy. And here's my daughter Marianne, and my Aunt Victoria, and Zebulon. Yes, that's Zebulon. All dead."

Then Rebecca felt a chill as she saw a young girl, her sketched-in features looking familiar. "Who's that?" she said, almost afraid to ask.

"Why, that's Suzannah Brand," Elizabeth Connaught said. "I had a daughter once, Marianne, but everybody says that Jeremy Brand killed her."

"That's not true!" Rebecca exclaimed.

But Elizabeth was no longer listening to voices of this world; her eyes had turned inward, and she moaned, "Dead, they're all dead."

"But why is Suzannah in that section?" Rebecca demanded.

Elizabeth roused herself long enough to murmur, "I heard Devroe say . . ." But then the light faded from her eyes. She sat listlessly, the threads of the unfinished panel trailing from her hand.

Rebecca ran from the room and rode back to Washington. She tried to convince herself that what Elizabeth said was nothing but the chatter of a madwoman. "She's been confined to that plantation for more than thirty years. How can you believe anything she says?"

But the incident so troubled her that by nightfall, she decided that she had to go after Suzannah herself.

"Where you a going?" Letitia cried when she saw Rebecca packing a small canvas bag. "Wingate said you was to rest. I'm going to get him right now. He'll give you what for."

Rebecca hurried to the door before Letitia could reach it. "Now listen to me and don't argue. You're to stay here and take care of Gunning and Bravo. Don't tell Bravo until I'm well gone, or he'll try to follow me. If you hear anything from Devroe Connaught, or if Suzannah should come to her senses and return home, then send Tad after me. Here's where I'll be going." She listed the towns on the stagecoach line that went from Washington to Pittsburgh. "From Pittsburgh I'll take the steamboat to Nashville. I'll leave messages at each of those places in case Tad should come after me."

"I'm going with you," Letitia said. "I can't let you go out there alone in that wilderness with Indians around and the like."

"Letitia, don't make this any more difficult for me. I need you here to run the house. I'll be all right, I promise."

Letitia hugged herself to keep from falling apart. She hadn't dreamed what she'd done for Suzannah would turn out this way. She went to the dresser drawer and took out a small pistol. "I'd best pack this in your bag for you," she said.

At daylight the following morning, Letitia and Tad took Rebecca to the temporary stagecoach station that had been set up opposite the Capitol Building. The stage offered the fastest service to legislators traveling to Washington from all over the twenty-four states. A cow grazed near the Capitol steps, its bell tinkling as it munched and moved.

The stagecoach arrived, the driver bringing it to a stop outside the station. Its horses were quickly changed by waiting stablehands.

Rebecca's eyes drank in every detail of the city at dayspring . . . the lifting light that shone off the buildings of white stone and mellow red brick. She had grown up with this city, grown as it had grown around her, and she loved it with the passion that came from knowing that she, too, had had a small part in contributing to its growth.

I may never see this again, she thought.

The stage came round, and the other passengers climbed in.

"Now you take care," Letitia murmured.

The two women embraced, then Rebecca climbed into the waiting coach. She was determined to bring Suzannah back safe and sound, or give her life to that end.

Chapter 4

FLEEING FROM the White House, Jonathan and Suzannah rode hard toward Georgetown. Suzannah couldn't quite believe that this was happening. She thought of her blue satin gown made for the inaugural ball at Carusi's, and to another ball at the Central Masonic Hall. But here she was, galloping toward the unknown with Jonathan. The thought frightened her, yet the realization that Devroe and her mother might be pursuing her at this very moment made her spur her horse.

As they approached the outskirts of Georgetown, Jonathan slowed to a canter. "We don't want to arouse suspicion."

Georgetown looked strangely empty, its citizenry having already flocked to Washington. Though Georgetown, like Alexandria, was fast losing its usefulness as a seaport as the Potomac silted in, its reputation as the most desirable residential area close to the capital had grown, and many legislators had taken quarters there. Some congressmen and judges had even been so daring as to move their entire families to the charming town—it had most of the amenities that Washington still lacked.

Suzannah pointed to an old brick house. "That house was built by my grandfather, Mathias Breech. Mother still uses it when she wants to get away from Washington. She could get a handsome price for it, but she just doesn't seem able to give it up."

Suzannah fell silent, remembering the time when she, Gunning, Bravo, and her mother had moved into the Georgetown house when her parents had separated. Circumstance lived with them also after Jeremy died in the accident at the White House. Then there'd been that terrible tragedy with Tanzy; Suzannah's father held the colored freedwoman in bondage for many months, claiming she was still his slave, though everybody knew otherwise. When Tanzy's husband, Eli, tried to rescue her, Zebulon bludgeoned him to death. Somehow, Tanzy got hold of a

35

pair of pruning shears, freed herself, and stabbed Zebulon. The wound wasn't immediately fatal, but for her attempt at murder, Tanzy was hung. But then Tanzy's hand seemed to reach up from the grave . . . the pruning shears had had manure on them, and Zebulon was felled with a fatal case of lockjaw. For three weeks Suzannah watched her father die a slow, agonizing death, his muscles tearing themselves apart in his violent spasms. Suzannah never got over the conviction that this was God's retribution for her father's transgressions. Yet she had adored him, loved his garrulous, demanding ways, the excitement he generated wherever he went. How could he have done such a dreadful, dreadful . . . ? Tears formed in her eyes as she stared at the house, as though it might hold the answers to the questions that had so tormented her.

"Don't be sad," Jonathan said. "You'll have your own home soon. Maybe not so fine as that, but I promise you, Suzannah, we'll have a place we'll be proud to leave to our children and grandchildren."

She smiled at him, wanting so terribly to believe him, wanting to leave her old way of life behind, that life of confusions and sorrows.

Once they were beyond the main street, Jonathan picked up their pace. "Knowing your mother, I'd say she's not about to let any grass grow under her feet. She's probably after us right now."

With that, Suzannah spurred her horse and soon outdistanced Jonathan. As she rode, the wind sang freedom in her ears. The miles sped beneath the galloping hooves as they pressed deep into the hills of Maryland. Spring had not yet greened the land, and pockets of snow still patched the meadows and hillsides. Here and there a crocus poked its hardy purple head above ground, a harbinger of all that was to come.

Miles later, Jonathan said, "We can stop whenever you're weary. It's a long way we've got to go."

"I'm all right," she told him. "But Jonathan, I must warn you about Devroe. I think he may come after us too. He isn't a man who likes to be crossed. He considers it an offense to his manhood."

"I've seen the man, taken his measure, and I'm not frightened of him."

"Oh, of course not, I wasn't suggesting that," she said quickly. "It's just that he'll come with his men, and they'll be armed."

Jonathan nodded. He knew she was right, and in this instance it was better to run than to fight.

As the sun waned, the afternoon grew much cooler. "I'm glad I wore my fur-lined cloak," Suzannah said. She smiled when she remembered how sly Letitia had been about suggesting she wear it. She'd known all along, and Suzannah was overwhelmed with a rush of love for her nanny.

They rode well past twilight, then fearing to injure the horses, they stopped for the night at a small farmhouse just south of Frederick, Maryland.

"Glad to see folks about," the farmer's wife said, and she did seem genuinely pleased to see the travelers. "Not much room in the house for you, seeing my youngest has chicken pox, but you're welcome to bed down in the barn."

Jonathan and Suzannah fed and tended their horses. "I never realized you could ride so well," he said.

"Oh, it's something that all the Brands do quite naturally. My father was the best horseman I ever saw, won practically all the races at the track in Washington. I remember a great black stallion he owned called Baal."

"Baal? That's an ornery name for a horse."

"Isn't it?" Suzannah said, while she curried her mare. "Father named it that because he said he always wanted to ride the devil. Now Gunning's named his horse Baal too. Gunning's the best rider and jumper in these parts. Even Bravo, who spends most of his time tinkering with his little inventions, he does himself proud on a horse. But then, nobody rides like Circumstance. When she's on a mount, she seems to be part of the animal."

"Her Indian blood, probably," Jonathan said.

After sharing the simple supper of the farmer and his family—five children ranging in age from four to sixteen years—Suzannah and Jonathan retired to the barn. There was little time for embarrassment or false coyness, and as the night deepened, it got so cold that they had to huddle in the straw to keep warm. They lay staring out the hayloft door, watching the moon move through the frosted sky.

He kneaded her soft, pliable fingers with his own rough-hewn hands. "I swear, Suzannah, I'm going to make the best life for us."

She looked at him through the darkness, seeing his wide bony shoulders, the long muscular line of his neck broken by his prominent Adam's apple, and the craggy, almost gaunt face

that showed he had little time for tomfoolery. He wasn't handsome in any conventional sense, he was far too thin, and most
of the time his hair stood on end like a porcupine's . . . yet he
was the one she wanted, and she wondered at the mysteries of
the human heart.

"You'll see," he repeated, taking her silence for doubt, "the
very best life."

"I know you will," she said. "And I'm going to help. I
realize I don't know much, but I can learn. I'm going to become
the best housekeeper and mother and wife on the Texas frontier!"

She said it with such naïveté that he flung himself back in
the straw and began chuckling.

"Why are you laughing?" she asked, annoyed. "Don't you
believe I can do it?" She clamped her hand over his mouth to
stop his laughter, and he grabbed her fingers between his teeth
and gently chewed on them. When she tried to pull away he
wouldn't let go.

"Stop! You'll wake up the whole farm," she whispered.
"Let me go."

"Never," he said, as he rolled to face her. They stared at
each other for some moments, knowing without words what
must be, then she slowly began to undress.

"Are you sure?" he asked huskily. "We can wait until we
get to the preacher."

She stood up to get out of her skirts, and at last she was
naked. She leaned over him, the dark fall of her hair gently
caressing his face. "I marry you in the eyes of God. I marry
you with my soul. And if ever I betray you, may my spirit be
taken down into the dark places."

He drew her down beside him and buried his head against
her breast. His hands moved over her body as if exploring a
new world. He wasn't an inexperienced man; he'd known many
women in his travels with Andrew Jackson, and in the brothels
of Nashville and New Orleans. But this was something new,
something different, something that he had always expected
would change him when he found it . . . and change him it did.

He experienced her not only as a woman, but as salvation.
Whatever had been denied him because of being an orphan,
suddenly that was in the past, for she was all things to him—
mother, sister, friend, bride—and he knew that the good Lord
had granted him this woman as an act of grace. "From this

moment on, I swear that I'll never, never look at another woman as long as I live."

Suzannah heard his words, but her body heard other, more insistent messages as his hands roamed over her, so gently that he might have been stroking a day-old fawn, his mouth so sweet on her flesh that when finally her nipples were taut, and her body flowing with joy, he entered into her world.

The pain was sharp, and frightening, but of mercifully short duration. And then a new sensation took over, one of fullness, of completion, and she was proud that this bone-hard man had chosen her to love, proud that he thought of her as more than a mere plaything. He would build a life for them—no, they'd build it together!—she thought urgently as she moved faster, harder in rhythm with him, pursuing the dream, tantalized by sensations sweeping through her body, swept to a climax so unendurable for her, for him, that when it did happen she thought surely she was about to die.

Then quiet, a return to a place where they lay dreamily, sharing promises and plans—promises never to be broken, plans made for the ages.

When Jonathan had fallen asleep, Suzannah lay awake, wrapped in wonder. With the secret knowledge of her sex, she knew that she'd conceived, knew it just as surely as she knew that the man who lay sleeping beside her loved her. And the joy of that made silent tears stream down her cheeks. She burrowed in the straw and grasped Jonathan's shoulder. "Thank you, God," she whispered.

Just before dawn, the darkness bristled with the distant barking of hounds. Jonathan sprang up, instantly awake, his ears tuned to the baying that echoed through the hills. He hopped into his buckskin trousers and flung on his shirt. "Suzannah, wake up," he said urgently.

She opened her eyes slowly, and still caught in the memory of the night before, reached for his leg. "Come back to bed. It's still dark outside."

"Listen," he said. "They've tracked us here."

Chapter 5

SUZANNAH HEARD the ululation of the hounds and understood at once. Within moments, she was dressed and ready. He saddled her mare and his own stallion, while she broke through the thin layer of night-ice that had formed on the water barrel and filled their canteens.

Then they were off, wheeling their horses west and away from the pursuing hounds. A few miles later, Jonathan found a stream and led their lathered mounts into it. "It's going to slow us down considerable," he told Suzannah, "but the dogs may lose our scent."

"It must be Devroe," she said with a sinking heart. "He's always talking about having the best tracking dogs on the Eastern seaboard."

"Damn! I wish we could stand and fight, but there must be at least half a dozen dogs, and like as not, as many men."

All that day they rode, stopping only once to let the horses graze and rest, and then they were off again. Keeping away from the traveled roadways, Jonathan led them deep into the wilderness of the Appalachian foothills.

The forest closed in around them, thick stands of pine and evergreen that blocked out the sunlight and chilled the air. A carpet of humus muffled their steps.

"How can you know where you're going?" she marveled.

"I'm no stranger to these paths. Been over them many times before. Now listen, Suzannah, we're going to Pittsburgh first. That's about two hundred and sixty miles from Washington, and as close as I can figure it, maybe two hundred miles away from where we are right now."

"Then we must spare the horses as much as possible," she said.

"Right. They're all we've got, and if something happens to them—well, let's not even think on that. If we're lucky getting

40

over the mountains and all, it should take us about ten days to reach Pittsburgh."

"After Pittsburgh, what then?" she asked.

"We'll take a boat down the Ohio, then up the Cumberland to Nashville, get off there, and load up a wagon with all I own. It's not much, just some furniture that the Jacksons gave me during the years I lived with them, but it'll give us a start. Then there's other things of mine—two rifles, saddles, and the like. Then we head into Texas."

"How long will that take?"

"A couple of months maybe, maybe less. Depending on the kind of weather we hit. It'll be spring by then, so there'll be some flooding. But we'll make it."

"I know we will."

They rode silently for a bit, hearing the mournful wind rustling the pine needles. Then Suzannah said, "You're worried about me, aren't you? Afraid I'm not going to be up to this trip."

"What put that idea into your head?"

"Oh, just the way you treat me. As if I were something that might break into a million pieces."

"It's a long, hard journey, Suzannah. One that's felled many a man in his prime."

She set her jaw resolutely and straightened in the saddle. I'm a Brand, she thought, and if anybody can do it, I can.

The Appalachian range reared before them and they moved higher into the cold, sharp air. They traveled from first light until it was too dark to move safely. Then they'd rest for the night under the stars, ears tuned to hostile sounds, arms twined about each other for warmth. Despite their exhaustion and hunger, their closeness would always lead to love. This effort, rather than tiring them, would enable them to face the morning with renewed zeal.

Food presented a problem; they'd soon run out of what little provisions they had, and Jonathan was afraid of using his rifle for fear the gunshot might give them away. Once he managed to snare a rabbit, and another time he was fortunate enough to catch a young wild turkey.

Despite the danger, Suzannah built a fire, plucked and gutted the bird, then spitted it and broiled it over the glowing coals.

"You never cease to amaze me," Jonathan said.

"Did you think I was only good for dancing a reel or serving tea? Why, Letitia taught Circumstance and me how to do this when we were eight or nine years old."

The following day it rained for six hours straight, turning the winding trail into a slogging mire. They dismounted and walked the horses, since any slip could easily break an animal's leg. Though the rain finally let up, a sharp wind from the northeast froze their breath when they talked. Jonathan searched out a recess in a cliff-face that offered them shelter from the wind; using his double-edged Bowie knife, he built a lean-to. They dried their clothes near the small fire then slipped under their saddle blankets.

Suzannah looked down the side of the mountain. The valley was fast losing its shape to the encroaching twilight. Ahead lay the summit of the Appalachians, and beyond that, the first stars flickering in the evening sky.

A whippoorwill sounded his last lone call, a bobcat snarled, and then all was still, a preternatural silence that lay like a comforting blanket over mountain and valley.

"It's very beautiful, isn't it?" she murmured. "I never dreamt it could be so beautiful."

He nodded. "It's calm, got its own rhythm. It allows a man to think, to know who and what he is, away from all the sham of the towns and the cities, and all the things that people think they have to do in order to please other people. The wilderness has its own still, strong soul—like you, Suzannah."

"Sometimes I think you see things in me that aren't there," she said softly. "I hope I don't disappoint you."

"You'll never disappoint me."

They made love again, this time fiercely, fearing that their pursuers might catch them and tear them apart, and that they would have only this brief time to remember. And when they were done, they made love again.

The following day Jonathan came upon an Indian camp. "Monongahelas," he said warily to Suzannah. "I can tell by their dress and ornaments." He kept his pistol in his belt, primed and loaded.

Using the universal sign language, he traded some of their salt for a quiver of arrows. But when he tried to barter for a bow, the Monongahelas refused. The chief, a surly-looking old man, pointed to Suzannah.

Jonathan shook his head vehemently.

"Oh dear, what is it?" she asked, a tremor in her voice.

"That's all right, Suzannah, I told them no."

"But what?"

"They want that cameo you're wearing in exchange for one of their bows."

Suzannah's hand flew to her necklace. "This belonged to my grandmother." Then her hand fell away from her throat. "But a bow's important, isn't it?"

"We'll get along without it."

She shook her head. "With a bow, you can keep us supplied with food, and silently, too. If we're still being followed, we need a bow." Without further hesitation, she took off the cameo. "Trade them. I know my grandmother would approve."

That evening, Jonathan killed a buck with a well-placed arrow in the withers. Suzannah had never dressed a buck, and Jonathan showed her how. He skinned it, cooked a portion of the meat, then salted the rest so that they could have it for days. He used the thickest part of the hide to make a pair of mocassins for her, her own shoes having long since worn away.

In this way, the days passed one into the other until at last they reached the summit of the mountains and then descended onto a rolling plateau cut through with narrow valleys and marked by precipitous bluffs. Several more days of weary traveling followed. Then, far in the distance, at the confluence of two rivers, the Monongahela and the Allegheny, the weary travelers could just barely make out the town of Pittsburgh.

Bone-tired, yet exhilarated that they'd accomplished this part of their journey, they began the final approach to the town.

Jonathan said, "When George Washington was just a youthful surveyor, he chose this spot to fortify. Because of its strategic position, he built a fort here to legitimize Virginia's claim to the territory. But the French beat Washington's men off, and erected their own stockade, called Fort Dusquesne. Then during the French and Indian Wars, the Americans recaptured the post and named it Fort Pitt. The town of Pittsburgh is really built around that old settlement."

"I'd no idea you were such a student of history," Suzannah said, delighted to learn about this new side of him.

"If you're around Andrew Jackson long enough, you can't help but absorb it," he said. "He's the one who really knows American history."

"But I thought . . ."

"That he was illiterate and coarse?"

"No, not that; my Uncle Jeremy fought with him at New

Orleans and he had nothing but high praise for him. And my mother and father were somehow involved with Jackson during Aaron Burr's trial. But I never realized that Jackson had the makings of a scholar."

"All that campaign slander made him out to be a nincompoop, but he's self-taught, and smart as a whip. Not only that, you Washingtonians are in for one great big surprise. Andrew Jackson, for all his abrupt ways, is a man of refinement."

Having seen his dignified deportment at the inauguration, Suzannah could half believe that.

"Most of Jackson's manners are due to Rachel," he said. "Though she was a frontierswoman, she had the instinct for gracious living, and taught him most everything he knows."

"Well, it's a pity she didn't live to see him sworn into office."

"Died of a broken heart, she did," Jonathan said grimly. "I can't count the times she told me, 'I'd rather be a servant in the house of God than live in that mansion in Washington.' But they killed her, all those political reporters with their insinuations and their damnable lies."

His face clouded with an anger that Suzannah had never seen before. Rachel and Andrew Jackson had raised him after his parents had been killed in an Indian raid, and Suzannah sensed how wounded he was over the injustice done to his foster parents. She reached over and took his hand, and they rode in silence for a bit.

Trying to rouse Jonathan from his mood, Suzannah said, "When Circumstance and I were little, Uncle Jeremy used to tell us about his adventures on the Lewis and Clark expedition. You know, Meriwether Lewis first went to Pittsburgh to get the corps outfitted, and in Pittsburgh, he bought Scannon, the Newfoundland dog. It cost him twenty dollars."

"That's a lot of money for a dog," Jonathan exclaimed. "I think Lewis must have been taken."

"Uncle Jeremy said Scannon repaid his cost ten times over, for he'd always warn the men when grizzly bears were nearby. Imagine how brave those thirty-two men must have been! To go where no white man had ever gone before—all the way across the continent to the Pacific Ocean."

"You liked your uncle, didn't you?"

"He was a wonderful man, kind and generous, and such an even disposition. Oddly enough, he didn't look anything like my father. Why, most times, you'd never dream that they were brothers. Half-brothers, really. They had such different likes. Except..."

He noticed the change in her tone, which suddenly sounded troubled. "Except what?"

She shrugged slightly. "I think they both loved my mother."

Her statement hung on the air. An uncomfortable moment passed. Jonathan cleared his throat and said, "Did I ever tell you about the first time I met her?" Of course he had, very briefly, but this seemed as good a time as any to fill in the details. "I was about sixteen, and General Jackson sent me to Washington with communiqués for President Madison. The British had just burned Washington and were about to do the same to Baltimore, so I went to join up with our militia. I got to Fort McHenry while the British were bombarding it, and I saw this woman standing in the lee of a farmhouse, watching the bombardment and writing something. I figured she was some kind of a spy, and that I'd best take her prisoner. Well, we had a little battle about that, and finally it all got straightened out, but you can understand how your mother and I got off to a bad start right from the beginning.

"Still, I thought that she was the most beautiful woman I ever saw. And she still is mighty handsome for a woman her age. That's comforting, because at least I know you'll last."

His attempt at humor had escaped Suzannah, who was still engrossed in her original thoughts. "No, I don't *think* that they both loved my mother, I *know* it. And though she never said anything to us, I believe that Mother wanted to divorce father because she planned to marry Uncle Jeremy."

He waited impatiently for her to exhaust this vein of conversation, for it was only making her sad.

"But then Uncle Jeremy had that dreadful accident... and the light just seemed to go right out of Mother's life."

"Suzannah, that's all in the past," Jonathan said gently. "We're starting our own life now, and I figure we're going to have enough troubles of our own to keep us busy."

Suzannah turned to him with a half-smile, and blinked back her tears. "You're right," she said softly.

Jonathan took her hand and pressed it. "Like I told you, I've been to Pittsburgh many times as a courier for General Jackson. In those years, this was the only city west of the Alleghenies that had any manufacturing at all. There were glass factories, supplying the windows for all the new houses going up in St. Louis, Louisville, Nashville, and New Orleans. Suzannah, do you know you can take a boat from Pittsburgh, go all the way down the Ohio River to the falls of the Ohio, change boats at Louisville, then go on to the Mississippi, and continue right on down to New Orleans? What's more, with a steamboat, you can come right back upriver again!"

She nodded, warmed by his enthusiasm.

"Wait till you see Pittsburgh. There are huge iron forges, and shipyards are springing up all along the riverfront. Right now, there are close to twelve thousand people there, turning out maybe fifty steamboats a year."

"Steamboats—that's what Mother's invested in. She thinks that until the railroads get a firmer foothold in the land—I mean, they're not always going to be drawn by horses—most of the country's commerce will be done on rivers."

"She's right there."

Suzannah rubbed her forehead. "It seems to me she said recently that they discovered a huge vein of coal right near Pittsburgh."

He nodded. "Bituminous."

"That's right. With such a cheap supply of fuel nearby, the city's bound to grow. In fact, Mother thinks that some of the great fortunes in America will be made here."

"I hadn't thought much on that," he said. "Guess it takes a special kind of person to have that kind of foresight. Your mother sounds like a real smart woman. I wish we could get along. We might even have something to say to each other."

"She is smart, and that's what makes it so difficult," Suzannah said, as they reached the outskirts of town. "If I could just dismiss her, then there'd be no problem at all. But I can't—because, well, she's been right so often in the past."

"Are you sorry you came with me?" he asked softly. "Because if you are—"

"No, no," she said hastily. "In this case, she's wrong about you and me. I know that in my heart."

Jonathan broke into a grin. "Well then, we've got to find us a preacher soon as we can. I can't go traveling all over America with an unmarried woman. Suzannah, you've got to make an honest man out of me."

She poked him playfully in the ribs. The prospect of a hot bath and a bed with a mattress made their mood lighten as they rode deeper into town.

"Let's go to the boat terminal first, see when the next paddleboat is going downriver," he said.

Pittsburgh seemed to be flexing its muscles; buildings were going up everywhere. The streets were unpaved, and the only sidewalks were hastily constructed wooden affairs. Over on Fifth Avenue, in the section of town called the Gold Triangle because of the way it jutted out into the junction of the rivers, townspeople bustled all about.

"Well, I see that Pittsburgh hasn't prettied itself up none," Jonathan said, grinning.

All along the riverfront, the massive forms of steamboats were loading and unloading their cargoes. Manufactured goods went to the frontier, while the raw materials were sent back from the interior to be traded and passed along to the East through Pittsburgh.

They reined in at the steamboat ticket station and Jonathan went inside. He caught sight of a handbill tacked on the wall. "Wanted, Dead or Alive," he read silently. "Jonathan Albright, for the abduction of Suzannah Breech Brand."

There was a full description of both of them, and then at the bottom, "A reward of five hundred dollars for the capture of Jonathan Albright, and another five hundred dollars if Suzannah Brand is returned to Devroe Connaught. Mr. Connaught can be reached through the offices of the *Pittsburgh Gazette.*"

Acting as casual as possible, Jonathan strode outside to Suzannah and said, "We've got to keep moving. It's clear Devroe and his men got here before us. We'd best be on the first boat out of here."

He pointed to a steamboat, the *Crusader,* with one or two passengers going up the gangplank. Burly Negro stevedores were loading the last of the cargo on the lower level of the boat. "That boat doesn't look very seaworthy, but we don't have much choice. Now Suzannah, don't look around. Just ride your horse right up that gangplank. If we're lucky, we'll just blend with the crowd. We can buy our tickets on board."

Suzannah tried not to look back, but like Lot's wife, she did. From the corner of her eye she thought she recognized the scarred face of Sisley Urquhart, one of Devroe's servants. As her mare clip-clopped up the gangplank she said, "I think we've been seen."

"Just keep moving," Jonathan urged her.

What seemed like an eternity, but was only several minutes later, the shrill sound of the steamboat whistle rent the air. Stevedores removed the gangplank and untied the heavy hawsers from the dock pilings. The paddlewheels began their slow revolutions, and the *Crusader* eased away from the dock and headed downriver into the Ohio.

Suzannah clutched Jonathan's arm. "We're safe!"

"Maybe," he said softly. "Maybe."

Chapter 6

SEVERAL DAYS before Jonathan and Suzannah had even arrived in Pittsburgh, Rebecca jounced along the rutted road on the stagecoach going to that river port. She drifted in and out of a fever, a fever that burned away all the defenses she'd built up through the years.

She saw herself at thirteen, bursting with energy . . . One particular day stood out in her mind, the day they'd laid the cornerstone of the American Palace, way back on October 13, 1792. That day had been chosen because it was the three hundredth anniversary of Columbus's discovery of America.

Even at thirteen, she had captivated twenty-year-old Zebulon Brand, and with youthful artlessness she'd flirted with him. She had barely acknowledged the presence of Jeremy Brand, for he was only ten years old, hardly worth notice.

But the years have a way of changing people, and Jeremy grew into a young man of broad shoulders and quiet assertiveness. Still, he stood in the shadow of Zebulon—Zebulon the adventurer, the reprobate, the rake who seduced women and made them ache for more. Only Rebecca was able to resist his formidable charms, which led him to an infatuation so unremitting that one day, maddened beyond reason, he tried to take her by force.

In the ensuing struggle, the Breech carriagehouse in Georgetown burned down. Zebulon, frightened of what Rebecca's father might do, enlisted with Stephen Decatur and sailed off to do battle with the Tripoli pirates, who were ravaging American shipping in the Mediterranean.

With Zebulon gone, Rebecca turned her attention to Jeremy, discovering at last that she preferred the constancy of his love. She tried to persuade him to enter her father's stone business— Mathias Breech had become quite prosperous by then, supplying stone and brick for the building of the American Palace

49

and other government buildings in the capital. But Jeremy had
plans of his own; he'd promised Meriwether Lewis that he'd
go with him on the Voyage of Northwest Discovery, to explore
the vast Louisiana Territory that President Jefferson had just
purchased from Napoleon.

For two years Rebecca heard not a word from Jeremy; the
nation came to believe that all the men on the Lewis and Clark
expedition had perished in the wilderness. Meanwhile, Zebulon
returned from the Tripoli Wars covered with glory, and he and
Rebecca gradually resumed their courtship. Just as she was
about to say yes to Zebulon's proposal of marriage, Jeremy
returned. But he had with him a daughter, Circumstance, be-
gotten of an Indian squaw, White Doe. White Doe had died
in St. Louis shortly after giving birth, but despite Rebecca's
entreaties, Jeremy refused to give up his child.

Enraged, Rebecca married Zebulon. In quick succession she
had two children, Suzannah and Gunning. The War of 1812,
the burning of Washington and of the White House by the
invading British army—Rebecca lived through it all. And
somehow survived. During those tumultuous years, when life
took on added meaning because of its very precariousness,
Rebecca came to grips with her own selfishness and stupidity
and realized that she truly loved Jeremy, had always loved him.

When the British captured him, and Sean Connaught planned
to hang him on trumped-up charges of being a spy, Rebecca
did everything in her power to free him, including helping
Jeremy's mistress, Marianne Connaught, in her own efforts to
save him. But the women's plan came to naught

The war dragged on. When the news of the Battle of New
Orleans, where General Andrew Jackson decisively defeated
the British, arrived in Washington, Rebecca's joy was tempered
by the sadness of not knowing what had happened to Jeremy.
During the war, Zebulon had jeopardized the Breech-Brand
business with his smuggling operations, and to recoup the family fortune, he sailed off on an illicit slaving venture. At that
moment, Rebecca took her courage in both her hands and
instituted divorce proceedings against him. She could no longer
tolerate his brutish ways, could no longer submit to a man she
didn't love.

It was while Zebulon was away at sea that Jeremy, by then
presumed dead by Rebecca, returned to Washington. With the
help of Marianne Connaught, he'd escaped from the British
and had fought alongside Andrew Jackson at the Battle of New

Orleans. He'd built the redoubts that had successfully stopped
the British assault. Jeremy had suffered his own tragedies,
including the death of Marianne at Sean Connaught's hands.
Jeremy subsequently killed Sean on the battlefield. In their
mutual sorrow and distress, Rebecca and Jeremy gravitated
toward each other, and she waited only for the moment that
Zebulon would return so she could obtain her divorce.

Then Rebecca received news that Zebulon had been lost at
sea. After a mourning period, she and Jeremy finally consum-
mated their love, a love that had grown despite adversity,
despite the passage of the years, to an incandescence that illuminated both their lives and taught Rebecca the supreme joys
of being a completely fulfilled woman.

But once more the fates thwarted her. Zebulon reappeared.
When his boat had broken up on a reef off Pensacola, he'd
been captured by the Spanish and the Seminoles, and held
captive in Florida for more than a year. Now he fully expected
to resume his life with Rebecca. Jeremy tried to take Rebecca
away then and there, but fearing that such a scandal would
harm her children, she remained at the house on New York
Avenue, though first swearing to Jeremy that nothing would
ever happen between her and Zebulon.

That night Zebulon forcibly took Rebecca. She fled to
Georgetown, and with Chief Justice John Marshall's help got
a legal separation. Nine months later she gave birth to a child.
At first Zebulon assumed that the boy, named Bravo, was his.
Rebecca's divorce dragged on for almost two years. During
this period, Zebulon's suspicions were kindled to the flash
point, for Bravo, with his tow hair and brilliant blue eyes,
began to look more and more like Jeremy.

Then the dreadful accident at the White House changed all
their lives. Jeremy, in the final stages of rebuilding the mansion,
plunged four stories to his death. Though no one ever questioned Zebulon's presence at the scene of the accident, Rebecca
always suspected his complicity. Whatever the truth, Zebulon
had eventually paid for his life of excess with a gruesome death.

Rebecca, feeling that she'd little left to live for, turned her
attention to her children. Gunning, whose wildness and zest
for life resonated a secret feeling in Rebecca's heart—he reminded her so much of her own youth. Suzannah, a child of
such extraordinary sweetness that Rebecca knew that someone
would take advantage of her. She'd tried to protect her daughter
by having her marry Devroe Connaught. The Brand-Connaught

feud seemed finally to have resolved itself, and Devroe could have given Suzannah the security that someone of her delicate nature needed. Then that lout, that uncouth frontiersman Jonathan Albright had kidnapped her.

"Well, he won't get away with it!" Rebecca cried aloud, and startled all the passengers on the coach. She felt wide-eyed and alert, and her fever had burned itself out.

"Pittsburgh!" the driver shouted as the coach pulled into the inn that served as a stage depot.

As soon as Rebecca entered the inn, she saw the handbill that Devroe Connaught had posted. Reading it, she experienced an uneasiness in the pit of her stomach. There was something so drastic in "Wanted, Dead or Alive." She'd intended nothing like that. All she wanted was Suzannah back . . . and hopefully, for her wedding to Devroe to take place.

She went immediately to the offices of the *Pittsburgh Gazette* and learned that Devroe Connaught was headquartered at the best place in town—Brown's Hotel, on Fifth Avenue. She hurried there and discovered him in his rooms.

He was dressed in a handsome brocaded robe, his thin face was lathered, and his man Sisley Urquhart was about to shave his sideburns and trim his moustache. Devroe's bodyguard, the giant Ebon, sat on the stuffed horsehair couch, arms akimbo.

Devroe jumped to his feet when he saw her. "Madam, I cannot believe that you were foolish enough to follow me here. This is nothing but a benighted outpost on the edge of civilization, and hardly fitting for a woman of your sensibilities."

"Devroe, if necessary I would journey to hell to protect my daughter," Rebecca said. She realized that her sudden presence here must have been a shock to him; nevertheless, she'd expected a somewhat warmer greeting. "Have you learned anything?" she asked.

"Nothing yet. We tracked Albright as far as the foothills of the Appalachians, and then the blackguard eluded us. But a farmer and his wife did tell us that Albright planned to go to Pittsburgh and then take a boat to Nashville."

Rebecca told him that was the information she'd prized from Letitia.

Devroe wiped his face clean; it had a pink, almost babyish sheen to it. "It sounds logical. They don't have the provisions or the horses to make it overland to Nashville. I have my men staked out all along the waterfront and at every ticket station, watching for them."

"Devroe, I must tell you, I'm very upset about your poster."

"Let me assure you, it was the only way to get some action from the law officials in this hellish town. What we both want is Suzannah, and we shall get her."

Somewhat mollified, Rebecca took her leave. She registered at the hotel and spent most of that day resting; the stagecoach journey had exhausted her. But the following day she began to haunt the waterfront, questioning stevedores and sailors about Suzannah. Nobody had seen a girl answering her description.

Another day passed, and then another, and Rebecca grew more agitated. Had Jonathan lied to Letitia about Pittsburgh in order to throw everybody off the track? Had he changed his plans? Then late one afternoon, while she was sitting in the lobby of Brown's Hotel sunk in hopeless gloom, she saw a great coming and going from Devroe's rooms.

First a breathless Sisley Urquhart went running in, and then Ebon lumbered out and headed for the waterfront. Instinct warned Rebecca that something important was going on. Unable to contain herself any longer, she hurried to Devroe's suite.

She found him practicing with his pistol, aiming, passing it to the other hand, then aiming again. He reacted to her interruption with mild surprise, then continued practicing. "This is a trait that most Connaught men have," he said. "We're ambidextrous. I'm a crack shot with either hand."

Rebecca had no time for his bragging. "What's happened?" she demanded.

"My man will tell you," Devroe said and nodded at Sisley Urquhart.

"I saw them half an hour ago," Sisley said. "They boarded an old riverboat, the *Crusader*. That man, Jonathan Albright, and your daughter."

Chapter 7

REBECCA GRASPED the arm of a chair for support. "You saw them? There's no mistake?"

"No mistake," Sisley said.

She pressed her fingers to her temples to ease the pounding. "You did nothing to stop them?"

"There wasn't time. The gangplank was already going up when I spied them."

"What are we going to do?" she asked. "Have we come this close only to lose them?"

"Madam, give me credit for having some small intelligence," Devroe said. "Having anticipated such a turn, I've made contingency plans, and have already engaged Captain Harmon of the *American Flyer*. I've sent Ebon to alert him. Captain Harmon was going downriver anyway, and in addition, he'll be paid handsomely to catch the *Crusader*."

Devroe's manner was so condescending that Rebecca felt her cheeks burning. Yet she was impressed with his foresight; the man was shrewd and efficient.

"The *Crusader* is an older steamboat and requires wood to fuel her engines," Devroe went on. "The *American Flyer* is a newer design and uses coal. Captain Harmon is laying in a stock of coal this very minute. The *Crusader* will have to stop along the Ohio River to pick up wood, but we won't. I expect we'll catch them within twenty-four hours."

"When do you plan to leave?" she asked.

Devroe's slitted eyes narrowed even further. "You're not thinking of going?"

"Of course I am," she exclaimed.

"That would be most unwise."

She straightened to her full height. "May I remind you that I'm Suzannah's mother? Whatever concerns her concerns me. I have every intention of being on that boat."

Devroe drummed his fingers impatiently as he argued with her, but Rebecca remained adamant. All things considered, it would have been simpler for him if she weren't along. Yet the more he thought about it, the more he believed her presence to be poetic justice. If she insisted on seeing what he had in store for Jonathan and Suzannah, then let her.

With a shrug, he said to Rebecca, "Come along if you insist. Captain Harmon plans to leave at dawn tomorrow. By then he'll have his cargo loaded. With a full day of light we can proceed at full speed. And now madam, if you'll permit me, I have my packing to complete."

Rebecca took her leave. She packed hastily, then went directly to the riverfront. "I'm not taking any chances on that boat leaving without me," she muttered to herself.

As far as the eye could see, steamboats were docked along the wharves. Finally, she found the *American Flyer* and boarded. A black cabin boy directed her to Captain Harmon, who was on the lower deck, going over bills of lading. He was a taciturn Scotsman with salt-and-pepper hair and a beard to match.

When Rebecca inquired about accommodations, Harmon shook his head. "I'm sorry, but every stateroom aboard the *American Flyer* is booked."

"I'm Rebecca Breech Brand from Washington, D.C.," she said. "Very shortly, I'll be Devroe Connaught's mother-in-law. If you'll just show me to my room—any room will do—I'll keep out of everybody's way." With an artless gesture, she slipped a gold coin into Harmon's ready hand.

The captain sang out for his second mate: "Donohoe!" An engaging-looking lad of about eighteen came running up. Fresh from the Louisiana frontier, he spoke with a strong southern accent. His hair was so black that it seemed to shine blue in the light. His skin was very fair with a line of freckles across the bridge of his nose. Patrick Donohoe wore his spanking-new mate's uniform with pride and was so eager to please that Rebecca liked him immediately.

"Follow me, Mrs. Brand," he said, and led her along the passageway to the lower level.

A gang of slave stevedores, stripped to the waist and with muscles gleaming, shoveled coal into the bins. Rebecca passed a jumble of machinery that ran the new boat. If Bravo were here, he'd be able to tell me what all the components are, she thought. Against the stacked bales of cotton and the crated manufactured goods huddled the poorest passengers. Most of them were immigrants, Irish, and German, and Swedish, come to America to pursue the dream of a better life.

"Most of these poor souls used the last of their money to secure passage into the interior. That's where land still can be bought cheaply," Patrick Donohoe told her.

Lifting her skirts, Rebecca climbed the ornate stairway to the upper deck, the domain of the first-class passengers. She followed Patrick Donohoe along the promenade where each cabin had the name of a state over its door.

"The steamboat entrepreneur, Henry Shreve—they named Shreveport, Louisiana after him—he decided that since all the first-class accommodations aboard his steamboats were called staterooms, he might as well name them after the states in the Union."

"Now that's something I didn't know," Rebecca said.

"Right above us is the hurricane deck, because it catches every breeze on the river. That's where Captain Harmon and the other officers live. Above that"—he pointed to a small post high above the officer's quarters—"that's the pilot's house. He really knows the river, its currents and sandbars and whirlpools and any other hazards. While this vessel's moving, nobody—not even the captain—can countermand the orders of the pilot. He's lord of all he surveys."

"How long have you been working on steamboats?"

"Going on two months now," Patrick said proudly.

"I think you're doing wonderfully well." She liked this kind of enterprising character, somebody who threw himself into his work with verve and industry. "This boat is really a whole world in itself," she said, her own natural curiosity taking in every detail.

He nodded eagerly. "And a better world than most."

"Do you plan to become a river pilot, then, or a captain?"

"Can't rightly say for sure, ma'am. You see, I lived with my folks in Louisiana, along with a whole tribe of aunts and uncles. Well, a few years ago, my uncle Luke Donohoe crossed over into Texas—why the Mexican government was practically giving away land. They settled in Brazoria County, and I went out there to work as his ranchhand. I liked it fine enough, but it was so lonely. Why, the closest female to us was a widow who lived fifty miles away. I could have tolerated that well enough, excepting she was fifty years older than me! Well, I'm young, and my feet are itchy, and they say that's the time to sow your wild oats, so I came east to do a little sowing. Begging your pardon if I'm being a little too direct, ma'am. Now what I want to do is see as much of this great country as I can."

"Well, if your travels ever take you to Washington, D.C., make sure you call on me. I know a number of young ladies who'd be delighted to meet you."

"Why thank you, ma'am." Patrick Donohoe stopped at a door and said, "This is your cabin."

"Tennessee" read the sign over the lintel, and Rebecca interpreted this as an ill omen. You're getting to be a superstitious old fool, she chided herself.

"If there's anything else you need, don't hesitate to call," Patrick Donohoe said, doffing his cap.

Rebecca nodded, gave him a generous tip, then closed the door after her. Once inside she had to sit down lest she collapse. "It's nothing more than fatigue," she said, trying to calm herself.

She looked around her room. It was well appointed, if a bit cold and colorless: white chenille bedspread, white muslin curtains at the window, the furniture all painted white. Her window faced dockside, and she could see all the activity on the riverfront.

A half-hour later she felt calmer and went about her toilet. She poured water from the pitcher into the washbowl and scrubbed her face. She unpinned her hair, replaited it into a coil, and piled the mass of titian hair shot through with gray atop her head. Feeling somewhat refreshed, she proceeded to the dining room for a bit of supper.

Men and women promenaded along the decks; some were young lovers, others not so young, and still others were very wise in the ways of love that they peddled. The women of fashion wore long full skirts, and bonnets a trifle larger than those now fashionable on the East coast. Many of the younger girls had Negresses for chaperones, but that only seemed to lend a certain *frisson* to their flirtations.

The dining room salon was the grandest room on the boat. The tables were laid with linen service, decent china, and a passing-fair imitation crystal. Bouquets of flowers graced each table. In a far corner a sign read, GENTLEMEN WHO PLAY CARDS FOR MONEY PLAY AT THEIR OWN RISK. Riverboat gamblers wearing tall hats sat at green baize tables with decks of cards, enticing the occasional rube who thought he could make a fast fortune on the river. Here and there Rebecca saw men she took to be planters. They'd come north to Pittsburgh with their cargoes of cotton or wheat, and were now returning home. The gaiety of the passengers was in direct contrast to her own state of mind, and Rebecca wondered, what is it in the Breech-Brand line that so figures our lives with turmoil and tragedy? Do we call it down on ourselves? Are we so intent on fulfilling our own destinies that we have no time for the ordinary daily commonplaces of living? That question had long perplexed her, and she knew it would continue to intrigue her until she died. "We do it to ourselves," she whispered. "This much I know. We call down the lightning. Thank God we're a family of valiant hearts. That is our salvation."

She ate lightly—some fresh vegetable soup, a slice of warm whole-wheat bread with rich country butter. The food lifted her spirits somewhat, and after circling the promenade deck, she retired to her cabin. A black maid helped her undress and unpack, and then she slipped beneath the freshly starched sheets of the bed and fell exhausted into a deep sleep. Several times during the night she wakened in terror. She'd never put much stock into anything as ephemeral as a mother's intuition, yet deep in her soul she knew that something was desperately wrong.

She awoke just before daylight and through her fogged cabin window saw Devroe Connaught, Sisley Urquhart, and Ebon come aboard. Three other men followed them, and Rebecca recognized them as Devroe's hirelings.

Slaves chanted in rhythm as they untied the hawsers holding the *American Flyer* fast to the dock. The slow revolutions of the paddlewheels on the sides of the vessel made the shallow-draft boat glide over the water, leaving only a frothing wake behind.

As they proceeded downriver, the fog grew more intense. Soundings were taken every few hundred yards.

Devroe angrily accosted Captain Harmon. "We'll never catch them at this speed."

"Fog's the same for them as it is for us," Captain Harmon said. "They've got to slow down too."

By ten that morning the fog had burned off enough for Rebecca to make out the riverbanks. She saw an occasional small town on some windswept bluff, saw the hamlets at the mouths of the smaller rivers and streams, saw the tiny wood-camps where destitute people eaked out their living by supplying cords of wood to the ravenous engines of the steamboats. She had never realized such a life existed, and it disheartened her to think that she was profiting from her steamboat venture in part because of these poverty-stricken people.

By noon, the last vestige of fog had dissipated. Captain Harmon's crew fired up the engines and built up steam pressure. The paddlewheels dipped faster into the water, and soon the *American Flyer* seemed to race along the waves. Rebecca stood at the prow of the boat, the quick wind in her face, searching the river for the *Crusader*.

Patrick Donohoe appeared at her side. "The captain says the *Crusader's* got a twelve-hour lead on us. We probably won't catch them until nightfall. So it's no good for you to be standing out here in the wind. Catch your death of cold, you will."

Rebecca just drew her light wool cloak more tightly around her. All afternoon she kept at her post, searching the river, hoping that just around this bend, or the next, she'd see the *Crusader* and Suzannah. She longed to hold her daughter, talk sense to her, tell her how much she loved her. She knew she could persuade Suzannah to come home. This interlude with Jonathan was nothing but a girlish infatuation. With kindness and a thoughtful explanation, how could Suzannah fail to see that? As for what might have happened between Suzannah and Jonathan, Rebecca couldn't bear to think of that.

Just before sunset, Captain Harmon and Devroe joined her at the prow of the ship. Devroe raised his spyglass to his eye.

"Do you see anything?" Rebecca asked hopefully.

Devroe handed the spyglass to the captain.

Harmon nodded. "Aye, that's the *Crusader*. I'd know those cumbersome lines anywhere. Pile on the coal!" he shouted to Patrick Donohoe, who relayed the order. Down the line it went to the engine room.

Devroe put his hand on Harmon's sleeve. "There's an extra hundred dollars for you if you catch them before nightfall." He didn't want to take any chance on Jonathan and Suzannah's slipping away in the darkness. Devroe's heart began to thud dully. He had six men, more than enough to take care of Jonathan. Devroe motioned to Ebon, who came up behind him. Making sure that Rebecca was out of earshot, Devroe said, "When we catch them, you know what to do?"

Ebon grunted with a gap-toothed grin. "Umm, break the man's back. Break him dead. Then bring the girl to you. If she fight back—" Ebon snapped his fingers. "—break her dead too."

"Good," Devroe said, nodding. "Very good indeed."

Chapter 8

ABOARD THE *Crusader,* Jonathan Albright noticed the plume of smoke from another riverboat. As he watched it through his spyglass he saw it gaining on them. "They're fools!" he muttered. "These waters are full of sandbars, and with the spring floods and the sawyers in the river, they'll snag one of those logs for certain. Punch a hole right through their hull."

Suzannah joined Jonathan and they watched as the pursuing boat closed on them. Both steamboats seemed to be riding on a river of fire as the last rays of daylight flamed the waters.

When Captain McLernan joined them at the stern, Jonathan said, "I believe that boat's trying to give us a race. What do you think?"

Captain McLernan nodded. "It's that confounded *American Flyer.* Captain Harmon thinks he owns the Ohio with that new boat of his. Well, there's a thing or two he'll have to learn about this river, about its shallows and its shoals."

"And a few things about passing another boat under such treacherous conditions," Jonathan said. "I think we ought to teach them a lesson. What do you say—are you game for a race?"

"Pile on that wood there," Captain McLernan shouted to his crew. "Let's show them our smoke."

The hands heaved wood into the boilers, and the paddle-wheels began to turn faster, sending a rainbowed mist of water high into the air. The exhilaration of the race swept through everybody on board, and soon they were urging the captain to go faster.

Twilight held them in its strange blue grip for half an hour, then darkness came over them. The ship's oil lamps and candles cast their flickering light on the river, and a ghostly reflection of their boat kept pace with them. Miles upriver, the lights of the *American Flyer* bore down relentlessly.

In the dining room and the gaming parlor, people began to wager on the outcome of the race; would they beat the *American Flyer* to the falls of the Ohio? Two black cabin boys leaned far out over the prow of the *Crusader*, holding up lanterns to light the way through the dark treacherous currents. What little light the lanterns offered couldn't possibly have made a difference, but at least it was something that one could do.

As night deepened, the smokestacks slashed a trail of sparks across the darkness. The boiler fires burned so hot that the smokestacks seemed to glow. Still, the shimmering outline of the *American Flyer* became larger and brighter as it closed the gap.

Suzannah stared at the pursuing boat. "It's my mother, isn't it?"

"We don't know that," Jonathan said. But he suspected as much. He checked the pistols in his belt: loaded and ready.

"Jonathan!" Suzannah exclaimed.

"Trust me. Nothing's going to happen," he said. Then he gripped her shoulders. "But I will tell you this. They're not going to get you away from me again. Not after I've spent a lifetime searching for you."

"Don't worry, I'm with you," she whispered.

At one point, the boats came close enough for Captain Harmon to hail the *Crusader*. "Captain McLernan!" his voice called above the whoosh of the paddles. "Heave to, we want to board you."

"Begone, you river rat! Nobody's boarding my boat while I'm captain!" Then the crack of a gunshot rent the air; the bullet imbedded itself in the wooden walls of the *Crusader's* upper deck. A woman screamed, and another passenger fainted. "Shoot at me, will you!" Captain McLernan bellowed. "If I had a cannon I'd blast you out of the water!"

The shooting incident infuriated Captain McLernan. He and Captain Harmon had a long history of antagonism on the river; this latest outrage wasn't to be borne. "They want to board us, boys. Well, they're going to have to catch us!" What had begun as a lark had suddenly become deadly earnest. "I don't know why they want to board, but I'll be damned if I'm going to let them."

Believing that the captain had a right to know the complete truth, Jonathan took McLernan aside and told him the entire story. McLernan listened intently, then said to Suzannah, "Is he telling the truth? Are you with him of your own free will?"

"I am," Suzannah answered with verve.

"That's good enough for me," McLernan said.

All through the night the riverboats raced. The *Crusader* would pull ahead for a bit, then the *American Flyer* would regain lost ground. Though the *Flyer* was obviously faster, Captain McLernan knew the river better and maneuvered more adeptly. Nobody slept—the excitement had become unbearable. About an hour or so after midnight, the cabin boy called up to Captain McLernan, "Engine room says we're running out of fuel! We'll have to stop for wood somewhere along the line."

"If we do, they'll catch us for sure," McLernan said.

"Some of these old wooden benches look expendable," Jonathan said.

McLernan thought only for a moment before nodding. "We were going to get outfitted with new ones on the next trip. So let's get rid of them now."

Jonathan and the rest of the crew fell to with gusto. The wooden benches were broken up and fed to the boilers. Once more the *Crusader* held her own. But the boilers were insatiable, and soon every piece of wood unnecessary to the flotation of the boat had been hacked to pieces and used for fuel.

By dawn, there was nothing left to burn; even some loose and rotted planks that had covered the paddlewheels had been ripped off, exposing some of the blades. Reluctantly, Captain McLernan pulled in to a wood camp. "If we move fast enough, we can load up and be away before they overtake us," he said. Though the stevedores worked furiously hurling the logs from one man to another, by the time they'd gotten a supply of wood aboard and a head of steam up in the boilers, the *American Flyer* had caught up with them, and was maneuvering to block their way.

"Do you think we should make a run for it?" Suzannah whispered to Jonathan. She pointed to the dense forest that lay just beyond the riverbank.

Jonathan shook his head. "I'm tired of running. They'd only keep pursuing us everywhere we went. Besides, like you said, we married each other in the eyes of God. You're my wife, Suzannah, and that's all there is to it."

They watched as the *American Flyer* lowered a rowboat. It carried half a dozen men and a woman. "It is Mother. And Devroe!" Suzannah whispered.

Captain McLernan said, "Suzannah, you go to my cabin. Stay there until we get rid of them."

Suzannah hesitated, but Jonathan agreed with McLernan. "Go, darling. It's best."

Suzannah climbed the stairs to the hurricane deck. She went into McLernan's cabin and closed the door, but from the window, she could watch everything that was going on.

When Devroe Connaught's party came aboard, Jonathan gauged them carefully... Six in all. None of them appeared especially tough, with the exception of a huge black buck who looked as if he could wrestle a bear to earth. And, of course, Devroe. That one had the cold flat eyes of a ferret, shrewd and dangerous.

Patrick Donohoe had also come aboard as the official representative of the *American Flyer*. He gave Rebecca his hand and helped her climb the steps.

Rebecca hurried straight to Captain McLernan. "Where's my daughter?"

Devroe's arm shot out, restraining her. "Madam, if you please, this is men's work, and we'll proceed legally." He handed Captain McLernan a warrant for Jonathan Albright's arrest. "And we demand the return of Suzannah Brand," Devroe said.

"But this here warrant says that Albright kidnapped her," McLernan said.

"That's right," Rebecca and Devroe said in unison.

"Well, that ain't exactly what Miss Suzannah told me," McLernan said, pitching a chaw of tobacco into the river.

"She came with me of her own free will," Jonathan said. "And as soon as we can, we're going to be married."

"Don't listen to him," Rebecca interrupted. "Mr. Donohoe, do something!"

Though Patrick had come aboard with every intention of getting Rebecca's daughter back for her, now he was of a very different mind. He didn't care much for this Connaught man, and since his natural sympathies went out to the underdog, he felt a kinship with Jonathan. "I think we ought to hear from Miss Brand," Patrick said.

"Shut your mouth!" Devroe said.

Rebecca whirled on Captain McLernan. "Yes, I want to see my daughter. I *demand* to see her."

Captain McLernan scratched his scraggly beard. "Guess we can't stop that, can we, Jonathan? She is her mother. Mrs.

Brand, Suzannah's in my cabin. Top deck."

Rebecca pushed her way past the men who were still confronting each other and went up the narrow stairway. When Suzannah saw her coming, she shrank away from the door.

Rebecca found the captain's stateroom and pounded on the door. "Suzannah, let me in!"

"The door is open, Mother," Suzannah said quietly.

Mother and daughter stood face to face. More than anything, Rebecca wanted to take Suzannah in her arms, wanted to comfort her, tell her all the things she'd planned to say: her concern, her worry, her love. Instead, she heard herself saying, "Suzannah, get your things. You're coming with me right now."

Suzannah stepped forward and grasped her mother's hands. "Mother, don't upset yourself. Are you all right?"

Rebecca pulled free. "Quickly now."

"Mother, please, listen to me."

"I'll listen when we're away from this foul place and this foul boat. Away from that . . . that . . ."

Suzannah clenched her fists and exclaimed, "Mother, listen! Don't say another word. For once in your life, just listen!"

Taken aback by her daughter's vehemence, Rebecca felt a wave of dizziness and pressed her hand against her heart.

"Mother, even if you have an attack now, that won't stop me. You *must* listen."

Rebecca tried to control herself.

"Mother, what would you have done if your father had forced you to do something you didn't want? Don't you see? I'm in the same predicament. I'm your daughter. The same feelings that you had, I have also. I can't be made to act as if I were some puppet of yours, living the life you want me to lead. I love this man."

"What do you know of love?" Rebecca demanded. "Some maudlin, mawkish, sentimental ideas of a schoolgirl. There are times, Suzannah, when you act like an infant. This man is trouble. I can see it in his face. And mark me, my girl, love dies with trouble."

"Mother, how can you, of all people say that? After all you've been through with father, and with . . . Uncle Jeremy."

"What do you mean?" Rebecca fairly shouted.

"I know everything," Suzannah murmured. "I know you loved Uncle Jeremy. You've never been the same since that dreadful accident at the White House."

Rebecca turned deathly pale. "What does that have to do with anything?"

"It has everything to do with it!" Suzannah cried. "If you were willing to risk everything you'd built because you no longer loved my father, but loved another man, then why can't you understand that I need to follow my heart also?"

"Oh, God, Suzannah, how can you be so blind, and so wrong?"

"If I'm wrong, as you claim, then don't I have the right to discover that myself? Would you want me to go through life feeling that I'd been forced into something I didn't want to do? You taught me everything I know about freedom of the spirit! And now you're asking me to go back on everything I believe. Why can't you see that?"

Rebecca had never known her daughter to be so fierce, had never realized that her gentle demeanor hid a backbone of steel. But Rebecca pushed all those conflicting emotions from her mind. "Suzannah, we'll talk about all this once we're back in Washington."

"I'm going to Texas with Jonathan."

"You are not!"

Suzannah's face set, and the determined look in her eyes spoke more eloquently than words.

Before Rebecca could say anything else, the door to the cabin swung open and Devroe entered. His contemptuous gaze passed from Suzannah to Rebecca. "Madam, I can't wait any longer. My men have disarmed Jonathan. Now we must be gone from here. We'll bring the kidnapper to justice and then have a doctor examine Suzannah. You know the terms of the marriage contract."

"I'll never submit to any such examination," Suzannah exclaimed, her face flushing with anger. "Nor will I ever marry you. Devroe think! I don't love you. Can't you see what a life of torment we'd have together?"

"I can appreciate how upset you are," Devroe said. "Without question, you're going through a momentary aberration. But I have every confidence that once I've gotten you back to civilization, you'll come to your senses."

Devroe was sure that the tall frontiersman had had his way with Suzannah, deflowered and besmirched her. And though that knowledge infuriated him, he took grim satisfaction in the humiliation he would soon visit on this girl and her mother. It would never balance the scales for all the anguish the Brands had caused his family, but it was a beginning.

He reached for Suzannah, but she slipped out of his grasp and darted out the door. She ran down the steps and toward the prow where she saw Jonathan struggling with Devroe's men. As she called his name her heart filled with resolve. She would stand with him, die with him if necessary.

Hearing her, Jonathan fought all the harder to break free of Sisley Urquhart, Ebon, and two of Devroe's other men.

The moment Patrick Donohoe saw Suzannah, any doubts about the course of action he would take disappeared. If he had any regret, it was that this extraordinary creature was already spoken for. He leapt on the back of one of the men holding Jonathan.

With the odds a little less overwhelming, Jonathan fought with renewed fury, and with a quick snap of his arms, he broke Sisley Urquhart's grip. But Ebon brought his fist down on the side of Jonathan's head, pitching him to the deck. Ebon kicked Jonathan in the ribs, then raised his foot again, this time aiming for Jonathan's face.

"Watch out!" Patrick Donohoe shouted.

Just then Suzannah reached them and flung herself at the black giant, beating at him with her fists.

With a sharp backhand he swept her aside as though she were a rag doll. The blow knocked her against Devroe, who'd followed her. He grabbed Suzannah's shoulders and tried to drag her away. She fell to her knees, trying to fight him off.

"Stop, you're hurting me," she cried.

Her cry roused Jonathan. He sprang from the deck and tackled Devroe; the force of his legs sent both men crashing against the flimsy wooden railing. With the air knocked out of him, Devroe gasped for breath. Jonathan hit him on the jaw with a left hook and followed it with a right cross that sent a tooth flying from Devroe's mouth.

Devroe spat blood, and then screamed at Ebon, "Get him off me! Kill him!"

Rebecca, who by now had also reached the fighting men, shouted, "No! No killing. All I want is my daughter." She knelt beside Suzannah, her arm around her shoulder.

Ebon knocked both women aside as he moved to tear Devroe and Jonathan apart. Ebon's hand closed around Jonathan's shirt and he half-lifted him off the deck. Jonathan kicked out at him and landed a blow to the knee that made his opponent drop him. Jonathan scrambled to get to Suzannah, only to find Devroe's other men closing in on him.

"Captain McLernan, oh, stop them! Help!" Suzannah cried, getting to her feet.

The captain and several of his men were already converging on them, and along with Patrick Donohoe, they managed to hold off Devroe's men. But Devroe, Jonathan, and Ebon were still battling it out. The fight carried them along the deck toward the center of the steamboat. The huge paddlewheel turned relentlessly, sending out sprays of water through its partially uncovered wooden housing.

Crouching behind Ebon, Devroe followed the big black as he forced Jonathan closer and closer to the paddlewheel. Devroe snatched his pistols from his belt, trying to get a clear shot at Jonathan.

Suzannah flung herself at Devroe, clawing for his eyes. He hit her, but she came at him again. He grabbed her arm, twisted it behind her back, then held her in front of him as he tried again to get a clear shot at Jonathan. Ebon had fought Jonathan to the rail and had him in a bearhug, trying to pitch him overboard.

As Rebecca saw the horror unfold, a jumble of thoughts overwhelmed her. She had caused this. If Devroe killed Jonathan, his blood would be on her hands forever.

Her jagged impressions were interrupted by the loud report of a pistol shot. She saw Jonathan reel away from Ebon as Devroe's bullet slammed into his shoulder. He slumped against the paddlewheel housing, as the turning blades continued their deafening revolutions close to his head.

As she saw Devroe aim his other pistol, it came to Rebecca that all these months she'd been duped. She'd been obsessed with Suzannah's material well-being, and Devroe had played on her fears, woven his web. All to get Suzannah in his power. The Brand-Connaught feud had never dimmed in his mind.

Moving with a mindless fury, Rebecca seized a belaying pin nestled in its holder near the ship's rail. As Devroe steadied his pistol, Rebecca screamed and brought the belaying pin down on the back of his head. Though she'd struck with all her strength, it was little more than a glancing blow. But it proved enough to deflect Devroe's aim, and his bullet missed Jonathan and instead smashed into Ebon's back.

The giant Negro reached behind him, his fingers tearing for the bullet. He lurched against the rail; it splintered beneath his bulk and then gave way. Ebon leaned back into the empty air, his hands grasping wildly for the rail. Devroe stared dumbly at him, reaching for the man who'd been his bodyguard, but Ebon fell, toppling into the river. His body thumped against the hull, hit the rudder, then was swept in the ship's churning wake.

Devroe turned, his slitted eyes fastened on Jonathan. Flecks of blood and spittle had formed at the corners of Devroe's mouth and they sprayed the air as he snarled, "No matter, we'll settle this as we should, between ourselves."

With that, he reached down into his boot, drew a long stiletto from its holder, and lunged at Jonathan.

Still dazed from the bullet that had torn through his shoulder, Jonathan barely managed to parry Devroe's thrust and deflect the knife.

Devroe slashed again, this time ripping open Jonathan's shirt and drawing a line of blood across his chest. The whooshing of the revolving paddlewheel muffled the screams of Rebecca and Suzannah. Devroe's face had turned into a madman's. But as he went in for the final kill, his anger, his need for blood made him reckless.

A lifetime as a soldier and Indian fighter had honed Jonathan's instinct, and he nimbly sidestepped the thrust. Devroe drew his arm back again, intending with a sideswiping motion to lay open Jonathan's throat. But his arm came too close to the paddlewheel blades. One blade snagged the ruffled sleeve of his shirt and before he could pull free it yanked his arm into its inexorable arc. Again and again the blades descended, first on his wrist, then his forearm and elbow, breaking and splintering bone.

The excrutiating pain made him lose his senses. Jonathan grabbed Devroe's suit jacket and hauled him away from the paddlewheel. But by then his entire right arm hung limp, bloodied and twisted.

Seeing the mangled arm, Rebecca began to scream, a shrill piercing wail, and Suzannah slapped her mother to make her stop.

"Oh my God, why, why?" Rebecca sobbed.

Suzannah held her mother in her arms, soothing her. In having to comfort her mother, she was able to contain her own horror at Devroe's condition.

With Ebon dead and Devroe unconscious and crippled, there could be no further battle. Captain McLernan brought the *Cru-*

sader into the first river port he came to, which happened to be Gallipolis.

The local doctor examined Devroe's arm and urged amputation. By then Devroe had regained consciousness. He lay in an agony of pain, but refused to have his arm cut off. With each pulse of pain that seared through his body he silently swore, "One day I'll use my arm again, use it to smite all the Brands and their offspring!"

Jonathan's wound turned out not to be very serious. The bullet had passed cleanly through his shoulder, and though he'd lost a great deal of blood, the doctor managed to cauterize the wound. "With the proper rest and care you'll soon recover," the doctor said.

After a day in the small river town, Captain McLernan gave the order for his ship to continue downriver.

Suzannah took a moment to say goodbye to Patrick Donohoe, who had remained aboard the *Crusader*. "Thank you for all you've done for us," she said. "Without your help, who knows what might have happened?"

Patrick grinned at her, feeling as foolish as a schoolboy. "I didn't cotton to that Connaught right from the start. So you're going off to Texas, then," he said softly.

She nodded.

"Well, I've got kin in Brazoria County, and I aim to go back soon, in a year or two maybe—so who knows? We may meet again."

Suzannah reached out and kissed him on the cheek. Then she walked away to where her mother was standing, leaving Patrick staring after her, his hand to his cheek.

With sinking heart, Rebecca watched her daughter approach. Suzannah took her hand. "Mother, I must go," she said gently. "I've got to nurse Jonathan back to health. As soon as he's well, we'll go directly to Texas. Otherwise, he'll forfeit all the land he's contracted for."

Rebecca couldn't speak, her mind and tongue still numbed by all that had happened.

"Mother, I love you. But you must let me have my own life."

Rebecca hung her head, trying very hard not to break down. "I just know that I'll never see you again, never. And it's breaking my heart."

"You will see me. I promise you. And your life will be filled with the new life of your grandchildren."

Rebecca started slightly and Suzannah smiled and finished, "Yes, Mother. And Jonathan and I plan to have as many as possible."

With the shriek of the steamboat whistle came the sing-song call of the mate: "All aboard!"

"Oh, Mother, please, I beg you, give me your blessing!"

Still unable to find her voice, Rebecca could only nod her head slightly. Suzannah embraced her. Then she hurried up the gangplank. She stood at the rail and waved at Rebecca.

He's taking her from me, Rebecca thought with an unreasoning flash of anger. I'll never see her again.

Rebecca watched Suzannah grow smaller and smaller as the *Crusader* headed downriver. And only when she could no longer distinguish her daughter from the other passengers did she allow herself to break down and cry. She stood on the windswept dock, watching the river and life take her daughter from her.

"Oh, dear God, watch over her," she whispered. "She's so fragile. So in need of your protection. Goodbye, my darling Suzannah."

PART TWO

Chapter 9

REBECCA RETURNED to Washington in a state verging on total exhaustion. But her physical condition was nothing compared to the malaise of her spirit. Though Suzannah had shown a spark of independence that Rebecca never knew existed, nevertheless she remained convinced that her daughter's pigheadedness could only lead her into a life of trial and deprivation. If she managed to survive at all on the Texas frontier.

But to be young enough and sure enough to gamble all on love—how she envied Suzannah that! What might her own life have been like if she'd listened to her heart and to Jeremy? But that was a question that could never be answered, a question that could only haunt her through whatever years remained to her.

As her stagecoach passed through the environs of the District of Columbia, Rebecca experienced the same familiar edge of excitement that she did whenever she returned to the capital. Her home...where she'd been born, grown up, suffered her defeats, and known moments of ecstasy. Whatever the quality of her life, she could fall back on that. The capital, the land, the nation did abide.

It was unseasonably hot for April, and the trees seemed to droop in the humidity. And it would get worse; Washington could be a hellish spot in the summer.

"But I am home," Rebecca said aloud as they pulled into the stage depot in Georgetown. She transferred to the Royal George, a commuter coach drawn by four cream-colored horses that ran between Georgetown and the capital. Two women sitting across from her were engaged in some serious gossiping, and intermittently, she heard bits of their conversation.

"I don't care what President Jackson says or how he defends her, the woman is nothing more than a brazen hussy."

"No decent person would acknowledge her, let alone speak to her."

"If her husband wasn't the secretary of war, she wouldn't be acting so high and mighty. They say that Andrew Jackson absolutely dotes on her, and *some* say that he—well, a Christian woman doesn't even like to consider such things."

So, it's Peggy O'Neale Timberlake Eaton they're talking about, Rebecca thought, her interest piqued. I wonder what she's done now?

The stage stopped. Both women got off, and Rebecca heard their final snatches of conversation: "If President Jackson isn't careful he's going to find himself shunned also..." "Why, they say she'll lift her skirts for anybody to get what she wants. And if Jackson keeps defending that trollop, I wouldn't be surprised if the entire government came crashing down around his head."

Ah, Washington, Rebecca thought with a rueful smile. City of rumor and innuendo, intrigue and back-fence gossip, all elevated to an art because of its effect on those in high places. Thus was it ever in the beginning, and thus would it always remain.

"Only one more mile now," she said aloud, thinking that it would be wonderful to see Gunning and Bravo, and then slip between the clean linen sheets of her own bed, sleep in the safety of her own house. The commuter coach stopped on Pennsylvania Avenue, at a point just a few blocks from her house on New York Avenue.

Taking only her valuables, she left her heavy luggage on the street corner, knowing full well that nobody would touch it. The pieces were clearly marked with her name and address, and more than likely, some passing neighbor would deliver it to her house. She approached the grounds of the White House.

"Well, this is something of a surprise," she said aloud. "The White House is still standing." With Andrew Jackson ensconced in the President's house, she thought that his adoring mob would surely have torn the place assunder by now. But she saw gardeners planting magnolias around the newly completed south portico. She remembered when Jeremy had worked with James Hoban to design the serenely beautiful semicircular portico with its six soaring columns. In fact, she was forced to admit, the freshly painted mansion and the well-tended grounds looked better than she'd seen them in years.

As Rebecca approached her neat, trim house on New York

Avenue and Eighteenth Street, tears started to her eyes. Suzannah might be lost to her, but she still had Gunning. And, of course, Bravo. She increased her pace, nearly breaking into a run as she passed through the wrought-iron gate.

She saw Letitia on her hands and knees, tending the vegetable garden on the southern side of the house. When the maid saw her, she let out a tiny cry, raised herself laboriously, and threw her arms around her mistress.

"The Lord of mercy, you home and *safe*," she cried. "You don't know how we been praying and crying and praying!" She dried her eyes on her apron.

"Where are the children?"

"Gunning's out, and Bravo's off somewhere playing down by the Potomac. Bravo says he's going to invent a better steam engine, and he near blowed up the basement the other day. All the preserves is ruined—jams and jellies everywhere."

Tad came running from the carriage house, where he'd been polishing brass and saddle-soaping the harnesses. Rebecca sent him off for her luggage.

Holding Rebecca as if she were some valuable piece of porcelain, Letitia led her into the house. Rebecca sat on the settee in the main drawing room.

"It's good to be home," she said. She still felt the tingling in her body from the stagecoach ride.

"And my Suzannah?" Letitia asked tentatively.

Rebecca told her as briefly as possible. For a moment she felt a resurgence of anger about Letitia's role in all this, but what was the use in holding a grudge? When she'd finished the tale, Letitia sat back and stared at her hands.

"'Pears to me that I'm never going to see my Suzannah again. And that hurts my heart like nothing I know. But if she be happy, then I got to be happy too, no matter what."

"Now stop crying," Rebecca said. "I've done enough crying for all of us. There's nothing that can be done about it now."

Then Rebecca's nostrils crinkled: she sniffed, aware of a faint, yet vaguely familiar, odor in the room. "What is that smell?"

"Oh, there's been lots of goings-on around here," Letitia said, shaking her head.

"What?"

"Best that Mr. Gunning tells you. He'll be home right soon. And that's all I got to say about that matter."

Rebecca didn't press her; whatever the mystery, it could

wait until she'd had a bath. She began to climb the stairs to her bedroom.

Letitia started up after her, in a state of growing agitation. As Rebecca entered her room she drew in her breath sharply. "Letitia, who's been using my room?"

Letitia kneaded her worn hands. Then she heard the sound of horses' hooves; grateful for the interruption, she ran to the window. "I think I hears Mr. Gunning. Yes'm, that's him coming along right now."

Rebecca stood at the window and watched as Gunning galloped up the driveway toward the carriage house, followed closely by a young woman whose face was hidden under a white veiled hat. An older gentleman, trying very hard to post in rhythm to his mare's gait, brought up the rear. Failing miserably, he looked like a disjointed marionette.

"Oh no," Rebecca groaned. "Not Audubert Villefranche. I could tolerate anybody but that man and his daughter."

Though Rebecca considered Audubert a pompous fool, she thought him harmless and somewhat pathetic. But his daughter Véronique was a totally different matter. Rebecca detested her, detested the air of artless innocence that failed to mask her true nature, that of a venal, self-serving little bitch.

The front door burst open and laughter filled the house— Gunning's deep, rich irrepressible baritone, Audubert's honking bray, and Véronique's brittle soprano. Rebecca winced. Gunning bounded up the stairs and stopped dead when he saw his mother.

Then with a shout of glee he rushed to her, swept her into his arms, and whirled her around. "How wonderful that you're here! Why didn't you write? Why didn't you let me know you were coming? Where's Suzannah? Devroe?"

The questions tumbled from him, breathless, demanding. Rebecca found herself still vulnerable to this elemental force that was her son, as vulnerable now as she'd been at the moment of his birth. She wanted to find comfort and strength in his embrace, she needed to cry for all that had happened. But she couldn't allow herself, not in the presence of Audubert and Véronique.

"But you have returned home," Véronique cried in her piping voice. "Washington has not been the same without you."

To be sure, Rebecca thought.

"And I have been desolate," Audubert chimed in, "asking

about you every day. You have been naughty, not writing to
your Audubert."

Rebecca sniffed again; this time she placed the odor: Audubert's ambergris perfume. It seemed to cling to everything
in the house, and Rebecca felt her gorge rise. She turned to
Gunning. "We've important family matters to discuss. I'm sure
the Villefranches would find it all very tedious."

Gunning's brows knitted. "But Mother, I wrote you—" He
slapped his thigh with his riding crop. "Of course, you didn't
get my letters. I've asked the Villefranches to stay with us.
With all of President Jackson's cohorts streaming into the capital looking for jobs, there's a fierce housing shortage. Since
you weren't here and our house was so empty—why, it was
the only Christian thing to do, don't you agree?"

Rebecca managed to hold her tongue, but she couldn't hide
the displeasure in her face.

With the timorous cry of a wounded nestling, Véronique
said, "But I will collect my meager things immediately and
move to another room." She began to clear the Hepplewhite
dresser of her clothes. She swept her unguents and lotions and
perfumes off the vanity top and into her cloth valise. "There,
your room is yours again." Then with a flutter of her hands
she tripped to the armoire, took out a frilly chemise, and clutched
it to her bosom as if she were naked underneath it.

"Charming," Gunning breathed. *"Charmante.* You see,
Mother, Véronique's been giving me French lessons."

Rebecca felt her stomach knot. She would have liked to
throw the Villefranches out, then and there, but sensed that it
would only drive Gunning closer to the girl.

Fortunately, Gunning detected her impatience. He said to
Véronique, "Don't worry, I'll take you to Gadsby's Hotel, put
you up there until I can get you permanently settled."

"Ah, what would I do without you as a protector," Véronique sighed.

Gunning grinned broadly at her, then turned to Rebecca.
"Mother, I'll see you in a bit." With that, he and the Villefranches left.

"What a terrible mess," Rebecca exclaimed irritably to Letitia.

"You're right about that."

Rebecca paced the room. "Now where can Bravo be? Send
Tad down to the river to get him."

Letitia did as she was told, then prepared a bath of warm water and scented oils, and helped Rebecca into the tin tub. She sank in it up to her chin, soaking off the grime and fatigue of her journey.

About half an hour later, Rebecca heard Letitia shrieking from the kitchen. "God, what now?" she called. She threw on a robe and hurried downstairs.

Bravo was standing in the entryway, a pool of water collecting at his muddled feet. He looked dazed, if not half-drowned, but he was still enough in command of his senses to fling himself at his mother.

She held him against her, unmindful of his sopping, dirty clothes, feeling his reedy body trembling with his exertions and with his joy at seeing her. He was only ten, but in the time she'd been gone, he'd sprung up like a sapling.

Amid hiccoughs, he gasped, "Suzannah?"

She told him.

"But—but is she safe?"

Rebecca nodded. "But what about you? What happened?" she asked.

It took Bravo several moments to quiet down sufficiently to explain. "I've been experimenting. Down at the Potomac. See, Robert Fulton thinks there's a way to make a ship travel underwater. I've been studying his plans since you left."

He went on to explain about a small, airtight vessel he'd built from a cask. "Using rocks for ballast, I did get it underwater. But then it foundered."

Rebecca held him at arm's length. "You almost drowned, didn't you?"

"Well, I did get a little wet," he said on a gurgling hiccough.

"Bravo, how many times have I warned you against doing such foolish things? You could get seriously hurt."

He toed the floor sheepishly while she chastised him. But moments later, his irrepressible optimism reasserted itself, and he blurted, "I know what I did wrong!" He started toward the door.

She grabbed his arm. "No you don't, my hearty. You're marching right up to your room. My first day home, I want to make sure you're safe and sound."

"Okay," he said agreeably. "I have things to read anyway, and I guess I can experiment tomorrow." He took the steps two at a time. Halfway up, he turned. "Don't worry, Mother, Suzannah will be all right. And Letitia and I, we prayed all the time that you'd be safe. Everybody did—Circumstance and Wingate too." Then he dashed upstairs.

Gunning returned at twilight. In the drawing room, he prowled the polished hardwood floors, which gave back the sheen of his knee-high boots. "I certainly hope you're in a better mood," he said.

"Now that I'm mistress in my own house again, I'm in a perfectly agreeable mood. Gunning, I've no intention of meddling in your affairs, but a word of caution. Make sure that you're not duped by Audubert. I've known him casually for at least thirty-five years, and he's something of a leech."

"I didn't realize you'd known him that long."

"He and your father were once involved in some harebrained scheme to sell building lots in Washington, when the government first moved here from Philadelphia."

"I can't imagine my father and Audubert being in business together."

"True, nonetheless. Their grandiose plan came to naught, principally because they overpriced the lots and nobody would buy them. They went bankrupt. Your Grandfather Breech had to bail them out. But then, can you imagine anything Audubert was involved in having any chance of success?"

"Frankly, no. On the other hand, he does go around claiming that he was once your swain."

Rebecca threw back her head and laughed, and Gunning joined in. "Beware, Mother, he says he's going to marry you."

"And why wouldn't he want to marry me? It would give him a home, a comfortable enough life in comparison to the gypsy existence he leads now. But have no fear. *This* Brand is immune to that kind of blandishment."

Her meaning wasn't lost on him, and he blushed furiously, all the way to his hairline.

Rebecca put aside the badinage and grew serious. She described what had happened with Suzannah. Her voice caught when she relived the gory details of Devroe's accident.

Gunning grimaced. "Lost the use of his arm—God, how awful."

She passed her hand across her brow, as if trying to wipe away the horror. "After the years of hatred and all the blood shed between our families, I'd hoped there would be peace between the Brands and the Connaughts. But Devroe fooled me completely. And now..."

"What's done is done," Gunning said reflectively. "We can't change Suzannah's stupid mistake, nor can we restore the use of Devroe's arm. Surely the man's intelligent enough to understand that."

"This has nothing to do with intelligence. I'm afraid his thirst for revenge will spill over to include all the Brands. Gunning, I beg you, be careful."

"Don't worry, Mother. I can take care of myself. But I'll keep an eye out."

"One last word before I collapse completely. I don't know what your relationship is with the Villefranche girl, and frankly, I don't care to know. But I consider myself a fairly good judge of character, and that young lady will cause you nothing but grief."

"In this instance, you're entirely mistaken. Véronique's given me nothing but pleasure." He raised his hands at Rebecca's scowl. "I give you my personal guarantee that she's as chaste as the most innocent virgin."

"But really—a toe dancer," Rebecca said with a shrug of distaste.

"You were a stone merchant's daughter," Gunning shot back.

"True enough, and I'm proud of it. But I never displayed my body in public, or for money. Anyway, I thought that Audubert and his troupe were going to New York months ago."

"There was a slight delay in their plans. But they're going in the fall, as soon as the theater season starts up again."

She shook her head slowly, unable to comprehend why Gunning couldn't see through this scheming minx. Lord, but men could be stupid when it came to women.

"And how is your own career coming?" she asked.

"It's tedious, that's the best I can say for it. I rather like the ceremonial part, but for the rest, it's drilling every day, and all sorts of other time-wasting nonsense. The day my hitch is over, I'm going to throw the biggest damned party that Washington ever saw."

"How is that you're off today?"

"Actually, I'm not, but I slipped my sergeant some silver dollars to check me off at roll call. I'll go back to Fort Myer later tonight."

"You're being foolish," Rebecca said, frowning. "I hope you never tangle with Andrew Jackson. He's a military man in the extreme—discipline is his watchword. Remember, he had eight of his own soldiers courtmartialed, then shot for desertion."

"Mother, you're always so full of cheer."

The clock struck the hour and Gunning said, "I'd better leave now. I've got to be in before final roll call." He took Rebecca's hands in his, kissed one, then the other. "Mother, we may disagree now and then, and even fight. But I do love you. I'm very glad that you're safe at home."

Then he bounded down the stairs, mounted his horse, and galloped off. Long after he'd gone, Rebecca listened to the phantom echo of the retreating hoofbeats.

Letitia came in and turned down the bed. She put a new candle in the candleholder, then closed the windows against whatever evil night humors might float in with the darkness.

"Gunning's so like his father," Rebecca sighed. "As tempestuous as a summer storm. I might have been a better parent to him if I didn't love him so much."

"Spoiled him rotten, you did, from the very day he was born. And you still does, because he reminds you of the way you used to be. Just as willful, just as headstrong, pushing his chin to the North Star, like you always did. And that's all I got to say about that matter."

"Oh, I can't argue with you tonight; all the fight's been taken out of me. How's Bravo?"

"Sleeping sound as can be. Probably forgot already that he almost drowned. Like as not he's off on some new adventure in his dreams."

"What are we going to do with that boy?"

"Love him. You worry so much about Suzannah and Gunning—but Bravo, he hardly gets any of the leftovers from your table."

"That's not true!" she protested a bit too vehemently. "Anyway, I was talking about his experimenting all the time."

"Leave him be, that's what. Because the good Lord gave that boy a gift. Sometimes he fills my head with such stories about what's going to be, it's enough to make my hair turn grayer. But he sees these things, truly, and so you've got to let the Lord work his miracles through him."

"Oh, what superstitious nonsense. I can see you've been going to those revival meetings again," Rebecca said irritably. Then feeling contrite, she reached across the counterpane and took Letitia's gnarled black hand. "Thank you for watching out for the children, and thank you for all you've done for me."

Letitia leaned over and kissed her mistress on her forehead. "I knows you're weary tonight. Sees it in your eyes. But I been with you long enough to know that by tomorrow you'll be up and raring to go, getting into more mischief. But tonight, rest easy in your bed. And let's say a little prayer for all our children, wherever they is."

"Amen," Rebecca murmured.

Chapter 10

WASHINGTON WAS practically deserted in the summer. Those citizens who could afford it fled to the mountains of Maryland and Virginia; the poor were forced to remain in the stultifying heat of the capital, perhaps to fall victim to the dread Potomac fever. The seasonal outbursts of the disease struck in early August and by midmonth had claimed the lives of scores of people, particularly in the Foggy Bottom district.

"I know we should all leave," Rebecca said to Letitia, "but this summer I just don't have the strength to get out of Washington."

"But you got the strength to go gallivanting from house to house, nursing the sick," Letitia said.

"Well, Wingate and Circumstance can't do it alone. Somebody has to help."

"Then you'd best wear this charm I done made for you," Letitia said, hanging a small bag of camphor around Rebecca's neck. "Keep the fever away from you."

"Keep everybody else away, too," she said, wrinkling her nose at the pungent odor. "Wingate says that camphor is just an old wives' tale."

"Them doctors don't know anything, 'specially these young ones that gets everything out of a book."

Early that morning, Circumstance and Wingate appeared at Rebecca's house. They dropped off their son Jeremy, so that Letitia could watch out for him and Bravo.

"Now you be careful with Jeremy," Rebecca said to Bravo. "And none of your infernal experimenting, promise?"

Bravo nodded and threw his arm over his cousin's shoulder. Though there was a six-year age difference between the boys, Bravo had a genuine affection for his cousin, and Jeremy idolized him.

Then Rebecca, Wingate, and Circumstance made the rounds

of those who'd come down with the fever. If by chance the
woman of the household was afflicted, Circumstance and Rebecca would do the chores, burn the bedding, and stuff new
pallets with fresh straw, prepare meals for the children, and
then move on to the next patient. Most of the older, more
affluent doctors had long since left the fever zone, but Wingate
remained, laboring on. With calm, quiet dedication he saved
those he could, and eased the passing of the others.

During the burning days of summer, the affairs of government ground to a halt. Most of the legislators, clerks, and judges
had left the capital in late spring. Only President Jackson and
his cabinet remained, struggling to make some sense out of the
"Ladies' War," as the prestigious *Times* of London had dubbed
the fracas over Peggy Eaton. Whereas Rebecca might have
once thrown herself into the fray, now she had little interest
in the scandal and less patience.

"How can these ladies carry on so with their charges and
countercharges when there are scores of people dying in Washington?" she asked Circumstance.

"If these so-called Christian ladies weren't so concerned
with themselves and their precious reputations, and just got out
and tended to the needy, we'd have a far more Christian city,"
Circumstance agreed.

Rebecca worked with Wingate and Circumstance from
dayspring till dusk, and sometimes long into the night. She
came to a new appreciation of these two young people who
gave of themselves so selflessly. Her appreciation grew to love,
and somehow this managed to soothe her anguish about the
loss of Suzannah.

One night, while Circumstance lay abed with Wingate, both
of them so exhausted from the day's labors that they couldn't
sleep, they talked about Rebecca.

"I've had so much difficulty with her," Circumstance said,
"especially when I was very young. I think she blamed me for
standing in the way of her marrying my father."

"But that was so many years ago," Wingate said.

Circumstance nodded. "Since then she's more than proven
herself my defender and friend. We'd have nothing if she hadn't
given us back the deed to this house when you and I married.
And she's arranged for the bank to send me a statement every
year about the income from Father's invention."

"Thank God for that," Wingate said. "It's kept us out of

the poorhouse." With the meager wages that a doctor earned, Wingate was hard pressed to provide enough money for the household. But with that extra money, young Jeremy should be able to get a decent start in life.

The haunting hoot of an owl made Circumstance huddle closer to Wingate. "I'm amazed at how hard Rebecca works. Was she really seriously ill? I've often wondered if she wasn't reacting just a bit too strongly when Suzannah ran off."

"Basically she's got a strong constitution," Wingate said as he gently kneaded her weary shoulder. "But her illness wasn't feigned. When Suzannah left, it was a genuine shock."

"Wingate, I love you."

He drew her closer and they made love, with the gentleness and passion that had graced their lovemaking throughout their married life. Shortly before their marriage, Circumstance had been waylaid by an unknown assailant in the Rock Creek woods; she'd been knocked unconscious and raped. Fearing that she'd conceived, and burdened by guilt, she'd refused to see Wingate. But when he discovered what had happened, he insisted that they marry. "If you have conceived, the child won't know the circumstances; it will only know the love we give it. Besides, if it's your child, how can it be anything but good and decent?"

Wingate's persistence finally won Circumstance over and they married. Ten months later Circumstance gave birth to a son, ruling out the possibility that her unknown assailant was the father of the child. Through Wingate's quiet, consistent devotion, Circumstance had fallen in love with him, deeply, and for a lifetime.

When at last their passion was spent, she lay with her head on his chest. "My darling, do you know something? I want to have another child."

He hiked himself higher in the bed, pondering this. "It might be better if we waited a bit. At least until my practice was more established, and we could afford it."

"At that rate, it might never be," she laughed, and he joined her.

"Now that I'm tending to President Jackson, more and more legislators are calling on me. Soon, maybe I can give you all the things you need to make your life a bit easier."

She gripped his arm fiercely. "Oh, Wingate, what does that matter? Our child will never go hungry. As you yourself once told me, we live and grow on the love we receive. Wingate, I'm so happy with you, so filled with life, that I yearn to pass that gift on. You've had brothers and sisters, but I was an only child . . . and oftentimes, it was so lonely. So if only for Jeremy's sake, please let him have a brother or sister."

Their talk, and her body trembling with desire, rekindled his own passion, and they made love again, this time with a oneness that had the rhythm of being in it, renewing their love, recreating themselves in the image of life.

At long last, summer burned itself away. With the cooling breezes of autumn, the fever epidemic abated. Slowly, the citizenry returned to Washington, followed hard upon by the legislators, and the capital's political and social life resumed. To Rebecca's great relief, Véronique and Audubert Villefranche left for New York City, there to seek their fortune on the stage.

"Mr. Gunning sure is moping around since that little Frenchie left," Letitia said to Rebecca.

"He'll get over it soon enough," she said as she cut the pattern for a new dress. "You know how changeable he is."

"Ain't that the truth! But I knows my Mr. Gunning, and this strikes me different. I ain't never seen him pine for so long."

"But Véronique's only been gone a few days."

"That's nigh onto an eternity for Mr. Gunning!"

By mid-October, social life had picked up considerably, and Rebecca received an invitation to tea at Margaret Bayard Smith's. She sent her regrets, only to receive another note from Mrs. Smith practically imploring her to come. "To discuss a matter of some urgency," the note read. Reluctantly, Rebecca accepted.

Margaret Bayard Smith's husband, Samuel "Silky Milky" Smith, had founded the *National Intelligencer* way back in 1800, and before he sold the newspaper to Joseph Gales in 1811, Margaret had reigned as editor of the society column. She still contributed some pieces, though not on a regular basis.

Rebecca had little patience with this sort of reporting; she deemed it somewhat frivolous. In a town that thrived on gossip and rumor, Margaret Bayard Smith had established herself as something of a power. "I don't want to go," Rebecca said to Letitia, "but I suppose I must."

Margaret Bayard Smith was about Rebecca's age; she wore her graying hair in fashionable shoulder-length curls. Her afternoon tea gown had a bib of lace and matching lace cuffs, and more bows than were seemly for a woman her age. Her greeting to Rebecca was effusive.

Rebecca was somewhat surprised to see the drawing room filled with some of the most distinguished ladies in Washington. Floride Calhoun, the wife of the Vice-President, chatted with Mrs. Samuel Ingham, the wife of the secretary of the treasury, while Mrs. John Branch, wife of the secretary of the navy, was in an intimate tête-à-tête with the Berrien girls, daughters of the widowed attorney general.

Rebecca's surprise was further heightened by the arrival of Emily Donelson, wife of Andrew Jackson's nephew and secretary, Jack Donelson. Emily served as the president's official hostess at the White House.

Margaret poured tea from the pewter Revere tea service. A plate of dainty sandwiches was passed around the crimson-satin room. The amenities dispensed with, Mrs. Ingham turned to Rebecca. "My dear, we've asked you here today to discuss a matter of vital importance. The scandal surrounding Peggy Eaton is casting such a bleak shadow on President Jackson's cabinet. Nobody can get any work done. All the talk is centered on her. If that woman is allowed to continue her scandalous behavior, it's entirely conceivable that she'll do irreparable harm to the President."

Chapter 11

REBECCA FIXED Mrs. Ingham with her penetrating gaze. "Surely the affairs of one woman couldn't have that profound an effect on our government."

"Since you were away from Washington during the spring, you've no idea of the *proportions* of the scandal." Margaret Bayard Smith had a curious way of emphasizing key words.

"News of the scandal has even reached across the Atlantic," Mrs. Branch said.

Floride Calhoun's teacup, held delicately between thumb and forefinger, paused midway to her lips. "Because of her unconscionable influence over our legislators, all of Europe is referring to that Eaton woman as . . . the American Pompadour!"

"To think that this woman who wields so much power was once a barmaid!" Margaret Bayard Smith exclaimed.

"Oh, Margaret, a moment please," Rebecca interrupted with a smile. "Surely you'll agree that one of the shining glories of this country is that an individual needn't be rooted forever in a former social position. Anybody who works hard enough, who has the brains and the will, can do anything. If Peggy Eaton managed to elevate herself, who are we to object? After all, my father was a stone merchant. Margaret, your husband started a small newspaper, and I remember very well that many a night you yourself set type so that the paper could be published in the morning."

Margaret Bayard Smith set down her cup with a clatter. "All of what you say is true. But neither of us has caused our government grave embarrassment. Neither of us has sown such dissension that an entire nation is shamed."

Emily Donelson leaned forward in her high-backed Chippendale chair. Barely twenty, she was considered by most people to be the prettiest girl in Washington, a title once claimed by Peggy Eaton. "Every day I see the terrible effect this scandal is having on my uncle," Emily said. "Coming so soon after the death of my dear aunt Rachel, this additional sorrow does nothing but weaken him."

Margaret Bayard Smith poured Rebecca another cup of tea. "I can see that this news has shaken you. My dear, of us all, you've lived in Washington the longest. You know everybody, including Peggy Eaton." She posed her next question very carefully. "Perhaps you're privy to some information about this infamous woman that will help President Jackson see the light?"

So this is the real reason I've been invited here today, Rebecca thought. "I know a great deal about Peggy Eaton," she began. "Her parents invited me to her christening. Of course, that was back in 1800, and there were only about two thousand people in Washington then."

The ladies leaned forward avidly, eager to pounce on any scrap of information that would help them in their crusade to destroy Peggy.

"Peggy's parents, Rhoda and William O'Neale decided to open an inn, and built Franklin House on I Street, right near former President Monroe's house. Franklin's quickly became the best boarding house in Washington—senators, congressmen, and even Vice-President Clinton had a suite of rooms there. So Peggy grew up with about seventy 'uncles,' all highly placed in the government.

"Peggy and my daughter Suzannah attended Monsieur Generes's dancing school together, though Suzannah was a good deal younger than Peggy. As a matter of fact, I recall a recital at the White House when Dolley Madison awarded Peggy three first prizes for her dancing skills."

"Wasn't that about the time that Peggy tried to elope with a Captain Root?" Floride Calhoun asked impatiently, trying to train her guns on the important issues.

"That happened when Peggy was fifteen," Rebecca said. "She was sent off to a finishing school in New York as punishment and stayed about a year. But she missed Washington, she considered it the most exciting place in all the world—as many of us do. When she finally returned, her father was experiencing some serious economic reversals, and Peggy went to work at the boarding house."

"As a barmaid!" Floride Calhoun said. "Shocking!"

Rebecca nodded. "The tavern soon became the most popular spot in all Washington."

"For obvious reasons," Mrs. Branch cut in, sharing a knowing look with the other women.

"I believe Peggy was about seventeen when she married John Timberlake. He was an unemployed purser in the navy, and to save money they lived at Franklin House. Then Peggy discovered that her husband had a serious drinking problem."

Floride Calhoun, her fan working in sinuous patterns, said, "Just about that time, Senator John Eaton, the richest man in Tennessee, moved into Franklin House. Eaton interceded for Timberlake and got him a position aboard the *Constitution* as purser. All very well, except that Timberlake would be going away on a four-year tour of duty!"

"Criminal!" Mrs. Branch exclaimed.

"If using one's influence was considered a crime in Washington, then all our jails would be full," Rebecca said mildly.

"But Senator Eaton did it to get Timberlake out of the way," Mrs. Branch said. "As soon as he was at sea, they began their . . . indiscretions."

"Do we really know that?" Rebecca asked softly. "Isn't much of the talk merely conjecture?"

"Why, you sound as though you're defending her," Mrs. Ingham said.

"Neither defending nor attacking," Rebecca said. "Merely following the dictates of the Good Book: 'Judge not, that ye be not judged.'"

Floride Calhoun stirred restlessly on the crimson damask couch. "Well, it is *not* conjecture that Timberlake drank himself to death aboard the *Constitution*. He discovered that Eaton and his wife were having an affair. In his deathbed note, Timberlake ended with the words *'Noli me tangere,'* 'Touch me not'—to my mind a clear indication that he knew Peggy had cuckolded him, and that he would have nothing more to do with her."

"That could mean anything," Rebecca said.

But Floride plunged on. "Further, it is *not* conjecture that Peggy O'Neale Timberlake had a miscarriage in 1822, at a time when her husband was at sea and couldn't possibly have been the father!"

"That is a damning statement," Rebecca said. "You know this for certain?"

Floride Calhoun snapped her fan shut. "Reverend Ezra Stiles Ely of Philadelphia, a most worthy man of the cloth and dedicated to God's truth, wrote to President Jackson himself, saying that he had learned about Peggy's miscarriage from a pastor in Washington."

"I'd no idea that the clergy had also become involved in this," Rebecca said.

"Of course they're involved," Margaret Bayard Smith said. "Are they not guardians of our morality?"

"And the name of this pastor in Washington?" Rebecca asked.

"None other than the Reverend John N. Campbell, minister of the Presbyterian Church, the very church that Uncle Andrew attends!" Emily Donelson exclaimed. "Reverend Campbell learned about the miscarriage from the doctor who attended Peggy."

"How did your uncle respond to these charges?" Rebecca asked the girl.

"Oh, he's so bedazzled by Peggy that he refused to listen. He insists that my Aunt Rachel liked Peggy—but in truth, she hardly knew her."

"Peggy and John Eaton lived together quite openly after Timberlake's death," Floride Calhoun said. "Those were the years when my husband served as John Quincy Adam's Vice-President, and Louisa Adams refused to allow Peggy into the White House. Not until Andrew Jackson was elected did John Eaton even entertain the thought of marrying her. You understand, Eaton couldn't serve in Jackson's cabinet while he was still openly consorting with this notorious whore. So he thought he'd give her respectability by marrying her. But once a whore, always a whore—and here we are, with Eaton one of the most powerful men in the government, and his scarlet whore reigning beside him, making a mockery of everything decent and virtuous in American womanhood."

"What's to be done?" Emily Donelson asked.

"Perhaps if there was less talk about it—" Rebecca began, but was quickly interrupted by Floride Calhoun.

"There are certain things which no Christian woman can overlook, and I for one cannot overlook whores."

Heads bobbed and nodded in agreement, lips became tightly pursed. The vehemence with which these women were attacking Peggy forced Rebecca to reappraise the situation. Clearly, this scandal, which she had first thought foolish, was reaching considerable proportions. If it continued, it could indeed cause irreparable damage to the country. But most of these women didn't seem to understand that, despite what they said to the contrary, they were interested only in achieving their own ends. Margaret Bayard Smith was involved because gossip was the natural manure of her life. Emily Donelson was young and didn't realize that she was being used; or perhaps she feared that Peggy Eaton would wield too much influence at the White House and usurp her own position as hostess. The Berrien girls, Mrs. Branch, and Mrs. Ingham were being drawn along in the wake of the strongest person in the room, Floride Calhoun.

And Floride has the most to gain, Rebecca thought as she studied her. The stakes were nothing less than the presidency of the United States. How Floride coveted that for her husband and for herself! Because of Andrew Jackson's failing health, he'd announced that he would only serve as President for one term. And the Calhouns wanted to make very sure of that.

John Calhoun, a consummate politician, had not only served as John Quincy Adam's Vice-President, but had been wily enough to throw in his lot with Andrew Jackson at the last election. But the role of second fiddle didn't suit him; he had his eye on the presidency, and this scandal might well give it to him. And all because of the indiscretions of a former bar-maid, Rebecca thought, feeling her anger grow. She had no special wish to defend Andrew Jackson, but she thought it stupid that the rise or fall of a man should depend on this idiotic scandal. Issues! Why couldn't the electorate concentrate on issues rather than on personalities? Are we forever to be bounded by our personal prejudices in our choice of leaders? she thought.

Then Margaret Bayard Smith cleared her throat. She was evidently disappointed that Rebecca hadn't come forth with more damaging evidence against Peggy, but she still wanted her on their side. "Rebecca, we know that you feel as we do and look with horror at this type of behavior. After all, we must do whatever we can to prevent our city from getting a reputation as a hotbed of sin and corruption."

"You see, there's to be a great ball at the White House," one of the Berrien girls bleated.

"This coming year," Emily Donelson said. "Uncle has asked me to be the hostess. It's to be called the Calico Ball, and all the ladies will be required to wear gowns made of calico."

Why calico? Rebecca wanted to ask, but Floride Calhoun was already racing ahead. "Under ordinary circumstances, the wives of the cabinet members would serve on the committee for the ball," Floride said. "But we've decided not to ask Peggy Eaton to be on the committee. We want you to replace her."

"If we band together and remain true to our principles as decent Christian women, we shall rid ourselves of the pestilence known as"—and here Floride Calhoun's voice grew heavy with distaste—"that American Pompadour."

If you believe it will be that easy, then you don't know Peggy Eaton, Rebecca thought. But it was useless to tell these women anything, their minds were so closed.

"Can we count on you, my dear Rebecca?" Floride asked.

"You may be sure that I'll act on my conscience," Rebecca said.

Chapter 12

REBECCA THOUGHT that she'd successfully avoided taking sides in the "Ladies' War," but several weeks later, she received a note asking if she would come to Mrs. John Eaton's house at three the following afternoon.

She debated whether or not to send her regrets. Her back ached, and the weather had turned dank and miserable, a cold that stabbed deep into the bones. "But if I don't go," she said to Letitia, "then Peggy Eaton will view it as a slight, since I accepted Margaret Bayard Smith's invitation. That can only make matters worse."

"Best you go," Letitia said. "We'll bundle you up real warm. Easiest way to grow old is to give in to your ailments."

"Are you accusing me of growing old?"

"Go."

A wind-driven rain lashed the capital when Rebecca set out the following afternoon. Tad drove the carriage to the Eaton house, which stood right opposite the British legation. Tad dropped her off at the porticoed entrance, then drove the rig into the carriage house to wait for his mistress. Rebecca noted that a number of carriages were there already.

John Eaton had built the fifteen-room Federal-style mansion for Peggy and staffed it with six full-time servants, some of whom were slaves. The rooms were spacious, with fourteen-foot-high ceilings. The fire blazing in the drawing room sparkled off the prismatic glass fireplace screen. Most of the heavy furniture had been imported from France; other pieces came from Baltimore, Philadelphia, and New York.

If I were a jealous woman, Rebecca thought, it would be easy to envy Peggy's rise from barmaid to mistress of all this. How it must rankle her enemies!

The butler announced her and Peggy came forward eagerly. The bronze-colored dress she wore set off her dark-brown hair

94

and eyes. Though she had two children and had just turned thirty, Peggy sported the figure of a young girl. She had a high, firm bust, a tiny waist, and long legs that gave elegance to her movements. But more than mere physical appearance, her attractiveness emanated from an inner vivacity. She'd been weaned on politics, had a keen grasp of political maneuvering, and in the Ladies' War, she would be formidable.

"Ah, my dear Mrs. Brand," Peggy said. "How good of you to come." She impulsively kissed her on the cheek. Since Peggy had not shown Rebecca such affection since she was a child, Rebecca was a bit nonplussed.

Like every other uncommitted female in the capital, I've become a piece of territory to be conquered by one side or the other, Rebecca thought.

"I believe you know everybody here," Peggy said, taking her around the room. Mrs. John Barry, the wife of the post-master general, smiled at her, as did Mrs. Amos Kendall, wife of the powerful politician from Kentucky. Mrs. Stephen Decatur curtsied to her; Susan Decatur was a lovely woman, but since the tragic death of her husband in a duel a decade before, she'd chosen not to remarry and lived a quiet life in George-town.

Then Peggy introduced Rebecca to a newcomer, a striking-looking woman stylishly dressed in the latest Parisian fashion. "This is Minerva Bankhead," Peggy said, "a new friend, but certainly one of my dearest. Her husband is the secretary of the British legation here in Washington."

Minerva Bankhead's brow furrowed. "Where have I heard your name before? Of course—at the Connaught estate a few weeks ago."

Rebecca felt her color rising. Seeing her discomfort, Minerva looped her arm through Rebecca's and drew her aside. "From the tales I was told about you, I expected you to be an ogre."

"I can well understand Devroe's feelings," Rebecca said. "He suffered a tragic accident, one that still makes me heart-sick."

"I knew Devroe Connaught for years in London before he emigrated to the United States. We all know he came here because his branch of the family was destitute, and the American Connaughts are very rich indeed. You're surprised by my candor? Well, Devroe is hardly my favorite person. Whatever happened between you, my guess is that he brought a good deal of it down on himself."

"I do appreciate your honesty." Rebecca said.

"If we're to be friends, and I hope we will be, then you'll find me outspoken in most things. For example, this brouhaha over Peggy Eaton. Such a thing would never happen in Europe; this backbiting gossip is so terribly provincial it's not to be tolerated."

"You must bear with us," Rebecca said. "We're a young nation, without the centuries of code and usage that you've grown up with. In matters like this we often err on the side of rigidity."

"If not stupidity," Minerva said.

Then the two women rejoined the party. Teaspoons clinked in china cups, eyebrows were raised over this or that piece of information, plans and counterplans were made in the Ladies' War.

"With all the scurrilous charges leveled at me, not one person has come forward with a shred of hard evidence," Peggy said. "As for those two sanctimonious preachers, Ely and Campbell—who are they to dictate morals to us? We'll see if they can stand up to the secretary of war and the President of the United States!"

Rebecca knew that under intense pressure from President Jackson, Reverend Ezra Stiles Ely had come to Washington, made a halfhearted apology to Peggy Eaton, then had hurriedly returned to Philadelphia. But Reverend Campbell of Washington had remained adamant in his charges against Peggy, and said that, if pressed, he would prove his case in a court of law. He'd even retained Francis Scott Key to represent him. President Jackson promptly boycotted Campbell's church, and declared he'd go back only if Campbell made an apology to Peggy—from the pulpit. Since doing so would have ruined Campbell's career, he refused. With the controversy now swirling around the ministry, Campbell was casting about for ways to extricate himself from this very difficult position.

"If Reverend Campbell doesn't apologize, I'll see to it that he's removed from Washington altogether," Peggy exclaimed. She turned to Rebecca. "My dear, you and I were born here, we have a natural love for this city. Why should we be at the mercy of these transient elected officials, who make their holier-than-thou pronouncements upon us, and then leave?" Peggy's tone was heated now. "Well, I too have friends in the government. Anybody I don't know in Washington isn't worth knowing. And as for Emily Donelson, she's nothing but a spoiled brat! She'd better watch her manners, because I've already spoken with Andrew, and he's assured me that if I'm not treated with respect in the White House, then he'll send the little brat packing right back to Nashville!"

Rebecca's eyes widened at that. Everybody knew that Andrew Jackson doted on his secretary, Jack Donelson, and on Emily. Both of them had been wards of Rachel Jackson's, and had grown up with the Jacksons at the Hermitage. That Peggy Eaton could make such a threat publicly meant that the Ladies War was creating a schism not only in the government, but in Andrew Jackson's family life as well.

Rebecca grew increasingly uncomfortable. To begin with, Minerva Bankhead's mention of Devroe Connaught had unnerved her. But she also realized that in accepting Peggy's invitation today, she'd tacitly thrown in her lot with the Eaton faction, something she had no desire to do. Above all, she wanted to remain aloof from this hennish backbiting.

She stood up. "Forgive me, ladies, but I must leave. There are so many chores to do at home."

"Oh, but we haven't even discussed our plans for the Calico Ball," Peggy said, rising to stay Rebecca.

But Rebecca started toward the door. At that moment the butler appeared and announced, "Secretary of State Martin Van Buren."

My nerves! Rebecca thought. Peggy's face was wreathed in smiles. And why shouldn't she smile? For the second most powerful man in the government to come calling on her was a coup, Rebecca knew.

"I had no idea that all of Washington's beauty was gathered in this one room," Van Buren said, as he greeted the ladies.

The man is a charmer, no doubt about it, Rebecca thought. And his manner was so reminiscent of Aaron Burr's. In fact, in appearance, there was a marked similarity between the two men. Short of stature, slight of frame, with fine-looking features and a profound intelligence. No wonder there'd always been rumors about Van Buren's parentage.

"But my dear Rebecca, what a fortuitous meeting!" Van Buren said. "After stopping to pay my respects here, I was going to call on you. To ask you to do me the honor of attending the Calico Ball with me."

From the corner of her eye, Rebecca saw the intensity of

Peggy Eaton's gaze. The thought that this entire thing had been
carefully arranged flashed through Rebecca's mind. And in it
all she saw the fine Machiavellian hand of Martin Van Buren,
"the little magician from Kinderhook, New York," a past master in the arts of political intrigue. Washington had long been
abuzz with rumors that Martin Van Buren had thrown in his
lot with the Peggy Eaton faction in the Ladies' War. By supporting Peggy, he hoped to gain favor with President Jackson,
and thereby erode Vice-President Calhoun's position. So far
he had succeeded admirably.

"Just what is this ball?" Rebecca asked.

"It's another of President Jackson's brilliant ideas to bring
North and South together," Van Buren said. "Grow cotton in
the South, manufacture it in the North, then sell calico throughout the world. Under our President's expert leadership, we'll
soon be competing with the great powers in Europe for our fair
share of world trade."

Rebecca couldn't dispel the feeling that Van Buren hoped
everything he was saying would be repeated to President Jackson.

"It's the duty of every patriotic female to do her part in
this," he continued. "That is why, my dear Rebecca, I know
you'll attend the Calico Ball with me."

"Oh my dear Martin," she said, addressing him in the same
coin, "I'm so terribly flattered by your invitation. But the Calico
Ball is weeks, nay months, away, and who can say where any
of us will be then?" With a promise to let him know, Rebecca
took her leave.

Outside, she breathed deeply of the rain-laden air. "My
Lord, but I'm glad to be out of there!"

That night, in the quiet of her study, Rebecca dipped her
pen into her inkwell. She hadn't written anything since Andrew
Jackson's election. Now, writing under her pseudonym, Rebel
Thorne, she demanded, "What is this foolishness called the
Ladies' War? Have we so much spare time that we can afford
to waste it on such inanities? Is this topic proper for the ser-
monizing of our esteemed reverends? Are the members of the
President's cabinet to be hamstrung in their official duties because of the pique of their wives? Ladies, desist! By cauter-
wauling at each other, you do nothing but bring down disgrace
on yourselves!"

Rebel Thorne then went on to excoriate both factions, ac-

cusing them of being vicious and self-serving. No good could
come of further concentrating on such a petty scandal, the only
result would be that the reputation of the United States would
ultimately suffer. Rebel Thorne concluded with, "In your zeal,
you are all acting like fools. Our President and our nation
deserve better. Again I say: Desist, or surely an outraged public
will bring down a plague on both your houses!"

The article appeared in the *National Intelligencer* later that
week and caused a sellout of that particular edition. Most of
the more reasonable legislators were grateful for Rebel Thorne's
outspokenness. Even President Jackson, who had an aversion
to Rebel Thorne, since that reporter hadn't supported him in
the preceding election, allowed as how this particular article
made sound sense.

But curiously, the people whom it should have affected most
remained immune. Rebel Thorne's continued appeal for reason
in the Ladies' War only served to harden the position of both
factions. By midwinter, the scandal had reached such untenable
proportions that Andrew Jackson was in a towering rage.

Chapter 13

"IT'S THE middle of the night," Circumstance said, rousing herself from her sleep. "President Jackson must be very ill to send for you at this time of night."

"I know," Wingate said as he hurriedly pulled on his trousers. "The messenger says that Jackson is having a bad attack."

Circumstance flipped aside the quilt and got out of bed. She wrapped a flannel shawl around her shoulders, went to the fireplace in the main room, and stirred the embers. She took the pot of hot water from the iron fireplace hook and brewed Wingate a cup of bracing peppermint tea while he gathered his instruments and medicines. Circumstance offered a cup of tea to Uncle Alfred, the Negro messenger who'd come from the White House, but the man shook his head. "No time for that, ma'am; the President, he surely got the powerful miseries. I been with him for years down Nashville way, and I never seen him took this bad."

Circumstance said, "You might as well get something hot in you while we're waiting for Wingate to saddle up the mule." Though the White House was close by, the weather was too fierce to walk.

Seeing the sense in what this woman was saying, the colored man cupped his cold hands around the mug of tea. Wingate came in from the shed, his hair hoared with pellets of hail.

"It's cold out there," he said, slapping his arms around his sides.

Little Jeremy had gotten up also and he handed his father a heavy woolen muffler. "Better take this, Pa."

Wingate lifted him in his arms and nuzzled his neck. "Thank you son."

"Can I go with you, Pa?"

Despite his young years, Jeremy had already shown a fascination for medicine. Often he helped his mother gather the herbs she used for her remedies, and if he happened to be with his father on one of his house calls, he never flinched when Wingate had to cut flesh, or set a broken bone.

Wingate shook his head. "You can't come with me. It's too late and too cold."

"But Pa, this is the President of the United States."

"Back to bed with you, and I'll tell you all about it in the morning."

With a hurried kiss to Circumstance, Wingate set out with Uncle Alfred, their heads bent against the driving ice storm battering the capital. Stubborn, the mule, hated being out in this weather and let her irritation be known with some sharp kicks and honking brays at the elements. The gusts tore at Wingate's muffler. Then seeing that Uncle Alfred's thin coat offered him little protection, Wingate unwrapped his muffler and gave it to him. "Take it," he called over the howling wind. "Otherwise you'll get sick and I'll only have to tend to you too."

Pennsylvania Avenue was treacherous under the icy coating, and more than once Wingate fought to keep himself in the saddle as Stubborn stumbled. He leaned over and patted her neck. "That's my good girl. When we get home I'll give you a nice rubdown and an extra feed of hay."

Stubborn turned her head and tried to bite him.

At last they reached the White House. The building's outline looked ghostly white in the slanting hail. Blurred aureoles of candlelight shone in the windows of the living quarters on the second floor. With the North Portico now substantially built, the area that former President John Quincy Adams had planted as his garden had given way to gravel footpaths, a driveway leading to the portico, and to the new carriage house and stable area where President Jackson quartered his prized racing horses.

Jackson needed familiar things about him, and in addition to members of his family, had brought his favorite slaves from Nashville to run the White House. His passion for racehorses remained one of his very few pleasures after Rachel died, and he often went to the National Jockey Club or other tracks in and around Washington to watch his Negro jockey ride his fillies Emily, Lady Nashville, and Bolivia.

Another black servant, with a blanket over his nightshirt, and with his nightcap pulled low over his ears, held his candle aloft and led Wingate through the cold and darkly ominous foyer, up the staircase to the upper floor.

For his living quarters, President Jackson had chosen two rooms at the end of the corridor on the southwest corner of the building. His private office was at the other end of the hall.

Handsome young Jack Donelson paced before the door of Jackson's bedroom. "Thank you for coming, Wingate. I'm sorry to get you out in such foul wêather, but Uncle seems very bad tonight."

"That's all right," Wingate said, as he shucked off his great-coat and brushed the sleet from his hat. "Most people tend to get sick at night; that's when the body's defenses seem to be the weakest. Tell me what happened."

"We had an early meal this evening. Well, words were exchanged at the table about . . . certain events here in Wash-ington. Uncle got upset; so did my wife, and she went to her room in tears."

Jack Donelson glanced down the corridor to the northwest bedroom facing Pennsylvania Avenue, which he and his wife used; the room next to theirs was the nursery for their three-year-old son. "About midnight, I heard a commotion coming from Uncle Andrew's room. I went in and found him com-plaining about pains in his chest. He looked awful. He hasn't had a decent night's sleep all week, and his mood is so mel-ancholy that frankly, I'm worried."

"You did right to call me," Wingate said. "Why don't you go to your room now? Get some rest yourself; I may be a long time. I'll call you when I'm done with the examination."

Jack Donelson nodded and headed down the corridor toward his room. Just then Wingate heard a woman coughing. It must be Emily Donelson, he thought. He didn't like the sound of the cough.

Wingate went into the President's room. Andrew Jackson lay in the tall, intricately carved fourposter; the mattress stood high off the floor to escape the floor drafts. The President was propped up on pillows, and in the yellowish glow of the oil lamps, he looked sallow and drawn. Deep lines furrowed his cheeks, his eyes were closed, and his breathing came in short irregular gasps.

Wingate regarded him intently. Jackson was still as lean and bony as he'd been when Wingate first met him in New Orleans fifteen years before. Once the general had been as strong as a hickory limb, which had earned him his nickname. But the campaigns fought against the Creeks in the South and against the Seminoles in Florida, and all the other battles fought for the nation, had taken their toll. His health had seriously deteriorated, and was aggravated by the grief that he was experiencing over the recent death of his wife.

"Mr. President, are you awake?" Wingate asked softly.

Andrew Jackson opened his eyes slowly. Of an intense blue, they seemed the only living feature in his face. "I'm awake." His voice was hoarse and weary.

"What's troubling you?"

"What isn't, would be the better question," President Jackson barked, and Wingate chuckled in spite of himself. "It's the pain in my chest." Jackson stabbed a long, calloused finger at his bony breastbone. "Can't sleep for the pain, can't turn without it piercing right through my body. But then you know that, Wingate; you've treated me often enough for it."

Wingate nodded. He unbuttoned the President's nightshirt, put his new stethoscope to Jackson's chest. The stethoscope was a straight tube of wood about twelve inches long with a slender brass earpiece. He heard Jackson's strong, rhythmic heartbeat. "Well, your heart is strong, and that's a relief."

After an intensive examination, Wingate determined that though Jackson still had the severe swelling of the feet and legs that had long plagued him, and a lung inflammation that caused him to cough up blood, the President wasn't dying.

He began to massage Jackson's shoulders and chest, easing the pain of an old bullet wound. In a little while the tight, drawn look on the President's face relaxed and his breathing became more regular.

"I remember when you did this for me at the Battle of New Orleans," Jackson said.

"That was a long time ago, General."

"Nigh onto fifteen years. You were only a lad then, but you brought me relief that night so we could fight the next day. General Pakenham and all his fancy red-coated boys—they'd beaten the great Napoleon, and thought that they would do the same to us. What were we but rabble and revolutionaries? How they coveted New Orleans and the rest of the Louisiana Territory, with all its wealth! They were going to conquer it all, and the United States too, and bring us back under the British heel."

Jackson harbored a deep hatred of the British. At thirteen, while serving as a courier for the American Revolutionary Army, he'd been captured by the British. An English officer had demanded that Andrew polish his boots. When he refused, the enraged officer struck the boy on the side of his head with his saber. Jackson still carried that scar.

"And Pakenham and his boys came charging at us that cold day in January. They were going to teach us a lesson, avenge the defeat they'd suffered during our War of Independence. But we rammed grapeshot and hot lead down their throats, didn't we, boy? And if I'd had a couple more regiments of Tennessee Volunteers and Kentucky riflemen, why, I could have taken the British Isles!"

Jackson's outburst gave him another stab of pain.

"General, it does you no good to excite yourself this way," Wingate cautioned him.

"It's that damned bullet again, isn't it?"

Wingate nodded. "You should have had it out years ago."

"But every other doctor I visited told me it was lodged too close to my heart to be gotten out safely."

"Rubbish," Wingate said. "We're making remarkable advances in medicine. It's not too late now. It's the bullet that's causing your persistent chest infection. If we remove it, it would relieve you of all your pain."

Jackson shook his head wearily. "No, I'm too old and far too tired to survive anything like that. Put me under the knife and I'd be sure to die on your hands. I got this bullet near my heart defending Rachel against one of her slanderers, and I'll be carrying it in me when I meet her by and by."

"At least let me take out the bullet that's in your arm. It's causing infections that are aggravating your condition."

Wingate's fingers moved deftly in the hollows of Jackson's ribs. The President closed his eyes and gave in to the gentle massage.

"Did I ever tell you about my duel with that Dickinson cad?" he asked.

He had; but as it seemed to ease Jackson to talk, Wingate listened while he recounted the event that had had such a dramatic effect on his life.

"Charles Dickinson was the best shot in Nashville," Jackson said. "He spent his time drinking, gambling, and practicing his sharpshooting. I didn't like him much, and he didn't like me neither. Well, one day—back in 1806 it was—we got into an argument over a racing wager. It was a stupid argument, as those things usually are, and though I'd never been one to walk away from a fight, I tried to calm Dickinson down. But Dick-

inson wouldn't be calmed, and then he did the unspeakable—
he profaned the sacred name of my Rachel, saying she was
nothing but an adulteress, that even the courts of the land had
proven that."

Jackson paused and heaved a huge sigh. "Oh, God, the
slander that poor woman had to cope with all her life! I'm
responsible for that, for it was I who insisted that we marry
immediately. Damn! Why couldn't I have waited and made
sure that Rachel's divorce from Robards was legal and proper?
But in those young days, when the blood runs hot, waiting is
the last thing a man wants to do.

"Well, Dickinson kept taunting me about Rachel. I demanded satisfaction, and we met shortly thereafter across the
Kentucky line.

"Rachel begged me not to fight, not on her account, but
how could I let such a dastardly lie go unavenged? You see,
lad, my mother, the dear saint, always told me never to take
an insult from any man, and to fight my own battles. And by
God, that's what I've done all my life!

"John Overton, my second, measured off eight paces, and
then he called to us, 'Ready?' Though my throat was dry, I
managed to shout back, 'Yes,' as Dickinson did. Then Overton
shouted, 'Fire!'

"I saw Dickinson raise his pistol, saw him aim, saw the
flash of fire and heard the loud report at the same time I felt
his bullet smash into my chest. But Providence must have been
watching over me that day. Because of the loose coat I was
wearing, Dickinson's aim wasn't true, and the bullet he'd meant
for my heart smashed my ribs instead and lodged in my chest.
But I didn't fall! No, I remained standing.

"'My God, have I missed him?' I heard Dickinson shout.
I felt the blood running down my side, down my leg, and felt
the stuff filling my boot. Never mind about that; I raised my
own pistol, aimed . . . and pulled the trigger. But the hammer
stopped at half-cock. I saw Dickinson's face go pale at the
misfire. It took all my ebbing strength to pull the hammer back
again. But I did, and fired, and this time the bullet found its
mark and killed him." Jackson paused for breath.

"I collapsed, and had to be carried off the field. Overton
rushed me to a doctor in Nashville, and he managed to stem
the bleeding, though they thought sure that I wouldn't survive.

"Later, I was asked whether or not I had any regrets about
killing Dickinson. Well, I believe that a man must be held

responsible for his actions, and he had defamed an innocent woman. I intended to kill him. I would have stood up long enough to kill him even if he had put a bullet through my brain. And so this bullet that I carry near my heart, I carry as a sort of penance for all the pain I caused my dear Rachel with my rashness."

Though Wingate had always been in awe of Jackson, he decided that he had to take a firm stand with him now. "General, that kind of melancholy talk does you no good. There's no reason you shouldn't live out your natural life. But your mood is so dark—no doctor can cure that. Nobody can cure it except yourself."

Jackson bolted upright in a flash of anger. "By God, Wingate, I'd thrash any other man who talked to me that way."

"That may be, General, but you know I'm right. You're beyond the point where you can think only of yourself. It's your country you must think of."

Jackson's shoulders slumped and he lay back. "You're right," he said at last. "I've no personal life left. The only thing is the country.

"Rachel never wanted me to run for this office," he said, his voice rising and falling in rhythm to Wingate's continued kneading. "But everybody told me that I had to run, that the little man in America looked to me, that John Quincy Adams and Henry Clay had made a corrupt bargain to deny me the presidency. In 1824, I did win the greatest number of popular votes, and even though I didn't have a majority in the electoral college, I did poll more than any of the other candidates."

Wingate nodded. "Like many other Americans, I believed that you'd been denied your rightful place."

"Out on the frontier, we're brought up with a different code than you city people," Jackson said. "An injustice done is an injustice that must be rectified. Otherwise, how is right to prevail? How is the country to grow as it should? And so I agreed to run in 1828 . . . and that campaign killed my poor Rachel. The lies and rumors in the newspapers, the innuendos that we'd lived in sin, when all that happened was an honest mistake. My God, we were married for *forty happy years* after that; wasn't that as important as one mistake? But damn them, they kept harping, lying—why, the press even claimed that my mother was a mulatto whore brought here by the British soldiers during our war to service their troops! But those reporters will pay. I believe in the First Amendment as much as anybody—freedom of the press and the like—but the press must also bear responsibility for what they say."

Several minutes later President Jackson said, "I think that's enough for now, boy. And thank you, the pain's eased considerable. I'd be obliged if you'd help me to my chair."

Wingate helped Jackson to a chair by the fireplace. The chair was a prized possession of his, presented to him by the people of Mexico. It had a carved mahogany frame and a hollow morocco leather seat that Jackson found particularly comfortable.

"Throw a log on the fire, will you?" Jackson asked. "I'd call the servants, but they've been up all night long."

Wingate stoked the fire, then put another log on.

"And come out of that corner," Jackson said. "Not even hell itself could warm that spot up." Jackson leaned back in his chair, resting his long legs on the middle bricks of the fireplace arch. Outside, the hail beat a staccato on the windowpanes, rattling them in their sashes. He reached for his long-stemmed Powhatan pipe and started to light it.

"General," Wingate began.

"I know, I know—I shouldn't smoke, but I'm too far gone now to be denied these pleasures. And it does help ease my worries. Believe me, lad, since I've moved into this Great White Prison, all I do is worry."

The fire cracked and popped as the two men stared into the flames. Jackson said softly, "I worry about the ordinary man, and how he's to make his way in this new land. I think the government should have a much more lenient land policy. Anybody who wants to, should be able to own land and farm it . . .

"Then I worry about the growing rift between North and South. I worry about the damnable tariff that John Quincy Adams pushed through Congress during his term of office, and I worry about the South's growing movement to have it annulled . . .

"I worry about our American settlers in Texas, and the repressive policies that Mexico is instituting against them.

"I worry about all the petitioners who come to Washington begging for positions. How am I to create jobs for all of them?" He paused for a moment and his face hardened. "And then I worry about this damnable Ladies' War. It does nothing but bring me grief; work cannot be done in my own cabinet; it's alienating my family . . .

"But I will not abandon John Eaton! He's been a true friend to me for many years. Why, I myself suggested that he marry Peggy O'Neale Timberlake. And he did. So why can't people leave them alone? My God, when I remember that it was the same kind of slanderous gossip that drove my Rachel to an early grave—No! I won't permit such injustice to continue. Those gossipmongers are only trying to embarrass me by sniping away at Peggy Eaton!

"What President can tolerate such division in his own house? My cabinet members say one thing to my face, but reveal their true animosities by allowing their wives to act disgracefully towards Mrs. Eaton. And the man behind the whole thing is John Calhoun. He stirs up dissension because he wants the presidency for himself. Oh, don't think I don't know that. He's a cold man, all head and no heart, and he doesn't understand the needs of the majority of the people. Thinks he knows so much because he went to Yale. Well, on the frontier, a man's value is measured by his common sense, and by what he can accomplish by the sweat of his brow. I'd hate to see how John Calhoun would fare out there!"

But we're not on the frontier, Wingate wanted to say; the political maneuvering in Washington isn't that simple. But he kept his peace.

The talk had roused Andrew Jackson out of his somber mood; he was ready to fight again. He ordered breakfast brought to his room and insisted that Wingate stay. Fatigued as he was, Wingate only wanted to go back home and crawl into his own bed, but when Andrew Jackson commanded, those around him obeyed.

Uncle Alfred brought a steaming pot of black coffee and Jackson poured himself a cup. He noticed the look of censure on Wingate's face, and said, "Wingate, I think you're a wonderful doctor, with the most healing hands I've ever seen on a man. And I promise to heed your instructions. Except I won't give up coffee or tobacco, so you might just as well save your breath."

Wingate threw up his hands, chuckling.

After a simple breakfast of wheat bread dipped in warm milk—Jackson had difficulty with his digestion—he sat back and lit a cheroot. "Tell me, have you any news whatever of your wife's cousin—what's her name?"

"Suzannah Brand. Now Suzannah Brand Albright."

Jackson nodded. "You know that the man she married,

Jonathan, was one of my wards? Raised him myself, when his parents were massacred in Indian wars. If Jonathan were here, maybe he could talk sense to Jack and Emily; they all grew up together. But no, the rascal had to abandon me and go off to Texas . . . Well, I'd probably have done the same thing for love."

"We haven't heard any news at all," Wingate said. "But then it does take a long time for the mails to get to Washington. And with Texas being a foreign country, who knows what their mail system is like?"

"Well, it won't be a foreign country for long," Jackson muttered. "Not if I have anything to do with it. This country has a destiny to fulfill, and that destiny is to occupy all the land from sea to shining sea. Hear me, Wingate—this nation and its people won't be satisfied until we've accomplished just that!"

Dawn had come when Wingate finally managed to take his leave. The President was already up and about, calling on Jack Donelson to get the day's events in order, putting time aside for Ralph Earl, his official portraitist and close friend who also lived in the White House, making plans for a meeting of his "kitchen cabinet"—men mostly from Tennessee, whom Jackson trusted and listened to far more than to his official cabinet. The informal group had gotten its name because the men came into the White House through the back door, the door closest to the kitchen.

When Wingate walked out of the north entrance, he saw his son sitting astride Stubborn. "Jeremy, what are you doing here?"

"When it got towards daylight and you still weren't home, Ma said that I could come and wait for you."

Wingate climbed up on Stubborn and rode with his son seated in front of him. It had stopped hailing, but the earth was crusted with ice, as were treelimbs and the cornices of houses and their roofs, all dazzling in the sunlight. As they plodded along, Wingate told Jeremy what had happened during the night.

"It's not easy being President, son. I don't believe it's a job I could handle well myself."

"I think I might like to be President one day," Jeremy said. "And live in that house."

"You know, your grandfather Jeremy Brand helped to build it."

The boy nodded. "Ma talks about him all the time, and once when she went to the White House basement to search out all his records, she let me come along. Did you like my grandpa?"

"Oh yes, I loved him. He was my best friend, and I wouldn't have met your ma if it wasn't for him. The world became a sadder place when he died."

Jeremy leaned back into his father's chest and Wingate's heart filled with love for this boy who was as gentle and generous as his mother. Soon, though, other thoughts began to intrude on Wingate. He was worried about the President's health. And also about Emily Donelson's. I should have taken time to see her, he thought. She was a fragile-looking creature, and that cough had sounded bad. The dissension in the White House over Peggy Eaton was taking its toll on everybody, that much was evident. "Something has to be done about it," Wingate thought aloud. "So at least the President can find some peace in his own house."

Chapter 14

"THERE'S A letter for you, Miss Rebecca!" Letitia cried, rushing into the house. For once, she forgot to wipe her feet on the doormat, and tracked in the powdery light snow that still blanketed Washington. Letitia clutched the letter to her breast. "Postman say it come all the way from Texas! Oh, pray the good Lord that it be from Miss Suzannah, and that everything be all right."

Rebecca and Circumstance hurried in from the sewing room, where they'd been preparing a layette. Circumstance was in her fifth month, and from the way she was carrying, low and wide, she and Rebecca decided it would be a girl. The blankets and baby clothes they were making were covered with pink ribbons. Hearing Letitia's commotion, Bravo and young Jeremy dashed up from the basement, where they'd been working on one of Bravo's new experiments, a way to increase the intensity of candlelight. For this they'd taken down every mirror in the house and carried them into the basement. Tad also came running in from the carriagehouse.

"Is it too late to catch Wingate?" Circumstance asked Tad. "I want him to hear this."

"He's long gone, ma'am," Tad said.

Wingate had left earlier for the White House, to look in on Andrew Jackson and also to treat Emily Donelson for her persistent cough.

Letitia handed Rebecca the letter. Rebecca stood in the center of the drawing room, clutching it. "It was mailed at the end of November," she said.

"But this is the middle of January," Bravo said. "Did it take almost two months to get here?"

"It did come all the way from San Antonio," Rebecca said, looking at the return address. "It *is* from Suzannah." She knotted her fists. "Oh please, please, let her be all right."

"Open it, mother, read it!" Bravo exclaimed, fairly dancing with excitement.

Rebecca ripped open the envelope and read aloud to the eager listeners:

"'My darling mother and brothers, I pray that this letter finds you all well. Jonathan and I arrived in San Antonio after a rather fearsome journey overland from Nashville. But perhaps I should start at the beginning. We loaded Jonathan's wagon with all our worldly possessions, which included a perfectly wonderful cast-iron stove, a spindle-back rocking chair that Rachel Jackson had given him when he was a youngster, a rosewood bureau, and various and sundry pieces of farm equipment—plows, axes, scythes, and the like, about which I know very little, but am quickly learning. One day in early May, we headed west toward our new home, and our new life. Oh, I want so desperately to forget what happened on the river, and all the anguish I must have caused poor Devroe Connaught. He must live with that affliction for the rest of his days, and I must live with the sad memory of it. Every night I pray for his forgiveness.

"'Jonathan and I didn't travel alone. We had in tow our most important possessions, a perfectly wonderful cow named Ruby Silverhorns, with the sweetest disposition, and what surely must be the meanest bull this side of the Appalachians, a snorting monster named Mean Red. Jonathan spent most of our money on them, for he says that these two creatures will provide for our livelihood. And I mustn't forget our dog. What breed she is, no one will ever be able to determine, but she's gentle and affectionate with us, and a terror to any wild animal that comes too close to our camp. Jonathan named her Monday, because that's when we found her—a frightened, abandoned pup, but she's grown into herself since then, and threatens to become a big dog.

"'We traveled for many, many weeks. The country is so enormous and so wondrous, and I kept thinking about the glorious tales that Uncle Jeremy used to tell Gunning, Circumstance, and me about his adventures on the Lewis and Clark expedition. How strange this will sound, but on our journey, I had the distinct impression that Uncle Jeremy's presence was with us. Or perhaps I only wanted it so.'"

At this point Rebecca's voice caught in her throat and she had to stop. Tears had also welled to Circumstance's eyes. "That's my grandfather," little Jeremy said proudly.

"Go on, mother," Bravo urged her.

Rebecca continued reading. "'Once we'd crossed the Mississippi near Memphis, we joined up with another family heading for Texas, the Kelleys. We were glad for the company and the extra rifles, particularly when a hunting party of Creeks followed us for three days. Fortunately, a herd of buffalo caught their attention and we were able to pass in peace.

"'How can I describe the beauty of our country? The endless, deep-green piney forests, the prairies covered with capricious wildflowers, the bounteous wildlife that grazes upon the breast of our Mother Earth. At night, as I lay staring at the endless heaven illuminated with an infinity of stars, I know in my heart that this is truly God's country.

"'At last we reached the ranchland that Jonathan had filed claim for, about fifty miles from the closest town, San Antonio. I was delighted with it, though it's very different from the terrain around the Chesapeake. Our acreage has some lovely groves of trees, a quick-running stream, and soil that Jonathan believes will prove very fertile, since it's watered by tributaries of the Guadaloupe River.

"'Happy though we were, Jonathan did find himself in an altercation with the local representatives of the Mexican government. They insisted that we had no true claim to the land, but Jonathan soon set them right. I haven't had time to study the situation thoroughly, but my understanding is that the new government in Mexico City, some thousands of miles from here, is refusing to allow any more Americans to settle in Texas. The Mexican army threatens to reoccupy the entire territory, by force if necessary. Stephen Austin will soon go to Mexico City to try to work out a peaceful settlement.

"'There are about eight thousand Americans in Texas now, and we're pressing for status as a separate province rather than being included in the larger province of Texas-Coahuila. Jonathan says we'd get better representation, and he's taken an active role in petitioning the Mexican government. But then, Jonathan takes an active role in everything. I've never seen such energy in a man!

"'After we got here and settled the issue of our right to our land—Jonathan's purchase was dated well before the new Mexican decree—we lived in our wagon for about a week. And then our neighbors began arriving, perhaps twenty in all: the Beacrofts, and the Caldeiras, and the Bybees, and our wonderful friends, the Kelleys, coming from as much as fifty miles away. The men carried their axes and saw and hammers, the women were laden with food and household necessities. They stayed with us for six days, and in that time we built a fine, flat-roofed timber-and-stucco house. Jonathan wanted the roof flat, because he plans to add a second story just as soon as possible. The timber was cut from our own forest, the material for the stucco dug from our own clay pit, a pit that I discovered after tramping about—Mother, you would have been proud of all that I remembered from Grandfather's stone works. The women helped me clear and plant a patch of land for a vegetable garden, and they made us presents of a hen, a rooster, and enough smoked meat and preserves so that we won't go hungry this winter.'"

Rebecca put down the letter and clutched her throat. "I must send her some money. I must—"

"Money won't do her any good out there," Circumstance said gently. "What she needs are goods—household necessities and clothes and farming implements from here in the East."

"Is that the end of the letter?" Bravo asked impatiently.

Rebecca picked up the remaining page. "'We've all settled in—Monday, Ruby Silverhorns, and Mean Red. And that's about all, except that I've saved the best piece of news for last, one that I hope will please you as much as it does me. The good Lord must know how very much in love I am with my Jonathan, for he's blessed us with a child, a fine healthy baby born the last day in November!'" Rebecca's voice had risen to almost a cry as she read the last sentence.

"A baby?" she exclaimed, her face lighting up. "Suzannah's had a baby?"

Everybody began shouting at once, laughing and hugging each other, and the boys let out a couple of Indian war whoops. "What is it?" Bravo asked. "A boy or a girl?"

"Oh my God, I don't know," Rebecca said, grabbing the letter again. "Where was I? Oh, here: 'Our neighbors, the Kelleys, bought land about fifteen miles away from us. But Mrs. Kelley couldn't get here in time—the baby came a bit sooner than expected—so Jonathan had to assist at the birth.'"

"Oh Lord, why wasn't I there to help my Suzannah?" Letitia wailed.

Rebecca stopped her with an abrupt motion of her hand and continued: "'He's such a dear child, and looks so much like grandfather, that I've christened him Mathias. Jonathan wanted to name him Andrew, after the President, but we finally compromised on Mathias Andrew Brand Albright. Now isn't *that* a name to reckon with? I hope it pleases you, mother. Jonathan is as proud as any father can be, and is already claiming that Matty could grow up to be President of the United States. Perhaps, I say, but first he needs to be weaned.'"

"I thought you said I was supposed to be President!" Bravo said to Rebecca.

"And me too," Jeremy chimed in.

"Hush and let me finish," Rebecca said. "'An Indian elder of a nearby Comanche tribe rode up to our ranch last week, wanting food and liquor. Jonathan said to give him the food, but no whiskey. The medicine man looked at Matty for a long time and said that he would be beloved by everybody, but that a star of danger hung over his head. The way he said it gave me a fright. But Jonathan claims that anybody on the frontier lives under a star of danger, and said that he wasn't about to let anything happen to any of us. Knowing Jonathan as I do, that made me feel at peace again. And now I hear Matty stirring, so I must tend to him. Please give my love to everybody in Washington, to my dearest brothers Gunning and Bravo, to my cousin Circumstance whom I miss so much that it hurts like a physical pain, and to Wingate and Jeremy, too, and to Letitia, bless her, and to Tad, and most of all to you, my dear mother. If I could have one wish it would be to hold you all in my embrace again and be warmed by your love. Your Suzannah.'"

"Why is everybody crying?" Jeremy whispered to Bravo.

"That's something that grown-ups do when they're happy," Bravo answered.

Rebecca dried her eyes, then took a bottle of sherry from the Heppylwhite sideboard and poured a glass for everybody, Letitia and Tad included. She gave Bravo and Jeremy just a drop, enough to wet their tongues.

She raised her glass. "Here's to Mathias Andrew Brand Albright. A new birth, and a new hope for the new year."

They drank up, then Letitia took the glasses out and disappeared briefly. Everybody was still in the drawing room, talking, conjecturing, making plans for things they were going to send off to Suzannah, when Letitia came back. She stood bundled in her heavy woolen coat, her overshoes pulled up as far as they would go, her woolen cap pulled down over her ears. She held her packed cloth valise in her hand.

"If you give me my wages for up to today, I'll be going."

"Where, in heaven's name?" Rebecca asked, thinking that

she might have said something that had inadvertently offended her.

"Why, to that there Texas. My Suzannah, she needs me now. I'll be a help to her. She can't raise a child without Letitia. You couldn't," she added belligerently.

"Oh, Letitia, it's wonderful of you to think of that," Rebecca said, and hugged her. But she went on to explain that Texas was thousands of miles away, and at Letitia's age, Suzannah would be saddled with somebody else to care for. "Besides, Letitia, I need you here. How could I ever get along without you?"

"You mean I ain't never going to see my Suzannah's child?" Letitia exclaimed.

"We'll go. We'll all go to Texas someday," Rebecca said.

"You promise?"

"I promise."

Chapter 15

THE TWENTY-FIRST Congress had convened around the New Year, and by the end of January, a furious debate precipitated a crisis in government unlike any that had occurred before. It arose because of the economic differences between the North and the South, but the confrontation between the two major spokesmen for their regions, Robert Hayne of South Carolina and Daniel Webster of Massachusetts, widened to include the issues of slavery, nullification, and states' rights versus national union.

"This debate has been going on since January nineteenth," Rebecca said to Bravo. "Here we are, a week later, and there's still no end in sight. I tell you, we're at a crossroads in our history. That's why you're coming with me to the Capitol. They say that Daniel Webster's prepared his final rebuttal to Hayne and will deliver his address today."

"But Mother, what about school?" Bravo asked. He attended school in Georgetown, preparatory to going to college there. Bravo had already decided that he wanted to go to college, and Rebecca supported him in this. She remembered when Jeremy had attended the school and gotten his degree in the sciences, and the same inquisitive streak and desire to "know" ran in Bravo's blood. Though the tuition was high, she paid it without question; what greater investment could there be than in one's children? And she was putting aside a goodly sum from the royalties of Jeremy's invention to make sure that any Brand offspring would have the opportunity for an education.

"What will I tell my headmaster?" Bravo asked.

"Tell him that you'll learn more about the workings of our government by seeing it in action than by sitting in any classroom. If your headmaster gives you any trouble at all, I'll write him a note. Now come along; we've got to get there early to find a seat. I've never seen such crowds as there've been this week."

Practically everybody in Washington was aware of the debate in the Senate, and partisans for both sides jammed the gallery of the chamber. Rebecca finally managed to find a seat in the back row; Bravo stood behind her. Along with the undercurrent of excitement that increased as the time for the debate grew near, a certain festive atmosphere also prevailed. Listening to the great debaters was as much a part of Washington's social life as going to the theater or to the racetrack.

The ladies had come in their finest clothes, their faces framed by gay bonnets. Some of the more enterprising women lowered baskets of fruit and cake to their favorite legislators on the floor.

The small semicircular chamber with its unadorned walls and domed roof had superb accoustics, a quality which invited the orators to indulge in grandiose eloquence. The senators sat at mahogany desks lined up on semicircular platforms, each row higher than the one in front of it, so that every legislator had an unobstructed view of the floor. Like the members of the House, the senators, unless they happened to be chairmen of committees, had no assistants or offices where they could work in private. Whatever work needed to be accomplished was done at their desks in the Senate chamber.

The crush of people in the chamber became so great that even the floor of the Senate was thronged with spectators. They crowded against the walls, and those who could find no other room stood in the spaces among the senators' desks.

Bravo caught sight of a young boy seated at the foot of Vice President Calhoun's chair on the Senate floor and waved excitedly to him.

"Who's that?" Rebecca asked.

"A friend of mine," Bravo said. "He works for the Senate as a runner. Pages, they're called."

"He looks awfully young."

"No, he's nine. He carries messages on horseback from the Capitol to all the federal buildings scattered over Washington. Other pages work in the House, and do the same for the representatives."

"Do they get paid?" she asked.

"Oh, yes. A dollar-fifty a day, and at the end of every congressional session, if they've done well, they get a two-hundred-and-fifty-dollar bonus."

"My, that can amount to quite a bit of money!"

"I've been thinking of becoming a page," Bravo said, "if I could fit it in with my school schedule. That way, I could earn enough money to pay for college."

Rebecca pondered that. She applauded Bravo's desire to contribute, but she wasn't sure that the atmosphere on Capitol Hill was appropriate for someone his age. These men are hard drinkers, she thought, womanizers, and God knows what else. Then she cut herself short. She was being foolish. Bravo could be trusted to make the right choices for himself. Now if it were Gunning, that would be a totally different matter. "How do you get the job?" she asked.

"A legislator has to recommend you."

"Would you like me to talk to Daniel Webster? Or Chief Justice John Marshall?"

"Would you, Mother? That would be wonderful."

"You see, not only would you be earning money for your tuition, but just as important, you'd be right at the center of power."

"Mother, I know you want me to be President," he said, gently jibing her, "but I don't want to go into politics."

"There are many ways to serve one's country," she said, cuffing him playfully. "And Bravo, we Brands are destined to that end. I knew it in my blood in my youth, and I know it now in my weary old bones. Your father served with Lewis and Clark—"

"My father?" he interrupted with a quizzical look.

"I mean your Uncle Jeremy," she said, trying to recover her slip of the tongue. She rushed on, lest Bravo ask further questions. "The sooner we Brands accept that it's our destiny to serve, the sooner our lives will be fulfilled."

Rebecca pointed out various senators to her son. "There's Thomas Hart Benton from Missouri. He fought a bloody duel with Andrew Jackson when they were both young men, but now he's Jackson's strongest supporter. And there's Daniel Webster." Up in the gallery, Rebecca pointed out other legislators, former President John Quincy Adams and his delicate wife Louisa, and various members of Jackson's cabinet, come to sound out the feelings in the Senate and then report back to the President.

Then all heads turned at a commotion in the gallery. Peggy Eaton, accompanied by Minerva Bankhead, swept in on a wave of floral toilet water, and flashing the most famous smile in all Washington. Though there wasn't a seat available, the gallant young blades fought to give up their places to the two beautiful women. With a lilting laugh, Peggy accepted two choice seats at the front rail of the gallery.

She caught sight of Rebecca and waved gaily at her; Rebecca acknowledged her with a gracious nod. But behind Peggy, off to one side, sat the other faction involved in the Ladies' War: the Berrien girls, dressed alike as the proverbial peas; Emily Donelson, looking beautiful as usual, but particularly wan; Mrs. Branch and Mrs. Ingham; and the formidable Floride Calhoun. These ladies immediately fell into animated conversation, making a great pretense of not noticing Peggy Eaton at all.

The chamber looked as if it couldn't hold another person when Senator Robert Hayne finally made his appearance. He was roundly applauded from the floor and the gallery. At thirty-nine, Hayne, a slim, blond, handsome southern aristocrat, was extremely popular in Washington social circles. Despite his boyish looks, he was an extremely effective debater. Ladies particularly thrilled to his passionate tones, and since he believed wholeheartedly in the cause he was espousing, his fervor usually swept away everything in its path.

Hayne hadn't quite finished the line of thought he'd been developing the day before, and after the roll call, he rose and briefly recapitulated his argument.

Rebecca listened intently, and even Bravo seemed interested. Hayne's point was that New England, because of its cheap water power, was rapidly becoming a manufacturing center. However, New England needed a high tariff to protect its infant industries against products that could be manufactured even more cheaply in Europe. Through the efforts of John Quincy Adams—here Hayne stopped and pointed deliberately to the gallery where Adams sat—such a law had been forced through Congress in 1828.

"That tariff is universally despised in the South," Hayne said in his deep, rich voice. "We've no need of it, and I oppose it as being nothing more than a sectional benefit. We assert our right to nullify this abominable tariff within the boundaries of our own sovereign state of South Carolina!"

A howl of protest rose from the northern legislators, while the states' rights sympathizers cheered themselves hoarse. John Calhoun, presiding over the Senate, allowed the commotion to roil for several minutes, then banged his gavel, calling "Order! Order!"

Rebecca said to Bravo, "There's the man who's behind the whole thing, John C. Calhoun. Hayne is nothing but his spokesman. Calhoun's written some brilliant tracts on the subject of states' rights. He believes that every state has the right to nullify what it considers unconstitutional, such as the law he calls the Tariff of Abominations. And if a constitutional amendment is passed which sides with the federal government, rather than with the individual states, Calhoun further claims that the state can secede from the Union."

"But doesn't that mean that *any* state that didn't like *anything* could eventually secede from the Union?" Bravo asked.

"Precisely the issue," Rebecca said. "The question is, will there be a Union or not?"

When order had finally been restored, Hayne continued his speech. In an effort to get the West on his side, he insisted that the South and the West needed to unite against the economic policies of the Northeast. He accused the Northeast of a deliberate effort to contain westward expansion for the sole purpose of retaining its cheap labor.

"If the poor cannot go west for new land and a new life, then they are forever condemned to spend the rest of their days in some hellish northern factory. The high tariff and western land restrictions create a dependent class of destitute workers in the cities of the Northeast. I denounce the government's attempt to utilize our western lands simply as a means to raise revenues, for this does nothing but increase the power of the federal government. The very life of our system is in the independence of the states. There is no evil more to be deprecated than the consolidation of the federal government!"

In his speech on January 25, Hayne's final comment had proven so popular that it had become the rallying cry for the proponents of states' rights. Now he chose to repeat it, "Once more I say, Liberty first, and Union afterward!"

Pandemonium reigned; the southerners were jubilant. Hayne had presented his arguments so brilliantly that it seemed impossible that anybody could refute them.

At long last the chamber quieted and Daniel Webster rose. His shoulders were broad, and his head massive. Jet-black hair and fierce black eyes that seemed to glow like anthracite had earned him the nickname Black Dan. He wore the clothes that had become his trademark, a dark blue coat with brass buttons, a buff-colored vest, and a high white cravat. His right hand rested on his desk, and his left hand hung at his side.

He began to speak, first lulling the chamber into an accepting mood, then gradually building to his attack. Alternately cajoling, then insisting, and finally demanding, he used his voice as a formidable weapon, and held the audience rapt with attention.

Rebecca felt her own blood begin to pound. How glorious, she thought, that such a debate could take place at all! In some of the monarchies of Europe, such a thing wouldn't have been possible.

Now Webster's left hand had worked itself behind his back, while his right hand made great looping gestures in the air. His stentorian tones reverberated through the chamber as he soared to the climax. "I declare that nullification is impractical, and unconstitutional. Further, it will bring this growing nation to ruin. I go for the Constitution as it is, and for the Union as it is! The Constitution is not the creature of the state governments. It is, sir, the *people's* Constitution, the *people's* government, made for the people, made by the people, and answerable to the people. The very chief end, the main design for which the whole Constitution was framed and adopted was to establish a government that should not depend on state opinion and state discretion."

The western legislators in the Senate chamber, a notorious bunch of ultranationalists, responded wholeheartedly to Webster's nationalistic fervor.

Then Webster lifted his eyes to the domed roof of the chamber. "When my eyes shall be turned to behold for the last time the sun in heaven, may I not see him shining on the broken and dishonored fragments of a once glorious Union; on states dissevered, discordant, belligerent, on a land rent with civil feuds or drenched in fraternal blood! Let their last glance rather behold the gorgeous ensign of the republic . . . not a stripe erased or polluted, nor a single star obscured, bearing for its motto, no such miserable interrogatory as 'What is all this worth?' nor those other words of delusion and folly, 'Liberty first, and Union afterwards,' but everywhere . . . that other sentiment, dear to every true American heart—Liberty *and* Union, now and forever, one and inseparable!"

A roar of approval swept the chamber, mingled with boos and applause. Realizing that it was impossible for the session to go on, John Calhoun called a recess. People filed out of the gallery and congregated in the Hall of Representatives, all discussing the debate.

Rebecca couldn't have been more excited.

"Mother, what will happen now?" Bravo asked.

"Impossible to tell," she said. "A great deal will depend on how President Jackson reacts."

"Is he for states' rights or for the Union? Do we know?"

Rebecca frowned. If the line were drawn, she didn't know where the President would stand. "You know that Jackson was born in Waxhaws—a small settlement on the border between North and South Carolina."

"So he's a southerner," Bravo said.

"Yes, and then he went out west to Tennessee. Wingate tells me that he opposes the tariff, and considering his southern and western background, it's easy to understand why. But he's also President, sworn to uphold the law, and like it or not, the tariff is the law. Well, we'll just have to wait and see how he declares himself. A determined President, acting from strength, can make all the difference."

People continued to mill about, congratulating either Robert Hayne or Daniel Webster. Peggy Eaton and Minerva Bankhead wended their way through the crowd, accepting the compliments of many of the legislators, particularly those who'd left their wives far away at home.

Then Rebecca stiffened as she saw Peggy and Emily Donelson come face to face. Though Peggy acknowledged Emily with one of her famous smiles, President Jackson's niece turned away without a glimmer of recognition. Peggy blanched.

Moments later, Peggy was inadvertently jostled by a woman known to be hostile to her. Her temper frayed by months of snubs, Peggy could control herself no longer, and invective suddenly poured from her mouth, her curses resounding throughout the towering lobby.

Silence fell over the crowd. Though Rebecca hardly considered herself a prude, Peggy's language was so foul that it was disgustingly offensive.

The matron quickly apologized, and when Peggy realized that the jostling had been unintentional, she calmed down. But her outburst had damaged her considerably, and further fueled the fires of those who insisted that she was unfit for polite society. Even Minerva Bankhead looked a little shocked.

Bravo saw his young pageboy friend and scampered off to

talk to him. Rebecca walked across the lobby to congratulate Daniel Webster, who was talking to John Quincy Adams.

Webster greeted Rebecca, and with a nod in Peggy's direction, he said, "Have you ever heard such an extraordinary outburst? And what attention was paid to it! Why, we senators can orate and declaim, but the Ladies' War rages on, crowding out every other issue of vital importance to the nation."

"You're right, and I've absolutely no idea what's to be done," Rebecca said. "People seem to have an insatiable appetite for scandal; they'd rather listen to gossip—the lower the better—than anything else."

Adams, standing several inches shorter than Webster, spoke up, "This whole Peggy Eaton affair exemplifies the immorality of the Jackson administration. The President of the United States surely should have more pressing issues on his mind than defending the virtue of a woman surrounded by suspicion and gossip."

Martin Van Buren brushed by them on his way to Peggy Eaton, whom he engaged in spirited conversation.

"And there's our Little Fox of Kinderhook, wheeling and dealing," Webster said. "It's odd, but the consequences of this desperate turmoil in the social and fashionable world may determine who shall succeed Jackson to the presidency."

Rebecca said irritably, "Oh, enough of her. Gentlemen, just how serious is this nullification movement? Is Robert Hayne just full of bombast, or is there a real danger?"

"Oh, there's a danger, no question," Webster said.

"If South Carolina declares the tariff law null and void, will other southern states follow suit?" she asked.

"Impossible to determine," Adams said.

"But if they did," Rebecca insisted, "would President Jackson have the manpower to put down such an insurrection? Is the army strong enough? Does it support him?"

Both men pondered her question without coming up with an answer, and Rebecca said, "What in heaven's name can be done?"

"Compromise," Webster said. "In a way that will satisfy both the North and the South."

Adams ran his fingers over his nearly bald head. "Compromise, perhaps, but that would work only for the immediate future. The issues go deeper, much deeper, and sooner or later we must address ourselves to the heart of the problem: slavery or abolition. True, the economic considerations are strong, but since this is a moral nation, the moral issue is the one that will determine whether or not there'll be a Union."

Rebecca mulled over what Adams had said. Of course he's right, she thought. The nation, by not addressing itself to the central problem, was merely buying time. Sooner or later the burning question would have to be resolved. Slavery or freedom, secession or Union.

Chapter 16

"WHY I ever agreed to go to this ball, I'll never know," Rebecca said as she straightened the bodice of her gown. "And, for my sins, with Martin Van Buren!"

"You still look real nice for a grandmother," Letitia said, sifling her laughter in her cupped hand.

"What kind of jewels can anybody possibly wear with calico?" Rebecca demanded. She tried various earrings and pendants, but discarded them all.

"You'll have a good time," Letitia assured her. "You told me Mr. Gunning was going to be there. And Circumstance and Wingate too."

Gunning, who still served in the President's ceremonial Old Guard, a division of the Third Infantry, had been assigned this evening to act as honor guard at the White House.

"I must say I'm excited about seeing Gunning," Rebecca said. "But as for the rest, it will be nothing but a bunch of backbiting females, and a lot of avaricious politicans jockeying for power."

"But you loves that," Letitia said. "You loves it since all the years I known you. And that's all I got to say about that matter."

"Honestly, you're incorrigible," Rebecca said, laughing. But you're probably right, she added to herself.

Martin Van Buren arrived toward dusk. He wore a tall hat and shoes with the heels built up; that and cheeks pink from the cold made him look disturbingly like an aging little boy. Rebecca felt so uncomfortable that she excused herself for a moment.

She hurried upstairs to her dressing room, took off her high-heeled, open-toed shoes, and substituted a pair of low heeled dancing slippers. Nevertheless, when she rejoined the secretary of state, she still stood a half a head taller than him.

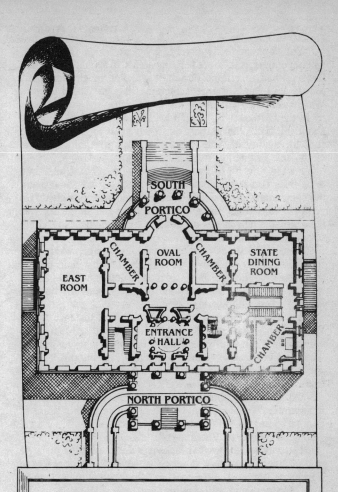

GROUND FLOOR PLAN OF WHITE HOUSE
DURING JACKSON'S ADMINISTRATION

"You look perfectly lovely, my dear," Van Buren said, waxing enthusiastic about her appearance to such a degree that Rebecca had to remind herself it was not an election year. Martin Van Buren wanted something, though. She'd lived in Washington long enough to know the signs.

In the carriage, Van Buren kept up a continuous dialogue about the ball. "Its purpose is to advertise to the world the superior quality of American calico. Did you know that the cloth came originally from Calcutta? Hence the name."

"I wasn't aware of that," Rebecca said. Trust Van Buren to be informed about whatever topic he discussed. He brought the same attention to detail to every issue he approached. He certainly earned her respect for that. What she didn't like was the sense that he was always plotting and planning. How could one relax with such a man?

"I ordinarily don't care for calico for evening wear," she said, running her hands over the dark blue fabric with its pattern of lighter blue flowers, "but when one's country calls . . ." She said it with just the proper tone of gaiety, and Martin Van Buren barked with laughter.

Van Buren's carriage took them the short distance to the White House. As they approached, they could see that every window in the house was ablaze with candlelight. Its pristine whiteness gleamed in contrast to the red-brick buildings of the Treasury and the Departments of the Army and Navy that flanked it.

"Do you know that I haven't been here since Jackson's inauguration?" Rebecca said. "I confess to a certain sense of curiosity mingled with dread."

"What for?" Van Buren asked.

"I keep wondering what Jackson's done. Will the place be in the same kind of mad disarray as the day his mob wrecked it? Has he turned it into a frontier cabin with animal skins all over the floors and walls? What?"

Van Buren smiled his enigmatic little smile. "All I will venture to say is that you may be agreeably surprised."

The carriage turned into the driveway leading to the North Portico, which had finally been completed. A black footman, dressed in an elegant black livery with highly polished brass buttons helped Rebecca out of the carriage.

She glanced at the grounds, taking in whatever she could in the failing light. "Everything looks so different. The approaches were much friendlier when John Quincy Adams had his flower and herb gardens planted here."

"Progress, my dear," Van Buren said. "Benjamin Latrobe designed that North Portico some twenty years ago. But it took Andrew Jackson to get the project moving. He's a man who gets things done."

"Martin, that sounds distressingly like a campaign slogan."

Rebecca swept into the Grand Entrance Hall. Soldiers of the Old Guard stood at attention at strategic points in the entryway and in the hall. Rebecca's eyes sought out her son.

Gunning stood straight as a ramrod, looking as handsome as any man had a right to look in his regimental uniform— white pants creased to a knife edge, dark blue coat with gold epaulettes, and wide white bands criss-crossing his chest. As she passed him he crossed his eyes at her and she burst out laughing, leaving Martin Van Buren quite perplexed.

They joined the people moving slowly toward the East Room where Jackson was receiving. "The entrance hall looks positively elegant," Rebecca said.

"The President's spent more than fifty thousand dollars refurnishing the mansion," Van Buren told her. "When John Quincy Adams was President, this place looked like the poorhouse."

"How quickly you've forgotten that Congress refused to appropriate any money for Adams!" Rebecca retorted. "A Democratic Congress, I might add."

Her remark might have floated over Van Buren's head for all the attention he paid it. "Fortunately, Jackson has an excellent rapport with Congress. They respect strong leadership and gave him the funds. And being a moderately wealthy man, he uses a good deal of his own money to operate the house."

A staff of sixteen servants tended to the needs of the partygoers, serving hors d'oeuvres from shining plates and liquors in the richest cut-glass tumblers and crystal wineglasses. When Rebecca commented on them as she took a glass from a waiter, Van Buren replied, "Jackson ordered twelve dozen of the tumblers, and eighteen dozen of the wineglasses."

The flower of Washington society, both social and political, had come to the ball—Webster, Hayne, Benton, most of Jackson's cabinet members and their wives. Doughty old Chief Justice John Marshall embraced Rebecca when he saw her.

Then Rebecca caught sight of Circumstance and Wingate.

Circumstance came to her and kissed her on both cheeks. "You know how I hate these big gatherings," Circumstance said, "but President Jackson's practically ordered us to come."

Wingate had recently operated on Jackson, extracting an old bullet from his left arm, one that he'd gotten in his duel with Thomas Hart Benton. The removal of the bullet had made a considerable difference in the President's health, and he'd insisted that the Granges attend the ball.

Circumstance, defying every canon of fashion, wore her hair loose, uncurled, and cut in a straight line about three inches below her shoulders. With absolutely no rouge, rice powder, or lip coloring, she looked distinctly out of place among the painted women.

There's something strange and primitive about this girl, Rebecca thought, something I'll never be able to understand. But I do adore her.

Rebecca's mouth fell open when she finally got into the East Room. Three glorious crystal chandeliers, ablaze with candles, reflected their prismatic light all over the forty-by-eighty-foot room.

"The East Room decorations cost nearly ten thousand dollars alone," Van Buren whispered to Rebecca. "Two thousand dollars went for those three splendid chandeliers."

Curtains of blue and yellow moreen set off the lemon-yellow walls, and a rich Brussels carpet of fawn, blue, and yellow, bounded by a wide red border, contrasted dramatically with the blue-damask upholstery used throughout. Rebecca assumed that most of the choices in color and fabric had been Emily Donelson's, and fine selections they were.

Two five-foot-high bronze doré candelabra flanked one of the fireplaces, their glow shining on the Gilbert Stuart portrait of George Washington. "The country has Dolley Madison to thank for saving that painting," Rebecca said to Van Buren. "She had it removed just minutes before the British burned the White House in 1814."

Rebecca's eyes swept the beautifully appointed room. "Frankly, I'm astonished. I've known this mansion under six presidents, and the East Room—which was never really finished—has never looked as beautiful."

Martin Van Buren nodded eagerly. "By making this house attractive, Jackson is giving the lie to everybody's fears that he and Rachel were nothing but frontier louts with no sense of decorum or taste."

Robert Hayne, the senator from South Carolina, paused to greet Rebecca and Van Buren. He flashed his boyish smile at them, then soon went off to talk to Floride and John Calhoun.

Rebecca turned to Van Buren. "What about nullification?" she asked. "Where does President Jackson stand on that?"

"About that, the President is close-mouthed."

"We all know he's a states'-rights advocate," Rebecca said, probing gently.

"Well, he is a southerner," Van Buren said. "But then again, he's also President of the United States."

Rebecca found Van Buren's refusal to commit himself infuriating. He was so adept at the verbal sleight-of-hand that nobody ever knew where he stood. But Rebecca wouldn't settle for this. "We know that Vice-President Calhoun advocates nullification. Would Andrew Jackson willingly preside over the fragmentation of his own nation? And if not, can two people with such divergent ideas exist compatibly as President and Vice-President?"

"Who can know?" Van Buren said. "When the President is ready, he'll make his views known."

I wonder if you *know?* Rebecca thought.

Van Buren went on: "I consider Andrew Jackson to be one of the greatest Americans that this country has produced, and certainly the greatest living American."

"I'm sure the President would be very pleased to know you feel that way," Rebecca said, suppressing a smile. It surely had not escaped Van Buren's notice that William Lewis and Ralph Earl, two Jackson supporters, were within earshot. Really, in spite of all his equivocations, the man was so transparent.

"Oh, but you must never tell him I said so," Van Buren said. "It would cause me untold embarrassment."

The laughter in the room sounded a little too loud, the voices a little too strained, and Rebecca became aware of a distinct edge of tension in the gaiety. Sooner or later Peggy Eaton would arrive. Then the ladies of Washington, and particularly the wives of the President's cabinet, would have to respond.

At last Martin Van Buren maneuvered himself and Rebecca close enough to President Jackson so that they could pay their respects. Jackson still wore deep mourning—a black suit and tie, a narrow black band around the sleeves of his coat. He bowed formally to Rebecca, and she curtsied.

"Mr. President, I cannot compliment you enough on the condition of the White House," she said. "You've given it back its former luster, and this room—every American can be proud of it."

"Thank you, my dear Rebecca," he said. "I might add that you have lost none of your own luster. If there's any change at all in the radiant creature I met back in 1807, that change is for the better."

Rebecca felt herself blushing with the compliment. As tough and strong as Jackson was with men, he was just as courtly and gallant with women.

"And the grounds also look beautiful," Rebecca said.

"Do you really think so?" Jackson asked, obviously pleased. "Let me show you something." Taking her hand, he led her through the crowd in the East Room and on into the Oval Room.

The Oval Room, considered by many to be the most beautiful room in America, was decorated in the French Empire style, which showed the influence of President James Monroe. The fabric on the Bellangé chairs and on the sofas was double-warp satin in a subtle crimson hue complemented by two shades of gold; an American eagle was woven into the center of a wreath of laurel, the classic symbol of victory. The oval Aubusson rug, woven especially for the room, was deep green velvet with the national arms in the center.

"The room is lovely architecturally," Rebecca said, "but the furnishings have always been entirely too crimson for my tastes."

"What would you prefer?" Jackson asked.

"I don't know—beige, or a subtle blue, to allow the beauty of the room to show, rather than overwhelming it with color."

"Well, perhaps someday another President will change it. Of course, if Rachel were alive . . ." He took her to the tall windows and they looked out into the garden, dimly lit by the candlelight coming from the rooms.

"I wanted the grounds to look as beautiful as possible," Jackson said. "You see, Rachel had a way with flowers; she could make anything bloom . . . flowers and people alike. That magnolia standing right there—I've planted it in her memory."

They stood quietly for a bit, engrossed in the beauty of the night and the shadowed garden. Rebecca thought, How wonderful it would be if I could plant something here in memory of Jeremy. After all, he did give his life for this building. I must speak to Circumstance about it . . . even if we have to plant something secretly.

"Incidentally, Rebecca, I recently received a letter from Jonathan Albright. I suppose you know that he's named me godfather to his son," Jackson said with a touch of pride.

"Indeed I do know, and I'm delighted. You may not know this, but Dolley and James Madison are godparents to both my daughter Suzannah and my son Gunning. I'm very pleased that my grandson is in such good company."

"Gunning? Why is that name so familiar to me?"

"My son is part of your regimental Honor Guard," Rebecca said. "In fact, he's on duty here tonight."

"Ah, yes, Gunning Brand. Tall, well-made young man. Headstrong, as I recall. Willful."

"Aren't they all at that age? And weren't you?" she added with a smile, knowing full well his reputation as a frontier hellion.

He smiled in return as they returned to the East Room.

Rebecca didn't quite know what had come over her. She was a woman over half a century in age, yet she was actually flirting with this man! She tried to regain her composure. It was unseemly to act this way—especially since she had come this evening with Martin Van Buren!

Then a low buzz swept the room, heads turned, fans were snapped open and fluttered nervously in the delicate hands of Washington matrons. Peggy and John Eaton had just made their long-awaited entrance.

Chapter 17

REBECCA WATCHED Peggy glide through the room with self-assured, casual grace. Peggy, with her dark-brown hair and dark eyes, had chosen a flamboyant red calico dress that put every other woman's gown to shame. She looked lovely, and she knew it. The unattached men in the room, as well as several who were spoken for, gravitated toward her, paying her extravagant compliments.

She does have style, Rebecca thought, a style edged with just a hint of commonness. She had something else that Rebecca couldn't quite analyze. An air of . . . availability was the only way she could describe it. Men were immediately drawn to it.

The Berrien girls turned their backs on Peggy. Floride Calhoun linked arms with Emily Donelson and drew her into the Green Room, and Mrs. Branch and Mrs. Ingham chose this moment to retire upstairs to repair their maquillage. Of the cabinet wives only Mrs. Barry, wife of the postmaster general, greeted Peggy. But surrounded as she was by dozens of legislators and foreign dignitaries, Peggy couldn't have cared less.

But what was happening wasn't lost on Andrew Jackson. His face turned such a glowering red that Rebecca experienced a moment of fright. She remembered his terrible temper. Even Thomas Jefferson had noted that, in his early days in Washington, "Jackson could never speak in the Senate on account of the rashness of his feeling . . . he would choke with rage."

"By the eternal, I won't let such outrageous behavior continue," Jackson exclaimed to Martin Van Buren. "John Eaton is my loyal friend! I'd sooner go to hell than desert him—no matter what lies some mealy-mouthed minister made up!" He turned to Rebecca. "You've known Peggy all your life, haven't you?"

Rebecca nodded, her mind racing. Peggy must have told him that. Ah! That was why Martin Van Buren had insisted she attend this evening's festivities. If she acknowledged Peggy at this public gathering, a battle would be won. Am I that important? she wondered. No, it's just that everybody is important in this silly petticoat war.

"And have you ever known this woman to be involved in immoral behavior?"

Rebecca couldn't tell him that for years she'd heard that Peggy slept with so many men that she scarcely remembered their names. "Mr. President, you and I have had circumstances in our own lives which make us a great deal more charitable than these dowdies here."

She hoped that he would understand her meaning and not involve her further in this inane fight. Jackson gave her a hard stare, then excused himself abruptly and went to Peggy, showering attention on her for all the room to see.

"What we're seeing," Van Buren mused, more to himself than to Rebecca, "is an example of misplaced loyalty. Because Rachel Jackson was hounded to death by her detractors, Jackson believes he must now protect Peggy Eaton from the same fate. It matters little if the charges against Peggy are true. Jackson's dug his heels in and he'll never budge."

Rebecca regarded Van Buren with new interest. This was the first time she'd ever heard him be so coolly analytical about the situation, and she was pleased at his insight. And you, my Little Magician, she thought, have enough intelligence to use all this to your own advantage.

The orchestra began to play; Peggy was swamped with offers to dance. She accepted the hand of the English minister, Sir Charles Vaughan, and gracefully showed off the new dance-steps she'd learned from Minerva Bankhead.

The awkward moment passed and Andrew Jackson came back to where Van Buren and Rebecca were standing. Laughter and music swirled and eddied around the elegant room, the candles burned brighter with the deepening night, and in the flush of wine and merriment, even the calico gowns took on a certain glamour.

With Peggy Eaton safely occupied on the dance floor, Floride Calhoun came out of hiding and she and her husband paid their respects to Andrew Jackson. Rebecca couldn't help but notice the stiff formality that now existed between the President and his Vice-President. It was in very marked contrast to the warmth that Jackson manifested toward Martin Van Buren.

Without question, in the first year of Jackson's presidency, Calhoun's star had waned and Van Buren's had risen.

When the Calhouns moved on, Jackson stared long and hard after them. "People say that Peggy Eaton has caused the rift between my Vice-President and myself. But it's a great deal more than that."

Rebecca looked at him encouragingly.

"Calhoun knew that because of my health I only intended to run for a single term. But thank the Lord—and Wingate— I'm feeling better every day. Calhoun's attitude may significantly alter my plans."

Van Buren beamed. Rebecca tried a gentle probe. "Do your differences center around nullification?"

Jackson's eyebrows raised in mild surprise. "Oh, my dear, these are problems that the delicate sex shouldn't trouble their heads about."

Though she loathed acting the part of the "delicate female," Rebecca attempted a lilting laugh. "Oh, General, don't you think that everybody who has an interest in this country should be concerned about such an issue?"

Jackson remained close-mouthed and Rebecca continued. "I went to the debates in the Senate. The people heard Robert Hayne, and the people heard Daniel Webster. But the people haven't heard from Andrew Jackson."

The President's eyes flashed and he fixed her with a penetrating stare. From his manner it was clear that he hadn't expected this kind of discussion from a woman. She felt as if his look was boring into her mind, trying to discern what she was after. Stiffening under his appraisal, she exercised all her will to face up to him.

Then the intense moment between them passed, and he was once more the charming, gracious Andrew Jackson, whose courtliness knew no bounds.

The laughter resumed, Baron Huygens of the Dutch legation asked Rebecca to dance, and she waltzed away, occasionally catching glimpses of the President, towering over the crowd.

She felt a bit unnerved by the glimpse she'd gotten into Jackson's character. She was convinced now that no matter what his cabinet said or did, Jackson was in total control of the executive branch of the government. Could that be why he chose weak men for his cabinet? she thought. So that the power would never go out of his hands? Who then is the real magician, she wondered—Van Buren or Jackson?

And he had resisted her every effort to learn where his real sympathies lay. But that was something he couldn't withhold from the country too much longer.

"Oh God," she whispered to herself, "I pray that he chooses wisely, pray that he chooses rightly. The country can't stand too much more of this divisiveness." Only a strong President could prevent the Union from fragmenting and becoming prey to the rapacious European powers.

For some reason, the statement that Benjamin Franklin had made at the signing of the Declaration popped into her head. July 4, 1776. . . . Since then the nation had survived for nearly fifty-four years, grown from thirteen states to twenty-four, with a population of over twelve million. But Franklin's astute comments then seemed even more appropriate today: "We must all hang together, or assuredly, we shall all hang separately."

For another half-hour Rebecca danced, sipped wine, and greeted old friends. She began to think that the ball was an unqualified success; fireworks had been avoided in the Ladies' War, everybody seemed to be having a festive time, and northern and southern legislators were making vigorous plans to capitalize on the production of calico.

But her lighthearted mood suddenly evaporated when she saw Devroe Connaught come into the room. She blinked, not quite believing the woman he had on his arm . . . but it *was* Véronique Villefranche! Rebecca didn't know which upset her more—seeing Devroe, or knowing that Véronique was back in Washington.

Rebecca couldn't tear her eyes away from Devroe. He was impeccably dressed, as usual; the clothes were the finest that Bond Street tailors could produce. He wore a black velvet coat with sweeping lapels, a pearl-gray waistcoat and trousers that matched, and a blood-red boutonnière in his right lapel. His right arm hung limp and formless; to give it any movement, he would grasp it in his left hand, place it in the position he wanted, either hooking it into his coat or waistband, and there it would remain until he moved it again. Sometimes he held the clawed hand in the other, kneading it as if to give it new life by his ministrations.

Devroe became aware of Rebecca's intense gaze; their eyes locked for an instant, then his lips parted in the suggestion of a smile.

Audubert Villefranche accompanied Devroe and Véronique, walking a few paces behind them. He beamed at everybody in a way that said, Look at the catch that my clever daughter has made! Then he spied Rebecca, and in a state of high agitation, tripped across the room to her.

"Alors, ma chérie, I have *so* much to tell you. Most of it good. The bad? Ah, that will pass soon enough." He made a low sweeping bow and kissed her hand.

"What are you doing here?" Rebecca blurted in a tone less than hospitable. "I thought you and Véronique had gone to New York."

"Mais certainement, we have been," Audubert said. "But the theater is closed for a fortnight." He coughed delicately. "Repairs. We might have been stranded but for our good fortune in bumping into Devroe Connaught. He was in New York on business and came to see Véronique perform. He insisted we return to Washington as his guests. Has there ever been a kinder man in all Christendom?"

Rebecca felt herself grow hot, then cold, and then a sense of foreboding swept over her, made even more nauseating by the overpowering odor of Audubert's perfume.

"Véronique scored a great personal triumph in New York," Audubert brayed in her ear. "Why, the city prostrated itself at her feet. She could have had her pick of *anybody.* But just between you and me, Rebecca, I think she still has a little place in her heart for your Gunning. And he for her. You should have seen them when they just met. Such a scene! Why, the sergeant had to come rushing over—but then, that has always been the quality of young love, *non?"*

"A sergeant?" she repeated. "Why?"

"You know how it is when there are two young cocks in the barnyard, and just one hen. I swear to you, Véronique cannot help the passion she stirs up in men. But Devroe's nose is not broken as we first thought—*non,* even the bleeding has stopped, as you can see."

"Audubert, make sense!" Rebecca fairly shouted at him. "What's happened to Gunning?"

"Nothing to worry about. The sergeant said that he would be relieved of his duty for the moment so that he could regain his composure."

When Audubert continued to babble in his own patois, Rebecca left the East Room and went to the foyer where Gunning had been standing. It was now occupied by another soldier. Then she spied drops of blood on the floor.

"Where is Gunning Brand?" she demanded.

Before the soldier could answer, the sergeant, an old career man, came over and took Rebecca's arm. "Come with me, ma'am," he said. "We don't want to create another scene." He led her to the Porter's Hall.

"I'm Rebecca Breech Brand," she said. "What's happened to my son Gunning?"

"He's all right."

Rebecca slumped with relief.

"It was the most curious thing I've ever seen," the sergeant said. "Everything was going just fine until that young couple came in—Devroe Connaught, the man said his name was. Well, he said something to Gunning, and Gunning broke our rule of silence and answered back, and before you knew it, they were at each other. It wasn't a very fair fight, because this Connaught is crippled. We had to pull Gunning off him."

"Where is he now?"

"We've sent him back to Fort Myer."

"What will happen to him?"

"A month or so in the stockade, I should think. Maybe more if Connaught presses charges."

The sergeant saw the look of deep concern on Rebecca's face and said, "Don't worry, ma'am. It's not such a serious infraction of the rules. And maybe Gunning has an explanation for what happened. But all he's got to do is serve out his time, and everything will be forgotten. A month isn't such a terrible long time."

"Caged up? You don't know Gunning."

PART THREE

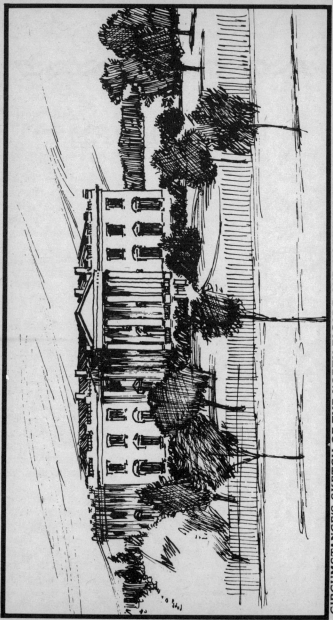

CIRCUMSTANCE'S SKETCH OF THE NORTH FAÇADE AND NORTH PORTICO OF THE WHITE HOUSE

Chapter 18

CIRCUMSTANCE STARTED when she heard the furious knocking at her back door. She put down the sketch she was drawing of the White House, gingerly eased herself out of her chair, and walked to the door, swaying ever so slightly. She was in the seventh month of her pregnancy, and her bigness made her feel awkward.

As she unlatched the door, it flew open and Gunning bolted inside, slamming the door quickly behind him. He put his fingers to his lips, then went to the window, drew aside the curtain and peered outside. "So far, so good. Nobody's followed me."

"What's the matter?" Circumstance asked, taking in his disheveled appearance, the hunted look in his eyes. He was wearing a formless gray tunic and pants that she recognized as army prison clothes.

"That night at the Calico Ball—well, when I saw Devroe come in with Véronique, and bragging to me about it, I guess I lost my head. I went for him. I got a month in the stockade, and that was increased to two months when I told the sergeant where he could stuff his filthy food. Then Véronique sent me a note from New York saying she thought Devroe was about to propose. Well, I couldn't let that happen, could I? Not after all she and I have meant to each other. So I escaped from the stockade."

"But that's madness!" Circumstance exclaimed. "You must go back. Perhaps they haven't yet noticed that you're missing."

"Too late," he said grimly, "I had to hit the guard to escape."

"Gunning, listen to me—"

He shook his head vehemently. "You listen to me. I can't go to my mother's house; that's the first place they'll look. So I came here. I need clothes—Wingate must have some that will fit me well enough. I need money."

143

She shook her head. "I won't help you. What you're doing is wrong. You'll only bring disgrace down on the family. If you can't think of yourself, then think of your mother."

"All I can think of is Véronique and Devroe. And if I don't do something about it, it's like to kill me."

She tried to block him, but he pushed her aside and went to the chest where Wingate's clothes were neatly folded. He shucked off his prison garments and stood in his underclothes, and she couldn't help noticing what a wonderful physique he had. Yet there was something about his presence in the room that frightened her, called forth unbidden memories, of a day years ago when she'd been hurrying through the Rock Creek woods and a stranger had accosted her . . . No, it can't be! She cried inwardly.

"Money!" he said curtly.

She shook her head.

He went into the kitchen and rattled the crockery. "I know you keep your household money here; I saw you put it in one of these things long ago. Ah, here it is." He counted the silver pieces and the paper bills. "Is this all you have? Circumstance, you don't understand! If they catch me they'll put me away for months—years, maybe. I can't let that happen. Not with Véronique and Devroe—"

"Sooner or later they're going to catch you," she whispered. "You can't keep running and hiding all the time. Go back now, Gunning, I beg you."

For an instant she thought he would listen to reason, but then he shook his head. "It's almost dark. I'll take Stubborn and be off. I don't want to get you or Wingate in trouble. If they find out, tell them I forced you to give me the things."

"What will I tell your mother?"

"Don't tell her anything. They'll be coming to her house soon enough. She'll find out then. But tell Bravo to meet me in Baltimore. Tell him to bring money."

Circumstance did not ask where in Baltimore they should meet, for she had no intention of going along with Gunning's wishes.

Without warning, he swept her into his arms and kissed her soundly on the mouth, a kiss with just a little too much fervor. Waves of nausea rolled through her and she thought she was going to throw up. She remembered that cold winter day six years before, when the blow on her head had knocked her unconscious . . . but just before she'd lost her senses, she'd felt a mouth searching for hers. And though he'd then been a lad in his teens, there was no question in her mind now but that the person who'd raped her was Gunning.

He saw her look, and hastily turned toward the door. "I've got to be going. Thanks, Circumstance. Tell Wingate I'll pay him back for everything."

When he was gone, Circumstance tried to collect her thoughts. If only Wingate would come home! But Jackson had called him to the White House late in the afternoon, and he might be gone for hours. Young Jeremy had gone down to the Potomac, hoping to catch some fresh fish for this evening's meal, and he might not be home until later.

"There's no other way. I've got to go and tell Rebecca myself," she said. Vague stirrings of pain moved through her abdomen, but since she'd had several of these false alarms before Jeremy was born, she paid little mind to the discomfort.

Thank God the snow's melted, she thought, as she started out. It was less than half a mile to Rebecca's house, she'd be there in no time at all.

She soon reached Eighteenth Street, but her legs were growing heavy, and then she stopped in her tracks with the first tearing pains. She started walking again . . . Now her only goal was to reach Rebecca's before she passed out. But when she finally got there, she found the place in an uproar. Military police attached to the Fort Myer were swarming through the house, while Rebecca futilely demanded an explanation.

Then Bravo saw Circumstance leaning against the door frame, and he ran to her. "Are you sick? Mother!" he called.

The commotion stopped momentarily. Letitia hurried to Circumstance and put her arm around her waist. "Nothing wrong with her that having that baby won't cure. Now all you people, clear out! This is woman's work, and shouldn't be no menfolk around."

She began to shoo the soldiers out of the house. They left with a warning to Rebecca that if her son did show up, she was bound to let them know, otherwise she would be guilty of harboring and aiding a criminal.

When the soldiers were finally gone, Rebecca went into the downstairs bedroom where Letitia had put Circumstance.

Rebecca brought in a pitcher of water and bathed Circumstance's sweat-beaded forehead. "I didn't think you were supposed to have the baby for another six or seven weeks."

Circumstance thought that the shock of recognition she'd

experienced with Gunning had brought on her labor. But how could she tell Rebecca that? What had happened was in the past, and she would never do anything to hurt this woman who'd been so good to her.

A spasm seized her body and Circumstance grasped Rebecca's wrist. "Gunning," she cried out. When the spasm subsided, she managed to blurt what Gunning had told her. "You must stop him," she whispered. "He'll listen to you."

Rebecca pressed her fingers to her temples, trying to determine what she should do. Her choices were clear . . . but no, she wouldn't leave Circumstance, not in her condition. Letitia was competent as a midwife, but she was getting old and somewhat trembly, and firm hands would be needed here tonight.

"Bravo!" Rebecca called.

Bravo came running into the room, wide-eyed.

"Your brother is in trouble. Mount up and ride out on the Bladensburg road. If he's going to New York to find Véronique, he'll have to catch the packet boat from Baltimore, and that's the road he'll have to take. When you find him, tell him that I *demand* that he come back and face the charges against him. They won't be too serious. We do have friends in Washington. Bravo, don't come back without him."

"But mother, you know he won't listen to me."

"Then you must *make* him listen. I don't care how you do it, but he mustn't get on the packet boat. If he does, his entire life will be ruined."

Circumstance cried out again, and Rebecca herded Bravo out of the room. "I'd go myself, but I'm needed here. Before you leave, send Tad over to the White House, tell Wingate what's happening. Now go, and don't forget what I told you." She leaned toward him and kissed his cheek. "I'm counting on you. Gunning mustn't make this mistake."

Minutes later Bravo was riding hard toward the road to Bladensburg. Within a mile, he left the government buildings far behind and was out in the countryside. The early April evening still had a touch of winter to it, but Bravo and the horse were both riding so hard that they were soon in a sweat.

The darkness closed around him, but he didn't have time to be frightened. The urgency in his mother's demand had fired him with resolve. "I'll stop him," he muttered, and the rushing night wind snatched the words from his lips. Then his horses' hooves were clattering over Tournecliffe's Bridge. Still nobody in sight. After nightfall, the roads out of Washington were apt to be deserted except for an occasional highwayman. Bravo reached Bladensburg and clattered through the stone-and-brick town. Some windows were thrown open at the unfamiliar sound in the night, but Bravo kept driving himself and his mount.

Baltimore lay some thirty miles beyond Bladensburg. Gunning couldn't have gotten this far already, not on that old mangy Stubborn. Could he have taken one of the back roads? Bravo wondered. There were one or two of those, and he rode hard for the first, which wound through a deep forest made even more impenetrable by the darkness. Still no sign of Gunning. Bravo dismounted and put his ear to the ground. He heard nothing, nor did he feel any vibration at all.

He estimated that almost two hours had elapsed since he'd started out. Two hours and not a soul had he passed on the road. He had no other choice; he'd have to ride on to Baltimore and haunt the waterfront. He was about to start out again when he heard the faintest tremor in the ground. It was coming from the direction that he'd just come from. Maybe I passed him in my haste, he thought.

About five or six minutes later, Bravo made out a dim form. "Gunning!" he yelled with glee and rode hard for him.

Gunning whipped out his pistol and aimed it at the rider bearing down on him.

"Gunning, don't shoot! It's me, Bravo," he shouted.

"Sneaking up on me that way, you almost got yourself killed," Gunning snarled.

"I'm sorry, I've been trying to find you for hours."

"It's this damned mule. She won't go any faster than it pleases her. Couldn't stop at any of the taverns and change horses; that might have given my whereabouts away. Did anybody follow you?"

"I haven't seen anybody on this road since I started out," Bravo said.

"Did you bring it?" Gunning asked. "Hand it over."

"What?"

"Don't be stupid, boy!—the money, like I told Circumstance."

"Mother didn't give me any money. She just said that you have to come back. Right now, before you make things worse. That's what Mother says."

"What does she know of any of this?" Gunning demanded.

"Does she know anything of the stupid regulations in the army that keep a man imprisoned for no reason at all? I'm not talking about my time in the stockade; I'm talking about every single damned day, taking orders from some flunky you wouldn't spit on, and being prevented from settling things between you, man to man."

"Gunning, what'll they do if they catch you?"

"They won't catch me. Bravo, give me your horse."

"Mother said to bring you back. No matter what, I had to bring you back."

Gunning reached for the bridle, but Bravo wheeled the mount and kept him out of Gunning's reach.

With a sudden lunge, Gunning caught the reins and, reaching up, hauled Bravo out of the saddle. As he tried to mount, Bravo clung to his brother's leg, "Gunning, don't, please! I promised—"

"Let go of me, you little bastard!" Gunning shouted. "Let go, I say!"

Bravo hung on desperately, even when his brother began to rain blows down on his shoulders and head, shouting all the while.

"You didn't do as you were told! You didn't bring the money! You've always set yourself against me! From the day you were born, you brought a dark cloud over the name Brand. On account of you, my father died!"

Bravo stopped struggling and Gunning shook him free.

"Gunning, wait! What do you mean? Wait!"

But Gunning was already galloping along the road to Baltimore, leaving a badly beaten Bravo behind. Bravo climbed up on Stubborn's back and began the slow ride back to Washington. He'd failed his mother—that was the worst of all.

What had Gunning meant? he wondered. Then he cast his thoughts back to the time when he and his mother had gone to the Capitol to listen to the Webster-Hayne debate. That day she'd let something slip about his "father" having gone on the Lewis and Clark expedition. When he'd questioned her, she'd quickly changed it to his Uncle Jeremy.

Now tonight, when he'd tried to stop Gunning . . . he touched his swollen face gingerly. Gunning had always been rough with him, often brought tears to his eyes, and had even shown him moments of cruelty. But never like this.

From the miniatures he'd seen of his Uncle Jeremy, Bravo

knew he looked more like him than the dark, fiercely handsome Zebulon. Suddenly, Bravo felt very alone. He whispered into the night air, and the ghostly words frosted before his eyes: "Who is my father?"

Chapter 19

THROUGHOUT HIS nightlong ride, Gunning's apprehension made him feel that military policemen were waiting for him around every bend in the road. But he reached Baltimore without incident, and in the morning he boarded the packet boat to New York.

Several days later, after a rough sea journey made even more uncomfortable by visions of Véronique and Devroe, Gunning arrived in the harbor of New York, and the packet boat docked at Wall Street. It was the first time that Gunning had ever visited the largest city in the United States, and he was amazed with its cosmopolitan air.

The city's fortune was its location at the mouth of the Hudson River. The river, when linked up with the Erie Canal to Buffalo on the Great Lakes, had made New York the gateway to the West. The city, with a population of over a hundred thousand, was growing rich on its trade in goods and immigrants—and from the look of things, it would grow richer.

Gunning bounded down from the gangplank to the cobblestoned street. He asked directions to the theater on Bowerie Lane and headed there without wasting time. "Why, *this* is splendid!" he exclaimed, looking at the row upon row of fine houses, most of them in the Federal style, that lined the streets. A commuter stage coach ran up Broadway, but Gunning, feeling very much the tourist, had a passion to see everything he could. He stared at the bakeries and the costermongers, the saddlemakers, shoemakers, clothiers, banks, emporiums. Why, I bet a man could get anything he needed here, he thought. This is really a city! It beats Washington all to hell and gone.

His need to cut his ties with Washington—he could probably never go back there again—filled him with resolve. "I'll make a new life," he swore inwardly. "With Véronique, I can do anything."

When he found the theater, he was a little disappointed with its size; from the way Audubert had carried on, Gunning expected something like the Colosseum in Rome. A theater poster announced a performance that evening of the Villefranche Dance Troupe, featuring "Véronique!" complete with a line drawing of a woman's ankle in toe shoes. Gunning flushed with anger and embarrassment; he didn't want anybody else to see those adorable legs. They belonged to him.

He didn't know where she lived; all his correspondence had been to the theater, and since the box office was closed, he had no choice but to wait until evening. He found a public bathhouse on the Bowery, where he sat in the steam room and soaked out his fatigue and worries.

While he was shaving, a man who looked like a derelict stevedore tried to panhandle him. When Gunning refused, the man got ugly and demanded money.

Gunning's eyes turned as hard as topaz and he flipped open his long straight razor. "Mate, I'd cut you up as soon as look at you, so back off."

With the razor being brandished in front of his eyes, the stevedore slunk off after easier prey. Refreshed, and full of renewed optimism, Gunning returned to the theater. He bullied his way past the protesting old man at the back door, then went down the long dark hallway in search of Véronique's room. At last he found it, and burst in.

Véronique sat at a dressing table, pencils of all colors strewn about, wiglets dangling from a screen, a pink costume with a tulle skirt hanging on a hook. He barely noticed the cramped quarters or the water stains dripping from the paint-flaked ceiling.

Véronique cried out when she saw his reflection in the mirror and half-rose from her cane chair. She wore the barest of undergarments. He swept her into his arms and his mouth found hers, but she squirmed out of his embrace. *"Mon dieu,* be careful! My makeup! I must give a performance in ten minutes."

"Come away with me, right now," he said, his hands roaming over her body.

She slapped them away. "What are you doing here? You have run away from the army?"

"No, nothing like that. Just a short leave of absence." He'd decided that he wouldn't tell her right away. No need to worry her unnecessarily. "What about Devroe?" he asked.

She started pushing him toward the door. "You must get out. I have to get dressed."

"I'll go only if I can see you after the show."

Her mind raced as she tried to remember if she'd promised to meet anyone else. She had, but she'd see that the man at the stage door canceled her appointment. "All right," she said. "But go."

Gunning went to the front of the theater and bought a ticket. He sat in the center and watched as an unsavory lot of people filed in. Most of them were men, and the few women who accompanied them looked a little suspect to him. On the other hand, he thought, maybe that was the way women looked in New York. Washington was notoriously stuffy.

The house lights dimmed, the curtain parted, and there she was, looking so beautiful in the pink footlights he could scarcely believe she was real. Véronique danced brilliantly that night. The knowledge that Gunning was in the audience, coupled with her embarrassment that he'd arrived so unexpectedly and discovered her in this rattrap, had made her nervous energy come to the fore. She danced a divertissement to Mendelssohn's *Midsummer's Night's Dream Overture,* and in the undulations of her long arms, the point of her toe, and the gossamer float of her costume, she created a sensation.

Gunning clapped until his hands were raw. After her encores he went backstage. "I didn't know that you could do anything like that! You were wonderful! But then you're always wonderful."

His crooked smile, a characteristic he'd inherited from his father, left little doubt as to what he meant.

"I must have something to eat," she said. "I am famished."

"All right, but you decide where. I don't know this city yet. But I plan to—I love this town! The excitement . . . everything."

"There is a wonderful place on William Street. Two brothers have recently arrived from Italy and opened this restaurant. They serve the most delicious pastries. It's called Delmonico's."

Audubert insisted on accompanying them: "I won't allow *ma jeune fille* to go out without a chaperon in this wicked city. Never."

The three of them repaired to Delmonico's, which lived up to Véronique's claim. "If we had something like this in Washington, they'd make a fortune," he said, relishing his pastry.

"Ah, what do you Americans know about food?" she asked. "You eat only to eat, but on the Continent we know the refinements of the art of cooking."

"And the refinements of most other things," Gunning said, trying to work his knee between her legs. But Véronique kept her legs close together. Gunning thought he would surely explode from the tension in his loins.

Afterwards, they walked back to the rooming house where Véronique and Audubert lived, a four-story dwelling near Lafayette and Prince Street. The night was balmy; the closeness of Véronique, her lilting voice, the smell of her made Gunning the happiest of men.

"Where are you staying?" she asked.

"I don't have quarters yet," he said. "Perhaps there'll be something here?"

Audubert frowned on that, but Véronique had other ideas. "Oh, I think probably," she said. They passed a fine-looking three-storied house, with dormered windows on the top floor. Véronique said, "I have never seen him, but they tell me that your President James Monroe lives in that house with his daughter, Mrs. Gouverneur."

"Really? Then I must call on him. He's a great friend of my mother's, and I've met him many times."

Véronique raised her finely arched eyebrows at that, and wondered how she might use such an introduction to her advantage. The Gouverneurs were among the richest families in New York, if not in all America. But then, so was Devroe Connaught rich, and lately he seemed to be paying her particular court. Though she wouldn't trust that man with anything.

Accommodations were found for Gunning in the rooming house where the Villefranches lived. That night, as he lay tossing and turning, he heard Véronique bustling about her room. In the middle of the night, driven half-mad by desire, he crept from his room, padded down the hallway past Audubert's open door—he was snoring soundly—and tried Véronique's door. Locked. But the lock felt flimsy; he set his shoulder to it, and with a little pressure, it sprang open.

Véronique bolted upright in bed, but he put his hand over her mouth. She shook her head vehemently. He kissed her, forcing her mouth open, thrilling to the tight warmness of her, and the delicate tongue that he used to dream about. His hands roamed over her body, finding her secret places, while she looked at him from the corner of her eye, once more amazed at his heroic physique . . . surely she had never seen anybody so well made, and always so ready to make love.

"I will not," she said simply, meaning it. "I love you— there, I've said it—but you cannot use me this way whenever you want."

"But Véronique, all I'm asking is that you do what we've done so often before," he whispered.

She let her head drop so that her hair hid her face. "I must tell you that Devroe Connaught has made certain . . . proposals to me."

"I'll kill him," Gunning said.

"Oh, no, you mistake me. He has been a gentleman always. I have not said yes to his proposal, nor have I said no, hoping that one day you would feel it in your heart to declare yourself. But now . . . if Devroe approaches me again, I must say yes to him."

He groaned. He wasn't stupid; he knew she was manipulating him—but in his passion, he didn't care. He persuaded himself that he really loved her, and thinking with the regions that lay below his belt, he blurted, "All right then, if that's what you want, we'll get married—"

"Oh, but how wonderful!" she cried. "We must tell everybody. Papa, the people at the theater."

"All right, we will, only tomorrow. Now—" He reached for her again.

She slapped his face resoundingly. "That most sacred part of me I have preserved for my husband. Not until our wedding night . . ." She scampered out of bed and stood at the door. "Now you must go or you'll wake everybody in the house."

He came at her again, his eagerness revealed by the jutting shape beneath his nightshirt, which gave him such a comical look that she almost laughed. Truly, God had fashioned man in such an awkward fashion. "Oh Father, everybody!" she cried out as his embrace threatened to breach her defenses. "Gunning has asked me to marry him!"

Candles were lit, people came running, Audubert stumbled into the hallway. When he learned the news, he invoked the blessing of God. The joy of the moment was so boundless that nobody bothered asking why the beautiful young couple were in their nightshirts.

• • •

Gunning Breech Brand and Véronique Villefranche were married the following day at New York's City Hall. The huge white marble building, with its gracefully arched windows and columns and a tall cupola surmounting it, was said to have cost more than a half million dollars when it was completed in 1812. Without question, it was one of the finest buildings in all America, and Gunning thought that it compared favorably with many of the government buildings in Washington.

Véronique suggested the civil ceremony be performed by a justice of the peace, claiming that she didn't have time to spare from the theater to plan a church wedding. Gunning, whose mind was on one thing only, acquiesced.

Dimly he heard the justice say, "For better or for worse, for richer or for poorer," and a curious change came over him. She was his wife now, and he would cherish and love her till death did them part. He would become a different person, making everybody proud of him. He knew he had those capabilities; it was only a question of channeling them. With her at his side, he knew he could do it.

He slipped the ring onto her finger, and kissed her gently, tenderly, trying to tell her that something new and wondrous was happening to him, and all because of her.

That night he made love to her, loved her as he'd never loved another woman. Sometimes the base carnality of his nature surfaced and in his passion they became like rutting beasts, and other times, he was as innocent and tender as he imagined Adam must have been when he discovered the delights of Eve.

Véronique found herself confused and overwhelmed by this man of insatiable appetite, using her first one way then another, but always giving himself so totally that it frightened her, for such passion was foreign to her experience. Once, at the height of their lovemaking, he stopped and stared at her, tears glinting in his eyes. "I'm just so happy I almost can't bear it," he said, and then continued.

The honeymoon night left her raw, wounded, drained, and fulfilled. Yes, she thought, I could learn to love this man. What woman wouldn't thrill to the endless pleasure he was capable of giving? Yet part of her was afraid to give herself completely. She'd lived by her wits for so many years, protecting herself and her father, that she'd forgotten how to trust another person, husband or not.

The following day they went shopping and bought a trousseau. He presented a letter of credit to a New York bank, drawn on his account in Washington, D.C. His mother had been banking his share of the Brand movable scaffold invention for years, and what better time to use the money than in starting a new life? Of course there wasn't as much as he would have liked; a great portion of it had gone to pay his old gambling debts, and to buy off some tavern wenches who claimed he was the father of their children. But it would suffice.

Véronique glowed in her new role. Now that she no longer seemed to be walking a tightrope; her dancing even improved.

A week after their marriage, Véronique was at their rooming house when two army officers came to the door. In quick order they told her that Gunning Brand was wanted for desertion; they'd traced him here through the bank drafts. He was to be placed under arrest and returned to Fort Myer.

"Impossible!" Véronique protested. "He is from one of the finest families in Washington. As soon as he comes home, I'm sure he'll straighten this whole thing out."

"When do you expect him?" the officer asked.

"Oh, not for two or three days," she lied. "He's out of town on business."

"We'll wait, if you don't mind."

"Ah, but I do mind," Véronique said, stamping her foot. "This is my home, and you cannot wait here."

But the officers weren't to be put off. They told her that if she aided and abetted him, then she too was guilty and could be prosecuted. Also, she was a foreign national, and that might make things all the more difficult for her. Slowly, Véronique realized the seriousness of this. Gunning had deserted. They were searching for him. The proud and precious moment of becoming Mrs. Gunning Brand had turned into something dangerous. She must save herself and her father at all costs. After all, she wasn't the one who had committed the crime, and she resented Gunning for placing her in this predicament.

An officer standing near the window stiffened. "Here he comes!"

At that moment, Gunning happened to glance up at the windows and saw the man in uniform. He immediately guessed what had happened. He whirled and sprinted down the street, turning the first corner he could, running hard, running away from more time in prison. Even so, he didn't think he could stand being away from Véronique.

He was in such superb physical shape that he easily out-distanced his pursuers, losing himself in the warren of narrow streets. But how to get in touch with Véronique? The theater—for they'd be watching the boarding house all the time now.

That night, he waited until her performance was done, and then risking all—they might be following her—he grabbed her when she got a block away from the theater.

"Why didn't you tell me?" she cried.

He looked around wildly, hoping they weren't attracting too much attention. "I didn't want to worry you. I wanted to marry you. I love you. I do! Now we must get away from here."

"Where?"

"West. They can't track us there. You'll see, I'll make a good life for the two of us. I can do anything as long as you're with me."

Her sharp, brittle laugh cut the night air. "West? Are you mad? Do you expect me to live among the savages? New York is bad enough compared to Paris. If you had told me what you'd done, I'd never have consented to marry you!"

"Véronique, I love you. Does that mean nothing?"

His plea, so young and naïve, reached her heart and she flung herself into his arms. "I cannot go with you," she said. "To begin with, it would be very foolish, for they will be watching for a young couple. You're better off alone. This is a big city. You can lose yourself among the thousands who live here."

"But then what?" he asked, confused.

"As soon as I earn enough money, or we can get whatever money is due you from your bank, we can take a ship to Paris. That's the center of the world anyway, where all life and art and love begins—Paris."

"Paris?" he repeated, not relishing that prospect at all. Yet in his situation, his choices were limited. "All right. But we have to make arrangements—where and how will we meet?"

"Write me care of the theater," Véronique said. "We'll manage it that way."

They passed a narrow, dark alleyway and he drew her inside. Bales of fabric were stacked in the fetid alley. He grasped her waist and before she could protest, lifted her atop one of the bales. He climbed up also and caught her in his embrace. He devoured her with his kisses, at the same time freeing her of her clothes.

For Gunning, it was a desperate attempt to hold onto the

women he loved, the woman he believed would give his life shape and direction. With her love, he knew he could be redeemed.

For Véronique, it proved to be a very different experience, on the one hand terrifying, yet also tremendously exhilarating. The brazenness of it, the fear of discovery at any moment, all proved to be a spur that piqued her to ecstasy, and persuaded Gunning that she loved him as no other man had ever been loved.

Afterwards, he handed her a letter. "I've written this for you. It will enable you to go to the bank and draw out money in my name. When we get enough, we can decide where to go." He gripped her shoulders and looked into her dark eyes. "I love you, my dear Véronique. I know that everything will work out for us."

"I love you too," she said, clutching the letter as if it were a life preserver. But that everything would work out for them—of that she was not so certain.

Chapter 20

WHEN BRAVO returned home from his encounter with Gunning, he found the household ablaze with light and in a frenzy of activity. Circumstance was still in labor. Tad had fetched Wingate from the White House, and there was a lot of hurrying back and forth to the kitchen and boiling of water.

At last, Circumstance was delivered of a tiny child, weighing less than six pounds. "But she's fine and healthy," Wingate said, and passed his swaddled daughter to Circumstance. "She's beautiful. She looks just like you."

Circumstance gazed at her daughter. The infant's complexion was darker than her own, the wisps of hair almost black, and her flat face and high cheekbones reflected centuries of proud Indian blood. "I never knew my mother," Circumstance said. "She died long before I was capable of memory. But something in my heart tells me that our daughter carries the spirit of White Doe in her. May we call her that?"

"Of course," Wingate said.

Then Circumstance thought a bit. "I remember the difficulty that I had growing up in Washington, the child of a mixed marriage. Our daughter will probably have even more difficulty, especially with a name like White Doe. Would just plain Doe be all right?"

"Whatever you want," Wingate said, stroking his wife's cheek. "Oh my darling, if only I could tell you how much I love you, how much my heart is with you."

"But you have," Circumstance murmured. She moved the baby closer to her. "This little one is proof of that."

"You must rest now," Wingate said. "Doctor's orders."

Circumstance smiled wanly. "Send Aunt Rebecca in first," she said softly. "I've something very important to tell her."

"Can't it wait?"

Circumstance shook her head.

Wingate went out, leaving Circumstance with her thoughts.
Gunning... the memory of that long-ago violence in the Rock
Creek woods made a shudder pass through her body. How
she'd loathed what had happened, how she'd loathed him. He
mustn't go unpunished!

Then the baby stirred and screwed up her little face, and
Circumstance's hatred gave way to other feelings, of warmth,
of love. Would it do any good to perpetuate the way she felt
about Gunning? she wondered. For him it had probably been
nothing more than a youthful experience, one of many, long
since forgotten. And yet, where was the balance of justice in
all this? "Oh, God," she whispered, "if only I knew what to
do."

She was still in this state of confusion when Rebecca walked
into the room.

"How are you feeling?" she asked softly.

"All right, though so tired and peaceful that I want to sleep
forever."

Rebecca leaned forward and peeked at the child. "She looks
like a wonderful little girl."

"I must ask you something very important," Circumstance
said, "and you must answer me with all the honesty in your
heart."

"Of course," Rebecca said, somewhat perplexed at Circumstance's sudden intensity. "What is it?"

"I've named my daughter Doe, after my mother. From her
appearance now, I know she'll grow up looking very much a
half-breed. I also know... that there was a time when you had
great difficulty about my having mixed blood."

Rebecca started to protest, but Circumstance stayed her with
a hand. "No, please, my dear, wonderful Rebecca. We both
know I'm speaking the truth. But in these last years I've come
to love you as if the same blood flowed in our veins. So what
I would ask you, is, if it wouldn't cause you any embarrassment, and if it pleased you... would you be little Doe's godmother?"

Tears sprang to Rebecca's eyes. She gripped Circumstance's
hand. "You do me an honor I don't deserve. You're right, I
was blind. But you've ripped that caul from my eyes. I can
think of nothing more wonderful than to have her as my god-
child."

Circumstance lifted the baby and held her toward Rebecca,
who cradled the child in her arms. "Hello, my little one," she

whispered. "I'm your godmother." Then she added under her breath, "And just let anybody in Washington dare to say anything against you!"

After leaving Circumstance, Rebecca went upstairs to Bravo's room. The boy lay sprawled on his bed; he'd fallen asleep waiting for her. She sat by his bedside and caught her breath when she saw his swollen face. Gunning must have beaten him. The battle between these half-brothers brought back the memory of what had happened between Jeremy and Zebulon. Oh Lord, she thought, is the same hatred to be perpetuated in this generation also? Is there never to be an end to it?

She buried her face in her hands and wept for all the pain that she knew lay ahead for Gunning. She told herself she should abandon him . . . but she couldn't. And tears wouldn't help. Something more useful was required.

"Rebecca, you know how sorry I am that this has happened to you and your family," President Jackson said to her.

When she'd requested an appointment with him, he'd agreed and received her in the Green Room. Jackson had redone this room also, but the color he'd chosen was such an odious green that it robbed his face of life, and Rebecca was certain that it was doing the same to hers.

Jackson held up a sheaf of papers, then laid them down on the couch near her. "I had the commander of Gunning's unit prepare a file for me. It's all here for you to see. Lateness, insubordination, then at the Calico Ball, he abandoned his post and attacked one of my guests, in my house! And a one-armed man at that."

Rebecca tried to explain the Brand relationship with the Connaughts, but Jackson wasn't receptive. "When he was put in the stockade for punishment, he overpowered the guard and escaped. Rebecca, how long do you think an army could maintain discipline if behavior like that went unpunished?"

"All I'm asking for is leniency," Rebecca said. "I ask it not as a lawyer, nor a military officer, but as a parent who loves her child. You would do nothing less for your children."

"As a parent, I most assuredly do sympathize with you. I know the pain that my own nephew and niece have brought me because of their actions. But as President, I have another, equally important function. The country must never believe that I cannot run my own household, or my own administration.

That's why I've asked Jack Donelson and Emily to go back to Nashville. If they can't honor my wishes in regard to Peggy Eaton, then I can't have them in my house. This same code insists that I deal impartially with Gunning Brand."

"What will happen to him?"

"It depends on how long he's absent without leave. If he returned to the fort of his own volition, it wouldn't be considered desertion. But if a significant length of time goes by, he'll be courtmartialed."

"A jail term?" she asked weakly.

"Most probably. Again, the extent of the punishment will be determined by the circumstances of his return."

Jackson rose and Rebecca knew that the interview was at an end. He took her hand and pressed it. "Rebecca, I am sorry. Perhaps he'll come to his senses and return, and this will resolve itself with less pain to you."

Rebecca left the White House, feeling more miserable than when she'd arrived. For the next few days she did whatever she could to locate her son—put notices in the papers, asked his friends if they'd heard from him. She thought of hiring a private detective—several of these men had achieved prominence in Washington for their investigative work recently—but with the paucity of information she had, none of them could help her.

The first week in April Rebecca received an invitation to the Jefferson Day dinner, which was to be held on April 13 at Brown's Indian Queen Hotel. Every year, the Democrats in Congress celebrated Jefferson's birthday—he was the founder of their party, and a man who believed in as little federal government as possible. Since feelings were running very high in Congress concerning states' rights and nullification, the dinner promised to be a lively affair.

Rebecca had no intention of going. Then one day Wingate came by and told her that it would be wise for her to go. "I know it's difficult for you, but you must keep up appearances. Besides, there'll be many people there who can ultimately help us in our cause with Gunning."

Rebecca didn't quite believe that.

"Circumstance doesn't want to go because she's still recuperating, so I've got an extra ticket," Wingate said. "Look, the President is sure to attend, since he's known to be the great restorer of Jeffersonian principles. If he goes, you can be sure that his cabinet members will too—and Vice-President Calhoun, of course, and everybody else of any importance in the Democratic Party. Already they're calling it a states'-rights gala. In fact, Van Buren claims that the entire dinner is nothing but a plot of Calhoun's."

"Van Buren sees plots in everything that concerns Calhoun," she said.

"But he says that Calhoun is going to use the celebration to gain support for the South."

Rebecca suddenly became alarmed. "You don't think that Jackson is going to champion the South's views on nullification, do you?"

"I wish I knew," Wingate said. "But on that problem, Jackson is still keeping his thoughts to himself."

"Well, then, I think I'd just better go to that dinner," Rebecca said.

As the day of the celebration grew closer, the *United States Telegraph*, the paper owned by Duff Green—a supporter of Jackson's known to be rabidly in favor of states' rights—printed the program for the Jefferson Day dinner. Rebecca read the list of the principal speakers with growing indignation. "Why, they're all states'-rights men!"

Thinking that they might have an opportunity to do some judicious lobbying with the legislators, Rebecca and Wingate started out early for the Indian Queen Hotel, located on the northwest corner of Pennsylvania Avenue and Sixth Street.

"I remember when this was the old Davis Hotel," Rebecca said to Wingate. "It was here in 1814 that the 'Star Spangled Banner' was first sung in public. Of course, it's been extensively remodeled since those days. But that sign—" She looked up at a crudely painted sign with a picture of Pocahontas that swung lazily in the breeze. "—that's always been here."

The four-story hotel, considered one of the finest in Washington, had been festively decorated for the occasion. A life-sized portrait of George Washington and two busts of Thomas Jefferson were prominently displayed. Evergreens festooned the door portals, and flowers were everywhere. Two long tables stood parallel to each other, with a cross table at the head, where the principal speakers and the President were to sit.

The ballroom began to fill with the prominent people of Washington—legislators, including more than a hundred congressmen in all; officers in the army and navy; civil officers in the government; and most of the distinguished citizens in the District of Columbia. People had come from as far away as Baltimore.

The affair had been organized with John Roane of Virginia officiating as president of the day, aided by Walter H. Overton of Louisiana, as vice-president.

President Jackson arrived at five o'clock in the afternoon, and was greeted with a ringing round of applause. The states'-rights people were confident that on this day the President would stand with them. After all, since the Hayne-Webster debate in January, the President had said and done nothing to make them believe that he was anything but on their side.

Dinner seemed interminable to Rebecca. Once the festivities began, the guests drank toast after toast. Rebecca counted twenty-four in all, and all but six of them mentioned the great principle of states' rights for which Jefferson had stood.

"Yet when Jefferson wanted to buy the Louisiana Territory, he consulted nobody—neither Congress nor any of the states—but acted on his own," Rebecca said sourly to Wingate. "Lord protect me from these people here, who will twist a man's words to their own ends."

Robert Hayne, chairman of the committee on arrangements, spoke long and eloquently on the glorious stand taken by Virginia in regard to the hated Alien and Sedition Laws, passed by John Adams back in 1799. Then, fixing Jackson with his gaze, he referred very pointedly to the course that Georgia had recently adopted in relation to the Cherokee Indians, how under the banner of states's rights, Georgia had achieved a great and glorious victory. He paused, raised his glass, and proposed his toast:

"The *Union* of the states, and the *Sovereignty* of the states!"

Rebecca thought that the toasts were bordering on sedition, and if *she* had had the platform . . . Many of them contained statements and sentiments that she knew Thomas Jefferson would have loathed. "How can Jackson just sit there through all this treasonous talk?" she exclaimed to Wingate.

Both Andrew Jackson and Calhoun were seated at the head table. Van Buren had been seated by the committee next to somebody known to advocate nullification. The moment was drawing close when Jackson would have to speak. At last, the regular toasts were concluded. The chairman rose and said, "Mr. President, we would be gratified if you would propose a toast on this glorious day, to our glorious Thomas Jefferson."

Jackson rose slowly. The people leaned forward expectantly. Jackson stood to his full height, his demeanor crowned with an air of purposefulness. His voice rang out:

"Our Union: It *must* be preserved!"

There was a long silence, and then an audible gasp when everybody realized what he'd said. The words seemed to reverberate around the room. "Our Union: It must be preserved," Rebecca repeated. "Amen, I say!" and she raised her glass to Jackson.

In the pandemonium, Hayne jumped up from his seat and ran to President Jackson. "Mr. President, I beg you, please put in the word *federal,* so that your toast can be reported in the newspapers as 'Our Federal Union.'"

"I'll be happy to insert that word," Jackson said. "I inadvertently left it out of my toast anyway. Report it as such."

"Hayne thinks that the word *federal* will make the toast less of an indictment against him and his followers," Rebecca said to Wingate. "But he's mistaken if he thinks the country will fail to get Jackson's meaning. Oh, hallelujah! I don't care what petty human qualities Jackson has, he came through for the Union, God bless him!"

At last, some order was restored. Vice-President Calhoun rose to try to salvage something from the devastation that Jackson had caused. He offered the next toast, "The Union," he said in a loud, clear voice. "Next to our liberty, most dear."

Then he launched into a lecture that somehow diminished the force of his brief statement. "He would have done better to have left well enough alone," Rebecca said.

Finally, Martin Van Buren rose to propose his toast. Rebecca heard the words, "Mutual forbearance and reciprocal concession. Through their agency the Union was established. The patriotic spirit from which they emanated will forever sustain it."

After the speechmaking was done with, Rebecca went up to Andrew Jackson and congratulated him.

He accepted her compliments modestly. He looked around, saw that he was within earshot of Hayne and Calhoun, and said, "I meant my toast to be a rebuke upon the seditious sentiments that were uttered in my presence."

"Bravo, Mr. President," she said.

"I've always felt that liberty was the final and necessary ingredient in my thinking about the government and its relationship to the people," Jackson continued. "But never through a fragmentation of authority into the diverse states. Freedom can only be achieved for the greater majority through a strong federal Union. And by God, that's what we shall have!"

At that moment, Rebecca could have kissed him.

A congressman from South Carolina came to say goodnight to Jackson. As was his practice, Jackson treated the legislator with great civility, even offering him his hand.

But the congressman was apparently uneasy with what had transpired. "Mr. President," he said, "I'm returning to South Carolina tomorrow. Do you have anything you want me to convey to my constituents, and to your friends back in South Carolina?"

The President thought for a moment, then said, "Please give my compliments to my friends in your state, and say to them that they can pass as many resolutions as they like about nullification. They can rant and rave and convene all sorts of protest meetings. But if a single drop of blood shall be shed there in opposition to the laws of the United States, I will hang the first man I can lay my hands on engaged in such treasonable conduct, upon the first tree I can find!"

The congressman's eyes almost popped out of his head, and he scurried from the room.

Rebecca left the Jefferson Day dinner in a far better frame of mind than she could have expected. True, nothing had been resolved about Gunning. But other, wonderful things had happened. She felt confident now that if President Jackson had anything to do with it, the Union would be preserved.

Chapter 21

"Is THERE any mail today?" Rebecca asked Letitia, as she'd asked her all during spring and the dog days of summer.

"Nothing," Letitia said. "Bills and things, but nothing from Mr. Gunning."

Rebecca drifted back to the chaise where she'd been reading a slim volume by a poet that was new to her, Edgar Allen Poe. One moody poem, "Tamerlane," intrigued her. But thoughts of Gunning and his welfare intruded, and she closed the volume.

After the Jefferson Day dinner, events had moved swiftly in Washington. Andrew Jackson's toast had left no doubt as to where he stood on the issue of nullification, and John C. Calhoun's star continued to wane as Jackson's choice as possible successor. As a consequence, the states'-rights faction in the government, and in Jackson's cabinet, increased its attack on Jackson's most vulnerable flank, Peggy Eaton, and salvos continued to be fired back and forth in the Petticoat War. In June, Emily and Jack Donelson left the White House and returned to Tennessee; their refusal to accept Peggy Eaton had forced their banishment.

With her own problems looming so large, Rebecca had thought she would have no patience or heart for the Byzantine plotting and planning in the capital. But curiously her situation had the opposite effect; each event called forth a heightened reaction from her.

One day her heart thudded when she learned that a reward had been offered for Gunning's capture and arrest. He was now considered a criminal. But then a new piece of information reached her. Monthly withdrawals on Gunning's account were being made at a bank in New York!

Further investigation revealed that "Mrs. Gunning Brand" had arranged for the transfer of funds, based on a letter of credit signed by Mr. Brand. Rebecca immediately went down to the bank and had Mr. Van Ness stop all future payments into Gunning's account. Since she controlled the disposition of royalties coming in from Jeremy Brand's invention, she was able to do this.

In her heart Rebecca knew whom Gunning had married, but she sent a private investigator off to New York anyway, praying that her fears wouldn't be realized. Two weeks later he returned with the disheartening news.

"Ma'am, I don't mean to be disrespectful," the investigator said to Rebecca, "but she's a saucy piece of goods, that Mrs. Brand. Said as how to tell you that she was Gunning's wife, and that he needed money for an ocean voyage—for his health, as she put it—and if you knew what was good for him, you'd send all you could to her—fast."

"Did you see him? Is he all right?"

He shook his head. "He's in hiding, ma'am. Nothing I did or said could make that little Frenchie say anything. Hard as nails, that one. Then she said that if you were thinking of coming to New York, to save yourself the trip. *She* was Mrs. Gunning Brand now, and she knew what was best for her husband."

"She's absolutely right," Rebecca said. "And I wash my hands of the whole thing." But as she paid the investigator for his services, her heart was bleeding.

Later that day she went to St. John's Church on Lafayette Square and prayed. She prayed for Gunning, a fugitive from the law, running—he'd always be running until he was caught. She prayed for Suzannah, living in some benighted place on the Texas frontier. And she prayed to God to absolve her of all her sins.

"Somewhere in my life, I've made all the wrong decisions," she whispered. "Everything that's happened so far, all the sadnesses and deaths, have flowed as a consequence of the error of my ways. I throw myself on your mercy, oh Lord, and I do willingly bare my own heart and soul for your chastisement, whatever that may be. But I beg you, spare the innocent, my children, for they've only inherited the sins of their fathers." She left St. John's, feeling somewhat less oppressed, but in her soul she knew that it would take something more than prayer to solve this situation.

• • •

The government returned to Washington in the fall of 1830. Bravo began working as a pageboy in the Senate. The Second Bank of the United States loomed as an issue, with the Webster faction pro-bank (Daniel Webster was the bank's lawyer), and Andrew Jackson dead set against it. The Indian Removal Bill had also divided sentiments in Congress, and long and eloquent speeches were made in the House and Senate. Bravo was intrigued with it all, and spent long hours discussing events with his mother.

The new year brought stormy, blustery weather, and Rebecca thought, it's winter in my heart. Then in January a letter finally did come, and Letitia shuffled into the house on her bowed and arthritic legs, wheezing for breath. "Postman says it's from Texas!"

Rebecca tore open the letter and read:

"My darling mother, I read and reread your letters and Circumstance's so often that the pages have fallen apart. Oh how I hunger for each piece of news about you and my family and Washington! The distances here are so vast, both during the day and in the starlit evenings, that loneliness can become a constant companion of the soul. Thank God I have Jonathan and Matty, who are both thriving. Whenever we have a visitor, they all comment on how active and bright Matty is. I suppose all parents say that, but he does seem to be an exceptional little boy. He's taken his first steps and can say Papa and Mama. At least, Jonathan insists that that's what the words are. Jonathan has been building the second story onto the house, and has almost completed it—and just in time too.

"I'm almost embarrassed to tell you this, for I had no intention of getting pregnant again so soon after the birth of Matty, but I guess the good Lord had other designs. This time, Mrs. Kelley was able to attend me and act as midwife. I'd done the same for her six months ago, and I was lucky that she did come. Mother, I thought there was something different about this pregnancy, but I didn't realize I was carrying twins!

"They are the most adorable little girl and boy, whom I've named Rebecca and Zebulon—Becky and Zeb for short. If there's anything wrong with their birth, it's that it's given Jonathan such a swelled head! All he does is strut around the house and sing while he's doing his chores, and if you'd ever heard him sing—*well!*

"I'll write and give you all the details as soon as I've a

moment, but with three little ones in the house now, it's all I can do to stay ahead of them. Please write as soon as you can. Your letters are all so welcome—and what wonderful news about Circumstance and Doe!

"Your loving Suzannah.

"P.S. I almost forgot to mention this. Do you remember Patrick Donohoe, that nice young man who was the second mate on the *American Flyer?* Well, last month he turned up here! I could hardly believe my eyes. He'd come to see his relatives who live on the Brazos River, about a hundred and fifty miles from here, and decided that he wanted to see how we were doing.

"He's not working on the Ohio anymore. He's progressed to first mate on a riverboat plying the Mississippi. He says that he prefers New Orleans, but I get the feeling that he doesn't know what he wants. I suppose that's usual for somebody his age.

"He stayed with us for several days, and he's so full of good humor that we had a lovely visit. Asked all about you, and kept saying that one day he'd come to Washington and just pop in on you. Jonathan and I owe him so much that if he does visit, I hope you'll be kind to him. He's gone back to New Orleans now, to the 'old fleshpot,' as he calls it—but his whole air of wanting to seem worldly only masks his shyness.

"I do hope he finds whatever he's searching for. I can't help but think that a good woman and a home and children would do him a world of good. But then, doesn't every woman think that about every man? Love to you all again. Suzannah."

The news of twin grandchildren sustained Rebecca for several weeks. She wrote Suzannah demanding to know all the details. Who did the children favor? How much did they weigh? Their coloring? She frequented the city market on Pennsylvania Avenue between Seventh and Ninth streets, buying things for the babies, and always including something for Matty. When she couldn't find what suited her, she would go to Georgetown or across the Potomac by ferry to Alexandria, there to search out the stores for fabric she then had made into baby clothes. Circumstance's child, Doe, came in for her fair share of attention also. In this way, she was able to keep her mind off Gunning and Véronique.

One blustery day at the end of March, a day more redolent of winter than spring, what Rebecca had feared most happened.

Bravo came running into the house, his face bloodless, a wild look in his eyes.

"I ran all the way," he said, panting and stumbling over his words. "A couple of my friends in the Senate told me . . . that some prisoners were coming in to Washington . . . and so I begged to be released for the afternoon, and I went down to the depot. It's Gunning."

"Tad! The horses!" Rebecca shouted as she grabbed her cloak. She and Bravo rode hard for the stage depot.

Her heart shriveled when she saw him. He was imprisoned, along with a half dozen other men, in a wagon with iron bars all around. "Like beasts," she whispered.

People milled around the wagon as though they were inspecting animals in a zoo. Summoning up all her courage, Rebecca came close to where he sat.

Feeling her presence, he lifted his head, and Rebecca's breath caught in her throat. Gunning looked dreadful—his high coloring faded, eyes sunken, a stubble of red beard on his sallow face.

They looked at each other for a long moment, he through wounded eyes, she through eyes blurred with tears. No matter what she felt about him, no matter how wrong he'd been, he was still her son . . . the son she loved to distraction. His imprisonment was her imprisonment also.

"I'm sorry you have to see me this way," he said dully. "Véronique and I were about to catch a boat to France, but just before we boarded, they caught me at the dock. They must have followed her. Mother, you must go to see her. She's here in Washington, and she's been absolutely wonderful to me. I know you two will get along as soon as you know each other better. After all, I couldn't be wrong about the two most important women in my life. Will you see her?"

Rebecca nodded.

"Don't worry about me. It's not as if I'd killed anybody, or stolen anything. I'll serve my time, I'll be out soon enough, and then I'll have my whole life ahead of me. Mother, I'm a different person, believe me."

"I do believe you," she whispered. "Where is Véronique staying?"

"I don't know exactly. But she said she'd follow me here. The city isn't so big that you won't be able to find her."

"I'll find her, I promise," Rebecca said.

Then the wagon master climbed back onto the high driver's

seat. He uncoiled his whip and sent it cracking through the air. "Move out of the way there," he shouted to the crowd. The horses strained at their traces and the heavy wagon lumbered forward on its final leg of the journey to the army prison at Fort Myer.

Rebecca and Bravo followed the wagon until it reached the bridge to Alexandria, then they turned their mounts and headed back home. "He'll never survive prison," she said to Bravo. "You saw the way he looked; can you imagine what a long prison term would do? And he is repentant, I *know* he is. Oh, God, if only I knew what I could do!"

For the next several days, Rebecca checked with every hotel and boarding house in the capital, but could find no trace of Véronique. If she was in Washington, she wasn't showing herself.

Late one afternoon, Rebecca and Bravo sat in the drawing room of their house; she'd just spent hours penning letters to every legislator she knew, asking for appointments to discuss Gunning's case. She'd even written to Chief Justice John Marshall; she had little hope that any of them could do anything, but any action was better than just sitting idle.

Bravo put the finishing touches on a reed whistle he'd carved for his cousin Jeremy. "Mother, will President Jackson really put Gunning in prison for twenty years? That's what I heard Daniel Webster tell Thomas Hart Benton."

"It's entirely possible," she said.

"I hate him!" he blurted. "Everything they say about him is true—that he's mean and vindictive, and never forgives a grudge."

"He's all those things and more," Rebecca said wearily. "Never forget that he's an army man who's always insisted on strict discipline. Gunning broke a rule, so now he must pay for it." She sighed and sealed her final letter. "If John Quincy Adams was still President, perhaps our problem wouldn't be as insurmountable. John was somebody you could reason with, and his actions were always tempered with mercy."

"And President Jackson is different?"

Rebecca nodded. "Jackson is no great thinker. In that respect, he's more like George Washington than, say, Thomas Jefferson. Jefferson left us the legacy of his profound political thought, that sense of dignity that every man has as his birthright. President Jackson simply doesn't have the mental fiber capable of that kind of thinking."

Bravo looked at her intently. "It strikes me that there's a huge difference between those two presidents, and I think I know what that difference is."

She gazed at him inquiringly, hoping that the fire that had always burned in her—the fire to know, to understand—had somehow been transmitted to her youngest child, this dreamer. "What is that difference, then?" she asked softly.

"Jackson is a frontiersman."

Her disappointment in what he'd said was so evident that he reacted as if she'd slapped him. He jumped to his feet. "You don't understand me!" he said angrily. "You never understand me."

"Oh, Bravo, please don't blaze into a temper tantrum—not when there are so many more important things to concentrate on."

"Jefferson thought. Jackson acts."

She sat up, immediately alert, for in his simple response he'd said something that she might not have been able to state so cogently. "Explain that, will you?"

He shook his head vehemently. "I've said it plain, and you understand it as well as I do. You're only testing me now, the way you test me all the time, and I've no stomach for it anymore." With that, Bravo dashed out of the room.

She watched him through the panes of the window as he ran along the walkway, then disappeared down New York Avenue. Her youngest . . . fast growing into a man. "Bravo," she whispered. "Bravo."

Several days later, Bravo strode boldly into Rebecca's sitting room, planted himself before her and said, "Mother, why is it that you don't love me the way you love Suzannah and Gunning?"

Her needle stopped in midstitch; she'd been embroidering a dress for little Becky. "Of course I love you, Bravo. I'm just upset about Gunning, that's why I haven't paid you too much attention."

Bravo shook his head slowly. "Don't make it worse by lying to me. It's always been this way, as long as I can remember. I don't mean to add to your worries about Gunning, so maybe it would be better for you if I went away. Because nothing I do seems to be right."

He backed out of the room slowly, waiting for her to say something, anything. But she was so taken aback that she couldn't speak.

"It has something to do with my father, I just know it," he said at the doorway. "Someday you're going to have to tell me the truth."

Chapter 22

LONG AFTER Bravo left, Rebecca worried his question. It had taken her so completely by surprise, had been stated with such earnestness, that it had demolished all her defenses. Does he have a right to know? she wondered. If I do tell him, then what happens to the family? I must pay more attention to him, she thought. Calm his fears. That's the answer.

At daybreak several days later, Rebecca said to Bravo, "Would you like to go riding with me?"

Since she usually went out alone, claiming that it was the only time she had for herself, Bravo was delighted with her invitation.

They rode north along Pennsylvania Avenue towards Georgetown, reveling in the sweet spring breezes coming in off the river. Bravo pointed at the construction going on. "There's a new house going up there, and another there. Pretty soon there won't be an inch of Pennsylvania Avenue left vacant."

In addition to the residences, dozens of billiard parlors dotted the avenue, along with tenpin alleys; Rebecca counted nine Fargo Banks in the short distance they'd ridden. "You would be wise to stay out of those taverns and billiard halls," Rebecca said to Bravo. "I know they seem heady when you're your age, but believe me, they're nothing but a waste of time."

Bravo broke into a canter and then a gallop, and Rebecca, throwing caution to the winds, raced after her son, galloping past the land that was being cleared, and all the new government buildings under construction. Washington was changing, no doubt about it; tomorrow it would look different from today, and in a decade it would be unrecognizable. What it would look like a hundred years from now only the gods knew.

After he'd given his horse his head, Bravo slowed down to a trot and Rebecca caught up with him. "You're riding well," she said. He rode better than average; the Brand blood had given him that as a legacy. But he was nowhere near as accomplished as Gunning, who rode as if he were a centaur.

Bravo seemed to fathom what she was thinking and said, "You're right, nobody rides as well as Gunning. He wins every race at the track, and I can never hope to compete with him there."

She felt the color rise to her face, and also felt the slightest edge of irritation that he'd discovered her thoughts so easily. Was there nothing she could hide from him?

Cautiously, she said, "Bravo, the other day you asked me a question. I decided that I should explain myself so that you'll know once and for all that I really do love you."

He brought his mount closer, and they rode in rhythm for a bit. "Every mother loves her children," she began, "but often in different ways and for different reasons. Suzannah, because she was my firstborn, holds a special place in my heart. It was through her that I experienced the first pain and the first pleasure of motherhood, and that memory is indelible."

She wondered if she was making any sense to him. Was he too young to understand what she was saying? But his expression appeared receptive, even encouraging. She continued, "Suzannah was clearly the gentlest of creatures, the one who needed guidance and protection the most."

He nodded somberly and brushed away the thick blond hair from his eyes. "I know that about Suzannah. I would do anything not to hurt her, because I know how easy it is to hurt her. But then I've been thinking, Suzannah is living on the Texas frontier. She's had Matty, and now the twins. So she's got to be a whole lot stronger than any of us thought, right?"

Rebecca's long fingers tightened on her reins. Any mention of Suzannah living on the frontier always struck a note of fear in her. She continued, "Then there's Gunning. He's got an enormous appetite for life, almost like a grizzly. But despite the trouble he's in, Gunning is the head of this family now. I know that sooner or later he'll find himself and bring honor to the name Brand."

"I wish I could let him know how much I like him," Bravo said ruefully. "Sometimes I think he likes me, but then there are other times . . . like when he shot the raccoon Circumstance gave me, remember? Said he thought it was a ferret eating our chickens, but he knew better than that. He killed it on purpose, and I don't know why."

Rebecca had never heard this tale before, but she thought better of saying anything. For Gunning knew . . . and every so often his unreasoned anger against his brother surfaced in an overwhelming rage.

A carriage drove toward them, and Rebecca recognized its occupants, John and Floride Calhoun. Calhoun tipped his hat to Rebecca, and Floride lavished a smile on her. Rebecca smiled back.

"I like it when John Calhoun presides at the Senate," Bravo said. "He's very smart, isn't he?"

"Among the smartest politicians I've ever met," she said. "And to my mind, one of the most dangerous."

"I hear a lot of the senators talk about Peggy Eaton," Bravo said. "Is she so terrible?"

"There have been . . . some unsavory rumors surrounding her, to say the least. But she herself isn't important. It's just that Calhoun believes Jackson will be so embarrassed by the scandal that he won't dare run for the presidency again. I wonder . . ."

"What?"

"Oh, nothing. I was just grasping at straws, thinking there might be a key to Gunning's situation in all this."

"Were you like Gunning when you were young?" Bravo asked. "You two look ever so much alike. Everybody says so."

"I suppose we do." She'd always thought that Gunning was devastatingly handsome, and it pleased her that people said they looked alike.

"But Bravo, getting back to you. I thought I was done with childbearing, but then you came along. They say that children of older parents are different than others, wiser. Both Circumstance and Letitia claim you have an old soul. Whatever that means. Most of the time I think you act the way you do just to devil me."

She said it with the suggestion of a smile, but Bravo misinterpreted her and said hotly, "Mother—"

She raised her hand quickly. "Bravo, I love you. If I haven't made that clear enough to you, then I beg your forgiveness."

She glanced at her son riding beside her and cried out inwardly, How could I love you? When every time I look at you I'm reminded of the cause of my grief? For Jeremy's death lay heavily on her conscience. She was certain that Zebulon had been instrumental in the scaffolding accident that had plunged Jeremy from the roof of the White House to his death. All this had happened because Zebulon had rightly guessed that he wasn't Bravo's father.

"Mother, whose son am I?" Bravo asked quietly.

"Why, your father's, Zebulon Brand."

"Mother, please don't lie to me. You know I don't look anything like him. And Gunning said—Mother, please don't cry. All I'm trying to do is find out the truth! Mother, *please,*" he cried out, his words like a prayer and a lament.

Rebecca reached for her handkerchief and dabbed at her eyes. "It's nothing," she murmured, "only a mote in my eye." She blinked, and in her swimming vision saw a carriage speeding toward them. "That driver must be a madman, galloping that fast on these rutted roads."

As the carriage thundered closer, she recognized the gold and black colors. "Dear God, it's the Connaught carriage!" The black horses swelled and plunged, and suddenly the carriage crossed over into their lane and veered directly toward them. "Bravo, watch out!"

Bravo shortened his rein and grasped it tightly as his spooked horse reared. Rebecca's mount stumbled into the ditch, but somehow she kept from falling.

Then the Connaught carriage left Rebecca and Bravo in a cloud of dust. "Did you see that?" Bravo exclaimed. "They did that on purpose."

He started to gallop after them but Rebecca called, "Bravo, don't. Help me." She was shaken, but otherwise all right, but she knew her call for help was the only thing that would keep him from pursuing the carriage. Bravo wheeled his horse and came back to her. He helped her dismount, and they stood by the side of the roadway.

"Mother, you're trembling."

"I'll be fine in just a moment," she said.

She was trembling, but not so much because of what had happened as because of what she'd seen. As the carriage passed her, she'd caught a glimpse of Devroe Connaught sitting in the back seat, a sardonic smile on his face. His right arm hung loosely at his side, but his other arm was looped over the shoulder of a woman sitting next to him, his fingers resting intimately on her near-exposed bosom. The woman was Véronique Villefranche Brand.

Chapter 23

BETWEEN FOUR and five in the morning, the dark hour when death often chooses its victims, and when babies are born, Rebecca woke out of a deep, disturbing sleep. She sat upright in bed, pulling the coverlet and her wits about her in the same motion.

An idea had come to her, but it was such a desperate one that she almost couldn't countenance it. Yet after seeing Véronique and Devroe in the carriage, she knew that only desperate measures could help.

At dawn, she went into her closet, unlocked her trunk, and took out a sheaf of papers. "Whatever I say, I'll need proof," she muttered to herself. "Otherwise he'll never believe me."

"My, you're up early," Letitia said, banking the fire in their cast-iron kitchen stove. "Never could learn one of these new-fangled things. Wasn't nothing wrong with the old fireplace; why'd they have to invent this? Food doesn't taste the same, anyways. What's you want for breakfast?"

"Just some tea. I'm so nervous I don't think I could hold anything else down."

After hurriedly gulping the brew, Rebecca set out from the house with a large oilskin envelope clutched in her hand. "Oh, God, give me courage, for Gunning's sake," she whispered as she turned into the gravel path leading to the north entrance of the White House.

The doorkeeper took her request for an interview directly to President Jackson. Ten minutes later he came down from his private quarters. He led her to the Red Room, which over-looked the south lawn and the magnolia tree that Jackson had planted in memory of Rachel. Somehow, this seemed like a good omen to Rebecca and gave her courage.

"Mr. President," she began, using this formal address so that he would know she was here on business, "it strikes me

179

that your administration needs a strong voice in the press."

Jackson regarded her with one of his penetrating stares, and Rebecca felt herself weakening. Remember, it's for Gunning, she told herself, and pressed on. "I know that for a long time you've been dissatisfied with the *United States Telegraph* being the mouthpiece of the Democratic Party. I also know that's why you had Francis Blair found the *Washington Globe.*"

"Yes, and he's doing a fine job for us," Jackson said.

"Admirable," Rebecca agreed. "In two or three years I'm sure that the *Globe* will have a healthy circulation. But in the meantime you're fighting both the *Telegraph* and the more conservative *National Intelligencer.*"

"And?" he asked, his one word indicating that she had only a little more time to make her point.

"You need somebody who has a following, a strong following, somebody that people respond to. Like William Lloyd Garrison, who's just founded the *Liberator* in Boston, though I know his antislavery sentiments aren't yours," she added hastily. "Or a pamphleteer the likes of Thomas Paine—"

"Would that he could be ressurected from the grave, these past twenty years," Jackson said.

"—Or a writer with the fire of Rebel Thorne."

"What? That dastard has been writing out against me ever since I ran for office. It was scandalmongers like Thorne that caused my poor Rachel's death."

"Rebel Thorne never *once* said anything against your wife. Whatever disagreements there were, were purely on the basis of issues. I've taken the liberty of collecting all of Rebel Thorne's articles; I've brought them here for you to read." She opened the oilskin pouch and spread the articles before him.

Jackson looked at one or two briefly, then grumbled, "What makes you think that a reporter of that persuasion would support me or my administration?"

"There are positions you share with Rebel Thorne."

"Such as?"

"An aversion to the nullifiers, and a conviction that the Union must be preserved."

Jackson's eyes narrowed. "Yes, as to that, I remember the articles he wrote during the War of 1812. And the last piece about Peggy Eaton seemed to have sound sense behind it. Do you know him, then?"

She pressed her hands together and nodded.

"It's always been my policy to meet a man face to face before I decide on the merit of the case."

"I doubt if such a thing is possible. One of the reasons for Rebel Thorne's effectiveness has been anonymity. In that way, his articles become the voice of the great majority of us, all yearning for expression. Take that anonymity away and—" Rebecca shrugged eloquently.

Jackson pondered that for a moment, then said. "My conditions are a face-to-face meeting, so I can take the measure of the man. Also, I need to know what he wants in return. No one undertakes such a task without wanting something. I have to know his price."

"It happens that I can tell you that," Rebecca said. "The price is clemency."

He looked at her, his eyes narrowing.

"Very shortly, a case will come up in Washington in which your voice can make a difference. Rebel Thorne asks only that though your judgment be within the bounds of the law, that it also fall on the side of mercy." She looked him squarely in the eye and said, "Mr. President, I am Rebel Thorne."

It took a moment for the words to register, and then Andrew Jackson barked, "Rebecca, you know I'm fond of you, you know I sympathize with your predicament, but this is a very poor joke indeed."

"It's no joke, I assure you. Nor would I have ever risked exposing myself if the situation weren't desperate. I'm prepared to raise up the standard of the Jackson administration and fight for it with all my strength. In return, I ask for mercy."

Jackson bounded to his feet and stormed around the room, stopping to say something, not finding the words, then pacing again. The rage worked over him, making him tremble, robbing him of the ability to speak.

"You and your kind killed my Rachel!" he exclaimed.

"If you believe that, then we have nothing further to say," Rebecca said, growing angry herself. "Rachel is dead. Nothing can be done about that. But the country is still alive—though barely, if the nullifiers have their way. You can wail and beat your breast about the past, or you can take command. The choice is yours." She stood up and started toward the door. She'd reached the portal when he shouted, "Stop!"

She turned to face him, her own blood pulsing in her. You must control your temper or all will be lost, she warned herself.

"Madam, if you were a man I would challenge you to a duel this very minute!" Jackson said. "I have never been spoken to that way in my entire life!"

"We are past the point in this country when matters can be solved by killing other people," she said. "It's a useless waste of valuable lives, and is counter to everything that this country is predicated on—Reason, and law."

"I find it disgusting and unnatural that a woman should have hidden behind a man's name and passed herself off as something which she is not."

"And I find it disgusting and unnatural that a woman is forced into such a mode because of the prejudiced thinking about the role and intelligence of women," she retorted. "Are Rebel Thorne's statements any less valid because you know that they were written by a woman? If that's so, then I say, for shame!"

"Madam, you go too far!"

"Forgive me, Mr. President, but I haven't gone far enough, nor have the women in this country gone far enough. We are more than chattel, we are human beings with wishes and desires and hopes of our own for this great country. Our voices deserve to be heard."

He looked so angry that for a moment she thought he might strike her. Hold fast, stand your ground, she said to herself. Show one sign of weakness and he'll demolish you. He's the President, elected by the will of the people—but nonetheless he is a man, not a king.

Their outburst had exhausted them and, chests heaving, they stood staring at each other. "I came here not to argue the case for women," Rebecca said at last. "It's a problem that confronts this nation, as it did during Abigail Adams's time, and I doubt that it will be solved during my lifetime. Though I never doubt that sooner or later it will be solved. But your concerns are more immediate. As I see it, your problem centers around your cabinet. Your own house is divided. Unless you act, and act swiftly, the Democratic Party will be rent asunder. Factions will begin to collect around John Calhoun, and he may emerge as the strong man in the Democratic Party."

"Never!" Jackson exclaimed. "The people, madam, the people will repudiate him."

"Not if they perceive you as being unable to run your own household." Rebecca began to take heart. After all she'd said, he hadn't struck her, nor thrown her out of the White House, though there'd been a moment . . . she began to speak quickly then, persuasively, outlining a campaign, snatching the ideas from her head even as she thought of them.

Jackson listened, his face gradually relaxing into a kind of grudging affirmation. "What of Peggy Eaton in all this?" he asked. "I will not abandon her and John."

"Peggy's importance will be relegated to its proper place. You know, Andrew," she said, risking the familiar address, "since time immemorial women have always been the greatest persecutors of their own sex. The women in Washington are particularly guilty of this obnoxious trait. But by the time I've done with both factions in the Ladies' War, I promise they'll never dare open their mouths again to spread slander and gossip."

Jackson's interest was evident now. "You believe that the course you intend to embark on will solve the problems of my cabinet? But you haven't yet told me how. By God, there are times when I wish I were rid of the lot of them!"

His statement flew like a dart into Rebecca's brain. "You must let me work this whole thing out, Mr. President. But naturally, I won't set pen to paper unless you give me leave."

Jackson stroked his chin. "This is a decision that I cannot make on such short notice. Even if I did decide in the affirmative, I couldn't guarantee anything specific about your son. Gunning's courtmartial, judgment, and sentencing will be done by his immediate superiors."

"I understand completely," she said. "One can only hope that those officers will understand that what he did, he did as a headstrong young man, and with love as his only motive." She paused and looked at him directly. "All of us have gone through similar experiences in our youth."

Then Rebecca took her leave. Once off the grounds of the White House, she leaned against the iron fence, fighting off waves of dizziness. The interview had exacted an enormous toll from her. When she finally arrived back at her house, Letitia took one look at her and immediately put her to bed. She fell into a deep, profound sleep.

Several days later, a wizened little man weighing no more than a hundred pounds came knocking at Rebecca's door.

"Looks like an undertaker to me," Letitia said, when she

announced the man's presence to Rebecca.

It was Francis Blair, owner and editor of the *Washington Globe,* the Jackson newspaper organ in the capital. "I'm here in the name of President Jackson," Blair said, speaking with a Kentucky twang. "Ordinarily, the *Globe* would be very happy to publish any articles of Rebel Thorne's. But in this instance President Jackson feels that because of our known partisanship to his administration, it might be wiser to publish in another newspaper."

Rebecca's elation was quickly tempered by two disturbing facts: that Blair now knew of her identity, and that Jackson had been canny enough to send an emissary to speak for him. If for whatever reason Rebecca's articles became an embarrassment to the administration, Jackson could always deny knowledge of any connections. Thus was it ever with politicians, Rebecca thought. On the other hand, she couldn't blame him for trying to protect himself. They were embarking on very dangerous waters.

Rebecca told Blair that she would deliver her first piece at the beginning of the week, and immediately set to work. Her first two efforts were so dull that she ripped them up. Then one night, she reached deep into herself, and poured out her feelings on the pages. She titled her article, "A City of Razor Tongues."

"A democracy? Why, the word is laughable here in the capital of the United States. This city, which should set the standard for all the highest aspirations of our people, has instead begun to reflect our baser instincts. For there is an aristocracy here in our city of Washington. Deny it if you will, but it is so.

"This aristocracy claims preference for wealth, and for the accidents of birth. They demand and get obedience from those not so fortunate in their circumstances. Hear me good citizens, the chief offenders are the delicate sex—yes, the women. Their tongues are like razors, and pity anybody who falls into their mouths! This tight little circle of women, aided and abetted by some sanctimonious clergymen, believe themselves to be the only guardians of our morality, and demand that everyone cringe before them. Piffle, I say, and paffle! Ladies, as long as your gossip was confined to the dank, dark corners of your own homes and minds, little harm was done. But when the poison spreads and threatens to stain the fabric of our government, when it makes us a laughingstock in the eyes of other nations around the world, then I and my fellow citizens cry out, Stop!

"This country has always been predicated on the individual's ability to rise within our society. John Adams was the son of a shoemaker, yet became the second President of the United States. Andrew Jackson, poor and orphaned at fourteen, nevertheless became a hero of this great country, and President.

"Why should not the same hold true for our women? And if a tavernkeeper's daughter rises to become the wife of the secretary of war, then who is to say her nay? Yet the naysayers are all about us, whispering behind their fans, pronouncing their moral judgments.

"There is only one possible solution to all this. If the cabinet members and their wives are so unhappy with their state of affairs, then LET THEM ALL RESIGN.

"If they are patriots, with the good of their country at heart, I repeat, THEY MUST ALL RESIGN. Resign and let the government get back to attending to the truly important matters—the Indian Removal Bill, the question of the Second Bank of the United States, the Preservation of the Union—instead of wallowing in the manure of gossip. All of you cabinet members who read this, search your hearts. I know you will all agree that the only sensible, patriotic course is to RESIGN."

When the article appeared, everything in Washington seemed to grind to a standstill. Stagecoach drivers sat high on their seats, reading; merchants left customers to their own devices while they read; an uproar was created in the House of Representatives when a legislator demanded that the article be read into the *Congressional Record,* while another congressman threatened to cane anybody who tried to do just that. The *National Intelligencer* sold out entirely within an hour, and pageboys ran from the House and the Senate to scoop up as many copies as they could find.

Behind the drawn curtains of the Calhoun, Berrien, Branch, and Ingham homes, the ladies were outraged.

Later that day, the President's mulatto servant, Uncle Alfred, appeared at Rebecca's doorstep.

"Mr. Jackson, the President, he wants to see you right away."

"What is it?" she asked.

He shrugged his shoulders. "I don't know, but he said he would skin me alive unless I found you and brought you right back."

"I take it he's angry."

"Like he been rassling alligators. Sent for Mr. Van Buren too, he did, and for John Eaton, and they all be there waiting for you."

"Letitia, don't hold dinner for me," Rebecca called to the maid. "From the sound of things, Gunning may soon have a cellmate."

Her attempt at levity couldn't mask her true feelings. She had risked all on this one gamble. Now it appeared she had lost.

Chapter 24

PRESIDENT JACKSON, Secretary of War John Eaton, and Secretary of State Martin Van Buren were gathered in the Map Room, which Jackson sometimes used for more intimate sessions with his cabinet officers. On the wall hung a large map of the United States, showing the twenty-four states of the Union. Other territories that the U.S. claimed were shaded; the Texas area had a heavy red-dotted line marking the Sabine River, the boundary line between Louisiana and Texas.

Other maps were strewn across the heavy mahogany table, but bunched on top of them were the crumpled sheets of the *National Intelligencer*.

As Rebecca entered the room, her eyes took in everything; she understood immediately that the men had been in conference when the newspapers were brought to them, and the news had obviously disrupted their meeting.

The moment Jackson saw her, he seized the crumpled sheets and threw them to the floor, grinding them under his heel. "That's what I think about this damnable article!"

Rebecca started to reply, but some cautionary note flashed into her mind. Jackson's anger lacked the consuming fire she'd experienced at their first confrontation. Was it an act, partly for Van Buren and Eaton?

"This is outrageous!" Jackson continued. "I never gave you leave to demand the resignation of my cabinet."

"No, Mr. President, you didn't," she said. "Because, as we all know, you are a loyal and devoted friend, such a thought would never have entered your mind." From the corner of her eye, she saw Van Buren and Eaton bobbing their heads.

"There's nothing to be gained from such a thing," Jackson continued. "I'd lose the two most valuable men in my administration."

"That would be a devastating loss," she agreed. "But you

187

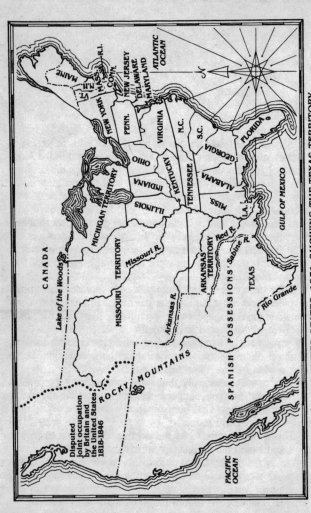

MAP OF THE UNITED STATES, 1831, SHOWING THE TEXAS TERRITORY

see, it would allow you to clean the Augean stables of the rest
of your cabinet. Then you could surround yourself with men
who truly share your own political philosophy." Rebecca knew
she wasn't telling Jackson anything he hadn't yet considered.
But now she was convinced that this exercise was for the benefit
of these two men.

"And, of course, the services of Eaton and Van Buren needn't
be lost to you at all. You could offer them the governorship
of some territory, or an ambassadorship, perhaps to the Court
of St. James's. Then as soon as the election campaign begins,
these men could be summoned back."

Rebecca could practically *feel* Van Buren's mind working.

John Eaton stared at his large hands. "This is all wrong.
Since it's my family that's the main point of contention, I'm
the one who should resign. Why should others suffer?"

Van Buren positively beamed.

Rebecca cut in, "John, if you are the only one to resign,
then the Calhoun faction will claim victory, saying that they
forced you out of office. The country would believe that Calhoun and his coterie are stronger than the President. But if Van
Buren and Barry resign also—for the good of the country—
then all the other cabinet members, who we know are hostile
to the President, will have to resign too."

"But suppose they don't?" Van Buren interrupted. "It's entirely conceivable that they wouldn't."

"If that were to happen, then President Jackson could demand their resignations, and the country would perceive it as
the only fair thing," she said.

Jackson slammed his palm down on the table. "I won't have
it!" In turn, he fixed Eaton and Van Buren with his piercing
eyes. "Both of you are abandoning me!"

Van Buren and Eaton let out cries of genuine protest, then
fell over themselves to assure Jackson that they only wished
to serve him and the country as best they could.

After another round of arguments, in which all of Jackson's
protests were beaten back, he grudgingly surrendered to his
two cabinet members. Then Jackson said, "But we're forgetting
the one person who's been most injured in all this."

"My God, Peggy!" Eaton exclaimed. "Washington is her
home."

"I'm sure you'll do a wonderful job of explaining to her
just how vital this is to the President," Rebecca said. "And it
is a wife's place to follow the example of her husband."

Van Buren nodded sagely, and Jackson's eyes twinkled.

By the end of the afternoon, and over the strenuous objections of Andrew Jackson, both Eaton and Van Buren agreed to tender their resignations.

Rebecca went home and collapsed.

On April 7, John Eaton resigned as secretary of war. On April 11, Van Buren resigned. Washington reacted with stunned surprise. When the other cabinet members partial to Calhoun balked at resigning, Jackson asked for, and received, their resignations. New cabinet members were appointed.

Jackson then nominated Van Buren to be minister to England. It was understood that when the furor died down, Eaton would become governor of the Florida Territory.

Without the Calhoun faction stabbing him in the back, Jackson was able to conduct his White House affairs with a good deal more efficiency. He was now determined to run for a second term. But he wouldn't commit himself as to his choice for Vice-President.

"I've kept my end of the bargain," Rebecca said to Letitia. "Now let's see if Jackson will keep his." She hadn't heard anything about Gunning.

But the entire affair affected her in a way she hadn't quite anticipated. Francis Blair told his typesetter that Rebecca was Rebel Thorne. The Lord himself knew how many people Van Buren and Eaton told, and in short order, most of Washington buzzed with the fact that the pamphleteer they'd read these many years was none other than Rebecca Breech Brand.

One afternoon, a group of ladies who considered themselves guardians of Washington's reputation came to call on Rebecca. They suggested that the neighborhood might be better served if she moved. "It's for your own good, dear," they told her. "In some distant town where you're not so notorious, you'll live this whole unsavory episode down much faster."

With her temper flaring, Rebecca showed them the door.

Late one night, some young rowdies serenaded Rebecca under her window with a scandalous ditty.

> Rebel is the Thorne I'd love to pluck
> But Rebecca is the woman I'd love to——

For their trouble, they received the contents of Letitia's slop jar. The serenading ceased.

A number of times Bravo returned from the Senate and from school with a bloodied nose, or an eye puffed and turning blue. "But I gave them better than I got," he said proudly to his mother. He also seemed to view her with a new respect that bordered on awe.

When Chief Justice John Marshall learned of the harassment the Brand family was suffering, he talked to the constable, and after a few more altercations, the harassment ceased.

But there were also positive aspects. Along with a dribble of hate mail, Rebecca received scores of letters praising her for her stand. Many letters were from women who'd felt the same restraints, and they took heart from her courage.

"Do you remember when I freed you?" Rebecca said to Letitia. "I felt that an enormous burden had been lifted from my shoulders. Well, I feel the same way now. The world knows who I am, knows what I stand for. I don't have to hide anymore, and what an enormous sense of freedom there is in that!"

When the date for Gunning's trial drew near, Rebecca learned to her great relief that the charges against him had been reduced from desertion to absent without leave. At the trial, he received a six-month sentence, with the option to serve his time at hard labor or to serve with an army unit soon to be assigned to the frontier. Gunning chose duty on the frontier. Though it was considered extremely hazardous, he leapt at this opportunity to redeem himself.

Before being reassigned, Gunning received a three-day pass to visit his family. When he arrived home, everybody had gathered to greet him: Rebecca, Bravo, Circumstance, Wingate, Jeremy, Doe, Letitia, and Tad.

There were shouts of welcome and hugs and kisses; Gunning ruffled Bravo's hair as if nothing but brotherly love had ever passed between them.

Gunning gave his mother a bear hug. "Thank you. All of Washington is abuzz with what you did. I know you risked it for me, and I'll never be able to repay you."

They stood before the tall windows, looking out at the vista that included a view of the south façade of the White House. Rebecca rested her hand on her son's arm. "I know you're capable of great and wonderful things. You've made a false start, but who amongst us hasn't? You mustn't let that stop you."

"I drink to you," he said, toasting her with his sherry glass.

"To the most extraordinary mother a son ever had."

Suddenly, all that she'd gone through was made worthwhile by his simple statement. "Gunning, if I had one wish for you . . . when you look back on your days, I don't want you to have any regrets. I never want you to think 'I should have done this,' or 'I'm sorry I didn't do that.' Whatever your secret dreams, at least try to realize them. Success or failure—well, that isn't nearly as important as the trying. Otherwise, you'll regret never having given yourself the chance."

He nodded. Feeling as though he'd just gone through the Valley of the Shadow of Death, he was ready to hear what she was saying—though she'd told him the same things for most of his life. "I'll do the Brand name proud, you'll see." Then he stared at his hand, turning the simple gold wedding band on his finger. "Not a word from Véronique all these weeks. Mother, did you ever hear any news of her?"

Rebecca debated whether or not to tell him, then decided it was his right to know. "I was hoping you wouldn't bring that up. I didn't want anything to upset this joyous day."

Gunning grasped his mother's hands. "You know where she is?"

"By accident, I discovered she was in Washington. I wrote her, telling her of your difficulties, but she never answered."

"Where is she?" he repeated insistently.

"Gunning, you're better off without her."

He gripped her hands as if to squeeze the information out of her. "Mother, I love her!"

"She and her father are staying with Devroe Connaught."

"I don't believe it!"

"Gunning, you're hurting me!"

"I'm sorry, I didn't—" He broke off and shook his leonine mass of hair. "With Devroe? But how can that be? She's my wife."

Gunning started for the door. "I'm going there. I've got to find out what's happened."

"Gunning, don't! Devroe's dangerous, he—"

But Gunning was already running from the house. He leapt onto his horse and galloped off. The wind was his carrier as he tore through the streets of Washington. In short order, he had left the city behind and was riding hard into the hills.

"There must be some explanation!" he shouted, but the wind only mocked him with its echo. "If he's done anything to her, I'll kill him!"

Chapter 25

ON THE side veranda of the Connaught plantation house, Devroe Connaught was concluding an intense conversation with Ludlow Parkhurst, a junior officer who served as a courier for the British legation in Washington. "When do you leave for England?" Devroe asked.

"The first available ship sails from Baltimore in two days," Parkhurst said. "The report you've given me will be in the hands of His Majesty's government within five weeks."

"Excellent. Now there are several final things which I will tell you and which you must commit to memory. I cannot stress their importance too strongly. Two situations in this country are about to work to our advantage. The first is the election in November of next year. There is a strong possibility that a man who wishes to disband the Union will run and be elected. Should that happen, it would provide Great Britain with a perfect opportunity to extend her influence in the southern states. Naturally, I will work for the election of this man, John Calhoun. Do you understand that?"

Parkhurst nodded.

"The second item, and possibly even more important to us, is that Mexico has rejected President Jackson's offer of five million dollars for the Texas territory. Further, Mexico has forbidden any more Americans from settling in its territory. We must form the strongest possible alliance with Mexico so as to thwart any further American expansion on this continent. It's entirely conceivable that I shall have to make a journey to Mexico City myself. I've had reports of a new man coming into power there, a general named Antonio López de Santa Anna. I'd like to know where this man's sympathies lie. If they're compatible with ours, perhaps I'll throw my support to him."

After drilling Parkhurst with his oral instructions, Devroe stood up with a gesture of dismissal.

Parkhurst bowed and left. Devroe paced the veranda, deep in thought. From an upstairs window he heard Véronique trilling a French country air; Audubert Villefranche lay in a hammock, snoring noisily. Devroe had put up with these two n'erdo-wells because they were an integral part of his plans concerning the Brand family. But the terms of Gunning's sentence had been a great disappointment; twenty years at hard labor would have suited Devroe better. At least that would have justified the expense he'd incurred in fetching Véronique and her father from New York last year. His thin mouth twisted into a grin when he remembered Gunning's reaction at seeing Véronique at the Calico Ball. Devroe couldn't have planned it better; Gunning's attack had landed him in the stockade. The rest had been simple: An anonymous letter to Gunning reporting that Devroe was courting Véronique in New York... Gunning's escape... and when the army's police had proven incapable of tracing him, Devroe's own superior agents had performed that task. With Véronique's help, of course. Like many women of her class, she had a passion for money—and enough sense to cast her lot with the winner. Though he had to admire the way she'd acted when they arrested Gunning at dockside. She had appeared almost remorseful.

Bringing Véronique back to Washington, and flaunting her in the faces of the Brands, had given him the greatest pleasure of all. Sooner or later it would flush Gunning out, and when it did...

Devroe heard the distant sound of a horn, a signal from the gatehouse, miles distant, that a visitor was approaching the plantation house. Devroe went to his study, where he had set up a telescope at a window that looked out toward Washington. Whoever was coming was still hidden by the foliage, and it would be some moments before he became visible.

He fixed his telescope on Washington, on the Capitol Building set atop its hill, then swiveled the sight down along Pennsylvania Avenue to the White House. The city was as decadent as any capital in the world—but in a peculiar way. On the one hand, its morality was determined by a handful of women led by sanctimonious ministers, as witness the Peggy Eaton affair. On the other hand, whorehouses had sprung up all over the city and were frequented by the legislators. It was a dichotomy as sick as it was vulgar; when Americans fell on their knees, they didn't know whether to worship God or Venus.

Then his eyes picked out a cloud of dust on the road. He watched the tiny form grow larger, until the rider became recognizable. A jolt of excitement coursed through Devroe. For an impossible moment, he felt that he'd regained the feeling in his right arm. But then that sensation died, leaving the arm limp and useless.

He hurried downstairs and said to the butler, "A man will arrive here in a matter of minutes. You're to let him in, and send him to the Mademoiselle Villefranche's suite. Do you understand?"

The butler nodded.

"If you make any mistake, I'll have you whipped until there's no skin on your back."

Since that had happened to him before, the slave nodded eagerly. "I understand."

Then Devroe bounded upstairs and went to the suite he'd given to Véronique. She was standing in front of the mirror, trying on one of the many gowns he'd bought her.

"Don't you think this green one is exquisite?" she asked, turning this way and that before the mirror.

Without a word, he went to her and tore the dress from her back. The suddenness so startled her that she didn't move when he did the same to her shift, leaving her naked. Up to now, their congress had always been slow and agonizing, fraught with difficulties. But as he shucked off his clothes she saw that he was more than ready. They fell into bed, rutting about in a tangle of arms and legs, growing hot and sweaty, he muttering gutter talk in her ear, she raking her nails across his back, leaving welts. She opened herself to him, arching her body to meet his, building to a climax slowly, but with such force that she cried out with each of his thrusts, *"Encore, encore, je t'aime!"* When she finally came to herself, she became aware of the tall form standing in the doorway. *"Mon dieu!"* she whispered.

Gunning lunged across the room. He grabbed Devroe's shoulder and hauled him off Véronique. In a mindless rage, his hands went to Devroe's throat. But Sisley Urquhart and the butler came running in, and with Devroe's help, they managed to subdue Gunning.

Straining to break free, Gunning stared in shock and revulsion at his wife. "How could you!" he cried.

"Tell him, dear," Devroe said. "Tell him how you sold him

to the authorities for a few baubles and some gowns."

Gunning saw the color rise to Véronique's cheeks, saw her eyes dart one way then another. When she started to protest her innocence, he knew she was lying. It had all been an act, everything. While he was getting ready to flee with her to Europe, she was busy betraying him.

Gunning's shoulders slumped, the fight gone out of him. He looked at Devroe. "Under ordinary circumstances, honor would demand that I challenge you to a duel. But my time behind bars has taught me a great deal, enough to know that she isn't worth it. You may have her."

Gunning shrugged off Sisley's and the butler's hold, and started for the door.

Devroe hadn't expected this reaction at all, and scrambled for a solution. "Ah, but the honor of my family demands satisfaction," he called after Gunning and strode to where he stood. "First you struck me in public at the White House. Now you've broken into my private chambers and laid hands on me again. I could shoot you right now and the law would be on my side. But as a gentleman, I demand satisfaction."

"Devroe, I don't fight cripples."

Devroe slapped him hard across the face with his left hand. "You'll find that even a crippled Connaught is more than a match for you and your filthy kind. I'll be at the Bladensburg dueling grounds at dawn tomorrow. Are pistols agreeable to you?" When Gunning didn't respond Devroe said, "Good. I'll bring them. And we'll make the distance six paces. I want there to be no doubt in your mind that at that close range, I mean to kill you."

Gunning turned on his heel and left.

When he returned home later that evening, Gunning found Rebecca waiting for him. "You were right," he said. "I discovered them . . . together."

"I'm so sorry," she murmured. "I would have done anything to spare you that pain."

He nodded dully. "Well, I suppose after all the wenching I've done, this is some sort of divine retribution. Though I've got to confess, I never thought it would happen to me."

"I know this is a blow to you, but in a year, perhaps less, you'll realize how lucky you were to have found this out now."

He smiled at her. "I think I realize that right this very moment. Goodnight, Mother."

When Gunning went upstairs, Bravo came running out of

his room after him. "What are you doing up?" Gunning asked.

"Waiting for you. Mother called the constable and everything, but he said it was out of his jurisdiction."

"Well, as long as you're up, come to my room. There are some things I've got to tell you."

Bravo padded after his brother; Gunning closed the door to his room after them. "Bravo, tomorrow morning, early, I've got business to tend to. Now I think everything will turn out all right, but you never know. So, if anything should happen, you've got to be the head of the family."

"You're going to fight a duel, aren't you?" Bravo said.

"You're not to say a word to Mother. Not a word. It would only worry her. Sometimes . . . well, there's no other way out of this."

Bravo nodded gravely. "Where's the duel going to be—Bladensburg?"

Gunning nodded.

"Can I come with you? You'll need a second."

Gunning shook his head. "Best if you didn't. It would only make me nervous. But don't worry. I can't afford to kill him. I'm in too much trouble with the army already to add murder to my account. I'll fire into the air."

"But what about Devroe?" Bravo asked.

"Oh, he's just doing this to save face. You know his right arm is crippled, so how's he going to shoot? Now go to bed."

Bravo started slowly toward the door and Gunning called to him, "Hey, Bravo?"

"Yes?" he said eagerly.

"If something should happen, then I want you to have my horse. And my pistols."

With a cry, Bravo ran to his brother and threw his arms around him. Gunning hugged him and said, "If ever I've been mean to you—well, you know I really didn't mean it, right?"

Bravo nodded. With tears in his eyes, he left the room.

Gunning roused himself at three the next morning. He dressed quietly and quickly, saddled his stallion, and was off before anybody in the house had wakened.

Except for Bravo. He'd spent a sleepless night trying to figure out what to do. But nothing came to him. By the time Gunning had galloped off, Bravo was already in his clothes and running for Circumstance and Wingate's house. "I promised him I wouldn't tell Mother," he said in jerky breaths as he ran. "But I didn't say anything about Wingate."

He pounded on their door, and after some moments Wingate opened it. Wingate had a look of sleepy-eyed resignation on his face, as if expecting a patient, but he became alert when he saw Bravo.

As quickly as he could, Bravo blurted out the story. Circumstance and Jeremy, both wakened by the commotion, joined them. "Gunning says that nothing's going to happen because Devroe's arm is crippled. But I don't trust that one. Would you go there? Please? I think it's best for somebody to be there with Gunning."

"You're right, lad," Wingate said. He hurriedly began to dress. "How much of a lead does Gunning have?"

"Ten minutes, at most."

"It's still dark," Wingate said. "Maybe we can get there before dawn, talk some sense into both of them. Jeremy, hitch Stubborn to the wagon."

Jeremy ran outside. Then Wingate turned to Circumstance. "Go to Rebecca's. Tell her to alert the authorities—though that probably won't do any good because the grounds are over the Maryland border. Tell her anyway. Bravo, come on."

As Wingate, Bravo, and Jeremy rode off in the buckboard, they saw Circumstance run from the house with Doe in her arms.

Several minutes later, Circumstance reached Rebecca's and wakened everybody. She told Rebecca what was happening. "But I understand that there isn't too much to be worried about," Circumstance said. "Gunning told Bravo that he wouldn't shoot at a man who couldn't fire back. So Gunning will shoot in the air."

Rebecca turned deathly pale. "Shoot into the air? Oh my God, no!"

"Why, what's the matter?"

"Oh, quickly, we've got to ride there! I've got to warn Gunning. Doesn't he know that Devroe is ambidextrous? He's just as deadly a shot with his left hand as he was with his right!"

Chapter 26

GUNNING REACHED Bladensburg shortly before dawn. The sky remained so heavily overcast that light barely tinged the edges of the clouds. The deserted dueling field lay covered in morning mist. Nobody was in sight, and for a moment Gunning hoped that Devroe had had a change of heart.

In this field, some ten years before, Stephen Decatur had been killed in a duel. Though the government frowned on dueling, the Bladensburg field had become a popular spot for gentlemen to settle their differences. The Valley of Chance, as it was called, was enclosed by the two hills, at the base of which ran a small brook. The hills concealed the meadow from the Baltimore–Washington turnpike. The District of Columbia line ran through this valley, so the combatants from Washington and Virginia would pass over the line into Maryland, thus evading the laws from their own territories. By now, the ground had been soaked with the blood of the wounded and the dead of more than fifty duels.

A few minutes later, Gunning saw the black-and-gold Connaught carriage roll onto the field. Devroe and his entourage emerged. Devroe wore a dark green coat, and lighter green pants; in the half-light, the clothes blended into the surrounding greenery.

That will make the clever bastard a more difficult target, Gunning thought. Sisley Urquhart, holding the case containing Devroe's dueling pistols, followed his master as Devroe approached Gunning. I wonder if I look as frightened as he does, Gunning thought.

Urquhart cleared his throat. "You will begin this duel by standing back to back. At my count, you will each take six paces away from each other. At my command, you will turn and fire at will. You are each allowed one shot."

Both men nodded. Sisley handed Devroe a pistol. He took

the shiny barrel in his left hand, then placed the butt of it in his right hand. The gun in his crippled hand hung limply at his side. Then Sisley handed Gunning the other.

Gunning couldn't help but notice Devroe's guns. They were the finest that English small-arms manufacturers could produce. But of what use would they be if Devroe can barely hold his?

"Devroe, there's no need to go through this," Gunning began. But Devroe turned his back on him. Gunning hunched his shoulders and turned also.

"One!" Sisley called.

The two men began to pace off the distance. With each step Gunning viewed the misspent life that had brought him to this moment. "The waste of it all!" he muttered to himself. And he swore that as soon as this was over it would be different.

"Three, four . . ." Sisley called.

"There's a faster way to get to Bladensburg than by this road," Rebecca called to Circumstance, who rode beside her. An old, shorter path lay through a forest, and there were two swollen streams to ford, but Rebecca wheeled her mare off the road and plunged into the thickets. Circumstance followed her. Rebecca had ridden this trail since girlhood and knew it well. She whipped her horse and the animal broke into a gallop, hurtling over fallen logs and stone fences, even as she cried, "Faster!"

Perhaps for the first time in her life, Stubborn seemed to sense the urgency in her master's voice and fairly flew over the road to Bladensburg. Bravo and Jeremy hung on as the wagon bumped over the road rutted with spring rains.

"Over there, look!" Bravo shouted, pointing to distant figures pacing in the field. "They've started already!"

"Five, six," Sisley Urquhart shouted.

Gunning and Devroe turned and faced each other. Devroe stood in profile, his crippled arm presented as a target. Slowly Gunning raised his pistol until it pointed straight up. Then he fired. The gun discharged harmlessly into the air.

Only then did a sardonic grin spread over Devroe's face. With great care, he took the pistol from his limp right hand and grasped it firmly in his left. He raised the weapon and took careful aim, giving Gunning enough time to realize that he'd been duped.

"For my father," Devroe whispered, and then fired.

The bullet struck Gunning squarely in the chest, and the force of it knocked him backwards. He fell to the ground and lay still.

Devroe handed the spent gun to Sisley, then took another pistol from Sisley. He walked over to where Gunning lay. His eyes were closed, his body motionless, the gouting chest wound forming a bright red stain on his white shirt.

Devroe nudged Gunning with his toe. "He's dead, or dying. No need to waste another bullet. Truss him up on the back of the carriage. Let his blood water the ground from here to Washington. It will give me the greatest pleasure to personally deliver him to Rebecca Breech Brand."

Sisley grasped one of Gunning's legs and started to drag him to the Connaught carriage just as Wingate, Bravo, and Jeremy drove up.

"Leave him alone!" Bravo screamed. Even before the wagon stopped he was off and running at Sisley. He hurled himself at the man, beating at him with his fists.

"Come away, Sisley," Devroe called. "We've accomplished what we set out to do."

Sisley dropped the body and retreated to the carriage. He climbed in and the carriage rolled away.

Rebecca, having cut through the fields, picked up the Bladensburg road again. She'd heard the shots, and her heart shriveled as she saw the Connaught carriage approaching her. Devroe sat in the back seat, laughing and chatting. He caught sight of her and tipped his hat gaily.

He's killed him! was Rebecca's only thought, and as the carriage rolled past, Devroe's high-pitched laugh seemed to confirm her worst fears. She spurred her horse to where Wingate, Bravo, and Jeremy were clustered around Gunning's body.

"Is he dead?" she cried as she dismounted.

Wingate turned to her, his stethoscope in his hand. "I can still hear a faint heartbeat. But he's critically injured."

Rebecca flung herself at her son's body, but Circumstance, who'd just arrived, grabbed her and drew her away. "You must control yourself," she said firmly. "Let Wingate do his work."

"He's bleeding too heavily to be taken back to Washington," Wingate said. "From the color of the blood I'd say that an artery's been severed. Unless I stop the bleeding . . ."

He took a cloth from his black bag, folded it into a compress, and jammed it against the wound. "Hold it there," he said to Jeremy. "Tightly."

Wingate looked at the sky. It hadn't gotten appreciably lighter. "I'll need a table to operate on and some light. Is there a house nearby?"

"Bladensburg is about a mile away," Rebecca said.

"We don't have that much time," Wingate said. "A minute can make the difference."

"Wait, there's a tavern just around the bend of the road," Bravo said, remembering the night when he'd tried to stop Gunning from leaving Washington.

"My God!" Wingate swore suddenly.

"What is it?" Circumstance asked.

"Look at his face. It's turning deathly pale." Wingate checked the other life signs. Gunning's skin was sweaty, and his every breath grew more labored. His lips and fingertips were also turning blue.

"Tell me what's happening," Rebecca demanded.

Wingate tore open Gunning's shirt. "The signs are unmistakable. I've seen enough cases on the battlefield to know. The bullet's punctured his lung, and air from the lung is escaping into his chest cavity. Circumstance, my scalpel!"

"What are you going to do?" Rebecca moaned, but Wingate was too intent on his patient to answer.

Rebecca's hand flew to her mouth as she watched Wingate make a deep incision into Gunning's chest, expertly moving the scalpel between the ribs. As the instrument sliced through the chest wall, the trapped air escaped with a loud hiss.

"Oh my God, you're only making it worse!" Rebecca cried.

"The air inside Gunning's chest was pressing against the punctured lung, constricting everything—not only the lung itself, but all the blood vessels," Wingate said. "Blood couldn't get to any of the vital parts of his body. With every breath he took, he was strangling himself a little more. Unless I had relieved that pressure, he'd have been dead in a matter of minutes."

They watched as the color gradually returned to Gunning's face. The blue color around his lips faded and his breathing became easier.

"But how is he still breathing if his lung is punctured?" Bravo asked.

"We all have two lungs," Wingate said as he continued to

work on Gunning, binding up the incision. "Gunning's second lung has taken over and is doing the work for both."

"Will he be all right now?" Rebecca asked.

"No!" Wingate barked. "All I've done is buy us a little time. He's still bleeding to death! Let's get him into the wagon and to the tavern."

While Jeremy held his hand tightly against the compress, the other four lifted Gunning's dead weight and hefted him carefully into the wagon. Wingate gave terse, exact orders. "Bravo, you get in and cradle your brother's head in your lap."

"Let me do that," Rebecca said.

Wingate grabbed her arm. "No, you're too heavy for the wagon. Just do as I say! Circumstance, you and Rebecca ride on ahead. Alert the innkeeper, gather all the clean cloths he has—sheets, pillowcases, whatever. And boil water. Jeremy, can you drive the wagon?"

"Yes, Pa."

Wingate climbed into the back of the wagon and held the compress against Gunning's wound. "As fast as you can, son," Wingate called to Jeremy.

Jeremy shouted to Stubborn and she took off at a trot. Every jolt made Bravo wince for his brother. Wingate said, "Don't worry, he can't feel anything. If we don't get him to the inn fast, it won't matter anyway."

Several minutes later they arrived and were met by the innkeeper, Peter Geary, and Circumstance and Rebecca. Wingate lifted Gunning under the shoulders and Mr. Geary grasped his legs.

"I've a bed in one of my empty rooms," Mr. Geary said.

Wingate shook his head. "I need a hard surface. A long table will do."

"In the main room, then," Mr. Geary said, leading the way.

"Why a table?" Bravo whispered to Jeremy.

"A bed is too soft. Papa must have a hard surface to keep Gunning from moving about. He'll probably tie him down, too."

In the main room of the tavern, they placed Gunning on the long trestle table. Wingate ran a length of rope over Gunning's ankles, holding him fast to the table. Then he tied down Gunning's hands. "Is there no way to get more light in this room?" he asked, glancing around.

Mr. Geary shook his head. "This is the best there is."

"Bravo, open all the windows," Wingate ordered.

Bravo dashed to each in turn and flung them open. But it didn't make much difference. The old stone tavern had been constructed during the years when Indians were still a menace, so the window openings were narrow and deepset. With the morning still heavily overcast, very little light reached the table.

Circumstance hurried in with kettles of boiling water and a basin. Wingate put his instruments in the basin and she poured the boiling water over it. Careful not to touch any of the cutting edges, Circumstance then laid the instruments on a cloth within Wingate's reach.

"I've got to open his chest, find the severed artery, and tie it off," Wingate said to Circumstance so that she would know the procedure. "If I can get the bullet out at the same time, so much the better."

He reached for a razor-sharp scalpel. About to make an incision, he shook his head. "There isn't enough light!"

Bravo raced around the tavern, returning with every available lamp and lantern. "It's a little better," Wingate said, "but it still isn't enough. Once I make the incision, I must see where I'm going. But quickly! We're losing him."

Bravo clutched his head in his hands, trying to think. He couldn't let his brother die for lack of light! Wildly, his gaze swept the room. Then he cried, "Go ahead, start! I'll be right back!"

He ran to the far side of the tavern, where a mirror hung on the wall. He tried to lift the mirror off, but it was bolted tight. Without a second's hesitation, Bravo picked up a tankard and smashed it against the glass. The mirror cracked, the pieces falling to the floor. Bravo picked up the largest pieces, four in all, each more than a foot square, and unmindful of the nicks and cuts they made on his hands, brought them back to the table. He gave sections of the mirror to Circumstance, Rebecca, and Jeremy.

"Do as I do," he said, and held his mirror so that it reflected the light from the lamps onto the table where Gunning lay. When the others didn't respond quickly enough, Bravo placed them strategically around the table. By tilting their mirrors, Bravo managed to focus much of the light on Gunning's chest.

"That's good, very good indeed," Wingate exclaimed. "Just hold the mirrors steady now. If any of you are squeamish, don't look at what I'm doing. But keep your mirrors still!"

Rebecca stared at Gunning's chest. It seemed that every

moment of her life had condensed down to this one instant.
As Wingate's scalpel cut into the flesh, she thought, I gave
life to that body, and now I'm watching it die. Everything in
her screamed out against this perversion of nature. The natural
order of the world demanded that the child survive the parent.
How else could life go on? Rebecca knew that if Gunning died,
she'd never survive it. If she could have substituted her own
body for his, she would have done so without pause, without
question. But the fates had decreed otherwise, and now everything rested in Wingate's hands.

Wingate made an incision more than eight inches long,
opening the flesh to the rib cage. The area immediately began
filling with blood, obscuring everything. Circumstance kept
wiping the flow away as best she could. Wingate then cut the
muscle tissue holding the ribs together. With a sure, firm motion, he separated the ribs. He saw the terrified look on Rebecca's face and said, "Don't worry, these ribs are like springs,
they have a lot of resilience. I've got to get into the chest cavity
in order to find the severed artery."

He wedged a block of wood between the ribs which kept
the gaping hole open. He worked his hand in, then pulled the
lung aside to expose the area where it was attached to the
windpipe, and where the heart was attached to the major ar-
teries.

The superior vena cava, the main vein draining blood back
into the right side of the heart, was uninjured, thank God.
Otherwise, Gunning would have long since been dead. The
bleeding must be coming from a smaller vessel. But it was
serious enough so that unless it was tied off, and quickly,
Gunning would bleed to death.

The warm smell of blood, mingled with the waxy odor of
burning candles and oil, permeated the room. The confined
space where they stood began to get very warm, and Jeremy
put down his mirror long enough to blot the sweat from his
father's forehead. Minutes ticked by, as inexorable as the pulse-
beat of blood.

"His limbs are getting cold," Circumstance said softly.

Wingate nodded and kept probing, trying to find the elusive
artery. And then he saw it. "It's the internal mammary artery,"
he said to Circumstance. It was a minor artery on the inner
chest wall, but it was draining the life out of Gunning. Quickly,
he grasped the spurting end closest to the heart with a delicate
pair of forceps.

"Hold this," he said. Circumstance deftly took the instrument from his hands without losing the end of the artery.

Wingate then took his suturing equipment, silk thread and needle, and tied off the end of the artery. The other end, away from the heart, had already closed off of its own accord. Wingate wiped away the blood, trying to see if there'd been any further injuries. But he couldn't find any.

"Now for the bullet," he said. He didn't tell the others that it was lodged perilously close to Gunning's heart. A mistaken move and the entire operation would have been in vain. In addition, lodged as it was, the bullet might be acting as a dam against the heart muscle. Pray God that the bullet hasn't penetrated the heart muscle itself, Wingate thought.

He took a heavier pair of forceps from the table and reached in, trying to extract the bullet. Three times the forceps closed around the end of the bullet, and three times Wingate lost it. Then with a final desperate grasp, he yanked and the bullet came free.

As far as he could see, the wall of the heart hadn't been punctured, and no further blood flow appeared. Gently, he extracted his hand, and dropped the bullet onto the table.

An audible sigh of relief escaped from Rebecca and Circumstance. But Wingate said, "No time for that yet. I've got to close him up." He took away the block that separated the ribs, and they sprang back into place. Then he sewed up the layers of muscular tissue and finally stitched up the skin.

He wiped the oozing blood from the scar, then bound the wound with clean bandages. Only then did he allow himself to sink to the bench. Circumstance hurried out and brought him a cup of hot broth.

Rebecca touched Wingate's shoulder. "We owe you his life," she murmured.

He patted her hand. "We mustn't speak too quickly. He's still in a very dangerous condition. He'll need weeks of bed rest to allow the puncture to heal."

"And the severed artery?" Rebecca asked.

"The other blood vessels will take over. We can thank God that Gunning's such a healthy specimen. Never seen anybody with such strong innards. An ordinary man would have been dead long ago."

Then Wingate turned to Bravo. "That was a smart thing you did. I couldn't have operated without that extra light. So you had a hand in saving him too. In fact, we all did."

He looked around at all their fatigued, sweat-stained faces. They crowded close and hugged each other.

Since it was impossible for Gunning to be moved, Rebecca made arrangements to rent a room for him. The landlord had a seventeen-year-old daughter, Kate Geary, a pretty, freckle-faced lass with a bright air and full of good humor, and she agreed to spell Rebecca and Circumstance while they were nursing Gunning.

Bravo and Jeremy cleaned up the mess from the operation. Unseen by anybody but Jeremy, Bravo pocketed the mashed bullet. "One day, I'll give this back to Devroe Connaught," he swore.

Chapter 27

FOR TWO WEEKS and more, Gunning hovered between life and death. From all signs, Wingate determined that the internal bleeding had stopped, but other complications set in. A fever from the operation sent his temperature soaring, and for three days Wingate, Rebecca, and Circumstance kept a round-the-clock vigil as Gunning struggled to hold onto the thin thread of life.

Kate Geary proved an invaluable aid, bringing in their meals, helping to change Gunning's sweat-soaked bedclothes and sheets. One night she took over Circumstance's watch after the exhausted woman had fallen asleep. As she sat by the bedside, Kate kept up an endless litany of prayer for Gunning's recovery. Even in his illness, she'd never seen anybody quite as handsome as this godlike creature. What a shame for life itself, she thought, if he were to die.

Gunning survived the fever, and as the summer waxed, he gradually fought off the ravages of his illness. One evening he was even able to hold down some chicken broth. A few days later Kate helped prop him up in bed, and a week after that, he took his first tremulous steps.

"I feel like a newborn babe," he said to Bravo and Kate, who stood on either side of him, helping him walk. Bravo made a point to ride out every day to Bladensburg. Gunning had lost close to twenty-five pounds, and the bones showed sharp in his ribcage and in his gaunt face. "Set me up in the field and I could pass as a reasonable scarecrow," he said, as they walked him around the room.

With Gunning slowly on the mend, Circumstance and Rebecca returned to Washington. Gunning wasn't yet able to travel, but Rebecca hired Kate to look after him. She liked the girl. Kate was full-bodied, buxom, and brimming with Gaelic charm she'd inherited from her loquacious father, and all tempered by a deep religious bent that came from her devout mother. She believed fervently, and without question, in the Lord. "He has a million eyes that watch everybody all the time," she once confided to Bravo, "and I'll never do anything to offend Him."

Bravo had fallen so desperately under her spell that he was almost ready to believe the part about the million eyes.

Kate's sincerity and good humor were so different from Véronique's ploys and deceits that in short order Gunning was also captivated by her.

President Jackson sent Gunning a note from Nashville, where he'd gone for the summer, expressing concern over his condition. As for the legal penalty for dueling, Jackson, with his own history of duels, was quite cavalier. He told Gunning he could join his army unit out west as soon as he was well, and no punitive action would be taken against him.

With Gunning's permission, Rebecca petitioned Chief Justice John Marshall to grant her son an annulment. Marshall set those wheels in motion, and since Véronique didn't contest it, the annulment was granted in early August.

One limpid afternoon, Gunning proved that he was well on the road to recovery; while walking slowly around the barn with Kate, he suggested a cure that would make his recovery complete. "Why not, Kate? I tell you it's the most fun in all the world. Once you start you'll never want to stop. And you know how much I adore you."

"Get on with you," Kate said, mimicking her father's brogue. "Mine's the only face you've seen for the past weeks, so it's easy enough to say you adore me. But as soon as you're well enough to go back to your fancy Washington, why, you'll soon forget Kate."

"How could I forget those blue eyes? That coal-black hair? Those freckles that I could bite off your cheeks and lips? I'll bet you have freckles all over—"

"Enough, Gunning Brand! I know all about you. Every young girl in this district has been warned about you. You're young and handsome and winning, and sure to set a girl's heart abeating, but you're also the devil incarnate, come to tempt us all, and I'll not be tempted."

"Oh, come on, Kate! My devil is nothing more than a little imp now, something you could easily handle." He swept her into his arms and tried to kiss her, but she broke free.

She grabbed a pitchfork and brandished its shiny tines at him. "Is that what you think of me? Something to be toyed with?" she exclaimed. "I'll not have it. I'll run this pitchfork through you if you so much as take another step toward me."

He slapped his thigh in glee. "Why, my Kate, there's nothing I like more than a lass with spirit!" He reached for her again.

But she jabbed his arm. With a yowl, he withdrew it quickly and rubbed the places where she'd pinked him.

"I'll walk with you no more if you keep that up," she said.

He held up his hands placatingly. "All right, I'll behave. But I warn you, Kate, I'll win you yet. Once I set my mind on something, I usually get it."

She tapped his chest lightly. "I can see that you do. And it near kills you."

With that, he burst out laughing. She tried to look stern, but his grin was so beguiling that she laughed also. They walked back to the inn through the sunset. The August haze made the landscape look like that in a dream. The lulling chirp of cicadas, a hawk floating lazily on the air currents, the honeyed smell of grasses and wildflowers, made them both feel utterly at peace.

He looked over toward the Valley of Chance, where his blood had soaked the ground. "You know, I almost died out there. But I wouldn't trade it for anything. Because something wonderful happened to me, I was given a second chance at life . . . There's so much I want to do, so much I can do."

He reached for Kate's hand; when his fingers twined through hers, she didn't pull away.

Gunning was sitting under an apple tree in the heat of late August, when he saw a lone rider galloping hard along the road from Washington.

The rider reined in at the inn, bounded inside, and several minutes later, Mr. Geary and his sons came rushing out. All the Negro help, slaves and servants alike, were herded into the outbuildings where they lived, and their doors slammed and locked.

"What's the matter? What's happening?" Gunning asked Kate, who'd run out to him, a pistol stuck in the band of her apron, and a rifle held in the crook of her arm.

"There's been a dreadful massacre!" she exclaimed. "The

slaves are rebelling in Virginia, slaughtering every white person they can lay their hands on. Da says we've got to arm ourselves!"

"What about Washington?" Gunning demanded. The population of blacks, both freedmen and slaves, had risen dramatically in the past decade; they represented at least thirty-five percent of the local population.

"The messenger says there's no trouble there yet, though everybody is taking precautions."

In the next few days, more news of the uprising came out of Virginia. Rebecca, who'd come to visit Gunning, brought all the local newspapers.

Gunning, now chafing under his confinement, had thought he was well enough to help Kate churn butter. But he'd quickly exhausted himself and lay sprawled on the grass. While Kate continued to churn, he read aloud from the *National Intelligencer*.

"On August twenty-second, Nat Turner, a slave preacher in Southampton County, led seventy or more slaves on a rampage, killing fifty-five white people, most of them women and children. The governor of Virginia immediately called out the militia, which put down the rebellion, killing at least one hundred Negroes in retaliation. Unfortunately, it was later learned that most of these poor souls had no connection at all with Turner's rebellion. The massacre has terrified Tidewater Virginia, where Negroes outnumber whites by at least sixty-five thousand people." Gunning looked up from the paper. "Good Lord, I'd no idea that white people were in such a minority there. Think of what the slaves could do if they really took it into their heads to have a full-scale rebellion."

"Lord have mercy on all our souls," Kate exclaimed.

Gunning continued reading. "The county is extremely puzzled by Nat Turner's actions; he was well treated by his master, and has been heard to speak highly of him and his family. Many Southerners feel that Turner, who unfortunately could read, had been influenced by abolitionist propaganda, mainly the incendiary sentiments of William Lloyd Garrison's *Liberator*."

"Well, this is going to make everybody in the South keep his rifle at his bedside," Kate said.

"It's far worse than that," Rebecca said. "It will bring down a curtain of censorship on the South. They'll refuse to listen to any viewpoint save their own. Think of how this has strengthened John Calhoun's hand. Nat Turner's done his people more harm than good."

Kate, in awe of Rebecca, thought her surely the smartest woman that God had ever created. All Kate dared contribute to the conversation was a weak, "What's to be done?"

"I don't know. But if the North persists in its uncompromising attitude about slavery, it will only give the nullifiers more ammunition to wreck the Union. The important thing is for both sides not to give in to hysteria. I understand that President Jackson is returning earlier than planned from Nashville. I'm thankful for that. What's wanted now is a firm hand. We've got to keep this contagion from spreading, or the Union will be ripped to pieces."

In mid-September, Wingate rode out to the Geary Inn to examine Gunning. "I believe you're well enough to make the trip back to Washington," he said. "Fairly soon, you should be able to join your unit."

Gunning let out a whoop that made Kate come running. "Did you hear that? I'm almost well."

Gunning made arrangements to leave the following day. Bravo and Tad would come out in the carriage and drive him home. That evening, with dusk almost giving way to night, he and Kate stood watching a flock of geese arrowing their way south.

"Soon you'll be going off like them," Kate said. "Off on your own adventures, and leaving us all behind. But that's the way it is with men, isn't it?"

"You could come with me," he said jokingly.

"Truly, you're the evil one's serpent for even saying such a thing," Kate exclaimed. "Would you have me be a camp follower?"

Suddenly Gunning became serious. "No, I mean it." He took both her hands in his. "Kate, I love you. Will you marry me?"

Her eyes, dark blue in the twilight, glowed for an instant, but then she lowered her head. "No, I can't marry you. You're being kind to me because I've been kind to you. It's not kindness I want, but love. I've been dreaming of that since I was a little girl, and I'll not settle for anything less."

"Oh, Kate, my Kate, what can I do to persuade you?"

"Nothing, I'm afraid. Once you're out of sight, well, that'll be the end of it."

"If I send for you, will you come?"

"Gunning, I'm not much like other girls—no good at flirting, and I don't say things I don't mean. So you've no call to try and deceive me."

"You'll see. I'll work my tail off to get my old rank back. That will make it easier for us to be married. I promise, I'll send for you."

He bent down and kissed her lightly on the lips. For a heart-stopping instant she kissed him back. Then she fled upstairs to her room and bolted the door. She threw herself on the bed and sobbed for all the things that would never be. Her heart warned her that once out of sight, he would forget her ... and she'd fallen hopelessly in love.

Chapter 28

VÉRONIQUE Villefranche Brand received the news of her annulment with mixed feelings. The law stated that she had never been legally married, but she found it impossible to erase Gunning Brand from her mind.

"He was a man who knew how to move me," she said to her father, "and one doesn't often find that in life."

"And Devroe?" Audubert asked solicitously.

Véronique gave a disdainful shrug of her shoulders.

"What are we to do?" Audubert lamented. "Now that he no longer needs you, he tells us to leave his plantation. We have been used . . . used!"

"Yes, *mon père,* I'm afraid you're right," Véronique agreed. "I must do what I can to rectify that."

"You have a plan?" Audubert asked.

Véronique would say no more, for though she loved her father, she knew him to be the worst of gossips. Her status as a single woman opened new possibilities, and she was determined to use it to her full advantage.

At what was to be their final dinner at the Connaught manor, Véronique dressed with particular care. Like many Parisian women, she did have a flair for clothes; whatever her situation, her wardrobe had always been distinctive, characterized by an understated elegance.

Her black silk taffeta gown rustled as she came downstairs to the candlelit dining room. Her hair, arranged in long curls, was artfully caught with a black velvet ribbon whose ends fell over her shoulder and rested on the pale white skin of her bosom. The only color she wore was the slash of vermillion on her lips. Worry, about what might happen to her and her father if her plan should fail, gave her piquant face a nervous animation.

Devroe sat at the head of the long mahogany dining table.

"Where's your father?" he asked, a trace of irritation in his voice. "Dinner can't be kept waiting."

"Papa is indisposed," Véronique said, "and begs your forgiveness." She'd instructed Audubert not to come to dinner this night; she needed to be alone with Devroe.

Devroe frowned and signaled the butler to commence serving. The first course, a crabmeat bisque, was placed before them. Devroe tasted a spoonful and pushed the plate away. "It's too cold. Send it back."

Because of Devroe's fear of a black insurrection, all the black help had been locked away for the night, and only a skeleton staff of white servants was left. The service was abominable.

A pistol lay on the table beside Devroe. He kept the keys to the gunroom in his pocket, and several times during the day, he'd check the room to make sure that none of the slaves had broken in.

"It's that damned William Lloyd Garrison," he said to Véronique, who sat at his right. "What can a newspaper printed in Boston, and funded by an ex-slave who lives in Philadelphia, know of our special problems here in the South? How dare the *Liberator* demand the absolute abolition of slavery?"

On this issue, Véronique rarely troubled herself. But believing that it would please him, she echoed Devroe's ideas. "How can they be freed if they can be taught nothing?" she asked. "Would they not just wander the streets and become a drain on the entire economy?"

"Exactly," Devroe said.

He had forty fieldhands working the plantation, harvesting tobacco and cotton, his major cash crops. Aside from occasionally amusing himself with one of the younger blacks, he paid little attention to them. Sisley Urquhart's long whip and leather truncheon kept them in line.

Devroe ran his fingers over his pistol. "This is like living in an armed camp. My Lord, why can't people just learn to keep their place? Then the world would run as smoothly as it was meant to . . ."

Véronique pushed forward her next question very carefully. "How does this slave insurrection affect your plans?"

"What do you mean?"

"Why, it serves your purpose for there to be friction between the North and the South, does it not?"

He looked at her sharply, but didn't respond.

During the meat course, a paillard of veal, Devroe suddenly slammed his pistol down on the table. "I cannot understand it! I aimed for his heart. I could have sworn Gunning Brand was dead. But these Brands lead charmed lives."

"I understand your disappointment," Véronique said sweetly, "but surely you will have a second opportunity to exact your revenge."

That thought seemed to placate Devroe. "Yes, I haven't finished with Gunning Brand, not by any means. And there's that little brat Bravo, and Madam Brand herself."

"That one!" Véronique exclaimed with a roll of her eyes. "She deserves the worst. You know, Devroe, together we could devise all manner of ways to even the scales of justice."

He stiffened at her presumption and said icily, "Incidentally, I've made arrangements for the coach to take you to the National Hotel in Washington early tomorrow morning. I've reserved the best suite for you and your father, and paid for a week in advance. After that, I assume you'll go back to New York."

Véronique raised her wineglass to her lips and looked at Devroe over the rim of the crystal. "I think not. Papa and I have decided to remain in Washington."

"Oh?" he exclaimed, not liking this turn at all. "I didn't think there was enough theater in Washington for you to advance your career."

"You're right. But I've been thinking of other endeavors. Several days ago, I rode into Washington and made inquiries at the French embassy. Ambassador Serurier told me that he could always use people who could act as interpreters—particularly since this madman Jackson has now taken it into his head to demand that France pay reparations for something that happened during the Napoleonic Wars! Can you imagine? Nevertheless, it is an opportunity for me, for I'm fluent in both French and English."

"They would never employ a woman," he said derisively.

"They would, providing the woman had information they wanted. Really, Devroe, your cook must learn how to make a chocolate mousse. I will show her."

Devroe opened the clawed fingers of his crippled hand and began to massage them. He tried to keep his voice level as he said, "I suppose that anybody would be prepared to pay for important information."

"Washington is a city of rumors," Véronique said, leaning toward him. "It is built on rumors, it thrives on rumors. Anybody with a soupçon of intelligence could put the pieces together and sell the product." She said with an air of artless innocence, "Did you know that Jackson wants to annex Texas, and has offered Mexico five million dollars for it? And did you know that Great Britain will do everything in her power to stop that sale? Why, messages fly back and forth across the Atlantic."

Devroe's bloodless lips tightened until they almost disappeared into his mouth. Obviously, this little minx had heard a great deal while she was his guest; he cursed himself for not being more careful. "Such information has been known to get a person in a great deal of trouble," he said, his voice edged with ice.

"Oh, I'm sure," she agreed. "Now if I were involved in such an undertaking, I would put all I knew into a letter, and give that letter to a reputable lawyer with instructions to open it and make the contents public should anything happen to me. Of course, I'm just a novice in these matters, but—"

Devroe bounded to his feet, knocking his Chippendale chair to the floor. He reached her in one stride, grasped her arm, and twisted it, forcing her off the chair and to her knees. "You dare to threaten me? What exactly do you know?"

She looked up at him, the expression on her face a mixture of fear and defiance. "I know all there is to know."

Her face twisted in a grimace of pain as he tightened his grip. "Specifics."

"A woman alone must protect herself. Look at what your reward to me would have been—a week in a hotel! After all I've done for you, is that fair?"

She moved her head closer to his body, feeling the thin fabric of his linen pants against her cheek. "There is so much we could do together, so much a woman could bring into your life. For one thing, I could give you an heir. Imagine how that would stop all the rumors in Washington. I care not if they're true; I am continental, and have sufficient sophistication. But the provincial ladies in Washington tend to talk suspiciously of confirmed bachelors."

He didn't say anything, and she hurried on. "I've proven that I hate the Brands as much as you do. Together we could bring them to their ruin. Think of it, Devroe, in me you'd have a helpmate to all your plans. And an heir to continue the

American branch of the Connaught line. The blood of aristo-
crats would flow in the veins of our children. Who knows to
what heights a superior child might rise in this land of inden-
tured servants and slaves and rejects of the world. Think of it,
Devroe. We might found a great aristocratic house here in
America. Why, if it were not for the French Revolution, my
father would still have all the lands that had belonged to our
family for generations. You know, Devroe, in France, the
Villefranche name commanded as much respect as the Connaught name in England."

Oddly enough, Devroe knew she wasn't lying. His own
investigations had unearthed the surprising fact that once the
Villefranches had been a solid aristocratic family. Still, they'd
fallen into a slough from which they would never recover. He
had more pressing problems than to bother about her past glories.

For a moment, he thought of getting rid of her entirely,
right here and now, then throwing her and her father into the
limepits on the estate. But then, she just *might* have written
everything down as she'd said. He couldn't risk that possibility.

He released his grip. "We'll talk of this some other time,"
he said, and abruptly started out the door.

She called after him, "Tomorrow perhaps? At dinner."

With an oath, he left the dining room. Then he came back,
picked up the pistol he'd forgotten, and was gone.

Devroe spent the night mulling over everything that Véronique had said. There were decided advantages to her propo-
sition. He wasn't a man motivated by love; that sentimental
tripe had never moved him. But she was a clever woman, one
with a sharp, incisive mind—see how she had fooled even
him! And she could bear him an heir. The full range of her
techniques had made him surprisingly virile with her, a feeling
he rather relished. The more he dissected her proposal, the less
distasteful it became. Then, of course, the change in their status
would give him one overwhelming advantage—a wife couldn't
testify or bear evidence against her husband.

By first light, Devroe had decided that he would marry her.
But he must find out if she had indeed written down all she
knew, and if so, destroy it. Then, if she continued to please
him, he would use her to produce an heir. After that, she might
be disposed of in any number of ways.

• • •

Early in October, without fanfare, Devroe Connaught and Véronique Villefranche were married in the main drawing room of the estate. At Devroe's insistence, Véronique had signed a prenuptial agreement renouncing all claims to the Connaught fortune. After the brief ceremony, Audubert cried into his lace handkerchief and then got sloppily drunk on peach brandy.

Elizabeth Connaught, looking like a wizened, painted doll in her pink ruffled dress, was let out of her quarters to peek at the ceremonies. But when she broke away from her attendant and began to dance around the room, Véronique ordered her shut up again.

Véronique's joy at the marriage was tempered with the realization that unless she was very clever, she faced the distinct possibility of being discarded by Devroe—or worse.

"I must make myself indispensible to him," she told herself as she prepared for the wedding bed. "I must run this plantation with an iron hand. Papa must stop being extravagant." She continued, reading off her duties as if she were telling beads. "I will cultivate all the ministers in Washington and begin to give parties that will aid Devroe's plans. Most important, I *must* produce an heir."

Yes, therein lay her safety. And on her wedding night, Véronique Villefranche Connaught labored energetically toward that end.

Chapter 29

"Now you dress warm, you hear? Wear your muffler, and don't get your feet wet."

"I'll be sure to tell that to my commanding officer," Gunning said to Letitia, as he hugged her goodbye.

Rebecca walked Gunning to the front gate, where his horse stood. "Are you sure you're well enough to travel? It's an awfully long way to the Kansas Territory."

"I feel fine," he said. "Besides, I'll be making the trip in stages. Harper's Ferry first, where I pick up a unit heading west. Then on to Louisville, then St. Louis, and from there it's just a hop and a skip to Kansas."

The federal government had begun its big push to force all the Indian nations in the East to move west of the Mississippi. This included the Cherokees in Georgia, the Seminoles in Florida, and the Creeks in Alabama. Around the Great Lakes area, the Sauks were also being pushed westward. The Kansas and Oklahoma territories were to be the new Indian homelands, and army posts were being set up there to make sure that all went smoothly.

Gunning mounted, made his horse rear in a final salute, then galloped off. Rebecca walked slowly back into the house. "They all grow up and leave us," she said to Letitia. "Suzannah in Texas, Gunning off to Kansas, Bravo will be starting college soon, and we're left all alone."

"That's the way it's supposed to be," Letitia said. "Them young ones, they don't want to be cooped up with two old ladies."

"Old? How dare you!" she cried indignantly. "I'm only forty-nine."

"I was there when you was born, and you be fifty-two if you're a day."

Rebecca shrugged. "How is it that men, particularly in government, don't reach their peak until they're in their fifties? Webster and Calhoun are about fifty; Jackson's sixty-four, yet nobody calls them old. But once a woman is past fifty, her life is over. Well, I won't accept that."

And Rebecca didn't. Her exposure as Rebel Thorne brought her a great deal of mail, including manuscripts from aspiring writers, both male and female, who wanted her criticism. She wrote encouraging letters to the young poet Edgar Allan Poe, whose verse she thought showed a streak of genius, or madness, or both. She began corresponding with James Fenimore Cooper, who was hard at work on the third volume of his *Leatherstocking Tales*. Even Washington Irving, America's great man of letters, deigned to send her a note. Written in his usual Olympian manner, it had the overall effect of damning her with faint praise.

She also received letters from politicians imploring her to use her pen in their favor. Among these was an urgent appeal from a political group in New York who wanted her support in forming a third party. Since this was the first time that question had arisen, Rebecca investigated it. George Washington had wanted but one political party in the country, but when Thomas Jefferson's more democratic viewpoint gained strength, two parties had formed. Usually, they were in opposition to each other, so that the people could have a choice. What would a third party do to the political system? she wondered.

This one was called the Anti-Masonic Party, and its energies were to be directed against secret societies, specifically the Masons. Many of the Founding Fathers had been Masons, and since Andrew Jackson had been a Grand Master of that august body, Rebecca correctly interpreted the formation of the party as a direct move against the President.

Rebecca saw Henry Clay's fine hand in all this. After Adams's defeat in 1828, Clay had gone back to Kentucky. But in December of this year, he had returned to Washington as the newly appointed senator from Kentucky. Life on the frontier had been a little too placid compared to the political intrigue in Washington. Now Clay was working feverishly to rebuild his political base so that he could run for President in 1832.

One crisp afternoon Henry Clay appeared on Rebecca's doorstep with two large smoked turkeys under his arm. "There's

one for you, and one for Rebel Thorne," he said, chuckling.
"I must say, my dear, you fooled us all."

Rebecca poured him a tall glass of Kentucky mash and
branchwater, Clay's preferred drink, and they toasted the coming holiday season.

"I'll get right to the point, Rebecca," Clay said. "I'm planning to run for the presidency."

"So I understand. How do you gauge your chances?"

"I've far more than a chance," he said. "I intend to win.
Jackson has injured himself gravely. This Peggy Eaton disease,
for example. Peggy is still the most powerful force in Washington, and her scarlet hue places an ineradicable stain on
Jackson's administration, which shall be infamous for all time."

"Oh, Henry, spare me. You sound like you're campaigning
already."

Rebecca had known Henry Clay since he'd first come to
Washington twenty years before. His political career had been
nothing short of meteoric. He was elected to the House of
Representatives in 1811. Along with John Calhoun in 1812,
he'd quickly established himself as a War Hawk—the name
given to legislators who urged the United States to go to war
with Great Britain in order to annex Canada. Though the plan
had failed miserably, Clay had survived that.

Virginia-born, he'd moved to Kentucky after his education.
He was tall and slender, and many people thought him handsome. The corners of his mouth were always turned up, as if
he was about to break out in laughter. His forehead was broader
and higher than most people's, which led him to believe that
he was smarter than most.

Through the years, he established himself as one of the new
breed of western statesmen. Called "the Cock of Kentucky"
and "the Western Star," he was unquestionably one of the most
brilliant Speakers that the House of Representatives had ever
had, elected without opposition so many times that Rebecca
had given up counting. Yet she'd never forgotten what John
Randolph, mad John Randolph, had said of Clay: "This being,
so brilliant, yet so corrupt, which like a rotten mackerel by
moonlight, shines and stinks."

Randolph's assessment had been harsh, yet Rebecca felt
there was an element of truth in it. Clay was prepared to say
or do anything to achieve his political ambition—the presidency. He was such a consummate actor that he managed to
fool all but the most observant. Every politician must be an

actor, Rebecca thought, for a certain amount of dissembling is necessary if one is to be all things to all people. She wondered if it might not also be true that the better the actor, the better the politician. Hadn't she seen Andrew Jackson fly into a rage, and all for effect? Clay, Calhoun, Webster—all used Congress as if it were a stage.

Clay's resonant voice interrupted Rebecca's train of thought. "If Jackson survives the Peggy Eaton scandal, then he will surely founder on the issue of rechartering the Bank of the United States."

Rebecca knitted her brow. "If I'm not mistaken, the charter isn't due for renewal until 1836. How can that possibly influence the election coming up?"

"Daniel Webster and I will push for a renewal of the bank's charter this coming year," Clay said triumphantly.

"But Jackson is sure to veto it," she said. "You know how he loathes the bank. In every message to Congress, he's attacked it."

"That's precisely the point," Clay said. "As soon as the country realizes that King Andrew is acting irrationally about one of our soundest institutions, they will repudiate him. I've had a count made, and three-quarters of the newspapers in this country are for the bank. Jackson will never be able to stand up against them. Rebecca, will you lend your pen to our cause? Are we to let this one man subvert the cause of democracy? You know in your heart how dangerous that can be."

"Henry, you're asking me to make a decision without first weighing all the issues."

"Weigh them, then. If you decide not to aid us, then all I ask is that you keep silent about this election."

Rebecca stood up and pumped the bellows to fan the fire in the hearth. Then she faced Clay, anger written on her features. "Since I and all those of my sex are denied the vote, my voice can't be heard at all in terms of the government. And do you now ask that I keep silent altogether? I'm afraid that's asking too much."

"Suppose I could arrange for a congressional committee to investigate your grievances? You know, for a long time I've been thinking of the inequity in our voting laws."

Rebecca stared at him; she wanted to scream, "You're a liar! You'd sell your soul if it could get you the presidency!" Instead, she said nothing.

Clay went on building a case against Jackson—the newspapers were against him...the South was ready to defect... "Rebecca, I'm going to beat this man," Clay finished. "When I win, you may be sure I'll remember those people who gave me their early support. I want you on my side."

"Henry, in the past I've had a great many problems with Andrew Jackson—"

"Haven't we all!" Clay responded with a disarming smile.

"But I think it's only fair to tell you that I'm coming to a new assessment of the man."

Clay stiffened. "Well, then, all I ask is that you keep an open mind."

"That's something I've always tried to do, Henry, something I hope always to do."

In the spring of 1832, true to his word, Henry Clay did maneuver a bill through Congress to recharter the Second Bank of the United States. True to *his* word, Andrew Jackson vetoed it. The bank was a private organization located in Philadelphia and run by the shrewd, competent financier, Nicholas Biddle. Much of the United States government's money was funneled through the bank. Biddle believed in a strict fiscal policy, in high interest rates, and in conservative banking practices. Though this policy suited the East Coast banking establishment, it outraged the westerners, who needed easy credit to buy land. The clash was essentially between the East and the West, as exemplified by two powerful men, Nicholas Biddle and Andrew Jackson.

Rebecca sat in her drawing room, reading Jackson's veto message aloud to Bravo. He lay on the floor, trying to decipher his textbook on logic.

"Jackson calls the bank 'un-American, undemocratic, unconstitutional, and injurious to the country, since it would make the rich richer and the powerful more potent.' Then he goes on to say, 'Shall the rights of the common man be respected or shall the rich rule the country again?'" She glanced at her son, "Bravo, what's the feeling in the Senate?"

"Pro-bank. They're going to try to override the veto, but they may not have enough votes. Everybody's lobbying, including Biddle. You see, lots of Congressmen owe him money, and he's hoping that will influence the way they vote."

"My, you learn a lot in your job, don't you?"

"Yes, and there's a lot that isn't very likable. Seems as soon as a man gets a little bit of power, it can change his whole outlook on things."

"Well, Jackson's thrown down the gauntlet. Unless I'm very much mistaken, Henry Clay is dancing a jig, because he thinks that Jackson's fallen into his trap. Well, at least in this election the issues are clearly drawn, and I think it's going to be a battle to the death."

As Rebecca suspected, Jackson's veto elicited a cry of rage from the entrenched conservative elements of the electorate, and more than eighty percent of the nation's newspapers came out against him. The President was clearly embattled, and if the election were held that day, Rebecca couldn't have predicted the outcome.

Early one morning, Uncle Alfred, President Jackson's servant, brought her an invitation. "President wants to know if you'll have dinner with him tonight at the White House."

"That would be very nice. Will it be formal?" she asked.

Alfred shook his head. "Most of the family be gone, and the President, he don't like eating alone. Besides, he's not feeling so good. Got the glooms again."

"I'm sorry to hear that, but we'll try to cheer him up."

Rebecca took a long bath in lightly scented rosewater and applied compresses of warm milk to her face, followed by an astringent made of lemon juice. She put the tiniest drop of belladonna in her eyes to give them luster. Then she brushed her gray-streaked titian hair until it sparkled, and coiled it into a chignon. She'd almost completed her toilet when she suddenly stopped. "Why in heaven's name am I doing all this?"

"You knows why," Letitia said with a roll of her eyes. "First Henry Clay comes calling, now the President."

"Oh, that's nonsense! The only reason they're pursuing me is because they think I can be of some help to them."

Nevertheless, when she left the house at twilight, wearing a new periwinkle-blue satin gown, she felt as lighthearted as a schoolgirl. And just as apprehensive.

Chapter 30

WHEN REBECCA arrived at the White House, she was struck once more by how wonderful the mansion looked. Not a day passed without Jackson making some kind of improvement.

But when she went upstairs, she found that the President himself was looking unwell, gaunt, fatigued, and low in spirits. He nervously fondled a miniature of Rachel that hung around his neck on a long black cord.

"I've asked to have dinner served up here," Jackson said. "I hope you don't mind. It's just that much easier for me."

"Of course I don't mind. It's the company that's important, not the place."

The sitting room was tastefully furnished, reflecting many of the things that Jackson and Rachel had shared at the Hermitage. Through the open door, she could see his bedroom with its tall fourposter bed. How odd, Rebecca thought, that the hero of the Battle of New Orleans and the President of the United States should nonetheless require familiar, sentimental things around him to make him feel comfortable. We are, all of us, ordinary mortals.

The veto was uppermost in Jackson's mind. "Nicholas Biddle runs the Second Bank of the United States as if it were his own personal fiefdom," he said hotly. "He has no concept of what the poor westerner must go through to buy, till, and own land. That's what we must have if this nation is to grow into its greatness—pioneers and settlers, building homes, raising crops, and children. And not hampered by the repressive banking policies of one man."

"But a sound fiscal policy is essential to the country," Rebecca argued. "Without it, we'd founder. The bank is a deterrent to the violent fluctuations in our economy."

Jackson shook his head vehemently. "The bank is using its enormous financial power as a political weapon! Biddle has lent money to scores of legislators. Why, Daniel Webster receives a monthly retainer from the bank! Do you think it's an accident that Clay and Webster have brought this issue up now? Of course not! The bank is trying to kill me, but I shall kill it!"

He'd gotten red in the face, and his breath came in choking gasps. This time Rebecca knew he wasn't putting on an act. His loathing of the bank was so strong that it would do no good to argue further with him.

"Where do you stand on this?" he asked.

"As Rebecca Breech Brand? or as Rebel Thorne?"

"Both."

She thought for a long moment, then answered as honestly as she could. "Though I don't agree with you about the bank, I do believe you're the man best qualified to lead this country. I'll do whatever I can to make that happen."

Jackson's features relaxed. "Everybody gives me advice; my nephew Jack Donelson, William Lewis, and the rest of my kitchen cabinet, Francis Blair and the other newspapers. I suppose you have something to add?"

How extraordinary, Rebecca thought. The President of the United States is asking for my advice. But with that came a wrenching pang of realization: Yet I don't have the right to make my thoughts known at the polls. I swear by all that's just and holy, one day, my daughter—or granddaughter or great-granddaughter—will have that right.

"You seem lost in thought," Jackson said.

Rebecca blinked. "My advice to you, Andrew, is first, to remain silent about Peggy Eaton. Clay will bring up the subject in the campaign, you may be sure. Second, avoid any more vetoes. Clay plans to make capital of the fact that already you've vetoed more legislation than all of our other Presidents combined."

"I believe in a strong chief executive," Jackson interrupted. "The President represents all the people, not just one state or region. I'm empowered by the Constitution to veto any law that I believe is unjust. Furthermore, I claim for the presidency not merely the power of approval, but the primary power, the power to *originate* laws."

"Then be prepared to have your opponents accuse you of usurping powers and acting like a king—which they're already doing."

Jackson grunted.

"Finally, you must choose a running mate who'll support all your political plans."

Jackson nodded slowly. "How John Calhoun fooled me! I offered him my friendship, but I never realized he was the man who, back in 1820, demanded I be censured by the Senate for my part in the Florida wars. When I found out and confronted him, all he could do was lie. If Calhoun had his way, he'd have me eliminated and take over the presidency himself!"

Calhoun, realizing that he had no hope of ever gaining the presidency through Andrew Jackson, had begun raising his powerful voice; as Vice-President, he presided over the Senate, and was doing whatever he could to thwart the policies of the administration. Now he was agitating for every single one of the southern states to join South Carolina in nullifying the hated tariff laws.

"Calhoun is a viper," Jackson continued, "and he'll do whatever he can to tear this nation apart. I'm talking about nothing less than the future of our country. Will it split into individual states again and become prey to the powerful European nations? Or will it hang together and grow into the greatest nation on earth?"

On this issue, his passion was as pure as a flame, and Rebecca warmed to the monumental surge and clash in the man. She wanted to comfort him, tell him that everything would turn out all right, yet she knew that ultimately, every President was alone and isolated in the office that demanded he be guardian for all the people.

Jackson cleared his throat. "I'm not well, Rebecca, and if I'm elected, there's the distinct possibility that I won't live to finish out my second term."

She knew that he wasn't being a hypochondriac, as so many of his enemies claimed, but that his fears were justified. For Wingate had told her how seriously ill he was. He could die at any moment.

"That's why my running mate must be the man best qualified to lead this nation."

Jackson took a sip of milk, about the only food he could easily digest. "I'll tell you something, Rebecca, but I don't want it to go beyond this room. I've decided that Martin Van Buren will be my running mate."

Rebecca feigned surprise, though practically everybody in

Washington surmised Van Buren would be Jackson's choice, particularly since Van Buren's appointment as minister to Great Britain had been thwarted by Calhoun in the Senate. Calhoun was convinced that he'd ended Van Buren's career. "This will kill him dead!" he'd said. "He will never kick, sir, never kick." When Jackson heard that he had flown into a rage. "By the eternal, they're trying to smash me, but I'll smash them!" he said. "I will see Van Buren as Vice-President, and then as President!"

Jackson regarded Rebecca. "Tell me your honest opinion of Van Buren."

"He's shrewd and clever, and a consummate politician, but I doubt that he can elicit the same degree of trust from the people that you do. One somehow gets the feeling that Van Buren accomplishes all he does by dissembling, rather than by really speaking his mind."

Jackson tried to hide his smile.

"Tell me the truth, Andrew. What do you think your chances are in this election?"

"I don't know. There are now many forces ranged against me. Monied people, the propertied class, a privileged part of society that's been entrenched in this country for generations. Whereas I must count on the common man."

"Then our only hope is that the people will want the Union. They know you're the only man strong enough to hold it together."

They looked at each other for a long moment, then Uncle Alfred came in to clear away the dishes. He lit a corncob pipe for the General, and then stood by his chair, expectantly.

"Thank you, Alfred, you can go to bed now," Jackson said.

Rebecca watched as the black man went into Jackson's bedroom and curled up on a pallet on the floor beside the bed.

Jackson called in to him, "Alfred, I won't be needing you tonight. You can go downstairs to the basement with the others."

"But I always sleep here!" Alfred exclaimed.

A thunderous scowl darkened Jackson's face. "Alfred!"

Alfred recognized the tone, hurried out of the bedroom, and disappeared downstairs.

Jackson said, "Alfred's slept in my tent or in my room for so long I can't count the years. During the wars, with the enemy all about, I knew I could sleep soundly if he was there, protecting me from spies or assassins."

"I would think the same thing applied here in the White House," Rebecca said.

Jackson barked with laughter. "Then when my illness became so severe, he refused to leave my side... many a night has seemed shorter because of his presence."

"You must feel proud and honored to have inspired that kind of devotion."

He nodded, then reached for her hand. "Rebecca, it does my heart good to see you. Not only are you the most intelligent woman I know, but you do have a way of making me see the comic side of life—the comic side of myself."

Rebecca felt herself blushing.

"We've both been scrutinized, and often condemned for our activities," he said softly. "Sometimes harshly, oftentimes unfairly."

She thought he was referring to her role as Rebel Thorne, but he went on, "When you came in tonight, looking so lovely in your blue gown, I remembered a night—oh, it was more than ten years ago, 1819, I think—when John Quincy Adams and Louisa gave a reception for me. Of course, we were friendly in those years. You arrived wearing an emerald-blue velvet dress, and you were with Jeremy Brand."

She felt her throat constrict, and didn't know what to say, except to murmur inanely, "You have a remarkable memory."

"You loved him, didn't you?"

She tried to find words to answer, but in the end could only fall back on the truth. "Yes, I loved him. Very much. Sometimes the gods simply cannot bear for ordinary mortals to be as happy as I was for those brief years. So the thread of fate is broken and we're left with our memories."

He reached for the miniature of Rachel that hung around his neck and stared at the portrait. "Yes, I felt that way about her. From the moment I met her, I never looked at another woman. Oh, I know what they say, that she was dowdy, and portly, and had no manners. All those things were raked up again and again in the presidential elections. But how wrong they all were. The woman had the same saintly qualities as my mother, and I loved her."

They talked far into the night. The embers of the fire burned down, and still they talked, with an ease that put Rebecca's heart at peace. Uncle Alfred peeped in once more, but at a stern glance from Jackson he retreated, to appear no more that night.

Then Jackson took the miniature from around his neck. "She's gone, and there's nothing to be done about it now."

Rebecca's heart began to thump hugely in her chest. For she'd noticed that when Jackson set the miniature on the table, he put it face down.

Just before dawn, Rebecca made her way back to her house on New York Avenue. She hurried through the streets, trying to get as far away from the White House as she could before anybody saw her. This city battened itself on gossip, and in an election year, it was the last thing that Andrew Jackson needed. She felt fiercely protective of him...nobody would understand what they'd shared; Washington would turn it into something sinful and ugly.

A group of drunken carousing legislators careened out of Lafayette Park, bellowing a popular ditty:

> General Jackson commands all
> Mr. Van Buren contrives all
> Mrs. Eaton rules all
> Office seekers approve of all
> The tariff men want all
> Trade and commerce suffer all
> The nullifiers threaten all
> Uncle Sam pays all
> Honest men are obliged to bear all
> If God has not pity on all
> The devil will take all!

The men were coming straight at her! Rebecca lifted her hood to hide her face and marched right past them. She thought she recognized Henry Clay...that one caroused at all hours. He squinted at her, but mercifully was dragged off by his compatriots.

When she arrived home, Letitia was pacing the hallway, waiting for her. "Where have you been all night?" she demanded. "Worried sick out of my mind. I was just going to fetch the constable." Then she saw the serene look on Rebecca's face and her hand flew to her cheek.

"Oh Lord 'a mercy! What you gone and done now? There's

nothing but trouble ahead, and that's all I got to say about that matter!"

Rebecca patted her maid's arm, then went upstairs. She drew the curtains and crawled into bed. Letitia was right. It was madness, and there could be nothing but trouble ahead. But she would have risked it again just to feel the tremulous joy of her reawakened spirit.

Chapter 31

IN THE early summer, Véronique Villefranche Connaught went into labor. Devroe happened to be in conference at the time with Ludlow Parkhurst, who'd just returned from England. Devroe found the intermittent screaming distracting and highly unpleasant.

"I'm going riding," he said to Sisley Urquhart. "Sound the horn when the boy is born."

He and Parkhurst rode out into the fields. They watched the blacks working with bent backs over the cotton plants, and occasionally heard the whirring of a whip as it cut through the air, followed by the cry of a slacker. "One must keep after them constantly," Devroe said. "It's getting so they're hardly earning their bread and board."

But the land was fertile, the crops good, the Connaught finances in excellent condition. And soon he would have an heir.

"I'm naming my son Sean Victor Connaught," Devroe said to Parkhurst, in a rare burst of camaraderie.

"It's a wonderful name, sir," Parkhurst said. "I do believe it has the ring of a Prime Minister to it."

Devroe smiled. He'd chosen the name Sean in memory of his father, and Victor after his Aunt Victoria, a woman of formidable intelligence and zeal. As for Véronique, as soon as she'd weaned the child, he'd decide what to do with her. As yet, he hadn't discovered to whom she'd entrusted her letter, but there weren't that many lawyers in Washington, and his informants were busily at work.

"I'm instructed to tell you that Intelligence is well pleased with your work," Parkhurst said.

"Excellent. And the funds they promised? I plan to go to Mexico very soon."

"They'll be sent to you through a courier, to be used at your discretion. I was told to inquire as to any recent developments in the election," Parkhurst said.

"There are changes every day," Devroe said. "The Peggy Eaton affair will work against Jackson, but not enough to do him mortal damage. But the Bank of the United States—there's the issue on which Jackson will fall. People respond to whatever affects their purses, and the entire East Coast establishment has risen up against him. Nicholas Biddle told Henry Clay that Jackson's veto had 'all the fury of a chained panther, biting the bars of his cage.' The veto is really a manifesto of anarchy, and Biddle believes it will insure Jackson's defeat. In addition, Biddle has spent more than a hundred thousand dollars, so far, to make doubly sure Jackson is defeated."

"A formidable sum," Parkhurst said.

"Democracy," Devroe snorted. "Little do these dolts realize that their system has already become corrupt. In 1828, more than a million dollars was spent by both candidates. In the coming election, double, perhaps triple that amount of money will be spent. Ultimately, money will be the single factor that determines who will be elected. Well, I too am prepared to spend whatever is necessary to defeat Jackson. Not only from the funds supplied to me, but also from my own private accounts."

"You're optimistic then?" Parkhurst asked.

"It's a foregone conclusion. Congress is up in arms against him for usurping their power, financiers and propertied people are solidly against him, and the newspapers are vicious in their attacks."

"Mr. Connaught, the ministry asked me to inquire about the broadening of the voting franchise and whether that might influence the election."

Devroe stiffened. He didn't like Parkhurst questioning his judgment, whatever the guise. "The ordinary voter in America does what he's told, and ninety percent of the newspapers are against Jackson."

"Still, suppose Jackson is elected? The ministry likes to be prepared for every eventuality."

This time Devroe couldn't hide his annoyance. "Even if Jackson is elected, I have personal knowledge that in November, right after the election, South Carolina will pass a resolution to nullify the tariff. If the Federal government refuses to abide by South Carolina's decision, then she will secede from the Union, and the rest of the South will follow suit.

Then we shall have two separate countries, North and South."

"God willing," Parkhurst said. "Well, then, I must be off to Washington to make my report." He wheeled his horse and rode off.

Devroe returned to the house about an hour later and found that Véronique still hadn't given birth. Her labor disturbed his dinner and his sleep, for it continued far into the night. Finally, toward dawn of the next day, the midwife came into his room holding a tiny swaddled infant in her arms.

"It's the most beautiful little girl I've ever seen," she said, holding the baby out to him.

Devroe stared in disbelief. Never had it occurred to him that it could be a girl! He moved the folds of the blanket aside and looked at her. He'd never cared much for babies, but this one did look less like a wrinkled old person than most. But a girl!

He handed the child back to the midwife, then went into his study, where he quickly drank himself into a stupor. This meant that Véronique would have to stay on, at least long enough for another try at producing an heir, and that prospect rankled. He decided that this would be an excellent time to go to Mexico.

The midwife brought the baby back to Véronique, who lay exhausted in bed. She took the child and placed her next to her bosom. "Did the master see her?" she asked.

"Yes ma'am."

"Didn't he think she was pretty?"

"Very pretty, ma'am."

Véronique gazed at the child, unable to hide her own disappointment. "You were to be my insurance, and now..." Tears rolled down her cheeks as she sobbed, "But I love you anyway. I shall call you...Romance. Romance Villefranche Connaught. I make you this promise: You'll never have to worry about anything in your life. Not a roof over your head, or the food in your mouth. This I swear."

At the end of October, scant days before the election, the campaign rhetoric heated to a boil. Bravo came running in one afternoon with the newspapers. "Have you seen these, Mother?"

Rebecca scanned the *United States Telegraph*. "I thought nothing could surprise me," she said, "but this passes the limit. The Clay forces are charging that if Jackson is elected, he will run for a third term, and then another, and another. 'The American people will find themselves with nothing less than a Caesar in the White House, a dictator!' What rubbish!"

She tossed the paper aside and turned next to the *Globe*. They were claiming that Clay and Calhoun planned to have Jackson assassinated, and that a fifty-thousand-dollar reward had been offered to anybody who'd do it.

"This is outrageous," Rebecca exclaimed, and rushed to her desk.

"Are we a nation of cutthroats and assassins," Rebel Thorne demanded, "or a democracy where the people's will can be heard? The newspapers speak of dictators and despots, of assassinations and murder, as if we were all nothing but common criminals and thieves, unable to solve our differences save by the gun.

"The fault comes from those men highly placed in office and from their spokesmen in the newspapers. The press prints its irresponsible, incendiary statements, all the while sanctimoniously hiding behind the First Amendment and Freedom of the Press. But does any sane, thinking person really believe that that's what the Constitution intended?

"We must have faith in ourselves, faith in our institutions, or we're lost. The issues in this election are clearly drawn. Peggy Eaton? An insignificant woman and little more than a footnote to history. The Bank of the United States? Admittedly, a more potent problem, and one that demands clear thinking. But the primary issue is: Shall we have a Union, or not? And if so, who is best suited to lead that Union? Though I have differed with Andrew Jackson on many issues, and probably will continue to do so—which is every person's right in a democracy—nevertheless, I believe that this man is most qualified to chart our course through the perilous times that lie ahead. My fellow Americans, think! Cast your vote for Andrew Jackson, and for the Union!"

In mid-November, before the election results were fully tabulated, South Carolina passed a resolution to nullify the Tariff of Abominations. If the federal government refused to honor that nullification, then South Carolina would secede from the Union in February, 1833.

To complicate matters, Robert Hayne had become governor of South Carolina. John Calhoun resigned the Vice-Presidency and was immediately appointed to Hayne's Senate seat by Hayne himself. Calhoun quickly became the champion for nullification, and now led the battle for nullification in the Senate.

Wingate was called to rush to the White House, where Jackson lay gravely ill. He found the President's bedroom crowded with army officers and officials from the Department of War. Jackson, though enfeebled, was giving terse orders.

"Gentlemen, with South Carolina's declaration, we are faced with a serious problem. South Carolina prepares for open rebellion. Her state militia is being called up, the federal forts there are slowly being surrounded by secessionists. I must muster one hundred and fifty thousand volunteers . . . We'll cross the mountains into South Carolina with a force so overwhelming as to render resistance useless."

Jackson began to cough violently then, and to spit up blood. Wingate herded everybody out of the bedroom and examined the President.

"I have tuberculosis, don't I?" Jackson said somberly.

"No, Mr. President, you don't. It's the old Dickinson bullet that's causing this. You're pushing yourself too hard. If you continue, I can't vouch for what will happen."

"Don't worry, I won't die just yet. I won't give John Calhoun that satisfaction!"

"Is this move by South Carolina as serious as it sounds?" Wingate asked.

"Far more so than you imagine," Jackson said, coughing. "I've alerted all the federal garrisons, sent money and munitions to Charleston, told the commanders of the fort there to watch out for an imminent attack. Particularly on Fort Sumter, which is vital to the defense of Charleston's harbor. If an insurrection does break out, that's as likely a place as any."

"I'd no idea—" Wingate began, at a loss for words.

"I can only hope and pray that the people of this great nation will give me a mandate to preserve the Union. Well, we'll know soon enough."

On December 4, the election results were finally tallied: The Anti-Masonic candidate, William Wirt, received 7 electoral votes; Henry Clay received 49; and Andrew Jackson garnered a thunderous 219. It was Jackson by a landslide!

That night, Washington was in a state of euphoric bedlam.

Torchlight processions wound through the streets, crowds stood in front of the low wrought-iron rail at the White House and sang:

> Here's health to the heroes who fought
>   And conquered in liberty's cause!
> Here's health to old Andy, who could not be bought
>   To favor aristocratic laws.

Then the crowd bellowed out in chorus

> Hurrah for the Hickory tree!
> From the mountain tops down to the sea
> It shall wave o'er the grave
> Of the Tory and knave
> And shelter the honest and free!

The moment Andrew Jackson knew that he'd been reelected, he appointed John Eaton governor of the Florida Territory. Peggy Eaton was aghast at the thought of leaving her beloved Washington, but when Jackson commanded, few would have dreamed of disobeying him. With Peggy removed from Washington, Jackson was sure that the Petticoat War would be resolved in favor of his administration.

Jackson also demanded that Congress pass a Force Bill, giving him the power to put down any insurrection against the Union, whenever and wherever it occurred.

In the Senate, Bravo listened avidly as the President's arguments for the Force Bill were presented to the tense legislators.

"The Constitution of the United States, then, forms a government, not a league . . . Each State, having expressly parted with so many powers, as to coinstitute jointly with the other States, a single nation, does not from that period possess any right to secede . . . To say that any State may at pleasure secede from the Union, is to say that the United States are not a nation."

To South Carolinians, Jackson had a special message: "Fellow citizens of my native state, the laws of the United States must be executed. I have no discretionary power on that subject . . . Disunion by armed force is treason. Are you really ready to incur its guilt? If you are . . . on your unhappy state will inevitably fall all the evils of the conflict you will force on the government of your country."

Bravo watched as the chamber erupted in shouts of approval and boos and catcalls. Staunch supporters of the Union were delirious with joy that Jackson had finally showed his true colors and were ready to vote him his Force Bill, while die-hard southerners pledged their support to South Carolina's cause.

The House of Representatives, always the more flamboyant of the two chambers, turned into something of a circus, with impassioned legislators outdoing themselves with histrionics. With the help of some of his pageboy friends who served in the House, Bravo sneaked into that chamber one day where Representative George McDuffie was holding forth.

McDuffie began pounding on his desk, stamping his feet, and shrieking so that everybody could hear, "South Carolina is oppressed! A tyrant majority sucks her life blood from her . . . they heap coals of fire on our heads—they give us burden on burden, they tax us more and more . . . the tyrant majority has no ears, no eyes, no form, deaf, sightless, inex-orable! Despairing, we resort to the rights that God and nature has given us . . . Secession!"

Taking heart from such support, Governor Robert Hayne of South Carolina made ready for war, and tried to enlist the support of other southern states.

This only increased Jackson's determination. "The Union must be preserved!" He thundered, and prepared to send two hundred thousand men into South Carolina to bring that state back into line. He also let it be known that he had said, "If South Carolina moves one more inch toward secession, I will arrest John C. Calhoun for treason, and hang him from the highest tree!"

"Bravo, will you be in for dinner this evening?" Rebecca asked. "You haven't been home in time all this week."

"I can't tell, Mother. Today, everybody in the Senate is expecting Calhoun to answer President Jackson. The debate may go on all night." With that, he ran out the door and rode off to the Capitol.

In the Senate chamber, not a sound was heard. John C. Calhoun held the floor. "The cast-iron man who looked like he'd never been born, and could never be extinguished," as he'd been described; was agitated beyond reason, frightened by Jackson's threat. He pushed several chairs together, en-closing himself in a sort of symbolic cage.

Calhoun's voice shook as he spoke sorrowfully of "the decay of that brotherly feeling which once existed between the States . . . to which we are indebted for our beautiful Federal System. I am weary, and know not if I can complete my remarks. But I must speak out for sanity and justice. The Force Bill not only declares war on South Carolina, but it decrees a massacre of her citizens! The President will be able to subject every man in the United States to martial law . . . and under the penalty of court-martial, compel him to imbrue his hand in his brother's blood!

"This bill has been said to be a measure of peace. Yes, such peace as the wolf gives to the lamb! Should this bill pass, it will be resisted at every hazard . . . even that of death . . . Thousands of her brave sons are prepared to lay down their lives in defense of the state . . ." Calhoun's voice rose to a hysterical pitch as he finished, "For merely daring to assert our constitutional rights, South Carolinians are threatened to—to have our throats cut, along with those of our wives and children!"

The people in the gallery gasped, and even Bravo's mouth dropped open. Never had he heard Calhoun use such inflammatory language; he'd always been the supreme intellectual, basing his arguments on law and logic. But now . . .

Then Calhoun trembled and rubbed his forehead, seeming to realize what he'd just said. "No, no, I go too far. I did not intend to use language so stormy."

Bravo heard Daniel Webster say to Thomas Hart Benton, "We've just witnessed the downfall of John Calhoun. Look at him, he's shaking like an aspen leaf. He's permitted himself to be unmanned in public!"

When the Force Bill came up for a vote on February 24, 1833, Henry Clay complained of "bad air" and left the chamber. All the southern senators, including John Calhoun, walked out. Only Senator John Tyler of Virginia remained, to cast the lone dissenting "Nay!"

Henry Clay, searching for ways to retain his potential as a future presidential candidate, pushed for passage of a modified Tariff Bill, which would reduce the tariff rates by twenty percent over a period of ten years. Calhoun, who hated Jackson even more than he hated Clay, agreed to support Clay's measures.

The South got an amended Tariff Bill, and President Jackson got his Force Bill. Then at the last possible moment, a weary messenger arrived from South Carolina. Governor Hayne and the people of that state, awed by the enormous gathering of federal forces on land, and naval forces in Charleston Harbor, and without any substantial support from any of the other southern states, capitulated to Jackson.

The crisis had been avoided. The states did not go to war.

About a week later President Jackson sent for Rebecca, and she joined him in the Oval Room on the second floor. He was looking out the window at the sweep of lawn leading down to the Potomac River.

"I've asked you here because I wanted you to have these," he said, and handed her a sheaf of papers. "They're my personal notes on the nullification crisis; someday posterity may want to know what happened here. I can think of no better person to entrust these notes to than you."

"Thank you, Andrew," she murmured. "I'll treasure them, and you may be sure I'll keep them safe." She let out a huge sigh. "Well, you've done it. Andrew, now that we've the benefit of hindsight, if you had it to do all over again, would you do anything differently?"

"Yes," he said without hesitation. "I'm sorry that I didn't shoot Henry Clay and hang John Calhoun!"

She started to laugh, though she knew he was deadly serious. "The important thing is that you've preserved the Union."

Jackson shook his head slowly. "It's only a momentary triumph. The coalition of Clay and Calhoun, combined with a host of nullifiers lurking in Virginia and South Carolina, portends no good but much evil. They won't rest here; the nullifiers in the South intend to blow up a storm on the slave question . . . This ought to be met, for be assured these men will do anything to destroy our union. They want to form a southern confederacy bound on the north by the Potomac River, and they would make Washington, D.C., the capital of their new southern nation. Make no mistake. This is a southern city, and if civil war had broken out, Washington would have sided with the South."

Reflecting on that, and on the existence of the flourishing slave traffic in the capital, Rebecca knew that President Jackson was right.

Chapter 32

"SUPPOSED TO be coming on to spring," Letitia said to
Rebecca and Circumstance, "but it's the coldest day I ever
recollect this time of year."

Though it was March 4, the temperature hovered at eleven
degrees; the freeze had crusted the heavy snow that lay on the
ground. Though Jackson's victory at the polls had been a stun-
ning one, no public celebration of the inaugural was planned
because of the fragility of the President's health.

"Don't know what for you're going, anyway," Letitia complained as Rebecca put on her fur-lined cloak. "Catch your
death out there."

"Andrew's asked Circumstance and me to be in the Presidential party," Rebecca said. "I don't want to disappoint him."

"Oh, so now it's *Andrew*," Letitia grumbled, but Rebecca
paid her no mind. Tad drove them to the White House in their
carriage; they got in line with the other waiting carriages that
would carry the President and his family. How different from
the day of his first inauguration, four years before, when he'd
walked to the Capitol on the crest of the public's adoration,
Rebecca thought. Though he was even more popular now, the
four years in the White House left him a debilitated man.
Whenever Rebecca saw him alone, which had become more
and more infrequently, he barely had the strength to sit through
dinner.

"There he is," Circumstance said, pointing.

Jackson appeared at the North Portico, and Rebecca and
Circumstance watched as Wingate and Uncle Alfred assisted
the President into his carriage. The carriage had been made of
wood from the U.S.S. *Constitution*, and it had a painting of
the ship on the carriage door.

"Doesn't Emily Donelson look peaked?" Rebecca asked.

Circumstance nodded. "Wingate says she isn't at all well."

Emily got into another carriage with her husband and her children. Jackson's close associates—Francis Blair, William Lewis, and Ralph Earl—followed in a third carriage, and then Rebecca's carriage fell into line behind them.

Beneath the horses' hooves and the carriage wheels, Pennsylvania Avenue had turned into a quagmire of slush and mud. A length of the roadway in front of the President's House was being macadamized, but the remainder was as rutted and muddy as on the day that Major Pierre L'Enfant had first laid out the city. "Sooner or later they'll have to pave the entire city," Rebecca said to Circumstance, "though with the speed that Congress works, I doubt I'll be alive to see it. Incidentally, how is your project coming?"

"Slowly, at best," Circumstance said. "Jeremy and little Doe seem to take up so much of my time. But on the other hand, it took Father ten years to help build the White House, and then another five years to rebuild it after the British burned it. It will probably take me that long to complete my history of the mansion."

"It's a very ambitious project," Rebecca said.

"Sometimes I think it will overwhelm me. But if I do a little every day—keep a journal, write down the anecdotes as I hear them—I think I'll be able to leave the American people a legacy of knowledge about their house."

"I know you've asked me so many times to tell you everything that I recollect," Rebecca said. "And I'm afraid I've been derelict. But I promise we'll get to work on it as soon as the weather warms."

"Oh, that would be wonderful," Circumstance said, and squeezed Rebecca's hand.

At the Capitol, President Jackson was met at the east front by the mayor of Washington and the council members.

"This is the first time that the city, as a separate entity, has taken part in any of the inaugural ceremonies," Rebecca said to Circumstance. "That's something you ought to incorporate into your history."

Precisely at noon, Jackson and Vice-President-elect Martin Van Buren entered the Hall of Representatives.

Rebecca and Circumstance made their way to their seats. "Van Buren looks like he's lapped up all the cream on the plate," Rebecca said.

"I would say he has," Circumstance said, smiling.

Jackson shuffled to the Speaker's seat, and Van Buren sat on his left. Jack Donelson sat on his uncle's right, looking very attentive to the President. Wingate sat on the sidelines, his black doctor's bag clutched in his hand. Circumstance caught his eye and he smiled at her.

When Jackson rose, he was greeted with cheers from the large assembly. Reaching deep into some untapped well of strength, he delivered his inaugural address in a firm, audible voice. His message contained nothing he hadn't said before. He deplored "the evils of the monster Bank of the United States," he insisted on the need "for a fair and less regressive tariff," and ended with his "absolute conviction that the Union must be preserved." Rebecca was heartened by the cheers and applause that followed his last statement. On this issue, the capital was still supporting the President.

Then Chief Justice John Marshall, looking as if he was bowed by his weighty black robes, came forward and administered the oath of office.

"Do you realize that Marshall's presided at the inauguration nine times?" Rebecca said. "He's sworn in every president that we've ever elected save John Adams and George Washington? What an extraordinary man!"

After the oath was administered to Van Buren, who didn't make a speech, the President and Vice-President departed.

Rebecca and Circumstance hurried back to the White House to help prepare for the open house. The mansion was to be open to the public from half past two o'clock to half past four. Though the weather was fierce, hundreds upon hundreds of people would crowd inside to wish their hero well.

As Circumstance labored to keep the festivities flowing, she made mental notes about the various changes going on. Work was in progress to transform the White House: The square in front was being macadamized at a cost of $115,000. The macadamized strip on Pennsylvania Avenue was only forty-five feet wide, less than half the width of the avenue, but it was to be widened the following year to make the streets passable in all types of weather.

The greatest improvement was that water was now being pumped into the White House—and into the Capitol and other federal buildings as well. This was a major project, with the work being done by more than a thousand newly arrived Irish immigrants. Congressmen and their aides were gleefully dismantling the hand pumps that had been in the Capitol yards.

The White House received its water from springs in the city block bounded by Thirteenth, Fourteenth, I, and K Streets, property bought by the government for that purpose at a cost of four cents a square foot.

Rebecca adored the luxurious plumbing system. "Do you realize that water goes directly to the kitchen and the pantry, and the shower rooms and water closets throughout the mansion?" she asked Circumstance. "I'm determined to do this with my house, and you'd be wise to do it also. I'll have the bank send you the money from your share of Jeremy's inheritance. There's no reason why you, Wingate, and the children shouldn't have life a little easier. This house does look wonderful though, doesn't it?"

Circumstance nodded. "Though Wingate tells me that President Jackson is constantly complaining because the maids can't keep the beds free of bedbugs."

"Well, in spite of all these modern advances, I suppose we'll never be rid of them," Rebecca sighed.

At the height of the open house, President Jackson crumpled to his knees. Wingate, standing nearby, caught him as he fell. He and Jack Donelson cleared a path and carried the President out of the East Room and to his quarters upstairs.

Wingate came down about an hour later. "How is he?" Circumstance asked at once.

Wingate shook his head. "Not good. It's plain exhaustion. The way the man drives himself, I doubt he'll live out his term of office. I told him that under no circumstances was he to get out of bed. Not even to attend the inaugural balls."

"That will be a great disappointment for the people," Rebecca said.

"Better a little disappointment than to lose a President," Circumstance said.

"Now he's developed neuralgia," Wingate sighed. "The pains are sharp and spasmodic along his nerves. He wanted me to bleed him, but the loss of more blood would only weaken him further, so I gave him your remedy."

"What's that?" Rebecca asked. "I've got a touch of neuralgia myself."

"It's little more than a counterirritant," Circumstance told her. "I make a warm plaster animated by cantharides."

"What in heaven's name are cantharides?" Rebecca asked.

"It's a preparation of powdered blister beetles, especially Spanish fly," Circumstance explained.

"I must try it," Rebecca said.

Washington was aglow with brilliance and pageantry that evening; one Inaugural Ball was held at Carusi's, and another, the Republican Citizen's Inauguration Ball, Civil and Military, was held at Central Masonic Hall. The President was represented at both by Emily and Jack Donelson, and by his adopted son, Andrew Junior, and his petite wife, Sarah.

At the height of the festivities, Rebecca slipped away and had Tad drive her home. There she picked up a jar of calf's-foot jelly, and a variety of puddings that she'd had Letitia prepare, and walked the few blocks through the snow to the White House.

Uncle Alfred let her into the mansion. It was strangely quiet, everybody being at the celebrations. She went upstairs and found Jackson in his sitting room, his legs covered by an afghan that she'd made him, his hand resting on his Bible.

"Hello Andrew," she whispered. "Are you awake?"

He turned to her, his eyes sunken and weary. She sat down beside him.

"How good of you to come and see me," he murmured, "when you should be out enjoying yourself at all these balls."

"They're not very festive without you," she said.

He attempted a smile. "There are times when I'm so tired I can barely think," he said. "Times when all I want to do is give up this mortal coil. I try to live each day as if it were my last, but the good Lord has kept me around for a purpose, I suppose."

"The Union," Rebecca said.

"Aye, the Union."

"You should be very pleased at how everything has turned out," she said.

"The biggest battle is ahead," he said. "There's the bank. I *must* get rid of it. It's a monster with no thought of anything save itself. South Carolina may lie dormant right now, but she's just waiting to foment rebellion again. Then there's the fate of thousands of our American brothers in Texas. Something must be done about them, we just can't leave them there at the mercy of the Mexican government. Every week they burden our settlers with new restrictions. Who knows where it will end?"

Rebecca stiffened, feeling a pang for the safety of Suzannah and her family, but she interrupted the President. "Andrew, stop. For at least one night, give yourself some peace."

"How can I?" he whispered. "Every day I must put on a false face of health and power, for the jackals and hyenas are always circling around, and if they sense how wounded I am, they'll pull me down." Tears started to his eyes. "I ask nothing for myself, but there's so much still to be done, and so little time left to do it."

He reached for the Bible and handed it to her. "Read to me, if you will."

"Is there anything particular you'd like to hear?"

He shrugged. "Anything will do. Sometimes, I just let the book fall open where it will, and sometimes I find truth and comfort there."

"All right, then," she said, and opened the book and let it fall randomly to a page. "It's the Second Book of Kings," she said, smiling. "That seems entirely appropriate, doesn't it?" She began to read.

"'In those days was King Hezekiah sick unto death—'"

Rebecca broke off, a chill coursing along her spine. How stupid of me not to scan that passage first! she thought and started to turn to another page.

"I want you to finish that passage," Jackson said.

"Oh, Andrew."

"Finish," he ordered in a commanding tone.

She turned back to what she'd been reading and began again. "'In those days was King Hezekiah sick unto death. And the prophet Isaiah came to him and said, Thus saith the Lord, Set thine house in order, for thou shalt die and not live.

"'Then Hezekiah turned his face to the wall and prayed unto the Lord, saying, I beseech thee, O Lord, remember now how I have walked before thee in truth and with a perfect heart, and have done that which is good in thy sight. And Hezekiah wept sore.

"'And it came to pass, afore Isaiah was gone out into the middle court, that the word of the Lord came to him saying, Turn again and tell Hezekiah, the captain of my people, Thus saith the Lord, the God of David, thy father, I have heard thy prayer, I have seen thy tears, behold, I will heal thee. On the third day thou shalt go up into the house of the Lord.

"'And I will add unto thy days, fifteen years...'"

Tears blurred Rebecca's vision and she couldn't go on. She

felt an enormous sense of peace, as though she and the President had just received some preternatural insight. Fifteen years. "Oh, Andrew, if only it were so," she whispered.

President Jackson was crying also, and the two of them sat there, sharing a communion far greater than any physical expression they'd ever known.

Chapter 33

FOR REBECCA, Andrew Jackson's assessment of the political situation proved uncannily accurate. Within the year, Henry Clay and Daniel Webster, aided by disenchanted Democrats like John Calhoun, coalesced their forces into a vigorous party opposed to Jackson. They called themselves the Whigs, after the British parliamentary group that had resisted the excesses of the English king.

Shouting matches in the Senate and House became more the rule than the exception, a good deal of the furor concerning the Second Bank of the United States. The bank's original charter still had a number of years to run, but Andrew Jackson began taking the federal funds out of "Biddle's Monster Bank" and putting them into several state banks, which quickly became known as "pet banks."

As Rebecca appraised the situation, it was a question of who would control the wealth of the federal government—the common man, or the entrenched vested interests? Would Congress and the bank prevail, or would the chief executive be triumphant?

One day in the spring of 1834, Rebecca heard the rap of the brass knocker on her door. "Letitia, will you answer it?" she called. But Letitia continued to mumble and complain to herself in the kitchen.

"Lord, what am I going to do?" Rebecca said to herself. "That woman is getting so deaf and ornery you've got to explode a cannon under her to get her attention."

Rebecca opened the door and saw a startlingly pretty, pale-skinned mulatto girl standing on her doorstep. She couldn't have been more than sixteen or seventeen years old and looked quite emaciated.

"I'm looking for . . ." Her voice trailed off, and she glanced around furtively.

"I'm sorry," Rebecca said, "but we don't have any work here at all."

"They're after me," the girl said plaintively.

"Who's after you? Who are you?"

Before the girl could answer she fainted on the doorstep.

"Letitia!" Rebecca shouted, and this time she heard and came running.

The two women lifted the young girl and half-carried, half-dragged her inside. Rebecca held some smelling salts under the girl's nose. The sharp odor pried her back to consciousness.

"Poor little thing is starving, is what," Letitia said. "Fix her up with a bowl of my ham-hock soup."

Between them, they led the girl down the corridor to the kitchen and propped her up at the solid pine table.

Letitia ladled out a bowl of soup. "Not too fast now, or you be likely to give it back. One spoonful at a time."

"What's your name?" Rebecca asked.

"Bittersweet," the girl murmured.

"Bittersweet—what a beautiful name," Rebecca repeated. "Now, child, who's after you?"

A look of panic crossed the girl's face and tears welled in her large brown eyes. "I won't go back there, I won't! I'll kill myself first!"

"My God, look at your feet," Rebecca exclaimed. "They're all cut and bleeding."

"Lost my shoes long ago. Been running for I don't know since when. Seems like years, but I guess it's only months."

"Who's after you?" Rebecca repeated, almost afraid of the answer. "Bounty hunters, isn't it?"

Bittersweet nodded. "I think two of them followed me to the river, but I managed to get on a ferry and be off before they knew it." The tears collected at the corners of her eyes and slowly spilled down her cheeks. "Seems they're everywhere. Every road I took, every town I passed through . . . a man, or maybe two of them, would look at me real funny, start asking questions, and then I'd have to be off again."

"Where've you come from?" Rebecca asked.

"Mississippi way."

"But that's a thousand miles!" Rebecca said. She felt terribly sorry for the child, but since Washington was a thriving slave center, bounty hunters were everywhere, and the laws against runaways were rigidly enforced. "Bittersweet, if any of those men followed you to this house—if they come after you, we'll have to give you up. You understand that, don't you? It's the law; we have no choice."

Her tears fell even more quickly. "I guess I always knew it would have to end like this."

"But why did you come to this house?" Rebecca asked.

Bittersweet looked from Rebecca to Letitia, then back to Rebecca. "I heard you call her by name, Letitia. And if that truly be her name, then I think she's my grandma."

The soupbowl slipped from Letitia's hands and fell to the floor, where it broke with a clatter. Letitia's hand trembled as she touched the girl's cheek. "Can't be," she whispered. "I'm as dark as the night, and you, you almost white."

"My father was white," she said. "He was the overseer at the plantation. He's dead now."

"Child, don't think you be putting some foolish story over on Letitia. What's your mama's name?"

"Martha. Though she told me that sometimes you called her Martha Abigail."

Letitia started to whimper. "Oh, my merciful God, can't be two alike with the same name. Martha Abigail, count of I named my baby after the first two First Ladies."

She reached for the girl and Bittersweet buried herself against her grandmother. "I been walking for so long, looking for you," she cried into her bosom.

Letitia stroked the girl's light-brown hair. "Don't you cry no more. You found me, I found you."

"Grandma, will they take me back? The men, I mean."

Letitia turned to Rebecca with an agonized look. "If you send her back, I'm going to die."

Rebecca couldn't quite see, because her own eyes were swimming. "Don't worry, Bittersweet, you're not going back."

"Even if they come looking here?"

"If they do, we'll hide you. Failing that, maybe I can buy you back. And if that doesn't work—we'll think of something."

Letitia grasped Rebecca's hands and kissed them. Then she turned to her granddaughter. "And my Martha Abigail?"

"She died, Grandma. She took terrible sick one night, and died. They never told me what from—overwork, most likely. That's when I ran away. I couldn't stand it there anymore. They were getting ready to . . . breed me. Mama warned me.

Told me to run, told me all she remembered about how to find you."

"How'd you get away?"

"Through the swamps. The hounddogs couldn't follow me. Then I just kept walking. Eating berries and roots, and oftentimes the bark from trees. Sometimes people were good to me, and sometimes they'd look at me kind of funny and I'd know that they suspected, so I just kept moving. My mama told me how she lived in Washington when she was a little girl, before she was sold. So every night, I asked in my prayers that my feet be guided here, so I could see you, Grandma."

"Take her upstairs and put her to bed," Rebecca said to Letitia. "You can use Gunning's room tonight. Tomorrow, we'll fix up something nice in the attic or the basement, whichever you prefer. Stay out of sight," she told Bittersweet. "We'll bring you your food. Then in a week or so, I'll start telling people that Letitia's getting too old, and that I had to hire somebody else. Within a month, I guarantee you'll be such a fixture here that nobody will pay you any attention at all. If we do run into trouble, then we'll spirit you north. I've heard tell of stories about an underground railway."

Bittersweet made a deep curtsy and looked up at Rebecca. "I swear on my mother's grave, you'll never regret what you're doing for me."

Letitia led Bittersweet upstairs. After they'd gone, Rebecca sat with a cup of cinnamon tea, and thought for a long time. The plan she'd outlined for Bittersweet sounded simple enough, but it was fraught with danger, both for the girl and for anybody involved with her.

Nat Turner's massacre had stirred up violent antagonism against blacks. The entire question of slavery was argued daily in Congress, with the southern legislators trying to push a gag rule through the House to cut off any debate, and John Quincy Adams eloquently leading the battle for freedom of discussion. But any citizen of Washington who publicly espoused abolition was liable to be tarred and feathered and ridden out of town on a rail. All runaways were hunted down mercilessly. Many people feared that if the slaves ever got the upper hand, they'd overwhelm the white society.

Around dusk, Bravo came home from his work at the Senate, and Rebecca explained the situation to him. "Besides the moral issue, the decision of what we do with Bittersweet has got to be yours also. It could affect your entire life."

"How so?" Bravo asked.

"If it were proven that we knowingly harbored a runaway, we'd have to pay a heavy fine, and probably be given a jail sentence."

He nodded slowly, then walked around the room in a long, loose-gaited stride. Bravo had shot up in the past years; his voice had deepened, and in certain stances he looked so much like his father Jeremy, with his penetrating blue eyes and thick thatch of white-blond hair, that the sight of him cut across Rebecca's heart.

"Mother, I don't think we can do anything other than give this girl shelter. After all, Letitia's part of our family."

"I was hoping you'd feel that way. Thank you, Bravo."

Later that night, as Rebecca lay abed, she thought, Before you knew Bittersweet was Letitia's granddaughter, you were prepared to turn her over to the authorities. Yet every child is *somebody's* daughter or son. What if a stranger came to your door with a similar story? What would you have done then? The question haunted her all through her sleepless night, as she knew it haunted many Americans. She couldn't help but remember what old Thomas Jefferson had once said, that the issue of slavery was like a firebell in the night . . .

Bittersweet turned out to be a blessing. After a few days of food and rest, she lost the look of constant fear. She chose to stay down in the basement close to her grandmother. The girl was a hard worker, and so grateful for being taken in that she couldn't do enough around the house. She even helped her uncle Tad in the stables.

With Bravo, she acted like a timorous woodland creature, probably because they were both at an age where they found each other attractive, yet knew that they must never do anything about it. But her presence proved to be a tonic for Letitia, buoying her up, despite her growing infirmities.

One day Bravo said to his mother, "You've been talking about modernizing this house a bit, haven't you? Well, now's the time to do it. There's no reason why we couldn't have running water piped into the kitchen, and even have water closets, the way they've done at the White House."

At first, Letitia resisted, convinced that the pipes would burst and that they'd all be swept away in a great flood. But at last she gave in to Bravo's pressure.

Rebecca went to the Metropolitan Bank, spoke to Mr. Van Ness, and borrowed a sum of money against the income from Jeremy's royalties.

"I had to pay astronomical rates," she told Bravo. "In an attempt to force Andrew Jackson to recharter the Second Bank, Nicholas Biddle has clamped down with a policy of tight money. Banks are failing everywhere; there's panic in the air. But Jackson is adamant—he wants the bank destroyed."

"What a pity," Bravo said, "that in this battle between Jackson and the bank, the country has to suffer."

As for Jackson, Rebecca continued to see him frequently, but he was so infirm that his family was always gathered about him to offer him strength and nourishment. The strain of his battle with Congress and the bank continued to age him drastically, and he suffered from increasing attacks of dropsy.

Wingate visited him almost daily now, and had even accompanied him when Jackson made a triumphal tour of New York and New England. At Harvard, he'd been awarded an honorary doctorate, much to the consternation of one of its illustrious alumni, John Quincy Adams, who complained that Jackson wasn't deserving of the honor, since he could barely read or write.

At his acceptance speech, however, Jackson won the hearts of the dour New Englanders when, after being addressed in Latin, he responded with the one Latin term he knew: *"E pluribus unum,* out of the many, one." Whenever he could, Jackson reiterated his conviction that the greatest challenge facing the nation was the preservation of the Union.

When Wingate returned from the tour, he told Rebecca that Jackson had been violently ill all during his travels, at times with serious bleeding from the lungs. "He seems to be living on will alone," Wingate said. "One night, when I was in his room, he kept reading a passage in the Bible—from Kings, I think it was."

Rebecca's hand flew to her throat.

"Sometimes I think he believes that if he dies, the Union will fall apart. So he's drawing strength from some deep part of himself to remain alive, and by his mere presence to hold the country together."

Rebecca nodded slowly. "I wonder if the office of the presidency itself doesn't exert some powerful, almost mysterious influence on the men who live in the White House, making them capable of even greater acts than they thought possible."

In her private thoughts, Rebecca reflected on the change in her own attitude, and in a moment of candor wrote to Suzannah: "There were times when I would have done anything in my power to see this man defeated at the polls, so convinced was I that he would bring the country to ruin. Now I pray fervently for his life. I think I know so much, but I don't know anything at all about people. Look at how I was fooled by Devroe Connaught, and all because of my own greed and stupidity!

"I am overcome by a hunger to see you and to know my grandchildren. I keep promising myself that I must go, and soon, before I'm too old to make that long and arduous journey. In the meantime, you must write me *everything;* do not leave out one childhood illness! And know that my thoughts, prayers, and love are always with you."

One morning, Rebecca said to Bittersweet, "I believe it's time that I showed you how to do the marketing."

Bittersweet hung back in fear. Up until now, the only time she'd been outdoors was to do the gardening and to help in the stables.

"Sooner or later you've got to go out," Rebecca said. "You'll be with me, so there's no need to be frightened."

"But what if somebody sees me at the market? What if they come after me?"

"If you send out such a message of fear, then you may be sure that somebody will get suspicious. You must *act* free, *be* free, otherwise it's you yourself who'll keep Bittersweet in bondage forever. Now come along."

Chapter 34

TAD DROVE Rebecca and Bittersweet over to Market Square, located on Pennsylvania Avenue between Seventh and Ninth Streets.

"Tuesdays, Thursdays, and Saturdays are market days," Rebecca explained to Bittersweet. "The farmers bring in their produce, and the best shopping is to be done early on those mornings."

Bittersweet stared at all the country people, black and white, who lined the footpaths with their old broken wagons hitched to decrepit mules. One black crone called to her, "Got every kind of herb and root to cure whatever ails you. Charms and potions, too. Just tell me what your trouble is and I got it. Only a penny a pinch."

"Come away," Rebecca said to Bittersweet. "I've tried them all, and none of them work."

Anything that anybody could possibly want in the way of food could be bought at the central market, right down to pineapples that had been imported from the West Indies, and ice selling at seventy-five cents per bushel. The ice fascinated Bittersweet. "It's warm out," she said. "Where does it come from? How do they keep it from melting?"

"Well, we're fortunate in both respects. We have ships and steamboats bringing us ice when it's available from Maine, all packed in sawdust. But when it gets really hot, we still have a supply, for there are two ice wells just outside Washington, and they're so deep that the water freezes down there and the ice is scraped off and brought to market. Though that costs a good deal more than seventy-five cents a bushel."

Rebecca stopped at a fishmonger's stall and looked at the fish neatly stacked, head to tail. "Fresh caught this morning," the man bawled.

"They weren't caught this morning," Rebecca said to Bittersweet. "See, the scales are no longer rainbow-hued, and the eyes of the fish are popping in their heads. We can do better than that. Shad and herring native to the Potomac are the best to be had anywhere," Rebecca said to Bittersweet. "Then about forty miles downriver are the ducking shores; from April to November the ducks and canvasbacks come to feed on the celery beds that abound there, and so we get wonderful fowl during those months. In the autumn, the forests of Virginia teem with wild turkeys, so if you remember those times of the year, you can usually get the best bargains."

"Yes, ma'am," Bittersweet said, struggling to remember it all.

Terrapin, venison, bacon, ham, smoked meats, freshly killed chickens, and others still alive and strutting around on long strings, not realizing what their fate was to be—all of this passed before Bittersweet's eyes.

Rebecca was so intent on making a selection of quail that she collided with a woman who'd just bought a freshly killed capon. As the blood splashed all over her expensive dress the woman let out an oath in French, and Rebecca turned to stare into the black and baleful eyes of Véronique Villefranche Connaught.

"I beg your pardon," Rebecca began as Véronique spat, "You stupid old fool!"

Véronique glared first at Rebecca and then at Bittersweet, trembling in an effort to vent her rage, then she turned on her heel and hurried off. She was followed by a nurse holding an exquisite little girl dressed very much like a doll, a second nurse carrying an infant swaddled in a blue blanket bearing the Connaught coat of arms, and two footmen, both with truncheons dangling from their belts and armed with pistols.

Rebecca had read the notices published in all the Washington papers announcing the birth of a son to Devroe and Véronique Connaught. The child's christening had been a gala event among certain segments of society. The boy was named Sean Victor, and Rebecca shuddered, remembering all the terrible connotations attached to those names.

Washington abounded with rumors that Devroe Connaught had suffered serious financial reverses because of the Bank War, and so Véronique had taken to parading herself everywhere in Washington, and always with the children, as if by her flawless appearance and full retinue of servants she would give the lie to those rumors.

Rebecca stared at Véronique, thinking, It's as though she feels she has no value, except through her children. Then she turned to Bittersweet, "That woman has no love for our family. If you should run into her anyplace in Washington, keep away from her. She's poisonous."

Letitia had told Bittersweet many of the details of the Brand-Connaught feud, and Bittersweet nodded at Rebecca's warning.

Though she felt somewhat unnerved by Véronique's appearance, Rebecca continued her marketing. She'd almost completed her shopping when she heard her name being called with some urgency. She saw Kate Geary hurrying toward her, her face flushed with excitement.

"Oh, Mrs. Brand, I'm that glad I found you! I went to your house and Letitia told me you'd come here. I've been searching for an hour."

Kate put her hand to her heaving bosom to catch her breath. More than two years had passed since Rebecca had last seen the girl. Now nineteen, Kate had grown into womanhood; it showed in her carriage, her body, in the direct, intelligent look in her eyes, so marvelously framed with jet-black lashes.

"Oh, Mrs. Brand, I'm so mixed up. I haven't told my father or my brothers, and Lord knows what they'd think if they found out. You're the only one I can talk to, that's how befuddled I am."

"What ever is the matter?" Rebecca asked.

Kate took a letter out of her reticule and opened the pages. "It's all here in this letter, and I'd let you read it but I'm afraid there are parts that might embarrass you, for to be sure they embarrassed me! It's from Gunning. He's asked me to come to him in the Kansas Territory. Says there's a wagon train heading out his way within the month."

Rebecca stopped in her tracks and felt her heart begin to palpitate. She'd received a number of letters from Gunning, all detailing his life at the army fort where he was stationed—the loneliness, the difficulty with Indians who were slowly arriving and being quartered on reservations, Gunning's disenchantment with only male companionship. But he'd never mentioned anything about Kate.

"Bittersweet," Rebecca ordered, "take these packages to Tad. You and he go back to the house. Kate and I will walk for a bit."

Bittersweet went off and Rebecca said to Kate, "So Gunning's asked you to come to Kansas, has he? And what have you decided?"

"I don't know what to do," Kate said. "That's why I've come to see you. I thought you might be able to..." Her voice trailed off.

Rebecca sensed that some very drastic measures were called for in this situation. She wanted to be kind, to reassure this girl who'd done so much to help Gunning. But that was the past, and now, the remainder of their lives were at stake. "How do you expect me to help?" she asked. Her words were ordinary enough, but her tone sounded accusatory. "Don't you know your own mind?"

"It's not my mind I'm uncertain of," Kate said, flushing. "But he's Gunning Brand. As handsome as any man has a right to be and spoiled rotten, as far as I can tell. Maybe even a little by you."

It was Rebecca's turn to blush, but she shot back, "You're worried about more than his being handsome. You're thinking that one day he may be comfortably well off, and you're the daughter of a tavernkeeper—and how would you fit into his world then? Isn't that right?"

Kate straightened. "I'll admit that's been on my mind a number of times. But it's not one of his fancy society girls he's asked to come out there now, is it?"

Rebecca hurried along, her skirts sweeping the dust. She was anxious to get away from the market, and from the curious looks they were getting from passersby. "No, Gunning didn't send for any of the girls in Washington he courted," Rebecca said. "It's probably because he knew none of them would go to that godforsaken wilderness. Perhaps they recognized that Gunning was really only interested in a little plaything."

"Well, if that's what was in their heads, then I'd say that Gunning was fierce lucky that they didn't come!"

"Has he asked you to go out there as his wife? Or..."

"Why, what a terrible thing for you to think!" Kate exclaimed. "I may be an innkeeper's daughter, but I'm no Peggy Eaton! Of course he's asked me to go as his wife!"

"What makes you think you could cope with life out there? The deprivation, the wilderness, the constant threat from Indians, never knowing if he'd come back from a scouting expedition? What in your poor circumscribed life has given you the strength that's required?"

They kept walking faster and faster as their words grew more heated.

"I'm a working man's daughter, aye, that I am, and I've worked hard all my life, but it's been honest work, and when I go to the man I marry, I'll go untainted by any other's hands. And if you love a man enough, if you put your faith in the Lord, then any woman can do anything. But I don't suppose that the likes of you would know anything about that, now would you? Raised with all your finery and maids and slaves and such, you probably wouldn't know what an honest day's work is all about."

"You're quite right," Rebecca retorted as they approached the White House and the South Portico became visible. "I usually leave the mundane tasks to the hired help."

"And you're saying that's all I'm good for?" Kate exclaimed. "That's what you're meaning now, isn't it?"

"You said it yourself. That's why you're so nervous about Gunning. You don't know if he would treat you as a wife or as a servant."

"Well, let me tell you something, Mrs. Brand! When I marry, my husband will know he's getting a wife who's a helpmate, one who'll stand beside him, work with him, love with him. He'll be getting a wife who's not afraid to dirty her precious hands."

"Oh, I'm sure you'll do perfectly well in the scullery, while Gunning is out romancing all the other belles in town."

Kate's face blazed with passion; she was so angry that she was almost sputtering. "If a man is happy with what he gets at his hearth, then there's no reason for him to wander. But you pinched society ladies—well, you're afraid to give of yourselves, afraid it might muss your hair or something."

They'd reached the house on New York Avenue, and Rebecca pushed her way through the wrought-iron gate, with Kate following her, still ranting about the slothful evils besetting women these days. "I'll tell you something else, Mrs. Brand. I'm surprised at how I misjudged you. I thought you were a decent type woman, and so smart, but now I see you for what you are, a silly misbegotten snob with no more idea of what brings a person happiness in life than that—that dumb door-post!"

They came to the door, and Rebecca grasped the girl's arm and pushed her inside.

"What do you think you're doing?" Kate cried. "I've nothing else to say to you."

Rebecca herded her into the drawing room. "Sit down and be quiet!"

"I will not! I was taught to respect my elders, but—"

"Sit down I say!" Rebecca ordered.

"I'll not be told to do anything by the likes of you!" Kate's fists knotted and her eyes visibly darkened.

"Have it your own way then—stand," Rebecca said. She unlocked her desk and opened a small leather case. She took out a necklace of beautifully matched pearls and held them up. "My husband brought these to me from one of his ventures in the West Indies."

Kate's eyes widened. "Are you thinking to buy me off with that? Have you no shame?"

Rebecca threw back her head and laughed. Then she moved to Kate and before the startled girl could stop her, she'd fastened the necklace around her throat. "I'm not trying to buy you off. But I did promise myself that one day I'd give this to the girl that Gunning decided to marry. As for Véronique ... well ..."

"I don't—" Kate began, holding the necklace in her hand. She'd never seen anything so fine in all her life, let alone had such a thing around her neck.

"Kate, you've seen enough of Gunning to know what he's like. God forgive me, but I probably did spoil him. Well, I had to be sure that you would be equal to all he'll put you through. And believe me, no matter what he says now, no matter how much love he professes, he'll put you through a great deal. It's in his nature. There are some people like that; they just can't help it."

"Aye," Kate said softly. "I've a feeling you're speaking the God's honest truth."

"But I believe that somewhere in all that mass of contradictions and confusions lives a very decent young man. I think you can help him become that man. At least, I pray you can. So go to him, Kate. And never forget that you're every bit as good as he is, if not better. It's not what you come from or where you've been that matters in this country. It's where you're going. And, my girl, I'd be willing to bet anything that you're headed in the right direction."

Kate stared dumbfounded, not daring to believe what she'd

just heard, wondering if this madwoman might change her mind again.

"Forgive me for baiting you as I did," Rebecca said. "But I simply had to know if you had the strength to cope with us Brands." She held out her arms, and with a cry, Kate bounded across the room and the two women embraced.

"Go to him then," Rebecca said. "Go to him with my prayers and my love."

Kate began to cry softly, but Rebecca held her at arm's length. "We don't have time for tears, my girl. There's too much to be done, too many plans to make. Letitia?" she called.

Letitia shuffled into the room, her eyes beginning to look milky from cataracts. "Letitia, will you brew some tea for us all? Enough for you and Bittersweet also. I have some news. Gunning's getting married. We've got to send Kate off to Kansas with a full trousseau. Everything's got to be ready within the month."

"Married? Less than a month?" Letitia repeated, astounded. "All I asked you was to go to the market and buy some food. I knew I should never have left you out alone."

Letitia went out, mumbling. "All my days, all I've been looking forward to is for one of these children to get married. A big wedding with lots of food and dancing. So first Miss Suzannah ran off, and now Mr. Gunning, he's off. That Bravo, he just better stay put!"

"You'll need money for passage, won't you?" Rebecca asked Kate.

She shook her head. "Gunning sent it to me. From the wages he's saved."

"Well, that's an encouraging sign! At least he's acting responsibly this time. But if you should get out there and find that he's changed, or that you've had a change of heart, then I want you to have enough money to get back home. I'll have my bank arrange it. Whatever you do, listen to your heart. A long time ago, Letitia gave me that advice. I didn't listen to her then, and I've regretted it ever since. Promise me that's what you'll do. Listen," Rebecca murmured, her fist clenched against her bosom. "Promise?"

"I promise."

Chapter 35

DEVROE AND Véronique Connaught sat at either end of the long dining table, finishing their dessert, a seven-layer chocolate cake. His Aunt Elizabeth sat between them; now little more than a wizened old woman, she'd been allowed out of her room to celebrate Devroe's return to the United States. With the years, Elizabeth had slipped deeper into her madness, and there were times when she acted like a child. This evening, she'd continually interrupted Devroe's tale of his travels.

"I'm very impressed with this new Mexican dictator, General Santa Anna," Devroe said. "Though he gained the presidency through a supposedly democratic election, he's very quickly seized power in that country."

"Like this Jackson then, *non?*" Véronique asked.

"Well, as dictatorial as he can be, Jackson must still take into account Congress and the Supreme Court, but Santa Anna answers to nobody but himself."

"I want more cake," Elizabeth interrupted.

"Hush!" Véronique said, "or I'll send you from the table."

Devroe continued, "I must say, Santa Anna and I got on very well. We understand each other, and our ends are the same—to stop further American expansion. He's firm in his conviction that the American settlers in Texas must abide by Mexican laws, or leave. Stephen Austin is constantly agitating for more concessions. In fact, Santa Anna told me that the Americans were becoming too troublesome and numerous for his comfort."

"It is Mexican land, and he has the right to chase them out, hasn't he?" Véronique asked.

"That seems to be his ultimate plan, but that requires rifles and guns and munitions for his army. Well, I arranged for a shipment of two thousand rifles and sufficient ammunition to be sent to him at the port of Corpus Christi. Our English gun manufacturers were very happy to have this windfall, and have promised delivery sometime next year. If things haven't quieted down by then, Santa Anna will march."

"There are times when your cleverness amazes me," Véronique said, and this time she wasn't dissembling.

Devroe patted his lips with his napkin. "I must say, Santa Anna seemed quite impressed also. He's asked me to act as sort of a military advisor to him. The man has pretensions of being a great general—he calls himself the Napoleon of the West—but except for a few skirmishes, he's yet to prove himself against the Americans."

"Will you do as he asks?"

"That depends entirely on the circumstances, and what's to be gained. Though when I think of it, being instrumental in humiliating these Texas-Americans does appeal to me."

Elizabeth clinked her fork against her wineglass to get Véronique's attention. "Who did you say you were? You're not my Marianne; no, of course not. She was much kinder than you. Then who are you?"

Véronique rolled her eyes heavenward. "Really, Devroe, have we not had enough of this? Now Aunt Elizabeth, it's time for you to go back to your room."

Véronique rose, went to Elizabeth, and grasped her firmly by the arm. Elizabeth pulled back, and as she did, she snagged Véronique's imported lace dress and tore it.

"You stupid, mad old creature!" Véronique cried, and slapped Elizabeth smartly across the face.

Elizabeth stiffened. Instead of crying as she usually did when Véronique abused her, this time some impulse in her brain made a sudden connection, and reason returned in a great surge. She half-rose from her chair, "How dare you strike me? I am the mistress in this house." Her eyes flashed from Véronique to the startled Devroe. "If you ever touch me again, I shall turn you out, both of you."

Devroe reached for the bell to summon Elizabeth's companion and have her taken away, but some warning instinct made him stop. He'd heard of cases in which people suddenly regained their reason. If such a thing were to happen to Elizabeth it would be deucedly awkward, particularly at this juncture.

"But of course you're right, my dear aunt," he said. "We're here at your pleasure, come to celebrate your birthday."

Elizabeth leaned forward in her chair, ready to do battle,

but Devroe raised his wineglass. "To your health." He drank the wine down and signaled to Véronique to do the same.

Muttering something about the bad manners in the young these days, Elizabeth finally drank her wine. Quickly discerning Devroe's intent, Véronique refilled all the glasses. "My dearest auntie, you must forgive me, or I shall be desolate. Allow me to propose another toast. May we all be here a year from now to celebrate your next birthday."

Elizabeth hadn't had this much attention in a decade, and she began to glow. Within the space of half an hour, she became so intoxicated that she didn't resist when Devroe helped her to her quarters.

He returned to the dining room and began prowling the room. Véronique, totally unnerved, said, "I have never seen your aunt like that. She appeared perfectly normal."

"I've seen it happen to her once or twice before," Devroe said. "But those other times, it lasted only a moment. Then the light died and she retreated to her memories. Tonight, however, her reason stayed with her for a long time, a disturbingly long time."

"Suppose she regained her full sanity—what then?" Véronique asked.

"She could have the courts rescind the power of attorney they've given me, and we'd live here at her sufferance."

"*Tiens!* Something must be done. How old a woman is she?"

"She's in her late sixties."

"Why, she could live another ten, fifteen years!"

"She could indeed, but I cannot imagine God being that cruel to us, can you?"

Véronique tapped her forehead. "I seem to recall a quotation from that lecherous old Benjamin Franklin: 'God helps them that helps themselves.'"

"A saying worthy of being remembered," Devroe said.

Shortly afterwards, Véronique retired for the evening. Devroe lingered over his brandy, then went upstairs also. He looked in at the nursery, where Romance lay sleeping peacefully, appearing very much a little princess. She really is extraordinarily pretty, Devroe thought, and he admired the way Véronique was bringing her up—with a firm grasp of her station in life.

Devroe tiptoed into the adjoining room where little Sean had turned his bed into a battleground. The covers were bunched

up and the pillow lay on the floor. Devroe picked it up and
gently replaced it. He leaned over and kissed the boy's forehead. Much as he would have denied it, Devroe loved his
children; in some curious way they had given him a tolerance
toward Véronique. She was proving a useful asset; his home
was always filled with the cream of Washington society and
the capital's most important legislators. Henry Clay and Daniel
Webster dined at his table, and often dropped choice tidbits
about what was happening in Congress. In addition, Devroe's
dealings with the British ministry were made that much simpler
when camouflaged by dinner parties, soirées, and balls.

It occurred to Devroe that he hadn't visited Véronique in
many an evening, and so he went to her room.

Véronique expressed delight at seeing him. In her artful way
she performed for him, rousing him to such a state of excitement
that their lovemaking proved quite satisfactory for both of them.

Afterwards, he lay with Véronique curled beside him. "With
Aunt Elizabeth at table, there was no chance to ask you about
the bank. Is there anything new?" Véronique said.

Devroe shook his head. "We've tried everything. Biddle
cut off all his money to all the state banks, recalled all his loans
from the western and southern banks, and has concentrated
most of his funds in the east. He hoped that way to get Jackson
to agree to the rechartering. But Jackson still refuses to budge,
and the people worship the old dictator with such idolatry that
he has unlimited powers. Jackson will bring the country to its
knees, and gloat over it."

"What will be the outcome, then?"

"The bank will not be rechartered, Biddle will lose millions,
the center of banking in the United States will probably shift
from Philadelphia to another city like Boston or New York.
I'm afraid that we shall suffer also."

"Seriously?"

"It could be. Especially if Aunt Elizabeth recovers and takes
it into her head to demand an audit of the Connaught accounts.
I did manage to recoup some of our losses by getting a group
of British banks to hold a large percentage of Biddle's notes."

"Ah, you're so clever about these matters."

Devroe sat up and swung his legs over the side of the bed.
"It took a bit of doing. The English banks balked at first, until
I persuaded the British government to guarantee any losses they
might incur. You see," he explained to Véronique in a rare
moment of candor, "if the English banks hold the American

notes, and if they wait for an advantageous moment and then call in their debts—why, that could wreak havoc with the entire American economy."

"That is a formidable plan!" Véronique's admiration was genuine. "This way, one can bring an entire country to its knees without firing a shot or risking a war."

"Precisely," Devroe said, impressed that she had caught onto the strategy so quickly. "These are modern times, and we must use modern means to achieve our ends. The power of brute force is giving way to the power of money."

"Then there is hope yet," Véronique said.

"If only Jackson were out of the way! Our task would be so much easier. I've never seen a man so close to death manage to cling so tenaciously to life."

"I understand he's received over five hundred threatening letters, all telling him that he must recharter the bank or he will be killed."

"Where did you hear that?" Devroe asked, intrigued.

"Oh, I thought it would be politic if I had Ralph Earl, Jackson's official portraitist, do a painting of me and the children. He's the rage in Washington—anybody who wishes to curry favor with the President has his portrait painted by Earl."

"My compliments to you, my dear, that's exceedingly clever. Oh, Lord, I thought I only had Andrew Jackson to worry about, but now there's also Aunt Elizabeth. Well, your quotation was quite appropriate. 'God helps them that helps themselves.'"

All during the autumn of 1834, Véronique paid great attention to Elizabeth, showering her with little gifts, helping her with her monumental petit-point canvas of Washington.

The winter was particularly miserable, but Véronique insisted they go riding every day, and Elizabeth, who'd been confined for so long, leapt at this chance of freedom. Véronique even suggested that they go ice-skating on the Potomac, but Elizabeth, not having been on skates for some thirty years, had the good sense to reject that idea.

Daily, Elizabeth did seem to be gaining a stronger grasp on reality, and this redoubled Véronique's efforts. They went out riding in a fine rain, and once even in a light snowfall, but the only thing Véronique got for her pains was a nasty cold. When all seemed doomed to failure, Elizabeth caught Véronique's cold.

"Do you think I should send for a doctor?" Elizabeth snuffled. "My maid says she heard tell of a wonderful one in Washington, a Doctor Wingate Grange."

"What do American doctors know?" Véronique said. "I will nurse us both back to health." She dismissed Elizabeth's personal companion and took charge.

Devroe's affairs in Washington became so demanding that he took a suite of rooms at Brown's Indian Queen Hotel on Pennsylvania Avenue and Sixth Street, N.W. Under the guise of buying and selling crops, and other capital investments, he was able to mask his true purpose, the gathering of vital information, particularly in relation to the growing turmoil in Mexico.

Having failed to have Jackson defeated, and smarting from the losses suffered in the Bank War, Devroe concentrated his energies on Texas. A number of outrageous demands by Americans had infuriated General Santa Anna, and he threatened to move full force against the rebels. Devroe did what he could to keep the Mexican government fully informed as to the political climate in Washington.

Several people attached to the British embassy reported directly to Devroe and acted as his couriers, among them Ludlow Parkhurst. One day, Parkhurst mentioned to Devroe that he'd met a strange young man at the Indian Queen Tavern.

"What caught my attention was that this man said that Andrew Jackson had killed his parents."

Devroe's eyes narrowed. "Who is he?"

"He's called Richard Lawrence, he's a housepainter, and he claims to be British. He came to this country several years ago and has been living in Washington. We hoisted a few mugs of stout—it's getting deucedly expensive, eight cents a mug—and all the time Lawrence complained bitterly that he couldn't get any work because Jackson was ruining the economy."

Devroe said no more about it, but for the next several days the thought kept titillating him—a man who claimed that Andrew Jackson had killed his parents? It was too fertile an opportunity not to investigate. He told the manager of the hotel that he wanted his suite repainted and would pay for the materials himself if they would pay the painter. He suggested Richard Lawrence. The management agreed.

In very short order, Devroe determined that though Richard Lawrence was young, a hard worker, and quite handsome, he was also extremely erratic, if not addled.

While he painted the walls a soft, muted green, he rambled on, and Devroe listened. "The bane of my existence is Andrew Jackson," Lawrence said. "As he is the bane of everybody's in this country. Did you know that he killed my parents? Well, he did. Shot them both dead. That's why I've grown this beard," he said, stroking the dark growth, "so that he won't recognize me."

"That's perfectly dreadful!" Devroe said.

Lawrence nodded solemnly. "It's Jackson's fault that I can't find any steady work. I don't know what I'll do when this job is over. Times are so bad that people are going hungry, and still he won't do anything about the bank."

Devroe encouraged him to go on. He also started an investigation of his own, and about two months later received news that Richard Lawrence's parents had never left England. Since Andrew Jackson had never been outside the United States, it was impossible that he could have killed them. Devroe was disappointed to learn that. But by that time, Richard Lawrence's fantasies had taken another turn: that he was the rightful heir to the British throne, and only Andrew Jackson stood in the way of his ascendancy.

"Oh, for the days when a man could settle his grievances by the code of honor," Devroe said. "That was by far the better way."

"I agree, absolutely," Lawrence said. "I've written to Andrew Jackson, challenging him to a duel, but he's never responded. The man is an unmitigated coward."

Day by day, in clever and devious ways, Devroe played out his silken skein of deceit, inflaming Lawrence until his hatred of Jackson was at a fever pitch. At one point, Devroe addressed Lawrence as "Your majesty," and the man accepted it in total earnestness.

"Once Andrew Jackson is gone, then everybody will know that I'm the rightful heir to the British throne." Richard Lawrence let out a huge sigh. "Since he won't respond to my challenge, I suppose I must take matters into my own hands."

Chapter 36

ELIZABETH CONNAUGHT'S cold grew worse, settling in her lungs. Véronique couldn't have been more solicitous. She insisted on feeding Elizabeth her meals herself and slept in her anteroom, the better to nurse her.

One morning, the chambermaid came to make up the room and she shuddered as she opened the door. The room was freezing; the windows were wide open, snow lay on the sill, and Elizabeth's covers were nowhere in sight.

Just then, Véronique appeared, and her mouth opened in horror. "You stupid girl, why did you open that window?"

"But I didn't, ma'am," the maid stammered. "I found it—"

"If I ever catch you doing anything like that again in a sick room, I'll have you whipped. Now get out!"

The chambermaid fled. Véronique clutched at her racing heart. Idiotic of her to have overslept. Heretofore, she'd always been up and about before everybody else; she would shut the windows that she'd opened the night before, cover Elizabeth with the quilt, and build a fire so that the room would be warm when the chambermaid appeared. "I will not fall asleep again," she promised herself. "Too much depends on this."

When the kitchen maid brought in Elizabeth's tray of food, Véronique would feed her one or two spoonfuls, and as soon as the maid had left, she'd throw away the rest of the meal.

Elizabeth grew so weak she was barely able to talk. Every so often she would have moments of lucidity and realize what was happening. Then she'd try to get out of bed, to tell everybody what was going on. But Véronique would push her back into the bed.

"You are so ill! You mustn't move—you'll catch your death."

Once Devroe came in and Elizabeth tried to tell him, but he shook his head and claimed that he couldn't understand her babblings. By week's end, Elizabeth developed pneumonia. She drifted in and out of delirium, imagining she saw the shade of her husband being bitten to death by a nest of writhing vipers...or she'd see Zebulon, and thrill to his magnificent manhood as he took her again and again. Sometimes the wraith of her Aunt Victoria would preach hell and damnation at her for all she'd done. But most of all, she hungered for the appearance of her daughter Marianne, gentle Marianne, who came to her, arms extended, to free her from this physical prison.

"This is my punishment for all I've done," she whispered one night to Véronique. "I don't have much longer; I must see a priest."

"Tomorrow," Véronique said. "I'll send for one as soon as the roads are clear of snow."

But tomorrow stretched out into another day, then another. At the end of the second week of her confinement, Elizabeth struggled to sit up in bed, and stretched her arms toward the light streaming in from the window. "Yes, my Marianne, yes," she whispered. "I'm going home to my Marianne."

She lay back then, a half-smile on her lips, the cares wiped from her face, the features so smooth and youthful-looking that she might have been the ravishing black-haired beauty who'd captured the heart of Zebulon Brand those many years ago.

Véronique searched for a pulse. She could find none. She placed a small mirror under Elizabeth's nose, and found no sign of breath. She forced herself to sit at the bedside for more than an hour. Then when she touched Elizabeth's fingers and found them stiffening with rigor mortis, she began to weep and wail.

All the servants came running. Devroe bounded upstairs and comforted his near-hysterical wife. "I'm certain that you did everything possible," he said.

After Elizabeth was safely buried, Véronique and Devroe shared a quiet moment and a glass of golden sherry. "She was a poor, benighted woman," Devroe said, "and caused the family untold grief."

"She will trouble no one any longer," Véronique said.

"It was very enterprising of you, my dear," Devroe said. "Of course, I've known what was going on all along."

Véronique looked at him levelly. "Whatever happened, was done for the security of our children."

"What if somebody should investigate?" he asked, toying with her.

"What would an investigation uncover? Just a woman judged insane long ago, who died of pneumonia. But think of where a *further* investigation might lead—why, to the Connaught accounts."

Devroe smiled. "Have no fear, my dear. I've no intention of saying or doing anything. I'm perfectly content to have things remain as they are."

"To the undisputed master of the Connaught estates, then," she said, raising her sherry glass.

"A pity that you preferred the dance to an acting career. Shakespeare wrote a wonderful part for a woman who helped her husband become king. I know you could have done justice to it."

President Jackson had taken seriously ill over the Christmas holidays, and so Rebecca could not see him until the very end of January. At his urging and invitation, she came to the White House on a wind-chilled day and found it still in a festive state. Fires roared in every hearth in the entire house. Uncle Alfred and the other servants served punch and cookies to the Jackson family. Jack and Emily Donelson and their children were there, as were Andrew Jackson's adopted son, Andrew Junior, his wife Sarah, and their newborn child, a little girl named Rachel.

The President sat in a rocking chair, covered with Rebecca's afghan quilt, dandling the little girl on his knees. Though his face was wreathed in smiles, Rebecca thought he looked dreadful, sallow and skeletal. With the children, Jackson was as loving as any grandfather could be. How extraordinary, Rebecca thought, that this fierce general, who'd slaughtered Indians and the British, could display a sensitivity to children that was akin to a woman's.

Jackson held the child up for Rebecca to see. "This little one is named after my wife. Oh, she's the delight of my old age. My joy and my succor."

Rebecca took the child and cuddled her. "You know, Andrew, I've never seen my own grandchildren, Matty or Zeb or Becky. Really, I must bestir myself one of these days and get out to Texas. Suzannah keeps asking me to come."

"Why not go, then?" Jackson asked.

"Oh, I suppose I'm afflicted with the creeping inertia that comes with age," she said.

"You? Nonsense. It's something else, isn't it?"

"Really, Andrew, you do have a way of probing right into the heart of a person." She stared out at the south lawn, bare and bleak this winter's day. "I simply don't get along with Jonathan Albright. It's as though there's something in our natures that just didn't mix, like oil and water," she added, smiling slightly at the cliché.

"But he's a fine man," Jackson said.

"Oh, I'm sure of that. Otherwise Suzannah wouldn't have chosen him. But if I go there, I have a feeling something disruptive will happen to make everybody miserable."

Jackson reflected for a moment. "You gave me some advice a while ago; good advice it was. Now it's my turn. People who live out on the frontier don't have time for the kinds of things you're talking about. All that wondering and backbiting and gossiping—why that comes from being citified. Don't live in the past, Rebecca. It's a new land and a new beginning for them. Why not allow it to be that for you?"

Rebecca felt herself gathering her energies to spring to her defense. But then she sighed wearily. "Thank you, Andrew, I think you're right. I'll write to Suzannah very soon."

"If you do decide to go, then we should talk," Jackson said. "There is a possibility that you could do some things for me."

"Oh? Like what?"

"Texas is in a turmoil right now. We'll talk about it fully when I've thought the situation out.

"Have you heard any news of Gunning?" President Jackson asked.

"Yes, and I'm pleased to say the news is all good from that quarter. Kate Geary arrived in Kansas safely, and they were married. Kate writes me religiously, every single week, but the conditions of the mails are such that I get batches at a time."

"I'm delighted to hear about the marriage," Jackson said. "That boy may make something of himself yet."

"Not a day goes by that I don't pray fervently for that."

Just then a pageboy arrived from Capitol Hill with some documents for the President. He read them briefly, nodded, and handed them back. "Excellent," he said. "My compliments to the Senate." The boy left.

"Good news?" Rebecca asked.

He nodded. "I've given France an ultimatum, and the Senate is behind me fully on this. France must pay the debt they've owed us for the past twenty years, or I'll confiscate whatever of their property I deem necessary."

Rebecca raised her eyebrows. "You know the dangers, I take it. This could lead to war."

"I also know the French. Unless they're threatened, they'll never pay. They've been dragging their feet since the Napoleonic Wars. Before I leave office I mean to balance the Federal budget—for the first time in our country's history, I might add—and this will help. I'm thinking of sending five or six of my warships to the French coast, as a show of strength— the way I did with the King of Naples. He paid his debt to us pretty fast. I bet it will make the French do the same."

When he talked of government affairs, Rebecca noticed that the old fire lit his eyes, and he seemed a youthful man again. But as soon as that passion was spent, he would revert to his old, infirm self.

"Will you be going to Senator Davis's funeral?" Jackson asked.

"Yes, I'll go," Rebecca said. "Warren Davis wasn't a great friend of mine, but he was certainly an acquaintance. You're not thinking of going, are you?"

"I fear I must," Jackson said. "Warren was the representative from South Carolina. If I don't go, then all the South Carolinians will say that I still hold a grudge against them for their nullification scheme. I don't want there to be any possibility for those wounds to fester, so I must attend."

"Then take Wingate with you," Rebecca said. "I'd feel much better if you did."

"I'll do that," Jackson agreed. "He's kept me alive this long..."

Seeing how fragile Jackson was, Rebecca made her visit brief. Emily Donelson walked her through the entrance foyer to the front door. Being far away from the roaring fireplaces, the hall was so chilly that Rebecca could see her breath.

"This house does have some serious flaws," Emily said with a resigned shrug. "It seems that I catch cold with the first gust of autumn wind, and the cold then lasts until spring." She turned her head and coughed. "It's not my health I worry about, but Uncle's. Then you know, he's also received so many letters threatening his life. But Uncle just rips them up and says, 'I try to live my life as if death will come at any moment.' Frankly, I don't know what to do."

Rebecca bit her lip. "I'd no idea he'd received that many threats. The funeral will be open to the public, with hundreds, perhaps thousands of people milling about. I doubt that anything will happen here in the capital, but why not have the President's guard accompany him? The funeral will have all the trappings of a ceremonial function, so the public will never guess why the guard's there."

"That's an excellent idea! I'm going to ask Uncle to do just that."

January 30 was a cold, foggy morning, the kind that Rebecca hated. Fog misted the windowpanes, and when she wiped them clean, all she saw was a shroud of fog obliterating the city. The dampness had gotten into everything, and Bittersweet could hardly light a match to get the fires started. Letitia laid out Rebecca's woolen underclothes, and when she dressed, she felt the heavy dampness of the cloth against her skin.

As Tad drove the carriage to the Davis funeral, he had to pick his way through the fog; it was so dense he could scarcely see the potholes. Fog continued to roll over the city in intermittent waves, sculpting the landscape, and leaving everything coated with a wet, heavy dew.

At last Tad reached the Capitol and Rebecca walked up the long flight of steps to the Hall of Representatives. President Jackson and his party had arrived shortly before, and she saw him surrounded by a coterie of friends and cabinet members. Levi Woodbury, the secretary of the treasury, held Jackson under one arm, and Wingate held him under the other. He looked as if he could scarcely get through the services.

Rebecca saw Devroe and Véronique Connaught among the mourners; Warren Davis had been a great friend of theirs, as were many southern legislators. Both Véronique and Devroe were wearing black, still in mourning for their Aunt Elizabeth.

The funeral services seemed interminable to Rebecca, but at last the final eulogy had been said. She watched Jackson stand, leaning heavily on the arm of Levi Woodbury. They moved slowly past the open casket, then went down the stairs to the portico of the Capitol.

A crowd had gathered at the line of columns, and among them stood a well-dressed, handsome young man with a black beard. Jackson got to within six feet of him when suddenly the man whipped a small pistol from his coat pocket and, at point-blank range, fired at the President.

Rebecca screamed and simultaneously took a step toward the man. Miraculously, the President was still standing, unhurt.

The gun had misfired. The man drew a second pistol from his pocket and fired again. But his second gun misfired also!

By now, the soldiering instinct in Andrew Jackson had been galvanized. With two shots fired at him, he lunged at his would-be assassin, his cane raised, and struck the man. Levi Woodbury, not knowing if the man was acting alone or if there were others, pulled the President back, while Wingate dashed in front of Jackson, shielding him with his body.

Davy Crockett, along with two other legislators that Rebecca didn't know, leaped on the attacker and wrestled him to the ground. Then the President's guard surrounded Jackson and he was rushed off to his carriage.

"Get us out of here," Wingate shouted to the driver. "Back to the White House!" Wingate loosened the President's shirt collar; his exertions coupled with the shock of the incident had left him gasping for breath.

Once they were back in the mansion, Wingate insisted that the President lie down. In the light of Jackson's health, the aftereffects of the assassination attempt might prove more dangerous than any bullet.

Rebecca hurried to the White House to find out how Jackson was, but the entire grounds had been cordoned off and soldiers patrolled everywhere. No one was being admitted.

Jack Donelson returned to the President's house about two hours later to report to Jackson. "The Capitol police questioned the man and he says his name is Richard Lawrence. He does odd jobs in Washington. The last one was housepainting.

"He claims that you murdered his father and mother, and that's why he wanted to kill you. But then he said that his father and mother had died in England. And that he was the rightful heir to the English throne, and you were keeping him from his inheritance. Clearly, the man is deranged."

"There's more to it than that!" Jackson exclaimed. "It's all part of some conspiracy. I wouldn't be surprised if one of my esteemed southern friends, like John C. Calhoun, was behind it."

Later that day, Richard Lawrence's pistols were brought to the White House, where Donelson inspected them. By some inexplicable coincidence, both of the guns had misfired. Though they were loaded with the finest dueling powder, only the caps had fired, leaving the powder charges intact.

"A ballistics expert just told me that the odds of two such

fine weapons misfiring simultaneously is one to one hundred and twenty-five thousand," Donelson told Wingate.

Jack Donelson then recapped one of the weapons, aimed it at a tree outside, and fired through the open window. The pistol went off with a loud report, and the bullet imbedded itself in the tree trunk. "Accurate and deadly," Donelson said.

"Could it be that the heavy morning fog caused the humidity to foul the firing mechanism?" Wingate asked the President.

Jackson nodded. "I've seen it happen often enough on the battlefield. Where is this Lawrence now?"

"They've put him in the city jail for the moment," Donelson said. "But they're convinced that he's insane, and they'll have him put into an institution."

"I say that man was hired by the likes of Senator Calhoun. He would have tried it himself if he'd had the courage," Jackson insisted. He gave orders that a full investigation be made to determine whether or not there had been a conspiracy.

Washington was in shock. Charges flew back and forth. When Calhoun learned that the President had accused him of being involved, he rose on the floor of the Senate, and white-faced with anger, shouted, "Andrew Jackson has become a dictator in this country! Anybody who doesn't agree with him is liable to incur his full fury! I don't have to repeat his own threats against me; everybody in Washington knows that he threatened to hang me. And now he attaches his own motives to innocent men. Gentlemen, beware, we have a new king on our hands!"

The newspapers in Washington followed predictable party lines. Duff Green of the *United States Telegraph* claimed that the entire incident had been engineered by Jackson. "It's his way of gaining sympathy because of the financial difficulty the country is in. All because he refuses to charter the Second Bank of the United States! Why, even John Quincy Adams, Jackson's bitterest foe in Congress, has now proclaimed his loyalty to the President. So Jackson's ploy has obviously worked," Duff Green concluded.

Francis Blair of the *Globe* expressed the sentiment of many Americans when he said that he thought Providence had been watching over the President that morning.

But it was Rebel Thorne, writing in the *National Intelligencer*, who put the entire issue into a new and frightening perspective.

"My fellow Americans. Something terrible has happened this day in America, something that has never happened before. A man with imagined complaints against President Jackson attempted to kill him.

"Oh, my fellow countrymen, I have a terrible suspicion that this assassination attempt will not be the last. As our nation grows, as malcontents begin to feel more alienated from our democratic process, they may seek recourse through violence.

"We have only one President, and we must do everything in our power to protect him. Can you imagine our horror if the assailant had been successful? Could we ever gauge this loss to the nation and to the world? Let this be a warning to us. We must act, and act with dispatch, to insure the safety of those whom we elect. If we don't, we shall descend back into the time of the barbarian."

For several days after Rebel Thorne's article appeared, Congress went through a great many motions, setting up committees, and investigative bodies, and studies, all aimed at unearthing the possibility of a conspiracy. But by the end of the week, their fervor died down, and within the month, the issue was shelved in some congressional committee, there to collect dust.

But having seen the assassination attempt with her own eyes, Rebecca still had nightmares, and she would waken from a tormented sleep, seeing the flash of fire, and hearing the loud report from the gun.

Chapter 37

"I'M BEGINNING to have second thoughts about this," President Jackson said to Rebecca. "It's developed into far too dangerous a situation now." She had come to call on him and they were in the sitting room. More than nine months had passed since the attempt on the President's life.

"That's precisely why I'm going to Texas," Rebecca said. "If it's as fraught with difficulties as we think, then this might be the time for Suzannah and the children to come back East with me, at least until the trouble dies down."

Jackson took a puff on his corncob pipe, then knocked out the ashes. "Each year, I get hundreds of clay pipes and briar pipes from well-wishers, but a corncob still tastes the sweetest."

"Don't let Wingate see you smoking," she said. "But getting back to Texas—I'm going anyway, so you might as well tell me what's on your mind."

"There's no way I can persuade you to stay?"

"None whatsoever. I'm determined to see my grandchildren before I go on to my reward. You'd do the same if it were you, you know that."

"But a woman!" he exclaimed. "Alone among the hostiles."

"Andrew, I'm going to be met by Suzannah and Jonathan."

Jackson drummed his fingers on the arm of his chair. "Well, if you're determined . . . What I'm about to tell you mustn't go beyond this room. And if you should ever find yourself in some sort of compromising situation, I'd have to deny we'd ever spoken."

Rebecca straightened in her chair. He'd certainly gotten her attention.

"I've been in close communication with Sam Houston," Jackson began. "You know he came to Washington some years back and asked if he could be my eyes and ears in Texas. I agreed. A finer man or soldier doesn't exist. He led the charge at Horseshoe Bend when we defeated the Creeks way back in 1811."

"I've pretty much the same opinion of Sam," she said. "I met him a number of times when he was serving in Congress, and, of course, I met him again in Washington at your first inauguration."

Jackson nodded. "That was before his ill-fated marriage. Well, we'll never really know what happened to that union, but it must have been terrible for Sam to leave his bride and go off and live among the Indians."

"But he's in Texas now, isn't he?"

"Thankfully, for us. Sometimes a great moment in a country's history can shake a man out of his own problems and be his salvation. I think Sam's got that opportunity right now."

"Do you want me to see him?"

"Of course, if it's convenient. But more than that, I need to know what's going on out there, not only in relation to what Texans want, but also how it would affect our own country. I want you to sniff the air, and if you choose to write about what's happening, so much the better."

"Write about it?" she repeated, with a touch of surprise. "But Andrew, you know my effectiveness as Rebel Thorne has been severely limited now that people know my identity. Why, I understand that there are some legislators who are discounting everything that I write."

Jackson nodded. "So I understand. But for all that, you've still got the common man's attention, and you could be a great help."

"All right then," she said, hiding her half-smile.

So there it was. A little rabble-rousing for the country. Well, the entire situation was terribly complex, but she tended to side with her fellow Americans. Also, she would feel that much easier if Suzannah and the children were living in a section of the country that had become part of the United States.

"General Santa Anna sent his brother-in-law, General Cos, to punish the Texans, bring them back in line. Well, those boys of ours showed the Mexicans a thing or two! Whipped them at Gonzales, at Goliad, and, now they've got General Cos bottled up in a town called San Antonio."

Rebecca felt a stab of apprehension. "Suzannah lives fairly close to that town—fifty miles away, if I remember her letters correctly."

"Proximity doesn't matter. If war does break out, it will

sweep across all of Texas before it's done."

"What are the prospects?" she said, almost afraid to ask.

"If Cos beats the Texans at San Antonio, that will be the end of their war for independence. But if Cos is defeated— well, after that it's anybody's guess. I figure that Santa Anna will gather an army, and head into Texas."

"Could the battle be going on right now? I mean, could Santa Anna be on the march?"

"I doubt it. The winters in Texas can be fierce, and if Cos has indeed been defeated, Santa Anna probably won't be able to move his army until spring."

"Then I must start immediately," she said, her trip given new urgency. Though she'd never paid much attention to omens and premonitions, the danger to Suzannah was too real to be dismissed. "How long will it take me to get there, do you think?"

"My couriers can make it in a little less than three weeks, but of course, they're riding hard and in relays. If you take the boat from Baltimore, then I'd say you'd be in New Orleans in about two weeks, and then it will be another two or three weeks before you see your family."

Rebecca stood up to leave. "Is there anything special you want me to tell Sam Houston?"

"Just that the United States is behind him. If I haven't come out vehemently on their side, it's because I must protect the presidential election next year. The Whigs will make an issue of Texas and the possibility of annexing it. The abolitionists will be against it, because Texas would come in as a southern state, and doubtless a slave state. The southerners will be for it, hoping to keep the balance of power in Congress. I must walk a very careful line here if I'm to get Martin Van Buren elected."

"I'll tell Houston," she said. "I'm sure he'll understand."

She took his hand and he held it in his firm grasp. Then their eyes met and held for a long moment. "Goodbye, my dear," he murmured. "I may be long gone when you return—"

"Andrew, stop that. Or must I read to you from the Bible again?"

He smiled and said, "You're right. We must trust in the Lord and allow His will to be done." He walked her to the door. "My dear, you write of what you see. These men, these Texans, are our American brothers. Some had fathers and grandfathers who fought at Valley Forge, and at New Orleans. They're fighting now for the same thing. Liberty."

Rebecca hurried home and made preparations to leave. She felt an imperative need to get to Texas as quickly as possible, and warn Suzannah of what the possibilities were, perhaps persuade her to return East for a time. Surely Jonathan would see the sense in that.

At home, Rebecca and Letitia packed trunk after trunk, loading them down with kitchen equipment, household items, bolts of cloth, a half dozen of Suzannah's old dresses, and an assortment of other items she thought Suzannah might need.

"I don't like you going out there alone," Letitia said. "Been asking you for weeks, why won't you let me come?"

Rebecca touched Letitia's arm. "I know Suzannah would adore to see you, but it just can't be. First of all, I can't afford it," she lied. "Second, it's a very tiring journey, and what if you should get sick? Don't you see, it's Suzannah I've got to worry about."

"What if I sent Bittersweet along with you?"

"That would make it easier for me, admittedly, but I could never ask her to go back to that part of the country again. It's just too risky."

In the last week of November, shortly before dawn, Rebecca started out for Baltimore. Tad was driving, and Bravo sat beside her in the carriage. They were silent for most of the journey, each lost in his own thoughts.

But when they reached the steamship *Columbia*, tied up at dockside, Bravo swung into action. As soon as his mother's trunks were loaded aboard, he motioned to Tad, who threw down a valise. Briskly, Bravo marched up the gangplank.

"Oh, no!" Rebecca said.

"Mother, I can't let you go alone. It's too dangerous. Frankly, you're not as young as . . . you think you are."

"Bravo, please, don't make this any more difficult for me. You mustn't interrupt your education. One of the Brands must be a college graduate!"

That was the consistent reason she'd given Bravo for not wanting him to come, but the real reason was that she couldn't bear to have another of her children thrust in harm's way.

"Mother, I've already talked to my professors and they've given me permission to take a six-month leave of absence. Six months is not going to make that much difference."

"Bravo, more than anything in the world I want you along. Don't you know how much easier it would be for me? But think. There's a house to be taken care of, a business to be watched over, and you're the only one we can trust to do that. So much of what the Brand family owns is in your hands. If something were to go wrong while we were away, you know you'd never forgive yourself."

She saw him wavering and said, "Then there's Bittersweet. What if some unscrupulous bounty hunter should take it in his head to arrest her as a runaway? With you watching out for everything, I'd be that much more at peace."

"All ashore that's going ashore," a mate shouted.

Rebecca led Bravo to the head of the gangplank. "I'll never forget that you wanted to come. God bless you." Then with a gentle nudge, she edged him down.

Stevedores cast off the ropes, the engines built up steam, and then the *Columbia* moved away from the quay and nosed out into the harbor. Rebecca stood and waved at Bravo—what a wonderful-looking young man he'd turned out to be, so much like Jeremy that there were times when she relived all that had happened.

She drew her coat closer around her, for the sea air was sharp. The gulls' piping cries followed the boat, and a mass of winter clouds furled across the leaden sky. As the boat passed Fort McHenry, she gazed at the flag that flew from its ramparts, remembering that night, twenty-one years ago, when she'd watched the British bombard the fort all night long . . . remembering when the fate of the nation hung by the thread of whether the defenders would be able to hold out against the might of the British invasion fleet. And here Rebecca had met Jonathan Albright. She'd been taking notes to use in an article by Rebel Thorne, and he'd mistaken her for a Tory spy. From that moment on their relationship had been doomed. And here her friend Francis Scott Key, while negotiating for the release of American prisoners aboard a British prison ship, had written the inspired words for "The Star Spangled Banner."

She leaned against the rail, remembering, and the wind whipped the tears from her eyes. Twenty-one years . . . it could have been yesterday, and all the events of her life seemed like ripples on the waves of this great sea, blending into a distant horizon, with an ultimate resting place of she knew not where.

What was the meaning, the purpose of it all? She wondered and felt herself sinking into a melancholy mood. And then she straightened and slapped her hand repeatedly on the rail, "For the moment, you know *exactly* what the meaning is and *exactly* where you're going. You're on a mission for the President of the United States. And you're going to Texas and Suzannah!"

PART FOUR

Chapter 38

THE STEAMBOAT hugged the shore, fighting the currents as they rounded Cape Hatteras. The late autumn air had a clarity that Rebecca found exhilarating, the fierce winter storms hadn't yet begun, and the wave swells couldn't have been more than two or three feet.

Several days later, they arrived in Charleston harbor. Rebecca borrowed a spyglass from the mate and peered at Fort Sumter, the federal fort that President Jackson had ordered reinforced during the nullification crisis. She could well understand its strategic importance, for as it guarded the harbor, it controlled shipping in and out of the busy port. A boom in cotton prices had made Charleston a wealthy city; she understood they shipped more than thirty million pounds of cotton each year.

"We'll have a six-hour stop in Charleston to refuel," the mate told the passengers. Rebecca was glad for the opportunity to get away from the confines of the ship. Wandering about the embarcadero, and through the streets of the prosperous town, she found it unlike any city she'd ever visited. There was an air of languid enchantment about its brick and stone houses; an unusual architectural detail was that the porches didn't face the street, but were built on the sides of the houses, and were usually screened by giant palmettos and magnolia trees.

But behind its charming façade, Rebecca found the city still seething with anti-Jackson feelings. Armed rebellion may have been avoided by Jackson's show of strength, but it lay just below the surface. She was glad to board the ship and be gone.

A brief stop in Savannah, then on to the tiny trading post of Jacksonville on the Florida coast, where they heard news of the Seminole uprising. This fierce tribe of Indians had defied

Jackson's order to move west of the Mississippi, and led by
their chief, Osceola, had hidden themselves deep in the Ever-
glades swamp of Florida.

By week's end, the steamship had reached Key West, the
southernmost point in the United States, a thriving seafaring
community with the dubious reputation of being one of the
richest ports per capita in all of the nation.

"Why is that?" Rebecca asked the mate.

"Salvage," he said. "They've got the most extraordinary
luck in salvaging shipwrecks." Then he added, "Rumor has it
that the townspeople of Key West make a practice of moving
the reef markers, thus luring unsuspecting ships onto the coral
reefs." Nevertheless the ship proceeded without incident.

The weather turned warmer as they headed into the Gulf of
Mexico, and Rebecca stared in amazement at the visible difference in the waters, the aquamarine of the Gulf current moving in the darker blue of the Atlantic waters. They reached
Pensacola, Mobile, and then, almost two weeks after they'd
sailed from Baltimore, they approached the Queen City, New
Orleans.

The boat was scheduled to dock here for two days, to unload
cargo, pick up new cargo, and refuel. Rebecca went ashore,
totally unprepared for what she saw. She recalled what
Thomas Jefferson had once told her, that because of its fortunate location
at the mouth of the Mississippi, New Orleans might one day
be the greatest city in the world. Right now it was the sixth
largest city in the United States, boasting a population of over
sixty thousand.

Steamboats of all sizes plied the Mississippi, and sailing
vessels flying flags from all over the world came to collect the
riches of the continent.

Suzannah had written and given her Patrick Donohoe's address in New Orleans, and on a lark, in addition to feeling a
curious interest in the young man, Rebecca decided to seek
him out. She walked the narrow streets, marveling at the distinctive and ornate architecture that Jeremy had once described
to her. The streets were crowded with young men, armed,
anxious, eager—and all, it seemed, on the way to Texas.

Rebecca finally found the address, a clean but dilapidated
boarding house on St. Charles Place, catering to riverboatmen.

The proprietor sized Rebecca up, decided that she was gen-
teel, and told her, "Yes, Patrick Donohoe's in New Orleans,

but he's between jobs, off on a tear, and hasn't been home to sleep for days now."

Rebecca left Patrick a note saying that she would be staying at Richardson's Hotel for two days, and would be pleased if he'd call on her.

A hot bath and a decent night's sleep in a bona fide bed felt like heaven to Rebecca. She rose early the following morning to do some shopping for Suzannah and the children. In the lobby of the hotel, she saw groups of men standing around and talking excitedly. Then she saw the bold headlines of the New Orleans newspaper—the new boldface type was an innovation that had caught on very quickly after its introduction.

"Texans Defeat General Cos!" the headlines screamed in glaring black print.

She bought a paper and read the account of the battle. A few hundred Texans had surrounded the Mexican general at San Antonio, and had starved him out. On December 5, Cos had surrendered, but was released on the condition that he never cross the Rio Grande River again to fight the Texans. All of Texas had gone wild at the victory!

Rebecca was wondrously pleased with the news, but as President Jackson had warned her, now Santa Anna would have no choice but to put down the rebellion, or face losing all of the Texas province, and his power base in Mexico as well. It made Rebecca's journey seem all the more imperative.

She spent most of the morning prowling the quaint shops, then, weary, she returned to her hotel. As she started up the stairs to her room, two men at the head of the flight began slugging it out. One of them came tumbling down the stairs, his body bumping on each step. With an oath, he bounded to his feet and made ready to charge up the flight when he collided with Rebecca. He stopped in his tracks and said, "Mrs. Brand? I've been searching for you all morning! Remember the first time we met, aboard the *American Flyer*? I told you we'd meet again, and here we are!"

"Patrick Donohoe!" she exclaimed.

"There, you see? I knew you'd remember me!"

"I must say I didn't recognize you at first with all those lumps and bruises on your face." He was also slightly inebriated.

"Are you coming back up here to get what you deserve?"

the riverman at the head of the steps shouted down to Patrick.

"I've no time for the likes of you now," Patrick called back with a dismissing wave of his hand. "I've just met a dear old friend." He winked at Rebecca. "You're a godsend, because I was getting the worst of it."

Rebecca took him downstairs to the dining room and they had a delicious meal of shrimp jambalaya. While they ate, Patrick told her all about his last meeting with Suzannah. He lavished such praise on Suzannah that it made Rebecca just a little uncomfortable.

Then Patrick poured out the story of what had happened to him in the past six years. "Worked the Ohio River for a few years. Fell in love half a dozen times—always to the wrong girl, of course, so I had to keep on searching for the right one, didn't I? Became first mate, then took all the tests for captain, but those old salts on the Ohio, why none of them are ever going to give up their commands, and they all live so long! So I thought I'd try my luck on the mighty Mississippi. I like New Orleans well enough, but the wine and the women—well, it does have a way of seducing you, and so I'm between jobs at the moment.

"Not that I care. You see, Texas fever's hit me, like it's hit everybody else in these parts. Why, they're pouring in from all over the country, far away as Boston and New York, and the fellow I was fighting, he's from Illinois."

"What were you fighting about?"

He stroked his chin. "I don't remember." Then his face broke into an engaging smile.

She laughed with him; she was pleased that he'd chosen to seek her out, and was spending time with her.

"Now what about you?" he asked.

"Why, as you may have guessed, I'm going to see Suzannah."

"Yes, I surmised that. I mean, for how long?"

"Several weeks, a month perhaps, depending."

He nodded, getting her meaning immediately. The bill came and Patrick scrabbled in his pockets, but Rebecca said, "Oh, no, I invited you," and paid it.

"This may surprise you," Patrick said, "but you and I are going in the same direction. If it's all the same to you, I'm going to make sure that you get to Suzannah's safe and sound."

"Oh, that's very kind of you, Patrick, but it's entirely unnecessary."

"No use protesting, Mrs. Brand. I was planning to go to the Brazos country anyway, to visit my aunt and uncle. Then I've been even thinking of joining up with Sam Houston."

"I suppose you need fare money," she said with a slightly knowing smile.

He sat back hard in his chair. "Now, that's not friendly for you to think such a thing of me! The truth is, I am short of money, but I'm so good at my work that I can get a job on any one of these steamships. So just tell me which one you're on and I'll go sign up with the captain."

"The *Columbia*."

"Aye, that's a fine ship—clean lines, sturdy and fast. She's the one they're loading up with the cannon and powder and ammunition. That's what Sam Houston called for, and we're going to bring it to him."

Rebecca went to bed that night still smiling at Patrick Donohoe's antics. Since he'd been under the influence of alcohol when they met, she never expected to see him again, but the following morning, there he was aboard the *Columbia*, looking clean and scrubbed and sober, and already hired on as an extra hand.

He'd been right about the cannon, two six-pounders were being loaded aboard, come as a gift from the citizens of Cincinnati to the people of Texas. At least a score of young men had also bought passage for Texas. A wonderful sense of comaraderie bound them, compounded of the call of adventure and the call for freedom and Rebecca found herself warmed by that unique American combination.

From New Orleans, the *Columbia* sailed to Galveston Island, part of the Texas territory now controlled by Americans. There, passengers who were continuing on, transferred to another steamer, the *Yellow Stone*, a smaller boat with a shallower draft, able to make her way up the Brazos River.

For twenty miles or so from the mouth of the river, the land remained flat, open savannah, broken by silvery patches of marshland. Upriver, the terrain gained slightly in elevation. The bottomland was obviously fertile, and Rebecca couldn't get over the gracious plantations that lined the banks of the Brazos. She cast her mind back to Suzannah's letters; none of them had remotely suggested this kind of leisurely life, and she mentioned that to Patrick.

"Most of the plantation owners in these parts come from

the South," he told her. "They've just transplanted their way of life out here, slaves and all. They can afford slaves, and the gracious way of life, but most Texans work damned hard for their living."

Though it was winter, and the sun little more than a pale orb in the yellow sky, the land remained verdant; cactus, yucca, pine trees, everything seemed to grow in this Texas heartland.

"It's a land worth fighting for, isn't it?" Patrick asked softly, as if reading her thoughts.

"I hope that another shot never has to be fired over it," she said. "But when you consider that seventy five percent of the entire population of Texas is American, well, it does give one pause."

"There's San Felipe de Austin," Patrick said, as they came within sight of the clapboard town. San Felipe, the leading town in Texas, was the seat of the provisional government.

San Felipe was bursting with its own inhabitants and with hundreds of new arrivals. The stagecoach on to Gonzales was scheduled to meet the *Yellow Stone*, and after a fretful night at the town's leading hostelry, Peyton's Boarding House, run by Mrs. Hamm, Rebecca and Patrick set out on the last leg of their journey.

"This stagecoach is somebody's idea of a joke," she said. It was little more than a squarish wagon outfitted with hard wooden seats, a wooden roof overhead, where Rebecca's trunks had been placed, and no glass in the windowframes, so that the dust kicked up by the horses' hooves quickly covered everything.

"I suppose it's not as fancy as what you're used to, but it'll get us there, and that's the important thing," Patrick said.

The miles sped beneath the wheels, jarring Rebecca out of her senses. "It's just uncivilized the way these Texans drive," she complained, but Patrick just laughed.

They reached the Colorado River and crossed it on a flatboat ferry that Rebecca thought would surely sink, but that somehow, miraculously got them to the other side. They stopped for the night, to give the horses a chance to rest and to graze. The half-dozen people riding on the stage fed themselves on hardtack and beef jerky, and prepared to bed down under the brilliant stars.

Rebecca wrapped herself in her heavy cloak, thinking, When I wake up tomorrow morning, my neuralgia will be killing me.

"Patrick," she called, "wouldn't it be nice if we had a fire? It would certainly cheer things up."

"It would. Especially for the Comanches," he said.

"Comanches?" she exclaimed. "My nerves! Who told you that?"

"Nobody had to. This is Comanche country. They're siding with the Mexicans, so that they can keep the American settlers from overrunning their hunting grounds."

Rifles crooked in their arms, the men spelled each other in two-hour watches. Rebecca couldn't sleep; every sound in the bush made her start, whether it be the cough of a puma or the screech of a hare impaled on the talons of a swooping owl. When daylight finally came, she was so irritable and stiff with pain, that she began to doubt the wisdom of ever coming out here at all.

But a tin cup of hot tea brought her to her senses. Now stop this, my girl, she remonstrated with herself. You're just showing your age. In another day you'll see Suzannah and the grandchildren, and everything will be all right.

They proceeded again, and as the stage pushed deeper into the country, they might go for ten, perhaps twenty miles without seeing a house.

"If a man had a mind to, he could do well out here," Patrick said. "All he'd need was a good woman to love, a few head of cattle and a bull, and God and nature would take care of the rest. Look at this wonderful land, a great place for—"

Oh, do shut up! Rebecca thought, annoyed by his constant exuberance. Then she immediately felt contrite. He was, after all, going miles out of his way for her. And why? she wondered suddenly. Certainly there was more involved here than mere friendship. Did it have anything to do with Suzannah? The way he talked about her, almost reverently . . . No, she dismissed that thought from her mind. But she would have to do something meaningful for him, perhaps stake him with some money, though he'd probably squander it all in the nearest bar or gambling hall.

At long last they reached the Guadalupe River, and the town of Gonzales. The stage rolled along the dusty main street with its two or three adobe buildings flanked by newly constructed clapboard buildings. Rebecca scanned the crowd waiting at the depot. Her heart leaped up with every form that seemed slightly familiar . . . but no, Suzannah was nowhere in sight.

Surely she'd come riding up at any minute. But the minutes passed. Lonely in the sobriety of the unmet, Rebecca watched with sinking heart as the people gradually disappeared, leaving her standing alone.

She walked over to the dispatcher and inquired if there were any messages for her.

He shook his head, and suggested that she try general delivery at the post office. The postman was due back next week.

Rebecca felt the tears well to her eyes.

"Now, now, Mrs. Brand," Patrick said. "I'm sure there's a perfectly reasonable explanation for all this. Maybe Suzannah's horse went lame, or maybe one of your grandchildren came down with a fever and she couldn't leave."

But everything he was saying only made her feel worse. "You've been to her ranch. How far from here does she live?"

"They live up to the northwest of here, midway between Gonzales and San Antonio—maybe fifty miles, a little more. But in this country, that's just a hop, skip, and a jump. If she doesn't show up by tomorrow morning, why, we'll just rent us a wagon and be there in a day or two." He scratched his head, "Though it will have to be a sturdy wagon, because of all your trunks. Learned a good lesson a long time ago: Travel light."

"The hell with the trunks!" Rebecca exclaimed. "I'm not waiting until morning. I'll leave them here and ride out on horseback."

He looked at her dubiously. "I don't know. It's an awful long ride to take just on horseback."

"If you're worried about my age, don't," she said. "I'm an excellent rider. You don't understand. Suzannah is very responsible. If she's not here to meet me, it's because something's happened. And I'm going to get to her ranch as soon as I can."

"Suit yourself." Patrick went to the stables to rent two horses. Rebecca had to put down an exorbitant sum of money as a deposit, but when she told the stable owner that she was related to Jonathan Albright, he said, "Put your money away. I'd do anything for Jonathan. Anybody around these parts would. You're lucky to have him as a son-in-law."

Rebecca doubted that, but kept her peace.

She and Patrick started out immediately.

"Keep a steady pace," Patrick said. "That'll get us there the fastest. Horse travels better that way anyway." They made slow, solid time, and Rebecca kept resisting an urge to break into a gallop. The first night out Patrick stood guard; every time Rebecca wakened she saw him peering intently into the darkness. Visions of Commanches and snakes and pumas kept filling her head, along with worries about Suzannah. It was surely the longest night she'd ever spent.

"I've never been so glad to see the sun in my life," she said. They mounted up and began riding again.

And then at long last on the second day, they reached the crest of a long rolling hill, and in the distance they saw a two-story house with smoke curling up from the chimney.

"That's it," Rebecca said without a moment's hesitation. "That's Suzannah's house. I'd recognize it anywhere from the description in her letters."

As they rode closer, she felt her apprehension grow. Yet everything looked so peaceful—and with that, she experienced a flash of anger. Maybe Jonathan just didn't want her there, and this was his way of telling her she wasn't welcome.

Then her horse spooked at the long tearing scream of a woman. Her mount reared, almost throwing her, and Patrick had to fight to keep his horse steady. The two of them looked at each other.

"It could be an ambush," he said, taking his rifle from its holder.

"I don't care!" Rebecca cried, spurring her horse forward.

Patrick galloped after Rebecca, and the two of them raced the last quarter mile to the ranch.

Chapter 39

REBECCA AND PATRICK reined up at the hitching post. They dismounted and started for the house. Patrick grabbed her arm. "Let me go first," he said, just as another scream came from the house.

Rebecca turned on Patrick and pushed him back. "You stay here. That screaming is a woman in labor." She opened the door and hurried in.

A jumble of impressions assaulted her—kettles on the boil in the large stone fireplace, the smell of sweat and blood, and a thin purposeful woman bending over a bed. The woman turned and it was Suzannah, and yet not her. She looked thinner, older, her face reflecting years of hard work, her spirit struggling to remain unbowed.

Oh God, what has that man done to my daughter? Rebecca wanted to scream, but her thoughts were cut off as Suzannah exclaimed. "Oh, Mother! I've never been so glad to see anybody in my life!"

There was hardly time for an embrace, before the screaming started again. Rebecca shed her cloak and rolled up her sleeves. "How long has she been in labor?"

"Almost two days now. If we don't do something, we're going to lose both her and the baby."

"A doctor?" Rebecca said, pressing her ear to the woman's distended stomach.

"Jonathan's gone to get one. But the closest is in San Antonio, and that's a two-day trip back and forth."

Rebecca looked at the woman, semi-conscious from the pain. She blotted the perspiration from her forehead and moistened her lips. "Who is she?"

"Mary Kelley, my nearest neighbor and dearest friend. I think I wrote you about her and her family. This hasn't been an easy pregnancy for her. She took ill in the beginning, and then last week she had some kind of seizure. So Sam brought her to stay with us until her time came. He's back at their ranch watching out for their children—they've got five; the youngest is two years old."

"Why didn't he send for a doctor, then?" Rebecca asked. "That does seem a little irresponsible."

Suzannah looked at her quizzically, then smiled. "Oh, Mother, women have their babies naturally out here. Mary helped me with Mathias, and then with Becky and Zeb, though that was an odd birth. Because just when I thought I'd done with Becky, I started going into labor all over again."

Another spasm contorted Mary Kelley, and she gripped Suzannah's arm, leaving fingernail marks in the flesh. The pain passed, and she released Suzannah and slipped off into a half-coma.

"Where are your children?" Rebecca asked.

"Jonathan dropped them off at Sam Kelley's before he went for the doctor. I thought it was better if they didn't see all this. Besides, I wouldn't have had time to care for them. I sent Enoch to the Kelleys' to do the cooking and things."

"Who's Enoch?"

"A black man Jonathan brought to help around the ranch."

"You own a slave?" Rebecca asked, scandalized.

Suzannah smiled and shook her head. "No, we freed him as soon as he was ours, with the proviso that he work off his price."

"Good girl," Rebecca said.

"I couldn't very well fly in the face of all the family had done, could I?" she said. "I remember that's what Uncle Jeremy did with Eli and Tanzy, before Father..." Her voice trailed off. "And that's what you did with Letitia and Tad."

"I want you to lie down and get some rest," Rebecca said. "You look exhausted."

"What about you?" Suzannah asked. "You've been traveling for more than a month."

"Oh, but I've had the *most* wonderful sleep these past nights," Rebecca said. "I'm as fresh as the first violet of spring. Now do as I say, because unless I'm mistaken, we're going to have our hands full in the next few hours. We'll need all our strength. Oh, before you lie down, I've a surprise for you. Remember Patrick Donohoe? Well, he's outside. He brought me here.

Would you see if he needs anything? A cup of tea, or coffee, perhaps."

Suzannah went out to the barn where Patrick had unhitched the horse and made himself at home; he was lying on the haystack. When he saw Suzannah again, he got the same sensation in his stomach that he'd gotten the very first time he'd laid eyes on her.

"Hello," he said softly, scrambling to his feet.

"It's wonderful to see you again, Patrick."

The color rose to Patrick's face, and as happened whenever he was around Suzannah, he found himself tonguetied.

Suzannah set down a pot of coffee. "I think you'd get a little more peace drinking it here than in the house," she said.

"Incidentally, your mother was so anxious to get here she left her trunks back in Gonzales. Four of them."

"Goodness, did Mother bring all that?"

Patrick nodded. Suzannah burst out laughing, and Patrick's laugh entwined with hers, and though it was only a laugh, he felt a degree of intimacy that sent a flush through his body.

"I'll bring out a bedroll for you," she said. "Thank you so much for bringing my mother."

"Well, you know she is going to pay me, and handsomely."

"Still, it was very decent of you, and I'm indebted." She smiled at him, then went to the barn door. "Patrick, you're welcome to stay as long as you like."

He watched her walk back to the ranch house, pliant as a willow. "You're welcome to stay as long as you like," he repeated in a whisper. "For the rest of my life, just to see your face the first thing in the morning, and the last thing before I close my eyes."

When she got back to the house, Suzannah lay down in the other room and in a matter of seconds fell sound asleep. Rebecca let her sleep as long as she could, almost two hours. Then Mary Kelley's spasms began getting worse; she called out for Suzannah, and Rebecca woke her daughter.

In a moment of lucidity Mary said, "Suzannah, I think I'm going to die. Would you tell the children and Sam that I love them?"

"Hush, you're not going to die. I'm not going to let you die," Suzannah said. "Mary, you must have a blockage somewhere, and that's keeping the baby from being born. It can't go on much longer. When you feel the pain coming on, you've got to push, push with all your might. Hold on to me and push."

Mary nodded weakly, and when the next tremor shook her, she did push, crying out in her anguish, but nothing happened. Suzannah peeled back the covers and gently began to massage Mary's stomach. "It must be a breech birth," she said to her mother.

Rebecca nodded. "Keep massaging her; perhaps the baby will manage to turn itself around."

Suzannah kept it up for as long as she could, and then Rebecca took over. Finally Suzannah grew desperate. "Mother, help me lift her off the bed."

"Why? What are you going to do?"

"I've seen some of the Indian women when they give birth. They squat, and that seems to make the child come out a little more easily."

"But that's the way of the savages!"

"Mother, I don't care whose way it is. If it can save Mary's life and the child, let's try it. We've got to do something, because she can't take this much longer. If this goes on she'll soon be dead."

Grasping the limp form of Mary under her arms, Rebecca and Suzannah helped her off the bed, and then made her squat on her haunches. The poor woman was so exhausted that she kept kneeling over, but Suzannah and Rebecca supported her. Ten minutes ticked by, the time marked by Mary's periodic screams and Suzannah's demand to push. The time lengthened to an hour. Then after another hour, with a terrible terrifying wrench, Mary screamed and the child started to come, its glistening head appearing, then its shoulders, and finally, Suzannah grasped the child and drew it out into life.

Mary collapsed on the floor. Suzannah cut the umbilical cord and tied it, then gave the baby to Rebecca. She leaned over Mary, "Oh my darling, you were so wonderful. It's a fine healthy boy, and you'll be fine also, just you wait and see."

She managed to get Mary back into bed, and Rebecca, who'd bathed the child, brought him back in his swaddling blanket and put him against Mary's breast. "The little thing is screaming his head off, so you've got to know he's healthy."

Mary managed a smile, and then fainted from her ordeal. Suzannah sat down at the hewn wooden table and rested her head on her folded arms. Rebecca came to her daughter and put her arms around her.

"That woman owes you her life, and her child's life also."

Suzannah looked up. "It's no great thing. It's just something we must do for each other. I know Mary would do the same for me, and that's a comfort."

Rebecca nodded. All the anger she'd felt at not being met, all the dark thoughts she'd had about Jonathan—how self-centered that all seemed in the light of what she'd just seen.

"Oh, Suzannah, I love you so much," Rebecca whispered, and mother and daughter held each other for a long time.

The following morning, Jonathan returned with the doctor, an elderly Mexican named Hernández. He looked in on Mary, pronounced her fit, complained that he didn't understand why he'd been called in the first place, charged them two dollars, and went off.

Jonathan barely had time to say hello to Rebecca. Then he said, "I'm off to the Kelleys' to bring back the children."

Though she was still weak, Mary insisted on going back to her own home. "I've been too much of a trial here already," she said, almost embarrassed.

No matter how much Suzannah protested, Mary would have it no other way.

While Jonathan worked to fix up the wagon a little more comfortably for Mary, Rebecca stole a glance at him. He looked more like a scarecrow than ever. But his face had weathered into a kind of granitic strength, and his rangy body moved with surety. Patrick gave him a hand; he put a mattress on the bottom of the wagon, then helped Mary and the baby in.

"Patrick, I'd be much obliged if you'd stay with the women until I get back. That is, unless you've got pressing business elsewhere."

"I'll be glad to stay. While you're gone, it seems to me that the north wall of your barn could use some mending."

"Couldn't pay you but a dollar a day," Jonathan said. "Though I know you're worth a lot more."

"Dollar a day sounds fair to me. Then maybe if you could help me cut a horse out of one of the wild herds, that would even it up."

The two men shook hands on it. Then Jonathan started off.

"I don't think I can stand this much longer," Rebecca said. "When will the children get here? I brought them some presents. They're in my trunks back in town."

"Oh, you shouldn't have."

"Nonsense. Christmas is almost upon us. I hope they like the things. Do you think they'll like me?"

"Mother, for heaven's sakes," Suzannah laughed. "They'll adore you, I know they will."

"Suzannah, I've never thanked you for naming the twins Rebecca and Zebulon."

"Mother, I can't think of anybody I'd rather name Becky after . . . though I must confess I had a little difficulty with Zeb. But then I decided that sooner or later I'd have to forgive Father, otherwise I'd spend the rest of my life trapped in recriminations."

Rebecca sighed with the memory of all that had happened. Then, remembering Andrew Jackson's admonition, "It's a new life for them," she shrugged her dark thoughts aside.

"I want to bathe, and put on a clean dress, and brush my hair," Rebecca said. The weather had turned mean again, and so they built a roaring blaze in the fireplace, heated water, and filled a barrel that Jonathan had cut in half.

"It's much easier when the weather's nice," Suzannah said, as she soaped Rebecca's hair. "Then we all bathe in the river. The children love it."

"Can they swim?"

"Oh, yes. Jonathan taught them almost before they could walk. He's so wonderful with them." She sighed, "They don't seem to pay much mind to me—I guess I'm too easy with them. But a word from him and you can be sure they pay attention."

"He doesn't . . . hit them, does he?"

"Only when it's necessary. And just to make sure the lesson's sunk in."

"Suzannah, are you happy here? I know I shouldn't ask such a question, but it seems such a hard life."

Suzannah poured the lukewarm water over Rebecca's head, rinsing her hair. "Sometimes, I confess, I remember how much easier it was when Letitia did my ironing, and I just sort of played house in the kitchen. But the Lord's given me children who are strong and healthy, and a husband that I love, oh so very much. Mother, aren't those the important things in life? Yes, I'm very happy."

Rebecca dried herself, then put on a simple blue dress of linsey-woolsey and sat before the fire. Her long hair crackled and snapped as she brushed it dry. It was more gray than titian now, but she still had a small streak of vanity about it. She braided it loosely and let it hang down her back.

"Suzannah, what of the rebellion? Do you think it's safe for you and the children to be here?"

"It's a problem that Jonathan and I have worried over ourselves. But you see, when our men defeated General Cos at San Antonio, he promised never to come farther north than the Rio Grande River."

"But surely such a promise won't be binding on General Santa Anna."

"Of course not. But whatever Santa Anna decides, we're hoping that he won't make a move until next spring. He'll be coming from Mexico City, and he'll need the new grasses to feed his army's horses, though Jonathan claims he can manage just as well on the mesquite that grows everywhere. At any rate, by that time we hope we'll be organized enough to present our petition to him from a position of strength."

"What exactly is it you want?"

"A more equal representation in the Mexican government. All our petitions get lost in the county seat at Coahuila. Is it so unreasonable to ask that our voices be heard?"

Rebecca sighed. "Well, the American colonies went to war over that in 1776."

"When Santa Anna came to power, he promised we'd be given a greater voice in our government. We hope he may yet keep his promise."

"Can you trust him?"

"Stephen Austin doesn't think so. He went to Mexico City to petition Santa Anna, and as soon as he got there, Santa Anna imprisoned him. Kept him in jail for more than a year! He's only just released him. That, more than anything, started the hotheads like William Travis talking about Texas declaring her independence altogether from Mexico."

The more Suzannah talked, the more concerned Rebecca became. Well, she could see that she had her work cut out for her, but she was determined to get her daughter and the children safely back East, at least until the situation was calmer.

Suzannah's face brightened at the sound of approaching hooves. She went to the opening cut into the wall of the house and pushed aside the oiled paper. "Oh, Mother, here's Jonathan with the children. But oh dear, what's wrong with Matty?"

Chapter 40

REBECCA STRAIGHTENED her dress, smoothed her hair, and followed Suzannah outside. She couldn't remember when she'd been this nervous. If she'd known the children individually from birth it would have been a different matter; they would have grown up being used to her. But they were grown and she was a stranger in their midst.

The twins, Becky and Zeb, sat up front with their father on the buckboard seat, along with their dog, Monday. Zeb was a fiercely handsome lad, five years old now, with traces of his grandfather Zebulon's wild good looks. When Rebecca saw Becky, she thought she was looking at herself as a child; she had the same kind of flamboyant looks, though her hair was redder in hue.

"Guess what?" Zeb shouted as he leapt from the wagon and raced to his mother. "Matty shot a skunk but it sprayed all over him and he stinks so bad that Papa made him ride in the back. He can't sleep in the house tonight, neither."

Zeb looked up at Rebecca with his merry red-brown eyes. "Hello. You must be my grandmother. How do you do?" He bowed stiffly and very formally. "Mama taught me how. How come your hair is all gray? Are you really too old to be taught new tricks? How long are you going to stay? Papa's been wondering about that."

Suzannah put her hand to her forehead in mortification, but Rebecca laughed aloud. "I'm certainly going to stay long enough to give you a kiss!" and with that she swung him into her arms and kissed him resoundingly.

Becky came up and curtsied. "Me next."

Rebecca put Zeb down and hugged the girl, reveling in her sweet smell, the bright inquisitive look in her eyes, green flecked with gold spots that seemed to catch and reflect the light. She had had that questioning look in her own eyes, oh so long ago.

"I think you're one of the prettiest little girls that I've ever seen," Rebecca said, holding her at arm's length.

"I can sew too, and Mama's teaching me how to read. I'm ever so much faster at it than Zeb, and even Matty. Even though they're boys."

"Being intelligent doesn't have anything to do with being a boy or a girl," Rebecca said.

"Zeb says it does," Becky said.

"I think he's mistaken."

"That's why I punch him every time he teases me."

"Where's Enoch?" Suzannah asked.

"I left him with the Kelleys to give them a hand, seeing how Mary's still bedridden," Jonathan said.

Rebecca started toward the wagon, where Matty still sat.

"Best not come too close," Jonathan warned. "If any of that musk gets on you, you'll wind up smelling like him."

"Hi, Grandma, hi to you!" Matty called, waving furiously at her. "Oh, I forgot," he said, then jumped up in the wagon, bowed low, then sat down again. "I'm sorry I got stunk up so bad, so would you please save my kiss for later? Tomorrow maybe. But I got that rascal, shot him dead! Isn't that right, Papa? He was raiding the Kelleys' chicken coop. Didn't I get him, Papa?"

"That you did, son, but you forgot to stay away from him like I told you."

"I was going to give the pelt to you, Grandma, for a Christmas present. But before he died, that mean old thing upped and squirted me all over."

He pronounced *thing* with a long *a* sound—*thang*—and why that should have tickled Rebecca she didn't know.

Jonathan went to the barn, got a shovel, and began to dig a shallow pit behind the house. "Suzannah, boil some water."

"Oh, dear, what are you going to do?" Rebecca asked.

"Bury him for a couple of hours. This is good rich earth, it'll leach the smell right out of him."

"Bury him?" she repeated. "That's barbaric. Isn't there any other way?"

"Nothing as fast. Don't worry, it won't harm him none. And he'll never forget the lesson." Jonathan finished digging and called, "Okay, Matty, out of your clothes." He took the kettle of water from Suzannah and poured it into the hole, stirring it up into a rich thick mud.

Rebecca watched as her grandson stripped off his overalls and stood naked in the afternoon sun. As she looked at the lithe body, saw his look of resignation and fear, she lost her heart to him completely. He hunkered down into the hole, and Jonathan shoveled the mud over him.

"Matty's getting buried!" Zeb chanted, dancing around the pit in a circle, while Monday chased him.

"It's not so bad, Papa," Matty said. "It's nice and warm."

Becky plaited some daisies into a wreath, put it on a long stick, and tried to crown Matty with the flowers, while Zeb raced around his brother with war whoops, throwing small pine cones at his head.

"I'll lick you for that, Zeb, just you wait," Matty called.

Jonathan looked sternly at his youngest son. "You have chores to do instead of deviling your brother, don't you?"

Zeb stopped dead in his tracks. "Yes sir." Then he took Becky by the hand, and they dashed into the barn. Rebecca sat as close to Matty as she dared, though when the wind shifted there were still strong traces of the odor.

She listened as Matty told her everything about Texas, the canyon draws where he and his father went to trap and capture wild horses, how he'd gone on round-up this past summer, and brought in the heads of steer, and how he'd soon learn how to put the Albright brand on their cattle. "Coming back here, we saw Indians watching and trailing us as we rode from the Kelleys'. Papa said they were Comanches, and that we'd best keep a wary eye out for them."

As Rebecca listened, she couldn't quite believe that Matty was six, the twins five, and yet they shouldered the responsibility of adults. Was there any time for childhood on the frontier? she wondered.

A few hours later, Jonathan dug up his son, plunked him in a barrel of hot soapy water, scrubbed him with carbolic soap—and then, when he was finished, rubbed down the boy's body with sage and sassafrass. "Good as new," Jonathan said.

"Thanks, Papa," Matty said, and hugged him fiercely. He seemed to do everything with that same passion and he turned to Rebecca. "I'm ready for my kiss now."

He threw himself at her and hugged her, and if Rebecca had any doubts about loving these children, they fled completely with his hug.

By some sleight of hand Suzannah had prepared dinner, and

everybody sat down at table—Jonathan, the children, Suzannah, Rebecca, and Patrick Donohoe. Suzannah said grace, and then everybody fell to eating. Potatoes that had been baked in the hearth, squash from Suzannah's garden, and a huge slab of beef that Suzannah had earlier cured and smoked, and now had broiled over the hearth coals.

After dinner, the children helped Suzannah clear the table and wash the dishes. Jonathan busied himself with barnyard chores, oiling and repairing traces. Then Suzannah read to the children from the Bible, teaching them words whenever she could.

Two hours after twilight, the children were already yawning, their eyes heavy with sleep. Jonathan had built the children their own room; Becky's part was separated by a cloth curtain, which now stood open.

Rebecca came in to say goodnight, and Matty said, "Grandma, tell us a story."

"Which one would you like to hear?" Rebecca asked.

"Tell us about Davy Crockett, who can lick his weight in alligators," Zeb said.

"No, tell us about Washington," Becky piped. "Mama says you know all the Presidents and go to the White House all the time. I'd like to see it someday."

"So you shall," Rebecca said. "All right then, here's the story about Washington. Once upon a time—oh, not so very long ago—the people in the government decided that they needed a new place for the capital of the country. The Northern states wanted the capital to remain in Philadelphia, which was a big and civilized city, but the South wanted the new capital to be located somewhere in its territory. So they compromised and put aside some land taken from Maryland and Virginia, which lay halfway between the North and the South."

By the time Rebecca had gotten to the laying of the cornerstone of the White House on October 13, 1792, "that date chosen because it was the three-hundredth anniversary of the discovery of America by Columbus," the children were fast asleep.

Rebecca bedded down on a pallet on Becky's side of the room. Suzannah had wanted to give her the main bedroom, but Rebecca refused. She woke up a number of times during the night, thought of the grandchildren, and hugged herself with happiness.

• • •

The days passed with a swiftness that Rebecca couldn't believe. From dawn to dusk, everybody seemed to find chores: stray cattle to be hunted for; the cow to be milked; butter to be churned; the soil in the garden to be broken up and fertilized; repairs to be made around the house. Already Becky sat at the spinning wheel and carded fiber to be made into homespun cloth.

Matty would always finish with his chores first, then he would beg to be allowed to take Grandma on a tour of their ranch. Off they would go to the cottonwoods lining the riverbank to catch some trout for supper, or they'd climb the hill just north of the ranch so that they could watch the sky on fire at sunset.

There were times when Rebecca became so enamored of this boy so full of life that she wanted to hug him. Well-formed and wiry, with dark hair that seemed to have just the right amount of curl to it, and a pug nose.

"Mother, I think Matty is exhausting you," Suzannah cautioned her.

"I know I'm doing things—*thangs*," she corrected herself, "that a woman my age shouldn't do, but I don't care," Rebecca said. "Tomorrow I'm riding out to the pond to see the badger, and if I'm lucky enough, Matty's going to teach me the difference between just an ol' bull snake and a diamondback!"

"Well, it is winter, so you'll probably not see too many diamondbacks. But if you hear a whirring noise, make sure you stay away. Don't forget to take Monday with you. She keeps our house clear of snakes."

"You've no fear about anything that the children do?" Rebecca asked.

"I did for the first year or so," Suzannah admitted. "Then I realized that my fear came from a lack of faith. Oh, they fall, and cut themselves, and get into mischief, and sometimes get hurt, but they've never been sick a day of their lives, other than the childhood ailments that everybody gets. And Jonathan has taught them how to take care of themselves, which is perhaps the greatest virtue of all. Why, I'd sooner be out in the wilderness with Matty than with a grown easterner."

"I suppose you're right," Rebecca sighed. "It's just that I was brought up so differently, with so many don'ts in my life."

"So was I," Suzannah said with a generous smile.

Rebecca laughed also. "Well, I can't pass the time of day with you any longer, Mrs. Albright; I've got to go riding with the best scout west of the Sabine River."

They took two of the horses from the corral; Patrick helped them saddle up.

"Why can't I go too?" Zeb complained as Rebecca and Matty rode off.

"Because you didn't finish your chores," Suzannah said. "If you finish them early tomorrow, then you can go along." Suzannah put her arm around Becky's shoulder. "I know you'd like to go also, but we've got so much to do to get dinner on the table. Maybe Matty will fill in for you tomorrow."

Becky chewed her lip, and didn't say anything.

Rebecca and Matty rode side by side for a bit. "I gave you the mare, Grandma," Matty said, "because she's the gentle one, and Papa said you might have glass bones."

"Oh he did, did he!" Rebecca exclaimed. "Well, I'll have you know that my bones are just as good as anybody's."

She increased her gait, and the mare responded. They came upon a small village of prairie dogs, and the whole town of the endearing creatures seemed to be out sunning themselves. At the sight of Rebecca and Matty, a few of the lookouts began to bark, their tails twitching furiously, and they dove back into their holes.

"Stay very still, Grandma, and they'll come out again, just watch," Matty told her. They did, and minutes later, a head popped out of a burrow, then another, and soon they were sunning themselves again. Two of them met on a mound, rubbed noses, and kissed, then stood there chattering, their arms around each other.

Suddenly a gray blur came racing out of nowhere, a coyote intent on a kill. The streaking animal spooked Matty's horse, and he bolted. Taken by surprise, Matty lost his reins, and dug his fists into the stallion's mane, hanging on for life.

Rebecca took off after him, whipping her mare. Matty's horse took the ditches and gullies and Rebecca followed, riding as she'd never ridden before, her only thought to catch the stallion before he stumbled and fell, or threw Matty. Gradually, she gained on the stallion. She leapt a small arroyo and managed to cut him off.

"Hold on, just hold on!" she shouted to Matty. Then she was within an arm's length of the dangling reins, and the

thundering hooves pounded the chant, "Catch him, catch him."
She reached down and grabbed for them, but missed the first
time. On her second try she snagged the dangling horsehide
and with a furious yank brought the animal up.

The stallion slowed, and Matty slid down out of the saddle.
Rebecca got off her mare also and clutched the boy to her,
feeling the quick beat of his heart against hers.

"Gee, Grandma, why didn't you tell me you could ride like
that? If I knew, I'd have given you the stallion. You could
have had more fun."

At last she managed to say, "I feel like walking a little. It's
not so far back to the ranch, is it?"

"Less than a mile," Matty said happily. "Thanks for catching
my runaway. Wait till I tell Papa how you can ride!"

"It might be better if you didn't mention any of this to your
father. Or your mother. Let's just keep it our secret."

"Okay, if that's what you want. I won't say a thing, my
word of honor." As they started back, Matty took her hand and
swung it to and fro in a long arc. "I like you a whole lot better
than I expected. Papa was anxious because he thought you
might be wearing your iron corset." He looked at her from
under his eyelids. "Are you?"

"That's just an expression," she said, feeling her cheeks
burning.

"Oh," he said, sounding a little disappointed. "Anyway,
Mama said you would be just fine, and Mama was the righter
this time."

Walking at a slow, steady pace, Rebecca gradually regained
her composure. What if something had happened to Matty just
now? She couldn't bear to think of that, for the boy had carved
a place in her heart that she hadn't even known existed.

"Grandma, I decided that I love you. Will you stay with us
forever?"

"I'll stay as long as I possibly can. You could always come
and visit me in Washington, couldn't you? Would you like
that?"

"I'd like it just fine. But I'd have to get all my chores done
for a month first."

When they got home, Matty kept true to his word and didn't
say anything about his runaway.

At dinner that night, Becky announced over the apple pie,
"As soon as I'm old enough, I'm going to Washington to live

with Grandma. And I'm going to be the first of the Brand women to go to college, and I'm not going to have to wash dishes or loom homespun anymore."

"Then I'm going too," Zeb blurted.

"I see you've been filling the children's heads with tales," Jonathan said mildly.

"Nothing that isn't a possibility," Rebecca replied.

"The way I look at it, there's no place like the frontier for learning the true values of life," Jonathan said. "Here's where a person can learn to depend on *himself*, without a lot of fancy book-learning."

"I see no reason why a person can't have both," Rebecca said.

Seeing that this was about to erupt into an argument, Suzannah interrupted. "Oh, stop, the two of you. The children have plenty of time to make up their minds about the course of their lives. Jonathan, I hope by that time you and I will have enough sense to let them decide for themselves. That goes for you too, Mother."

Suzannah rarely said or did anything to contradict her husband, but when she spoke her mind, Jonathan listened. He'd learned that behind her gentle manner was a backbone of steel. What's more, she was usually right.

After dinner, Rebecca went out to the front porch and joined Jonathan, where he sat bundled in his sheepskin coat, puffing on a corncob pipe. "I'm sorry if I said anything to offend you about the children," she began.

"I don't know what it is between us, Mrs. Brand, but whenever we're together, I'm reminded of a blacksmith's anvil and hammer."

"To begin with, you could stop calling me Mrs. Brand. We are family, you know."

"I only knew but one mother in my life, and that was Rachel Jackson. So, if it's all the same to you, Mrs. Brand will do me just fine. And no offense meant."

Rebecca bit her lip. "As you like. I just wanted to tell you that I think your children are extraordinary. Bright and just bursting with energy and life. So obviously you've done a wonderful job raising them. But I do hope that when the time comes and they're ready to step out on their own, you'll encourage them."

He turned from her and looked to the distant hills whose purple outline was being dissolved by the encroaching night.

"I'm building a life out here for Suzannah and me. We're doing it by the sweat of our brow. I hope it's the kind of good life that my children will want to choose. But like Suzannah says, time enough for them to decide when they're ready."

She'd hurt him, that much she could see, and she searched for some way to make it better. But she shrugged hopelessly at the impasse that existed between them—one, she feared, that would remain between them for the rest of their lives.

As adroitly as possible, she changed the subject. "Jonathan, no one must know this, but I'm here on an unofficial mission for President Jackson."

He looked at her in surprise. "You?"

"Why not?"

"Well, it's just that . . ."

"That I'm a woman, isn't that right?"

"Yes, in part."

"President Jackson knew I was coming anyway, and asked me to find out everything I could about the situation here. You know that his dream is to annex the Texas territory."

"It's my dream also. I'd rather have my children living under the American flag than depending on the whim of that dictator in Mexico City."

"But if Santa Anna marches on Texas, what then?"

"Oh, he'll march all right," Jonathan said. "The only question is when he'll do it. And where we make our stand."

"Is there no way to prevent war from breaking out? Settle things peacefully with Santa Anna?"

"I wish there was. No man with any sense likes war. But Santa Anna isn't to be trusted. Says one thing, then changes his mind whenever it suits him. We've got to be ready for any eventuality."

"And are you?"

"Not yet, we aren't. Mrs. Brand, I know you think I've been avoiding you during your visit here, but that isn't so. The reason I've been gone so much is because I've been riding to Goliad, and Gonzales, and San Antonio, scouting for Sam Houston. Trying to learn what I can from our people and from our Mexican friends. There's a lot of them who distrust Santa Anna just as much as we do."

"Would they side with you if it came down to that?"

"Many would. One of our biggest headaches right now is the Comanches. Every time the Mexicans make a move toward us, the Comanches try to take advantage of it. Matter of fact,

Sam Houston's been planning for a long time to ride out against them, settle things once and for all, so that if war with Mexico does come, we'll have one less enemy to worry about."

"Would you be going with Houston?"

"Most likely."

"You'd be leaving Suzannah and the children alone, then?"

"I don't like to, but there's no other way. I've scouted for Sam Houston before—why, I was with him and General Jackson when we fought the Creeks at Horseshoe Bend. Every man's got to do his share to get rid of the menace. I've already talked it over with Suzannah, and she understands. Besides, Enoch will be with her, and so will Patrick Donohoe. He's agreed to stay on at the ranch until I get back."

Rebecca didn't like the sound of that, but after what had happened this evening, she didn't want to run the risk of angering Jonathan further. "Does anybody have an overall plan for Texas? Something that I can take back to President Jackson?"

"I can't say that there is an overall plan. We should get our convention going fairly soon, to set up a provisional government. Delegates are waiting for the word right now. But tell General Jackson that we've got some good men leading us. Of course, he knows Sam Houston and trusts his military judgment. Stephen Austin is basically a peaceable man, but ever since he was thrown in jail by Santa Anna, that's changed; he led our men against General Perfecto Cos at San Antonio. Then we've got a couple of bad apples, like Colonel Fannin, who heads up our forces at Goliad. Fannin's got the blood of a turtle—slow to make up his mind, slow to move. He's got all the trappings of a military man, and none of the backbone. The sooner Houston gets rid of him, the better."

"What about this Jim Bowie I hear so much about?"

"There's a man who's bigger than life. Bowie knows the country, knows the Mexican mentality. He married a Spanish girl and had a fine family, but he hasn't been the same since they all died of cholera back in 1833."

"That must have been the same epidemic that struck Washington and moved on to decimate the rest of the country."

"We heard tell that the plague was coming," he said. "But once it got here, there was nothing to do but ride it out. The Kelleys lost one of their children, but the good Lord must have been watching over us, because it never touched our ranch.

But it wiped out Bowie's family completely, his wife and both his children."

"How awful."

"And he's still grieving. So much so that it hurts to look at him. Oh, he tries to hide it—lots of drinking, carousing, and brawling—but it's all to cover up his pain. Sometimes when I look in those gray eyes of his, I wonder where he gets the strength to go on."

"I know what you mean," Rebecca murmured.

"Bowie's in San Antonio right now. Arrived there yesterday, and sent a messenger here to tell me. You were out riding with Matty when he came. He's carrying orders for me from Sam Houston."

"Is there any chance that I could meet Jim Bowie? Get the measure of the man? If I ever write about your cause, the cause for Texas, it would help enormously."

Jonathan stroked his chin. "You must know how unusual it is for a woman . . ."

"Suppose you told Bowie that I came directly from President Jackson?"

"He might just do it then. You see, Old Hickory is one of his heroes. Look, I've got to ride into San Antonio tomorrow, see what Bowie's got to say for himself, and get my own orders. You might think of riding with me."

"I'll be ready at dawn."

Chapter 41

IN THE middle of the night, Rebecca's sleep was disturbed by the sound of repeated coughing. She tried to make out who it was, but couldn't, and when the coughing stopped, she drifted off to sleep again. Hours later, when she saw the first hint of dawn, she roused herself quietly so as not to waken anybody, only to find that she was the last one up.

Suzannah and Becky already had breakfast on the table—sizzling bacon and freshly gathered eggs, both scrambled and poached. Matty had milked the cow, and came in with a pailful, and Zeb stumbled through the door, his arms loaded with firewood.

At the table, Rebecca asked, "Who's catching cold?" The children shook their heads in turn. "Patrick, was it you in the barn? I did hear somebody coughing last night."

Then Matty burst out laughing. "Grandma, that was the panther you heard." Zeb and Becky joined in the laughter.

Jonathan said between sips of coffee. "The cat was a ways off, maybe half a mile or a mile. But at night, sounds carry on the prairie."

"Oh, my nerves!" Rebecca exclaimed. "A panther that close? Isn't that dangerous?"

Jonathan nodded. "He's raiding livestock, so he must be too old to hunt his natural prey. The ranchers around here have been after him for months. He's a smart, slippery cat, but we'll get him."

Breakfast was hearty and filling, and Rebecca's usual sour mood at this early hour gave way before the children's cheerful chattering. No question about it, she thought, being around young people made you see the world through their eyes, and that in turn made you feel younger.

The sun had fully risen when Rebecca and Jonathan set out, the children's shouted goodbyes echoing in their ears. The morning was cold, overcast and gray, muting the landscape's subtle shades of brown and mauve, and the blue-grays and greens of the evergreens. As far as Rebecca could see lay rolling hills, cut through with streams and lakes, all hinting at the fertility of the land.

"It's very different country from what I'm accustomed to," she said to Jonathan. "The Chesapeake area is such a wonderful marriage of land and water. But this endless prairie with its rolling knolls is very beautiful in its own right."

"The first time I ever saw this land, I got the feeling that I'd lived here before...that if I looked over my shoulder I would see my past, and if I looked straight ahead, then there was my future," Jonathan said softly.

She glanced at him; this glimpse into a gentler side of his nature had taken her by surprise.

"I know you think this is a hard life for Suzannah and the children, Mrs. Brand. But I believe that you get out of something whatever you put into it, and by dint of their daily labors, Suzannah and the children own this land."

"Providing General Santa Anna permits it. What if he should march? What would you do with Suzannah and the children?"

"Move them to safety, of course."

"Then why not let them come to Washington with me? I plan to leave sometime in mid-February. Don't concern yourself with their passage. I'll take care of that, and gladly."

He set his jaw and said, "It's not their passage I'm thinking of. Just suppose that when trouble came, every family decided to leave. Wouldn't Santa Anna deserve to conquer this land?"

"But this is their safety," she interrupted.

"Mrs. Brand, just a minute. Suzannah's been telling me a lot about you, I guess hoping that if we knew each other better, we might be friends. She told me that when the British invaded Washington and put it to the torch, you refused to leave. Not only that, but you stood on the roof of your house dousing the sparks flying your way from the burning White House. Well, if you were ready to do that to save your home, can't you understand that we're ready to do the same thing to save ours?"

Unable to find any effective answer to that, Rebecca shrugged hopelessly, and they continued their trip in silence.

They reached San Antonio in midafternoon. Mexicans wearing bright-colored serapes and large straw hats moved slowly along the narrow streets. Everything appeared unhurried, as if the entire pale-adobe town hung suspended in some sort of a dream. Even the river that looped around the town appeared sluggish. The square, ponderous San Fernando Cathedral with its squat steeple dominated the main plaza. Several peons lounged against the church's sun-warmed wall listening to a guitarist strumming a haunting Spanish melody. Only the bullet pocks in the buildings' walls gave mute evidence of the battle that had recently been fought here between Mexico's General Perfecto Cos and Stephen Austin's Texans.

After taking Rebecca on a brief tour of the town, Jonathan doubled back east about a half mile to the Alamo Mission. It was a large rectangular complex consisting of a roofless adobe church, abutted by low one-story outbuildings which long ago had housed the mission's monks, but which now quartered one hundred and fifty Texans.

Some of the men were fresh-faced recruits who'd journeyed from all over the United States to heed the Texas cry for freedom; some were hardened, leathery-looking ranchers, anxious to hold on to their newly won victory. Looking at them, Rebecca remembered the long-ago days of the battle for Washington . . . the bombing of Fort McHenry—and fires long banked in her rekindled. Jonathan took her across the enclosed grounds to the west side of the complex. The buildings comprising the west wall housed the artillery command post, the officers' quarters, and Bowie's headquarters.

When they entered the low-beamed room, Bowie's face opened in a smile. He embraced Jonathan, clapping him on the back. Rebecca could literally feel their intense comaraderie, the common goal that bound these two men.

"This is my mother-in-law," Jonathan said.

Bowie gallantly bowed, brought her a chair, inquired if she wanted anything—wine, food, fruit. Rebecca declined, but all the while observed the man. Bowie was so tall and raw-boned that he seemed to fill the room. But it was more than mere physical presence; his energy and the force of his personality dominated everything. She found him quite good-looking, with sandy hair and gray eyes that turned to gunmetal when he gave orders to the men who continually came into the room, seeking his advice. Yet once past the surface handsomeness, Rebecca couldn't get over the feeling of sadness that seemed to underly his nature.

When she explained why President Jackson had asked her to be alert to the problems in Texas, Bowie acted surprised. "I didn't know they had women writing for newspapers."

"Oh yes, more and more," she said, smiling.

"How long will you be staying with us, Mrs. Brand?"

"Perhaps another month, providing I don't wear out my welcome." She smiled lavishly at Jonathan. "Who knows? In that time, I might even be able to learn some new tricks."

Jonathan turned red to the roots of his hair, but when she laughed good-naturedly, he burst out laughing also. "That ought to teach me never to say anything in front of the kids."

"You must let us enterain you, then," Bowie said to her. "Though we're on the edge of the frontier, some of us still remember how to treat a lady."

"That's very generous of you. I will be going through San Antonio again when I leave."

Bowie looked at her quizzically, since a normal journey back to the United States wouldn't have taken her by this route.

Rebecca said, "I plan to catch the English schooner at Corpus Christi; I understand that one docks there every month."

"But that's going right into the heart of territory still controlled by Mexicans," Bowie told her.

Rebecca then told him the special nature of her mission for Andrew Jackson. When she finished, she swore him to secrecy; the fewer people who knew her plans, the greater the possibility of their success. She had every confidence that this man would keep her secret.

From where she sat in the room, Rebecca could see the area that had become the parade grounds of the mission encampment. As she watched the men going about their duties, and others drilling, she noticed a rider mount up and canter toward the main gate. She started to her feet and ran to the window, straining for a better look at him. Something about the way this man carried himself . . .

"Jonathan, come quickly!"

But by the time Jonathan reached the window, the rider was out of the gate and lost to sight. "Who was it?" he asked.

"I don't know. I thought I recognized something familiar about him." She turned to Bowie. "The man who just rode out of here. Youngish, in his late twenties, I'd say. Could you tell me who he is?"

"That's a little difficult, Mrs. Brand. There are about a

hundred and fifty men here, and since I only got here a few days ago, I hardly know them all. Could you be a little more specific?"

"Well, this man might have had a crippled arm."

Bowie shook his head slowly. "I can tell you there's nobody like that in my outfit. First thing I did when I arrived was to check on the men's fitness. Outside of a drinker or two, they're all in sound shape."

"Perhaps this was somebody from San Antonio?" she said.

"That could be; there's a lot of coming and going between the town and here. Wait a minute, I did meet a seminarian who's doing a tour of the local shrines in the area. Now his arm was broken, had it tied up in a sling. Said he fell off his horse."

"Did he have an English accent?"

"Well, Southern accents and English accents can be pretty close, especially when you mix them with all the other accents we've got floating around here."

"Do you remember his name?"

"David Carrington, I think it was. Yes, that's it, because he said that the Carringtons were from a long line of preachers."

Jonathan touched Rebecca's arm. "You thought it was Devroe Connaught, didn't you?"

She shook her head slowly. "It was a trick of the sun in my eyes. I left Devroe Connaught back in Washington. I'm sorry, forgive me for interrupting."

Jonathan turned to Bowie. "What's the news from Sam Houston?"

"Jonathan, he wants you to go to Washington-on-the-Brazos as soon as possible. The convention's gotten underway, and he needs you as a spokesman for this part of the country."

"Well, I've been expecting that, and putting it off as long as possible. I don't cotton much to politics. What about the Alamo?"

Bowie strode to the window and looked out at the complex. "Houston said that when I got here, I should blow the place up. So that if Santa Anna does come this way, he wouldn't be able to use it."

"Good idea. When are you going to do it?"

"I thought at the end of this week. Then I'd pull our men here back to Gonzales. But now that I've seen the place, I'm not so sure."

"What do you mean?" Jonathan asked.

"More and more, I get the feeling that maybe we should make a stand, defend the place. Jonathan, you know as well as I do that San Antonio's the key, the gateway to all of Texas."

Jonathan bounded to his feet. "You mean you're going to disregard Houston's direct orders?"

"Take it easy, Jonathan. I'm not saying I won't follow his orders, and I'm not saying I will, but I've got a feeling that Houston's wrong on this one. If Santa Anna sweeps through San Antonio, then there's no natural barrier or fortification to stop him between here and the Louisiana border. Every man in Texas will tuck his tail between his legs and run. But if I can show the rest of the territory that we can stand up to Santa Anna, hold him at bay, maybe even win, then all of Texas will know that he isn't invincible. They'll take heart, and—who knows?—maybe even make a nation out of this place. You see, Jonathan, I believe there's a whole lot more at stake at the Alamo than military strategy."

"You know what you're saying, don't you? When Santa Anna does come, he'll come with an army. If you do decide to make a stand and help doesn't arrive..."

"But help will arrive," Bowie said. "Santa Anna probably won't move his troops until spring. By that time, you politicians will have ironed out our new constitution. Houston will have raised an army, and the Alamo will be our first line of defense."

"That's all fine, providing Santa Anna sticks to your time-table," Jonathan said. "Suppose he doesn't?"

Bowie shrugged, and for an instant, Rebecca saw the weariness in the droop of his shoulders. Then he straightened and said, "That's why every man is here of his own free will. Nobody's been ordered to stay. You don't get a decent fighting force that way. Men have got to believe in what they're fighting for in order to win. So I've given every man the right to leave whenever he wants, no questions asked. I understand that Lieutenant Colonel William Travis is due to arrive soon with a few hundred men, and once he gets here, I'll have a better idea of what I'm going to do."

"Houston doesn't even realize that you're considering defending the Alamo, does he?" Jonathan asked softly.

"Not yet, but I expect you'll tell him when you get to Washington-on-the-Brazos."

"That's your final word on it?"

"Like I said, I haven't made up my mind, but that's the way I'm inclining."

Rebecca realized that once this man did decide on a course of action, nothing short of death could stop him.

"Jim, I think you're wrong," Jonathan said. "But I've always admired your courage and I admire it now. If you're thinking of staying, then I'm for staying here also and helping you."

Jim Bowie grinned and grasped Jonathan's shoulders. "Thanks. But Houston would really skin me alive if I kept you here. Especially since he's talking about going after the Comanches once and for all. I'm sorry to lose a good man like you, Jonathan, but you've worked with Houston before, you know each others' minds, and I guess you're needed more there."

Then Bowie gripped Jonathan's hand hard. "Spread the word. Tell everybody that if we do decide to make a stand, we'll need all the help we can get. I'll send couriers to let you know how things develop."

Jonathan and Rebecca walked out into the weak sunshine of late afternoon and saw details of men busily trying to repair the crumbling outer walls of the mission.

"I would say that Mr. Bowie's pretty much made up his mind, wouldn't you?" Rebecca asked.

Jonathan nodded.

"It looks so vulnerable. Do you think they can defend it?"

"Let's hope there won't be a need. Bowie's right in thinking that if we don't stop Santa Anna somewhere, he'll sweep clear across Texas. But I don't think the Alamo is the place. We beat Perfecto Cos because we had him bottled up in the town while our men had all the mobility. If the situation's reversed, especially with Bowie's small force, then Santa Anna stands every chance of beating us."

"You think Bowie realizes that?"

"He's too smart not to."

"I can't get over wondering—would Bowie be doing this the same way if his wife and children were still alive?"

Jonathan reflected on that, but said nothing.

They got back to the ranch very late that night, but Suzannah was up and waiting for them. Patrick Donohoe was sitting in front of the fireplace whittling whistles for Zeb and Becky. When he saw them come in, he rose, stretched, and excused himself. Rebecca also understood that Suzannah and Jonathan wanted to be alone, and she slipped into the room where Becky lay sleeping, curled in a sort of question mark. Rebecca pushed aside the curtain and peered at the two boys. They both lay quietly, but she noticed that Zeb's position was the mirror image of Becky's. It was uncanny—even in their sleep the twins seemed to have some sort of communion.

Jonathan and Suzannah sat before the fire, watching the logs burn down to embers, feeling the cold in the corners of the room steal toward them.

Jonathan cleared his throat. "I didn't want to say anything in front of your mother, because this is something that only you and I can decide. You know I may be gone for a time. Maybe a few weeks; it could be as long as a month. I hate it, but it's something that's got to be done."

"I know that," Suzannah said quietly.

"Well, she wants you and the children to go back to Washington with her during that time."

"Do you want me to go?"

"You'd be safer there than here."

The fire crackled and an ember popped onto the hearth. Suzannah brushed it back into the fireplace. "Jonathan, what if every woman in Texas felt that way? Why, we'd have no homeland at all."

"It would only be for a while."

"Oh darling, if anything were to happen to you . . . I wouldn't want to go on living. No, not even for the children. If I went to Washington when I could be here helping you, and something awful did happen, I'd never forgive myself."

"What if she just took the children back?"

"Then you and I would just sit here, worried to death that they were catching some Eastern disease. Jonathan, we're making a life here. Unless we do everything we can—I mean *everything*, including fighting for what we've built—then we don't deserve to keep it. I'll tell you what: I'll go to Washington if you go."

"You know that's not possible."

"Then it's not possible for me either. Come, Jonathan, let's not waste any more time talking about it when we've so little time left."

She leaned back and lay across his lap. He gazed down at her and whispered. "I think you're the most wonderful woman that God ever created. A man couldn't be more blessed than to have your love, and I consider myself the luckiest man in the world."

He bent to kiss her, tenderly and passionately all at once. The house creaked in the wind as they took off their clothes. He threw another log on the fire, and the light flared up, playing over their nakedness—her thin, pliant body made more womanly by the birth of three children; his lean, spare, muscled physique. He drew her to the bearskin rug in front of the hearth and they made love, their hands roaming over each other's body, as if desperate to imprint everything wonderful and familiar about themselves.

"A month," she whispered. "That will be like a lifetime."

One side of their bodies grew hot from the fire, but they were unmindful of that. Arms and legs twining, mouth to mouth, they became as one, their slow, deliberate motion reaffirming the years of their love, the hardships and sadnesses, the laughter and the joys. All of this they relived in each other, as they renewed and restated their eternal vow to love, and honor, and cherish. They moved faster, building to a climax so inexorable that neither could control it, and he had to bury his mouth against her shoulder to keep from crying out and waking the household.

Slowly, they returned to a place where the world gradually made itself felt again...the sighing of the wind outside, the crackle and pop of the fire. When she looked at him, she saw that he was crying.

She cupped his face in her hands. "My darling, what's the matter?"

He shook his head, "There's nothing wrong. I'm just crying for the beauty of you. After seven years...I love you more and more each day."

She smiled at him, feeling her own tears welling. "Then I ask only one thing of you."

"Anything."

"Come back to me."

Chapter 42

"WHEN WILL you be back, Papa?" Becky asked.

He picked her up and kissed her. "Soon as I can."

"Well, I don't want you to go," she said, tossing her light auburn hair.

"Me neither," Zeb said, hitting his father's leg. "Every time you go away, that means extra work for all of us."

Jonathan put Becky down, then placed his hand on Zeb's shoulder. "I know, and if it was up to me, I'd never leave. But there are things happening in this country, wonderful things that may mean a very different life for all of us, and we've got to do more than our share."

Zeb hung his head and nodded. "I understand, but I don't like it anyway."

"Now you children listen," Jonathan said, and recognizing his tone, they clustered around him. "You're to listen to your ma and do whatever she says. Matty, you're the oldest, so keep an extra careful eye out for your brother and sister. Zeb, you mind now, none of your shenanigans. I know I can count on all of you."

Jonathan kissed Suzannah, then mounted up and rode east toward San Felipe, some ninety miles away. Once there, he'd head north up the Brazos River until he joined Sam Houston at Washington-on-the-Brazos.

The family stood at the door, watching and waving until he was no more than a tiny speck. Then Suzannah said, "All right now, when Papa gets home, let's make sure that everything's done like he asked. That would be the very best present we could give him."

Deny it as she might, Rebecca felt a burden lift from her shoulders when Jonathan left. She'd come to like him, and she appreciated the effort he was making for Suzannah and the children, but she was never truly at ease around him. With him gone, nobody stood between her and the children.

These were her happiest days. Her grandchildren talked to her constantly, confiding their desires, and Rebecca listened and encouraged them. If their chores didn't get done exactly on time, was that such a crime? The days sped by, the weather as changeable as a woman's mind, and Rebecca knew a fullness in her heart that warmed and nourished her. Each of the children had such a distinct personality: Zeb could be a hellion, no doubt about it, struggling with his brother and sister for a place in the sun. Becky was by far the brightest of the three, caught somewhere between the desire to please her mother, and her boredom at the constant repetition of the household chores. Rebecca spoke to her like a confidante: "It doesn't have to be like this, Becky. The world is opening up. There are lots of different ways a woman can succeed. You could be a lawyer, go into politics, study medicine, become anything you want."

"Can I be married and happy like Mama and Papa too?"

"Of course! All you must do is find the right husband. When you're grown and ready for that part of life, why the entire world will be a different place. Whatever you do, my Becky, you mustn't settle for just being another pretty girl. Because you are pretty, very pretty, and I have a feeling that people will only see that part of you. So you've got to make them take notice that you've a great deal more."

"I will, Grandma, I promise."

Of all her grandchildren, Rebecca responded to Matty most strongly, perhaps because he presented the least problem. His expression was one of constant surprise and wonder at the world, whether he was showing her the trees heavy with honeybees down at the river, or routing out a groundhog tearing up Suzannah's vegetable patch, or helping Patrick clean out the stables. His every antic delighted Rebecca, and she found herself so beguiled that she would have given him anything he asked for. Yet he never asked, but always gave of his time and energy. At the moment his greatest interest was in everything about her and her life in Washington.

"I can't wait to meet my Uncle Bravo. I know I'm going to like him. And what about Cousin Jeremy? You say he's already helping his father with medical chores? And my Uncle Gunning's in Kansas? Maybe we could ride up there someday when there's not so much to do around here."

"We'll do it some day," she said. "That's a promise."

• • •

"Can three weeks have flown by already since Jonathan left?" Rebecca asked one day in February. "It doesn't seem possible." She was in the kitchen, helping Becky and Suzannah sweep the puncheon floor.

"It seems like yesterday and also a thousand years ago," Suzannah said. "Well, maybe he'll be back soon."

Outside, Matty and Zeb were in the corral, feeding the livestock. "Grandma, Grandma, look what I can do!" Zeb called.

Rebecca threw her woolen shawl around her shoulders and went outside.

Zeb was sitting on the split rail fence trying to lasso a yearling steer, just for practice. Matty, busy hauling some hay from the barn, called to his brother, "You better cut that out, Zeb. If Papa caught you deviling that steer, he'd tan your hide good."

Zeb paid no attention to his brother, but continued tossing the lasso. One lucky throw looped around the steer's head, and Zeb yanked hard, tightening the noose. The terrified, lowing steer began to buck and kick, pulling on the rope. Zeb hung on with all his might, but the animal yanked him from atop the fence to the ground.

Rebecca ran to the corral and opened the gate, hardly hearing Matty's shout, "No, Grandma, don't open it!" She was concerned only with getting to Zeb before the rampaging animal trampled him. Suzannah and Becky came running out of the house.

Rebecca snatched Zeb up. Other than having the wind knocked from him, he was all right.

Before Matty could shut the corral gate, the steer was out, trailing the lasso behind him. "Damnation, now look what you've done!" Matty yelled at Zeb.

Zeb started to give chase, but the steer had too much of a head start. Within moments, it disappeared into the golden prairie grass.

"It's my fault," Rebecca said. "I shouldn't have opened the gate."

"No, it's his fault," Matty exclaimed, pointing at his brother. "Papa's told him time and again not to torment the livestock, and he just won't listen."

"Well, after all, is it so serious?" Rebecca asked, trying to placate Matty. "He'll come back after a while, won't he?"

"Grandma, I'm surprised at you. If somebody put a noose

around your neck, would you come back by yourself? What if that rope gets tangled in some bushes? Why, unless we find him and free him, that steer can get stuck someplace and starve to death. Come on, Zeb, we got to go get him."

"He'll only go a little ways," Zeb said. "We'll find him sure."

"Don't you think you should wait for Patrick to help you?" Rebecca asked.

"He's out on the range with Enoch and Monday—won't be back until dark, and that crazy steer's liable to hurt himself by then."

"I'll go with you," Rebecca said.

"That's all right, Grandma, I can handle this alone," Zeb said. "Me and Matty." Then he touched his brother's sleeve, "You won't tell Papa, will you?"

"You got to promise never to do it again."

"Okay, I promise."

Matty glowered, and then said, "All right, I won't tell. Now let's hightail it after that critter."

Both boys mounted the mare and set off. Rebecca and Suzannah went back into the house. "Do you think they ought to go alone?" Rebecca asked her daughter.

"They've been out alone before," she said. "The steer will most probably run himself out after he's gone a mile or so."

"I just don't feel right about it," Rebecca said. "Why in heaven's name did I leave that gate open? I'm going after them."

"Don't get lost, Mother. And make sure they get back before dusk. The prairie is funny—all of it looks so much the same that you can lose your way without realizing it."

Rebecca saddled a horse and rode out after the boys. About fifteen minutes later she heaved a sigh of relief when she spied them in the distance, and galloped to them.

"Don't get ahead of us, Grandma," Matty called. "You're liable to mess up the trail."

Rebecca fell in behind them, marveling at how Matty and Zeb were able to follow the trail. Trampled grass, a broken twig, fresh spoor—all of these led the boys forward.

About two miles from the ranch they came to a series of gullies that slashed the terrain. They followed the trail deep into a narrow ravine, the walls of which were about fifteen feet high.

Zeb turned to look at Rebecca. "The dumb thing's gone down one of these blind draws. We'll catch him for sure now—didn't I tell you?"

The arroyo became too narrow and treacherous to risk the horses slipping and possibly breaking a leg, so they dismounted, tied both animals to a stunted mesquite bush, then pushed deeper into the ravine on foot.

"This is eerie," Rebecca said, glancing around at the shadowed arroyo. A number of varieties of cactus clung tenaciously to the rock, and Matty said, "Watch out for those spines, they can hurt."

Then they heard the steer lowing piteously.

"That's him!" Zeb said excitedly.

Matty stopped and held out his arms so that Rebecca and Zeb couldn't pass him. "Something else is here."

"What?" Zeb asked, inching closer to his brother.

"I don't know. But listen, the horses are acting up too."

Behind them, Rebecca could hear the animals whinnying. "Come on, let's get out of here," she said, feeling increasingly uncomfortable in the tight, confining space.

Just then, Matty turned a bend in the ravine and saw the steer. It was wild-eyed with fright; the trailing rope had snared between two rocks, and in trying to free itself, the animal was only pulling the noose tighter.

"That's all right, boy, it's okay," Matty called reassuringly, as he came forward, his hand extended. "We'll get you free in no time."

The steer lowed again, its eyes rolled back in panic. Matty stopped. "More than a snagged rope is scaring that steer."

A movement above him made Matty turn. He looked up and saw the panther crouched on the lip of the ravine, its long tail lashing to and fro. The big cat turned its sleek head to the side and snarled, revealing teeth at least an inch and a half long.

"Oh my God," Rebecca whispered, and at the same instant cursed her stupidity for not bringing a rifle. Her impulse was to pick up the children and flee back to the horses, but that would have meant running directly beneath the panther.

"Grandma, don't move!" Matty warned her in a whisper. "If you do, the panther will spring. Just stand dead still."

With her heart beating loud enough to burst, Rebecca did as she was told.

• • •

"Then when I get to Washington to live with Grandma, I'm going to college like she wants, and I'll be a lawyer or a doctor, or I'm not exactly sure, but I'm going to be *something,*" Becky said, as she continued to furiously shell peas.

"I think that's wonderful," Suzannah said, "providing that's what *you* really want to do. But just remember that when Grandma leaves, you can always change your mind."

"I won't change my mind," Becky said resolutely. "I—" She broke off in midsentence and stared straight ahead, her eyes fixed on some distant point. The bowl tipped in her hand and the peas fountained all over the floor.

"Becky, what's the matter?"

Becky stood still, not moving, not saying anything.

Suzannah had seen this happen too often before with Becky and Zeb not to pay it mind, and she waited anxiously.

At last, Becky's mouth began to work and she whispered, "Zeb's in trouble. They're all in trouble."

"Where?" Suzannah asked.

"I don't know, Mama."

Suzannah gripped her daughter's arms. "Are you certain?" Becky nodded and Suzannah said, "Then think, Becky, where?"

Tears started to Becky's eyes and she shook her head help-lessly. Suzannah went to the fireplace wall and took down the rifle that hung there. She also took the pistol from the dresser drawer. She started out the door and Becky cried, "Mama! Take me with you. Maybe I'll know when we get closer."

Suzannah quickly saddled the old gelding, the only horse remaining, then, lifting Becky up in front of her, she galloped off.

"Listen to me," Rebecca said urgently to Matty and Zeb. "If we stay here much longer, it's going to get dark and we'll be at that creature's mercy. I'm going to start climbing up the ravine wall. As soon as the panther comes for me, you two run as fast as you can out of here. Just keep running and don't look back."

"No!" Matty exclaimed. "Don't you know anything about panthers? He'll go after the first one who runs. Our only hope is to keep facing him down, make him back off. He's after the steer. See the way his pouch is hanging under his belly? He hasn't eaten in a few days. But he's old, and there's three of us against him, and that's our strength."

The great cat snarled, as if understanding Matty.

"Grandma, give me your shawl," Matty said.

"My shawl? What for?" she began, but Matty gestured impatiently. She took it off and handed it to him.

Matty inched forward slowly toward a candelabra cactus. It was near the cat, and as Matty came closer, the panther lashed out with its paw with lightning speed, its talons extended.

Rebecca moved to drag Matty back, but he shrugged out of her grasp. "Zeb, throw a couple of rocks at him, make him get away from the cactus."

Zeb picked up a few rocks and hurled them at the cat. The first two missed, but the third struck him on its hindquarters. The cat hissed viciously, then leapt across the arroyo. It prowled along the edge, ready to spring down on them from the other side. Then Matty looped the shawl around the cactus and began to tug at it.

"Grandma, it's too strong for me alone. Grab one end of the shawl and help me pull. Zeb, you keep throwing rocks at him, keep him off balance." Matty handed an end of the shawl to Rebecca, and with the two of them yanking at it, the brittle stalk broke at its joint and tumbled to the ground. It was about two and a half feet long, and its milky sap began to ooze from the broken end.

Matty wrapped the shawl around that end. "Papa once told me that if I ever found myself without a weapon, a stalk of cactus would keep anything away."

The spines of the cactus pierced through the shawl and needled into Matty's hands, but he set his jaw and held the cactus in front of him, brandishing it like a weapon.

The panther's growl rumbled deep in its stomach, and when it opened its jaws the roar was one of rage. It bared its fangs, the topaz eyes burned a brilliant red, and then its muscles bunched up under its hide.

"Watch out, Matty, he's going to jump!" Rebecca cried, dashing forward to take the brunt of the animal's attack.

As the panther sprang, a rifle shot cracked. The cat took the bullet in its chest, spun in the air, and landed on its feet, about two yards from Matty. In its death throes, it screamed and bit at its hide, then sprang at the boy, claws unsheathed. Matty swung the cactus and hit it on the snout just as another shot rang out and killed the beast.

Rebecca fell to her knees and clutched Matty and Zeb to her as Suzannah came into sight.

Rebecca started to talk incoherently, and Suzannah lifted her to her feet. "Mother, you can tell me about it later. It's getting dark. We need to be back at the house before nightfall."

Zeb untied the steer and led the lowing animal out of the arroyo. When they reached their horses, they mounted in silence; the family reached the ranch as night settled over the prairie.

Chapter 43

SUZANNAH SPENT the better part of an hour picking the spines out of Matty's hands. She managed to get all of them out of the right hand, but the left proved more difficult. A number of times she had to probe deeply; tears started to Matty's eyes and rolled down his cheeks, but he made no sound.

"That's about all we can do for tonight," she said, realizing that Matty couldn't stand much more. "We'll soak your hands in warm water tomorrow. If there are any spines left inside, they'll work their way out."

Because Matty found it difficult to use his hands, Zeb helped his brother undress. As he pulled off Matty's boots he said, "I'm sorry, I really am."

"That's okay, Zeb. We got that old steer back, that's the important thing."

Suzannah cut a stalk off an aloe plant, laved Matty's hands with the sap, then wrapped his hands loosely with bandages. Then she put the children to bed. When she'd gone, Matty called through the curtain to Becky's side of the room, "Thanks for coming, Becky. We'd have been in a mess of trouble if you hadn't brought Mama."

"I love you, Matty," Becky said. "You too, Zeb, and I'm not going to let anything hurt you. Now goodnight."

About half an hour later, Patrick Donohoe, Enoch, and Monday came in from the range, and they listened in stunned silence to the tale. "Damn," Patrick swore softly, "that's the story of my life. I'm never around when I'm needed."

Suzannah touched his arm lightly. "It's not your fault. How could you have known?"

Rebecca, who'd barely recovered, said to the men, "It was the most extraordinary thing I've ever seen. The boy isn't yet seven years old, yet he stood up to that panther as fearlessly as a grown man."

"Jonathan's taught the children that," Suzannah said. "To believe in themselves, and to use their good common sense."

"It would never have occurred to me to use that cactus as a weapon," Rebecca said. "Lord knows what might have happened if Matty hadn't thought of it. And thank God you came when you did."

"How did that happen?" Patrick asked.

Suzannah rubbed her eyes. "Becky and Zeb are tied together by something I really don't understand. Sometimes Zeb will start a sentence and Becky will finish it. Then there are other times when one of them will know when the other is in trouble. It's almost frightening. But I thank the Lord for giving them that gift."

"I've heard of cases where twins had that ability," Rebecca said, "but I never believed it until this day."

"What about Matty's hands? Will they be all right?" Patrick asked.

"We'll know better tomorrow," Suzannah said.

All that night, Suzannah kept a vigil at Matty's bedside; she'd doze off occasionally, but would snap awake at his slightest cry, and soothe him back to sleep. By the time dawn came, Matty's fingers were so swollen that his joints were indistinguishable.

Suzannah tried to get the remaining spines out of Matty's left hand, and when she had no luck, she asked Patrick to help. But Matty's hand was now so sensitive that every probe was an agony.

"I think we'd best leave the boy alone," Patrick said.

"Don't you worry none about your chores, Matty," Zeb said. "Becky and I are taking care of them all. You just rest your hands and get them all better."

As the day progressed, Matty began to run a low fever, and by nightfall, his entire body felt hot to the touch.

"I think he needs a doctor," Patrick said. "Somebody's got to cut those damned things out."

Suzannah nodded. "I'll hitch up the wagon tomorrow morning and take him into San Antonio. There's a doctor in town, old but reliable."

"Not that ancient man who came to help Mrs. Kelley with her baby?" Rebecca asked.

"Yes, old Dr. Hernández."

"Oh, I wish there was an American around. Wait, maybe

Jim Bowie's got somebody among his men? Suzannah, you stay at the ranch, and I'll take Matty in to San Antonio. I wouldn't know how to run things here as well as you. Everything would just fall apart."

"I can't let you go alone, Mother, not with all the rumors we've been hearing."

"I'll go with your mother," Patrick said. "Enoch can stay here to keep an eye on you and the children. I don't think we'll be gone longer than two, three days at the most."

Suzannah sighed. "I don't like it, but I must say that sounds like the best plan. All right, if Matty's not better by tomorrow morning, that's what we'll do."

The following day, Matty appeared to be worse. His eyes were glassy with fever and his entire body ached. Patrick hitched up the wagon. Suzannah laid Matty on a blanket and covered him with another.

Zeb watched wide-eyed, so upset that he could barely hold back his tears. When Patrick and Rebecca rode off, he ran alongside the wagon until they reached the first rise of hills, then he just stood and waved.

Patrick kept the horse to a slow, steady gait to prevent Matty from being bumped around; consequently, they didn't reach San Antonio until late afternoon.

"I think we should stop off at the Mission first," Rebecca told Patrick. "See if Jim Bowie does have an American doctor among his men. If not, he may know of a better doctor than Hernández."

When she and Patrick reached the Alamo, she was impressed with how much progress had been made in fortifying the mission. The gaps in the walls had been filled in with rubble and bramble, and gun emplacements had been fitted on top of the walls, including one for the eighteen-pound cannon at the southwest corner.

When Rebecca finally located Bowie, she was appalled at his appearance.

"I know," he said, seeing her shocked expression. "I've been ill for the past two weeks—some sort of walking pneumonia, I think."

Rebecca explained her problem, and Bowie said, "The best doctor in town is Enrico Hernández. Fact is, he's the *only* doctor in town. I'm sure he'll help the boy."

"You'd do well to see the doctor yourself," she said.

"He'd only tell me what he's told me before, to get some rest."

"It looks to me like you should be in bed."

"There's no time for that now, not with everything going on here."

At that moment, a tall, well-built man in his late twenties came into the room and Jim Bowie introduced him. "This is Lieutenant Colonel William Travis. He arrived with reinforcements the first week in February. Not as many men as I would have liked, but that's when I decided to defend the Alamo."

"Any news of Santa Anna?" Rebecca asked.

"Just the usual inconclusive rumors," Travis said.

"Nevertheless, Mrs. Brand, I wouldn't hang around San Antonio unnecessarily," Bowie said.

"Just don't believe anything that the Mexicans in town tell you," Travis said. "We have our own lookouts posted everywhere, and they've seen nothing."

William Travis was a native South Carolinian, and though his manner was typically southern, gracious and courtly, Rebecca took an immediate dislike to him. She knew her reaction was unreasonable on such short acquaintance, but she bristled at his air of self-importance.

"Oh, Mrs. Brand," Jim Bowie began, then had to stop in the midst of a fit of coughing. "Davy Crockett and a dozen of his Tennessee volunteers arrived also. Mighty welcome they were, too."

"Davy Crockett?" Rebecca said in surprise. "Really, that man has a knack of turning up in the most unusual places."

"I knew he'd spent some time in Washington, so I mentioned your name, and he said he knew you."

"Yes, we met during the time he served in Congress. Look, gentlemen, as soon as I've taken my grandson to the doctor, I'd like to come back and talk to both of you, and to Mr. Crockett, if possible."

"As pleasant as that sounds, I doubt I can spare the time," Travis said.

Rebecca stiffened inwardly, but tried to keep the peace. "What happens here is of the utmost importance to President Jackson and to the people of the United States."

"Then they should send men and munitions," Travis said. "Nothing less will do." He bowed and excused himself.

"That's a difficult young man," Rebecca said to Bowie.

"Don't mind him. He's just wangled a lieutenant colonelcy from the governor, but he wanted to be a general, so his nose is out of joint."

Rebecca took her leave, then she and Patrick rode the half-mile to town and found Dr. Hernández's house just off the main plaza.

Dr. Hernández, in his late seventies, moved with infuriating slowness, but to Rebecca's relief, his manner was full of concern. "How long have the boy's hands been this way?" he asked.

"Two days," Matty spoke up, his voice slurred with fever.

"The spines in the left hand will have to be cut out," Hernández said. "Where are you staying?"

"I haven't made any arrangements yet," Rebecca said.

"Well, you won't have trouble finding a room in San Antonio," Hernández said. "Everybody is leaving. General Santa Anna is on his way here."

"What? Are you sure?" Rebecca demanded.

"Certain. He crossed the Rio Grande—oh, a week ago. We warned all you Americans at the mission, but," he lifted his shoulders wearily, "nobody will believe us."

"I'd heard rumors about Santa Anna," Rebecca began, "but not that he was expected imminently. Why didn't Bowie or Travis say something?"

"Because they prefer to think it's some kind of Spanish trick meant to get you out of here to avoid battle," Hernández said. "Well, my maid and her children have fled, so you can have their room if you like."

"That's very kind of you. It will make it so much easier if we don't have to carry my grandson around."

Rebecca took Matty into the small, neat adobe room, made him comfortable, then rejoined Hernández. "Just how serious are Matty's wounds?"

"Serious enough. If you'd let them go any longer, blood poisoning would have set in. He could have lost the hand, or if the poison traveled into the blood . . ."

Rebecca felt a sinking sensation in the pit of her stomach. "But you can cure him?" she asked quickly.

"Everything with the help of God," Hernández said. "Soak his hand in cold water for as long as possible. It will hurt at first, but then it will go numb. There must be as little swelling as possible so I can see to operate. Once the foreign matter is out of his body, the fever will drop and he'll be fine."

Rebecca followed the doctor's instructions. The following morning, he operated. One of the spines had worked its way deep into the fleshy part of Matty's palm, and Patrick held Matty's wrist firmly when Hernández cut. Rebecca couldn't help but notice that old Dr. Hernández's hand had a distinct tremor, and she wished that Wingate were here.

But at last, Hernández extracted the final spine, a nasty-looking barb more than an inch long. Matty pressed his bloody palm with his fingers and a smile broke out on his face. "It's still sore, Grandma, but nothing like the way it hurt before."

Patrick ruffled Matty's hair. "You did good, boy, I couldn't have been as brave."

They made Matty comfortable in the small room. Then Patrick said, "Mrs. Brand, if it's all the same to you, I think I'll ride back to the Alamo and give our men there a hand. Looks like they can use all the help they can get."

"Can I go, too?" Matty said excitedly.

"No you cannot, young man," Rebecca said sternly. "You're still running a fever, and the doctor said you're to stay in bed. Patrick, when will you be back?"

"Soon as it gets dark. Wouldn't feel right leaving you and Matty alone at night."

"Thank you, Patrick. All right, then, we'll see you later."

Matty fell asleep and Rebecca began to write in her journal, making as detailed an account of the Alamo and San Antonio as she could remember. Several hours later, there was a knock on the door and Rebecca opened it to see the giant form of Davy Crockett filling the doorway. At the sight of her, he took off his coonskin cap and tossed it into the air. It landed on Matty's bed and woke him.

"Rebecca Breech Brand—I'd have wrassled a passle of alligators just to see your smiling face again!" He lifted her in the air and whirled her around. Matty watched with awe; his grandmother knew the famous Davy Crockett!

Rebecca had always considered Crockett a man of good intentions but also something of a naïve buffoon. But at this moment she was delighted to see him.

Crockett's fame was legendary. He was the greatest marksman of his day and his bravery was unquestioned; the tales surrounding him were as colorful as the man himself. All this had gotten him elected as a Congressman from Tennessee. His

behavior at first amused most of Washington. He'd quickly
established himself as an anti-Jackson man, and was taken up
by the Whigs, notably Henry Clay. When he'd lost his bid for
reelection, he was instantly dropped by the Whigs, and Crockett
said, "To hell with Washington, I'm going to Texas!" Rebecca
hadn't seen him since the January day in 1835 when the deranged Richard Lawrence had attempted to assassinate President
Jackson.

After the greetings were over and a wide-eyed Matty had
been introduced to Crockett, Rebecca said, "This fortification
of the Alamo—is it wise? If Santa Anna does come, you'll all
be trapped inside."

"I know. I've always hated being cooped up, but help's on
its way. Travis says so."

"What if he's wrong?"

"Afraid it's a little too late to change our plans now, Rebecca."

"As soon as Matty's fever goes down, I'm riding out of
here," she said.

"If there's anything I can do to help, let me know," Crockett
said. "Well, I'd best be getting back, but I couldn't resist seeing
you."

They parted with an embrace.

"Mr. Crockett, you forgot your coonskin cap," Matty called.

Crockett turned in the doorway. "Well, seeing as how I've
got me a couple of others, why don't you keep that one for
me, boy, till we meet up again."

Shortly after nightfall, Patrick returned. His face glowed
from his exertions; a passion that Rebecca had rarely seen in
him shone in his eyes.

"These men, they're joined together at the heart," he said.
"I've never felt so proud to be a Texan, or an American."

"Oh, Patrick, don't tell me..."

"Yes, I'm going to fight with them. What else can a man
do? Of course, I'll see you get home first. But then I'm turning
right around and coming back here."

Rebecca didn't even try to argue with him. She'd seen that
look too often before in the eyes of zealots and patriots; nothing
could change his mind. In an odd sort of way, she envied him
his calling, wished that she might feel it again, rather than this
overriding caution that age had brought. Her heart had burned

like that a long time ago . . . But Matty was the most important consideration now, and she'd have to get him out of San Antonio the minute he was able to travel.

The next morning, Tuesday, February 23, Matty seemed to be his irrepressible self. His fever had dropped considerably, and he spent the morning fidgeting in bed. "When can we go home, Grandma? My hand is almost better—look!"

"At this rate, in another day or so. But you were pretty sick, and I wouldn't want you to have a relapse."

About eleven in the morning, the bell in the tower of the Cathedral of San Fernando began to toll. The ringing grew in intensity, and Rebecca went out into the street to find out what was happening.

She shaded her eyes and peered at the tower; the American sentry stationed there, Daniel Cloud, was swinging wildly on the bell rope. Then she saw a detail of men riding hard from the Alamo to the cathedral; she thought she recognized Patrick Donohoe among them. The men disappeared into the church's entrance, and a few minutes later appeared high up in the belfry. Sure enough, some minutes later, Patrick came running out of the cathedral and down the street toward her.

"What's happening?" Rebecca demanded.

Patrick panted for breath. "Dan Cloud thinks he's spotted Santa Anna's advance guard!"

Chapter 44

"ARE YOU certain Cloud saw them?" Rebecca demanded. "Remember, there were false alarms all day yesterday."

"Well, he did act jumpy," Patrick said. "I tried to spot them, but didn't see anything."

Rebecca's mind worked furiously. Matty was still too feverish to travel with complete safety, but remaining in San Antonio seemed far more dangerous. "Patrick, let's get out of here."

"Right. I'll hitch up the wagon. You get Matty," he said, and started for the stable.

Rebecca ran back into the house and quickly packed their things. Then she wrapped Matty in a blanket. "Can you walk?" she asked.

"Yes, Grandma."

She took his hand and started toward the door. He broke free of her. "I forgot something!" He ran back and rescued Davy Crockett's coonskin cap.

When they reached the front door, Dr. Hernández stopped them. "It's no use. The townspeople tell me that Santa Anna's cavalry is already surrounding the city. The roads to Gonzales and Goliad are all cut off. Stay here; you'll be safer."

"But surely they'll let us pass," she said. "What would they want with an old woman and a little boy?"

"Don't go," Hernández repeated.

"Come on, Mrs. Brand!" Patrick shouted.

She and Matty hurried to the wagon and climbed up beside Patrick. Rebecca had thought that hardly anybody was left in town, but the lookout's alarm flushed the residents from their houses. The Mexicans were scattering into the surrounding countryside; the Americans and some of the sympathic Spaniards, were streaming toward the Alamo to take refuge there.

"What do you think, Mrs. Brand?" Patrick asked as they

339

neared the mission, which was off to the left of the road. "Would we be safer in there?"

"No!" she said sharply. "Jonathan warned me not to get trapped there. We'll keep on going."

"All right, then," Patrick said, and whipped the horses. They reached the outskirts of town and were almost in the countryside when Rebecca grabbed Patrick's arm and pointed to a copse of trees. A Mexican lancer outfitted in a shiny breastplate and helmet had just ridden out of the woods and was riding hard toward them.

Patrick grabbed his rifle and placed it next to him, out of sight. "Be ready for anything," he whispered to Rebecca and Matty.

The Mexican cavalryman, swarthy with a heavy black moustache, overtook them and grabbed their horse's bridle, bringing them to a halt. "Get down," he said, in barely comprehensible English.

"Wait, you don't understand," Rebecca began. "We're only trying to get home. My grandson is ill, he's—"

"Get down, I say!" the lancer ordered. "We have need of your horse and wagon."

"Now wait a minute," Patrick began, but the lancer drew his saber and charged at him. With a single fluid motion Patrick grabbed his rifle and fired, catching the man in the stomach at pointblank range. He toppled out of the saddle.

"Hang on!" Patrick shouted, and brought his whip down hard on the horse's flanks. They bolted forward, bumping and careening along the grassy road.

Alerted by the gunshot, three other Mexican lancers who'd been in the copse came riding after them. Rebecca glanced behind and saw the cavalrymen gaining on them, the sun glinting off the shiny steel of their drawn sabers. She clutched Matty to her, covering his body with her own. She saw a lancer galloping up closer on Patrick's side, his saber raised.

"Behind you!" she screamed. Patrick swerved the wagon into the man's horse, sending him tumbling off the road.

Patrick laughed aloud. "Only two more to go and we're free!"

But suddenly his body arched convulsively as a bullet caught him in the back, and then another ripped through his neck. He fell against Rebecca. "Nothing I ever do . . . turns out right," he gasped, blood trickling from his mouth. "Tell Suzannah I—"

His dead weight fell across her lap. She clutched him to her, trying to find signs of life, and then her endless scream, "Patrick!" tore across the plain.

A soldier grabbed the bridle and stopped the horse. Another cavalryman prodded Patrick's body with the tip of his lance, and he toppled off the seat and onto the road to lie there in a crumpled heap.

Horrified at what had happened, Rebecca nevertheless knew she had to protect Matty. She begged, pleaded, offered the Mexicans money if they would only let her and Matty go. But her horse and wagon were what they were after. Besides, one of their men had been killed, another wounded. Releasing her was out of the question. Making a wide circle around the Alamo, the lancers led Rebecca and Matty back to the main plaza of San Antonio.

They got there just as General Antonio López de Santa Anna was making his triumphal entry. His personal guard of thirty resplendent dragoons preceded him, their lances held with the glittering tips pointing skyward.

Stunned by Patrick's death and terrified for Matty's safety, Rebecca could only stare at the procession. Santa Anna sat tall in his gold-embossed saddle. His white, gold, and blue uniform was gorgeous, and silver fairly dripped from his epaulets and froggings. An intricately worked silver sword that must have cost thousands of dollars hung at his side. He looked to be in his early forties, and Rebecca loathed him on sight.

Convinced that only desperate measures would save her and Matty, she said to the lancer holding her, "Tell General Santa Anna that I'm an emmisary from President Andrew Jackson of the United States, and I wish to speak to him."

The lancer paid not the slightest attention to her, probably because he didn't appear to understand one word of English.

Rebecca turned to her grandson. "Matty, this is important. There's Dr. Hernández's house right over there. Go and get him and bring him back."

In the confusion of the parade, Matty slipped away from the soldiers and ran to the doctor's house. Minutes later, the gentle old man hurried to Rebecca. In a rush, she told him what had happened. When he heard that Patrick was dead, he held his head in both hands and cried, "Oh, war, war! Why must the young always be the victims?"

He listened with growing disbelief as Rebecca explained what she wanted him to do. How could it be? he asked. Even

if it was true, El Presidente Santa Anna would never listen to
a woman. Such a thing was unheard of in Mexico.

"Please!" she cried. "You must do it. You must try! Think
of all of the lives that can be saved if only Santa Anna will
listen. *Please*."

Dr. Hernández regarded her keenly. She was in a state of
shock, to be sure, but she wasn't lying, nor did he think she
was deranged. He noticed that her breathing had become labored and a heavy blue vein pulsed in her temple. Fearing that
any further agitation might have serious consequences, he said,
"All right, I'll try."

He went from one officer to another, repeating Rebecca's
request for an audience with the general. At last he was directed
to Ramón Caro, Santa Anna's secretary, a man known for his
ability to capitalize on any opportunity.

Ramón Caro approached Rebecca and ordered the lancer to
stand aside. With Dr. Hernández acting as interpreter, Caro
listened to Rebecca, his thin, sharp face twitching. When at
last she was done, he stroked his chin thoughtfully and inti-
mated that though El Presidente's time was of the utmost importance, he might be persuaded to grant such an audience.
Then Caro waited expectantly.

Rebecca stared at him blankly, and only when Dr. Hernández nudged her did she realize that Caro expected a bribe. She
gave him what money she had, about fifty dollars. Caro pocketed it, then said, "I understand the little boy isn't well. We
aren't barbarians, so I allow you to go back to Dr. Hernández's
house; he can look after him. Naturally, you will be placed
under house arrest. I have been informed of the death of the
lancer."

"What about the audience with General Santa Anna?" Rebecca asked, her heart sinking.

"The general will deal with you at his leisure."

Rebecca and Dr. Hernández were taken back to his house,
and a guard was posted outside the door.

"What's going to happen, Grandma?" Matty asked.

"Don't worry, everything will be all right," she said. But
all she did was worry, unable to think of a way out of this
awful predicament.

For a full day, Rebecca waited for some word from Santa
Anna's headquarters. From the window, she watched as thou-

sands upon thousands of Mexican soldiers filled the town: the personal dragoons of Santa Anna in their red and blue uniforms, the cavalry riding in tight formation, and then the common soldiers, dressed in loose-fitting clothes that had once been white. After the rigors of their eight-hundred-mile march from Mexico City, through desert and over mountains, their uniforms were now an indeterminate gray. Hundreds of supply wagons rumbled through the streets, loaded with foodstuffs and munitions. Mules dragged caissons with small eight-pound cannon. Trailing after the supply train came the *soldaderas*, the wives and children of the enlisted men, and the camp followers.

That day, Mexican patrols went out to probe the strength of the Alamo, and Rebecca started at every crack of rifle fire. She wondered if help would come to relieve the mission, but even if it did, how could they hope to hold out against this superior Mexican army? Nobody in Texas had ever dreamed that Santa Anna would come in such force.

Again and again she reviewed what she would say to Santa Anna when they met. She knew she didn't have much chance of influencing him, but that didn't matter. If she could slow him down for even an hour, that was one more hour gained for the men inside the mission.

Weighing most heavily on her mind was that she and she alone was responsible for Suzannah and Jonathan being here in the first place. If she hadn't been so opposed to their marriage, they would have settled within the United States, in some place like Nashville. Or Jonathan might have remained an aide to President Jackson, and she would have had her family safe around her in Washington.

"If it takes my last breath, I *will* make it right for them," she whispered to herself. "I *will* get Matty out of here. I've got to believe that, or we're lost."

Another day passed, peppered with more gunfire, and Rebecca thought she'd go mad. Everytime she tried to go out the door, the sentry pushed her back inside, and once he even prodded her with his bayonet.

The following morning, Ramón Caro appeared at the house. "You are fortunate, madam. Someone in our headquarters has interceded for you, and El Presidente will grant you an audience."

What Caro said made no sense. Who in Santa Anna's headquarters knew her? But there was no time for questions. Caro

and the sentry escorted her and Dr. Hernández across the plaza
to a building near the cathedral which Santa Anna had set up
as his headquarters.

She couldn't help noticing the blood-red flag that flew from
the church steeple, and wondered what it meant. The dragoons
guarding the doors to Santa Anna's sanctum gaped at her when
she passed through. Rebecca made sure to keep her head high
as she was brought into Santa Anna's presence.

She hadn't known what to expect, but she'd never expected
this. Santa Anna was wearing a beautifully brocaded lounging
robe and red slippers. The room was elegantly furnished with
personal possessions that he'd brought all the way from
Mexico City—an ornate French escritoire, campaign chests,
and in one corner a solid-silver chamber pot.

Rebecca noticed an antechamber just beyond this room;
there were several Mexican officers sitting there, and some
civilians, but she couldn't make out who they were.

General Santa Anna understood only a smattering of English
so Dr. Hernández was pressed into service as an interpreter.

Though her heart was pounding fit to burst, Rebecca lost
no time. "General, I'm here on a mission for the President of
the United States. I am Rebecca Breech Brand, but I also write
newspaper articles under the name of Rebel Thorne." She had
hoped that her pen name might be familiar to him, but Santa
Anna gave no sign of recognition.

Rebecca continued, "I've come here hoping to tell your side
of the Texas story to the rest of the world."

Though she knew that she'd probably compromised President Jackson's position, she felt that under the present circumstances he'd understand and forgive her.

Santa Anna stared at her. "I suppose you have papers to
prove that you come from President Jackson?"

"My mission is one of peace. Surely one doesn't need papers
for that. I feel sure that if we exercise reason and mercy, terrible
bloodshed can be avoided."

Santa Anna began paring his nails with a set of gold man-
icuring implements. "Señora, this is a valiant effort on your
part, and at any other time, I might applaud it. But in my
country, women know enough to stay at home where they
belong, without meddling in the affairs of men."

Rebecca turned to Dr. Hernández. "Tell him that I had heard
that El Presidente was far more reasonable than this. Tell him
I'm disappointed."

When Dr. Hernández heard Santa Anna's reply, his face colored.

"What did he say?" Rebecca asked. "Tell me!"

Hernández cleared his throat. "He says that your disappointment means nothing to him, it is like an annoying fly that he squashes. Just as he will squash all the traitors to Mexico who are in the Alamo."

Rebecca felt her temper flaring. The sight of Patrick being killed before her eyes, the sound of the constant bombardment of the mission, the fear of what might happen to Suzannah and the children—all these conspired to rob her of her caution, and she blurted, "Such a man doesn't deserve to be the leader of his nation."

Santa Anna's face darkened, and he jumped to his feet. Suddenly he no longer needed an interpreter. "Enough, Señora Brand, or Rebel Thorne, or whoever you claim to be. You have my permission to go, before you anger me further."

"How typical of you to assume that only you can be angered by this conversation. I assure you, President Jackson will take it as a personal insult that you've treated his emmisary in this fashion."

Santa Anna drummed his fingers on his campaign desk. "Women," he groaned. "Will they never learn their place? Señora, a good horsewhipping would help you to control your tongue."

Rebecca blanched. Every insult she'd ever experienced because of being a woman rose to her gorge. She wanted to do something that would annihilate him! But all she could manage was, "You were born of a woman, through a woman you have your heirs, and even in your own profession, there was a woman who proved herself far greater than any man."

Santa Anna looked puzzled for a moment, then his face lit with recognition. "You speak of Joan of Arc?" His mocking laugh was close to an insult. "You too have visions?"

His aides began laughing and slapping their thighs, calling her a fool and an imbecile.

When the laughter died down she said, "Indeed I do have visions. I have visions of people allowed to live peacefully on soil they've tilled. I have visions of a just and decent Mexican government responding to the claims of all its citizens. And if that is not forthcoming, sir, than I have visions of men fighting for what is theirs by right of their own free birth."

Santa Anna slammed his sword on the table. "Beware, Señ-

ora, you speak treason, and in my country, that is a crime
punishable by death, with no regard for sex."

"You dare threaten an envoy of the President of the United
States?" she demanded. Rebecca knew she had no official status, knew that in this instance, Jackson would have to deny
her. But Santa Anna didn't know that. Her rage at this man
overwhelmed her. Yet she couldn't think of that. She must
think first of the men at the mission, do whatever she could to
prevent more bloodshed.

"General, I ask you to put aside our personal animosities
for the moment. If I've angered you, I apologize. I ask you
only to think of this current situation. When all of your army
has gathered here, I understand that it will number more than
four thousand men. There are about one hundred and seventy-
five men inside the Alamo. Reason dictates that against such
odds, your army must be victorious. But how do you think the
world would perceive such a victory?"

"They would perceive it as I mean them to, that General
Antonio López de Santa Anna, the Napoleon of the West, is
invincible! Señora Brand, if you are wise, you'll tell your
ingrate countrymen that their position in Texas is hopeless. I
have come to crush these perfidious rebels!"

A chorus of agreement came from the men at his side.

Santa Anna continued, "I gave these rebels at the Alamo
every opportunity to surrender. They would have been treated
fairly. But they spurned my offer, and now they must die! Do
you hear? Write that in your newspapers. That everyone in
Texas who opposes me will die!"

He'd worked himself to such a fever pitch that Rebecca
knew there was no reasoning with him. Gone was her attempt
at conciliation, gone her belief that she could help the defenders
of the Alamo. All that was left was her loathing of this despot,
this man who boasted that he would kill anybody who opposed
him.

"You claim that the Americans spurned you," she said.
"Well, then, how could they believe you? Why *should* they,
after all your broken promises? When Stephen Austin came to
appeal to your sense of honor, you threw him in prison! Perhaps
men in Mexico bend their knees to a dictator, but never Americans."

He moved toward her, his hand raised as if to slap her, and
had she shown any fear at all, he would have. Instead, she

took a half-step toward him, her chin thrust forward. He stopped right in front of her, his baleful face inches from hers.

"The American cause here is lost. Tell that to your President Jackson! Don't you think we know that he encourages these rebels? Well, this is our answer! The red flag flies from the top of the church steeple. Do you know what that means? No quarter! None!"

"You know very little about Americans," she said, in a low and deadly tone, for every vestige of her own control was gone. "And you know even less about the settlers here who call themselves Texans. I'm proud that my daughter is one of them, proud that my grandchildren claim this soil by right of occupancy, proud that they seek redress against their grievances. And I shall tell them what our forefathers told their children when confronted by oppression. I shall tell them to fight."

"Tell them too that they shall all die! This I swear."

"There are things more precious than mere life. There are beliefs, there are ideals, there are visions. Not of the way this world is, your world of injustice and inequity—silver chamber pots while poor peons starve—but of the world as it might be. These Texans have that vision. And that, sir, is why we shall ultimately win."

In the deathly silence that followed, she heard the slow rhythmic sound of somebody clapping. Even before she turned to face the man who was coming out of the antechamber, she knew that it was Devroe Connaught.

Chapter 45

DEVROE HELD his crippled hand firmly against his abdomen, and with his left hand continued clapping in a slow, ominous cadence. Then he broke off and said, "Brava, madam, a very pretty speech. But then you always did know how to make pretty speeches. Pity you've chosen to come down on the side of the miscreant and the criminal."

How to describe her conflicting feelings . . . ? Surprise certainly wasn't one of them, for somewhere deep in her being she'd always suspected that the man she'd seen at the Alamo a month before was Devroe Connaught. Nor did she have to ask such mundane questions as, What are you doing here? Obviously, he'd been studying the fortifications and reporting that information back to General Santa Anna.

The deviousness of Devroe's undertaking nearly overwhelmed her. This man professed American citizenship, the better to intrigue against his adopted country. Visions of that old harridan, Victoria Connaught, of the master-spy Sean Connaught, and of poor sweet misguided Marianne clouded Rebecca's memory. The Connaught family had always been a nest of Tory vipers, and such they would always remain. And now fate had chosen Devroe Connaught to be her nemesis.

Devroe said to General Santa Anna, "You've seen for yourself, your excellency, that this woman is dangerous. That's why I arranged this audience. Her claim to be on a mission for the President of the United States? Laughable. Without question she's a spy, and should be dealt with as a spy."

"That's a lie!" Rebecca exclaimed.

"You have evidence of this?" Santa Anna asked Devroe.

"Indeed I have. I've seen her in intimate conversation with Jim Bowie. We know she was involved in the killing of one of your cavalryman. At this very moment, her son-in-law, Jonathan Albright, one of the leaders of this insurrection, is at

Washington-on-the-Brazos, plotting treason against your excellency."

"Formidable charges," Santa Anna said, glaring at her.

Devroe's thin lips parted in a half-smile. "I'll have a firing squad assembled immediately."

Rebecca felt waves of dizziness engulf her; Devroe grasped her arm in his steely grip and propelled her toward the door.

"Just a moment!" Santa Anna ordered. His slippers whispered across the floor as he moved to Devroe. "When I employed your services, I made it clear that in all matters the final decisions were to be mine."

"Of course, your excellency."

"This woman is more important to me if she remains alive."

"But your excellency—"

Santa Anna cut Devroe off with an abrupt gesture. "Let her witness our conquest of the Alamo. Let her see firsthand the full fury of the Mexican fighting force. And if the truth comes from her pen, then perhaps the United States of America, and this Andrew Jackson, will believe what I've been trying to tell them. That their days in Texas are over. Now release her."

Devroe's hand fell away from Rebecca. "As you wish," he said stiffly.

Santa Anna turned to an aide. "Take her back to her quarters and keep the guard posted. I'll send for her when I want her."

Rebecca and Dr. Hernández were escorted back to his house.

Matty came running to meet them and she hugged him fiercely. "Grandma, you were gone so long I was worried about you."

Dr. Hernández wiped his brow. "I too was worried. Madam, I believe you are truly mad. I know of no other explanation. Talking to El Presidente that way—I thought surely he would have you shot right on the spot!"

Rebecca slumped to the couch and Matty sat beside her. "In my country, we're allowed to speak our minds to our leaders. Though I must confess I was terrified. I know I lost my temper, but I couldn't help it. Oh, Lord, what's to be the end of this senseless business? Even if help does come to relieve the Alamo, we're trapped here, right in the middle of the Mexican camp."

Dr. Hernández mixed a draught and handed it to her. "Drink this, it will calm you." Then he mixed one for himself.

Rebecca took a number of deep breaths, as Wingate had

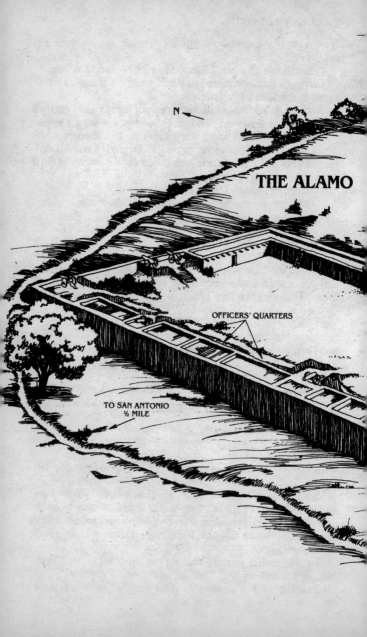

N

THE ALAMO

OFFICERS' QUARTERS

TO SAN ANTONIO
½ MILE

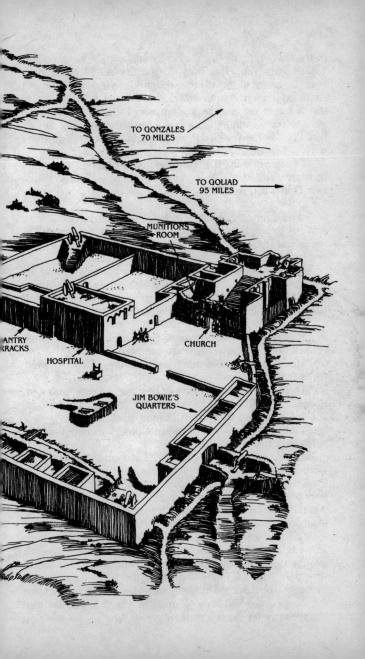

TO GONZALES
70 MILES

TO GOLIAD
95 MILES

MUNITIONS
ROOM

ANTRY
RACKS

HOSPITAL

CHURCH

JIM BOWIE'S
QUARTERS

instructed her, trying to calm her racing heart. "Listen, doctor, I must warn you. That man Devroe Connaught has a long-standing hatred of me and of my family. No matter what Santa Anna says, Devroe can't afford to let me go free. He knows that if I ever get back to Washington, I'll expose him. He'll have to try something, and you're in danger also if you stay here. You've been so kind to us that I couldn't bear it if anything were to happen to you."

"I'm an old man," Dr. Hernández said simply. "Too old to be frightened either of living or dying. So here I'll stay. Whatever God wills, so be it."

Twice during the last days of February, General Santa Anna sent for Rebecca and took her on a tour of the Mexican encampment. "As you see, we have successfully moved our gun emplacements closer and closer to the mission."

He gave the order, and a gunner put a burning taper at the touchhole of the cannon. The explosion nearly deafened her. Moments later she saw a puff of smoke as the cannonball slammed into the northeast wall of the mission.

"Already the wall is beginning to crumble," Santa Anna said. "And the *norteamericanos,* they cannot fire back at us, because they must save their ammunition!"

"This is a despicable thing you're doing," Rebecca whispered.

"There will be no prisoners in this war," Santa Anna continued. "All will be put to the bayonet. When I am finished, not one American will be left alive in all of Texas!"

"You'll speak differently when Colonel Fannin and Sam Houston get here," she said.

Santa Anna laughed delightedly. "Let them come! You think we don't know that Travis sends messengers back and forth from the mission? We allow those couriers to get through our lines because we *want* Sam Houston to come with his men, so that they too can be annihilated! How can this rabble stand up to an army trained in the tradition of the European art of war?"

Suddenly, the eighteen-pound cannon atop the Alamo's walls answered the Mexican's fire, and a geyser of earth spumed into the air about forty feet away from them. Santa Anna turned very pale, and then he galloped off the field. Rebecca was hurriedly taken back to Dr. Hernández's house. Later she learned that Santa Anna had been so upset that he'd treated his men outrageously for the rest of the day.

• • •

The afternoon of March 5, a bitter norther struck the San Antonio area; Rebecca was grateful, for it forced a cessation in the fighting. The ground froze hard; the Mexican army took shelter in their redoubts and in the lee of buildings.

By nightfall, the wind eased up somewhat. Rebecca sat at the desk, making futile stabs at recounting the course of the siege. She found it an almost impossible task. The men in the Alamo were going to die; it was as certain as the sun rising tomorrow. And she could find little comfort in the fact that they were dying for the cause of liberty.

About one o'clock in the morning of March 6, two soldiers barged into the house and ordered Rebecca to dress. She knew then that this was the day of the final assault.

Santa Anna's plan was simple: he would attack the garrison from all four sides simultaneously. There simply weren't enough Americans to cover every part of the wall. Shortly after two o'clock, the order to move forward was given, and under cover of darkness the Mexicans crept even closer to the mission, then began to race forward. Suddenly the eerie notes of the *degüello* were sounded on the bugle, the signal that no quarter would be given.

Rebecca put her hands to her ears to block out the chilling call of death.

Cannons roared, rifles fired, the shouts of the charging Mexicans mingled with the screams of the fallen. Wave after wave of the troops raced forward from all directions. In the darkness, the flash of rifle and cannon fire sporadically illuminated the rectangle of the Alamo.

The Americans were using their Kentucky rifles with a range of over two hundred yards, while the Mexicans' principal weapon was a rifle of Napoleonic-War vintage, purchased from Great Britain. Rebecca's heart leapt up when she saw the Mexican line falter, then turn tail and run back out of range of the Texas sharpshooters.

She heard General Santa Anna berating Devroe Connaught for the quality of the arms. Devroe said, "Your excellency, none of us expected you to move so quickly against Texas. That's why you didn't receive the new shipment of arms. But I assure you, nine hundred new rifles are due at any moment in Corpus Christi. They'll be in your hands by the time you're ready to push on to finish Sam Houston."

Watching his men retreat, Santa Anna cursed, "A momentary setback. But we must not hesitate. Prepare to attack again."

The division commanders regrouped their troops. Once more the bugle sounded, and once more the Mexicans moved forward. This time, though, the cavalry followed close behind so that the foot soldiers couldn't retreat. With shouts of rage, the Mexicans charged across the open ground, exposing themselves to the withering fire from the fortress. They fell by the score, and even the cavalry turned and galloped out of range. The second assault wave was beaten back.

Rebecca began to take heart. Could it be that Bowie, Travis, Crockett, and the rest of the Texans would hold off this mighty force?

By the time the Mexican regiments had been reorganized and the decimated ranks filled with reserve troops, dawn was breaking, streaking the eastern sky with red.

"This time the mission *must* be taken," Santa Anna said. "Throw in all our reserves. Lives do not matter—I can replace a thousand soldiers by conscripting men in this area alone, but first I must prove that we are invincible. Take the Alamo!"

The haunting notes of the *degüello* sounded again, the troops moved into position, and then the relentless force of thousands upon thousands of Mexicans charged forward.

Rebecca saw the first wave of men felled by the fusillade of fire from the fortress, but others took their place, screaming their hatred of the Americans. She saw scaling ladders set up against the walls, saw Mexicans reach the top rung only to be picked off again and again by the sharpshooters. But the Texans couldn't load their rifles fast enough to hold off the hordes overrunning them.

Then her heart sank as she saw Mexican troops pour through the breach in the north wall.

On orders from Santa Anna, an aide handed Rebecca a spyglass. She lifted it to her eye and saw men atop the ramparts using their rifles as clubs to try to beat back the tidal wave of Mexicans. But the wall, the first line of defense, was breached, and she saw the Texans retreating toward their second line, the barracks and the chapel.

By early morning, the last of the defenders were cornered in the chapel, and the Mexicans, by dint of sheer numbers, finally overran that. And then the firing died down, until the only sound left was the moaning wind.

General Santa Anna, his aides, and Devroe Connaught entered the smoldering ruins of the mission. Santa Anna motioned for Rebecca to be brought in also. She struggled to keep from retching at the sight of the carnage; men lay everywhere, twisted into fantastic shapes by death.

Other than Travis's black slave, there were no male survivors; every last Texan had been shot and bayoneted, their bodies mutilated beyond recognition, for an orgy of bloodlust had overtaken the Mexicans in their final moment of victory.

"I want to see Jim Bowie, William Travis, and Davy Crockett," Santa Anna ordered.

Travis's body was located at the northeast corner of the wall; Devroe Connaught identified him. A black bullet hole was drilled squarely in the center of his forehead. In sharp contrast to other mutilated Texans, his body was unmarked. Travis's slave, Joe, was brought to Santa Anna.

"Did your master kill himself?" he asked.

Joe shook his head. "Mr. Travis, he got shot right at the very beginning of the fight. I saw the bullet hit him square in the head."

They found Davy Crockett's body at the southern palisade, and Rebecca counted no less than seventeen Mexican soldiers lying dead all about him.

Finally, they discovered Jim Bowie's body in the chapel, where he'd been laid up, ill unto death. Mrs. Dickinson, one of the women survivors who'd been nursing Bowie, stared at Santa Anna's group with glazed eyes.

"Bowie hid here in bed like a woman, didn't he?" Santa Anna said.

Mrs. Dickinson, clutching her infant daughter, Angelina, shook her head vehemently. "Jim Bowie was so ill he could barely raise the pistols that Davy Crockett left for him. But when they forced their way into the chapel, he half rose out of bed and fired away, each bullet hitting its mark. When his pistols were empty and they came at him with their bayonets, he fought with his knife, killing at least two more. But then they plunged their bayonets into him, again and again, until there wasn't a part of him that hadn't taken the knife."

"Enough!" Santa Anna commanded, and turned on his heel and left.

Stunned into silence, Rebecca walked outside into the mission courtyard. She looked about her at the smoldering ruin . . . all the fathers who would never hold their children again . . . the husbands who would never love their wives . . . How could anybody ever tell this tragic tale?

Santa Anna had the bodies of the fallen Mexicans prepared for Christian burial. As for the Americans, he ordered them to be heaped into a pyre and their bodies burned. Rebecca watched as the mound grew taller—one hundred and eighty-two bodies in all, men from all over the United States who'd come to Texas for the common dream of freedom, consigned instead to a fiery grave.

"There you see it, Señora Brand," Santa Anna said. "That is the fate of anybody who opposes me. That is the word you must take back with you to the United States."

Tears streamed down Rebecca's face and she sobbed unashamedly as she watched the smoke curl upwards, carrying the ashes and spirits of these men into the sky.

Chapter 46

IN HIS official dispatches to Mexico City, General Santa Anna claimed he had killed seven hundred Texans at the Alamo and had sustained losses of only seventy dead and three hundred wounded. Rebecca knew these figures were ridiculous, for in their defeat, the Texans had inflicted a terrible blow against the Mexican army: more than six hundred killed or wounded.

Fourteen people within the Alamo survived the massacre, ten Mexican women and their children, and three Americans— Mrs. Dickinson and her daughter Angelina, and Travis's Negro slave, Joe.

With characteristic shrewdness, Santa Anna freed Mrs. Dickinson and Joe at the same time as he freed Rebecca and Matty. "They will go back and report what has happened here, and it will strike fear into the hearts of all the remaining settlers." He gave Mrs. Dickinson and Rebecca each a blanket and two dollars, and sent them on their way.

After a tearful goodbye to Dr. Hernández, Rebecca and Matty joined Mrs. Dickinson and Joe for the first leg of the journey. But when they reached the point to turn off toward the Albright ranch, she and Matty struck out on their own, over the objections of the others.

"We'd be much safer in a group," Joe told her. "Lots of Indians around here."

But Rebecca had only one thought, to get back to Suzannah. It was something of a miracle that they'd survived at all, and she knew that Suzannah would be out of her mind with worry.

"Do you think you can walk that far?" she asked Matty. "Just tell me when you're tired and I'll carry you."

"Why, walking is a real simple thing. Once Papa and me were riding on his horse and it came up lame. We walked fifteen miles back to the ranch, and tweren't nothing."

"Good boy," she said.

Since there was no visible trail, but only the tall golden
prairie grass, Rebecca consistently drifted off the course, but
Matty, his eyes always on the sun, kept correcting her. They
walked all that day, and far into the dusk. They found a hollow
with a few dwarf oak trees growing in it, and decided to rest
there for the night. Matty cut open a barrel cactus, extracted
a white pulpy mass, and gave half to Rebecca. "Papa taught
me this," he said. "There's enough water in it to keep you from
going thirsty."

He started to chew his wad; Rebecca popped the sticky
substance in her mouth and did the same. It tasted awful, but
it did prevent her mouth from being totally dry.

"Why, Mr. Albright, that's excellent! I do believe that I'll
have another portion," she said to Matty. He laughed with
delight and gave her some more.

They huddled against the base of an oak, wrapped themselves in the blanket, and went to sleep. Rebecca kept the boy
against her, shielding him from the wind. She looked up at the
sweep of stars, and gave thanks.

It was well past dawn when Matty shook her awake. Her
bones were stiff and she groaned with the effort of straightening
out. "Grandma, somebody's coming."

She sat up, alert, but saw nothing. Matty put his ear to the
ground and motioned to her, and when she did the same, she
heard the vibrations through the earth.

Several minutes later, she saw a rider approaching . . . and
made out the form of Devroe Connaught. She wanted to scream,
to run to the ends of the earth and hide, but she grabbed Matty
and flattened herself against the ground.

Devroe passed them, only to come circling back. He stopped
less than ten feet away from them. "But how charming to find
you here, Mrs. Brand," he said, doffing his hat. "You'll be
pleased to know that General Santa Anna is still in San Antonio,
awaiting reinforcements, before he pushes on to Gonzales to
annihilate Sam Houston. So I just thought I'd use this time to
settle old scores."

With a slow, deliberate motion, he took his pistol from his
belt and checked the chamber. "Why don't you run?" he asked.
"That might provide us with some amusing sport. Or would
you prefer to beg? That too could be amusing. And your last
moments on earth should be amusing, don't you agree?"

"Devroe, for the love of God," Rebecca began. "Do what

you want with me, but spare the boy. He's only a child, he knows nothing of what's between us."

"He's a Brand," Devroe spat. "And I'll see them all wiped off the face of the earth. Nothing less will ease my soul." He raised his pistol and pointed first at Rebecca and then shifted his aim to Matty. "Now which shall it be? You first, Mrs. Brand? Or perhaps the boy first, so that you'll feel that same exquisite moment of pain that I felt when I heard about my father's death. Yes, the boy first."

"No!" Rebecca screamed, and hurled herself in front of Matty. In the cruelty of his expression, she saw the seething current of insanity that coursed through all the Connaughts.

Devroe laughed, and circled his horse, round and round, faster and faster, while Rebecca tried to keep him from getting a clear shot. He kept tormenting her until she fell to her knees in exhaustion.

"You leave her alone!" Matty shouted, clenching his fists.

Bracing his pistol against his crippled arm, Devroe took careful aim at Rebecca. Matty sprang for his leg and tried to pull him from the saddle. Devroe fired, but his aim was deflected enough so that the bullet passed through the fleshy part of Rebecca's arm. Matty hung on to Devroe's leg, and the horse whinnied and reared, its forelegs thrashing the air.

Devroe lashed out with his leg, throwing Matty to the ground and knocking the wind out of him. He lay there, gasping for breath. Unable to reload while in the saddle, Devroe dismounted and drew his sword. Matty saw Devroe coming toward him and scrambled away.

Devroe stalked him. "By nightfall, the buzzards will have eaten their fill of both of you." He brought his sword around in a sideways swipe. Matty tried to duck it but the blade glanced off the side of his head and bit into the bone.

Rebecca screamed and went for the man, her fingernails raking for his eyes, her teeth seeking to tear out his jugular vein. She fought as one possessed, to avenge herself on this madman who'd haunted her and her family, to save this child whom she loved more than life itself.

Though able to use only one arm, Devroe was still the stronger, and his punch caught Rebecca on the jaw. She fell to the ground, stunned, fighting desperately to clear her senses . . . then she saw the form of the barrel cactus that Matty had cut in half the night before.

Devroe had gone back to Matty, and when he saw that the boy was still alive, he prepared to run his sword through him. Making sure to avoid the needlelike spines, Rebecca grabbed the cactus and sprang.

Sensing somebody behind him, Devroe turned, just as Rebecca, with all her strength, hit him in the face with the cactus. He screamed as the spines stabbed into his eyes.

His hands flew to his face and he dropped the sword. She lunged and seized it. Through the blood streaming between his fingers, he saw her stumbling toward him with the sword, her ravening face twisted with fury.

Devroe turned and dashed for his horse. He mounted and tried to run her down, but she took refuge behind a tree and when he passed her, she swung at the horse's flank, tearing open the flesh.

Blinded by the blood in his eyes, and fearing that she might cripple his mount, Devroe galloped off.

Rebecca knelt by Matty's body, keening over him. She searched for a heartbeat, and miraculously, found one. He's only unconscious, she thought. He'll be all right—God in heaven wouldn't take this child from me. When she lifted him, she saw that one whole side of his head was bloodied. She tore a strip of muslin from her petticoat, tied it around his head, and managed to stem the bleeding.

Then she picked Matty up and started walking toward the ranch, walking with strength, with determination. She would get him home. She would save him. And she would see Devroe Connaught in hell!

About two miles from where Devroe had attacked them, Matty regained consciousness, and looked at her through puffed eyes that were fast turning black and blue.

"Oh, Grandma, I hurt," he whispered.

"Darling, I know, and I never saw anybody as brave as you. But you're going to be all right, I promise." She kissed his head.

He closed his eyes and slipped back into unconsciousness.

She walked faster, faster. After the first miles, she thought her arms would drop with fatigue, but then she reached a state of no longer feeling them, no longer feeling anything save the rhythmic pace of one step after the other, each step bringing her closer to the ranch and to safety. She thought that she had hurt Devroe Connaught badly, but he might still take it into his head to come after them.

Matty regained consciousness a number of times, and each time Rebecca took hope. She kept talking to him, telling him how much she loved him, telling him all the things they would do as soon as he was well.

Late in the day, she began coming to familiar landmarks...the stream which she slogged across...the line of honey trees...the ravine where they'd encountered the panther...and then finally she saw the ranchhouse.

She started yelling when she was half a mile away, and kept yelling through some haze of madness, until finally Suzannah spotted her and came running. Becky and Zeb raced after her.

"Matty!" Suzannah cried. "Oh, what happened?"

"Devroe Connaught," Rebecca whispered through swollen lips. "But Matty will be all right. He *will!*"

Suzannah took the boy from her mother, and with the weight taken from her, Rebecca fell to her knees. "Go on, go," she called to Suzannah. "Get him into the house. I'll be all right."

Zeb and Becky helped her to her feet. "What's the matter with Matty?" Zeb kept asking. "It's not my fault!"

"Hush," Becky said to him. "This is different from his hands."

Suzannah laid Matty on her bed, and then with a damp cloth, wiped the caked blood away from his head. She saw the depression in his skull and moaned, "Oh, God, I think his skull is fractured."

Rebecca started to rant, "Devroe did it! And Patrick Donohoe is dead. Everybody's dead!"

"Mother, control yourself!" Suzannah said sharply. "None of that's going to do Matty any good."

Rebecca buried her face in her hands and sobbed until she thought she had no more tears left. At last she managed to stop, making the noises a small child makes after a spate of crying. While Suzannah bathed and dressed Matty's wound, Rebecca managed to tell her what had happened at the Alamo.

"I'd cry if I could," Suzannah said, "but there isn't any time for tears."

"Jonathan?" Rebecca asked.

"No word. We were pinned down here for days by the Commanches," Suzannah said. "That's why I couldn't get to San Antonio. The Commanches know something's going on, and they're all too ready to take advantage of it. They rode off after Enoch shot and wounded one of their braves."

"Suzannah, General Santa Anna is sending out patrols to

wipe out every single American family in this vicinity. We must get away from here."

Suzannah blinked, then nodded. "I'll send Enoch to warn the Kelleys. They've got a large, two-horse wagon. It will take all of us."

"Where will we go?" Rebecca asked.

"Gonzales. That's the closest place, and it's where Sam Houston would naturally bring his men. We'll fight from there."

"Suzannah, I don't think we can. You should see Santa Anna's army. He's so strong, so determined—"

Matty stirred and opened his eyes for a moment. He recognized his mother, whispered "Hello," then drifted off again.

Suzannah kept a vigil by Matty's bedside. Once during the night he sat up as if nothing was wrong with him. But when he tried to stand, he keeled over. Suzannah knew that there was something terribly wrong with her son, something that only the finest doctor could cure . . . if it could be cured at all.

Dear God, she prayed silently. He's innocent. Spare him . . . if it's a life you want, take mine.

The next day, after being alerted by Enoch, the Kelleys arrived with their wagon loaded down with their children. Suzannah had already packed a few meager things, then she barred and shuttered the house. "I'll be back," she whispered.

Then with Zeb and Becky looking forlorn, Rebecca appearing more dead than alive, and Matty drifting in and out of consciousness, they started for Gonzales, fleeing the scourge that was General Antonio López de Santa Anna.

Chapter 47

ON MARCH 11, after a five-day forced march from Washington-on-the-Brazos, Sam Houston and a force of three hundred men reached the town of Gonzales. Houston had come in answer to Colonel William Travis's last plea for help. But now whatever fighting took place would be done under a different banner, for the provisional government at Washington-on-the-Brazos had declared Texas independent from Mexico and had named Houston commander-in-chief of the army.

Jonathan Albright, elevated to the rank of colonel, rode alongside Houston. They found the citizens of Gonzales in a profound state of shock. Just that evening, two Mexicans had ridden into town with horrifying news about the Alamo. Thirty-eight men from Gonzales had gone to fight with Bowie and Travis at the mission, and the probability that they were dead devastated their families.

Immediately on hearing the Mexicans' tale, Houston shouted, "Lock them up, they're nothing but spies!" The protesting men were hustled off to the local jail.

"Sam, you know as well as I do that those men aren't spies," Jonathan protested. "I've known them for years. They wouldn't lie about something as vital as this."

Making sure that nobody could hear him, Houston said, "I know, but if I don't throw them in prison, we're going to have a full-scale panic on our hands. I'll send out Deaf Smith and a scouting party. He'll find out the truth soon enough."

Jonathan checked his pistol, then picked up his rifle. He started toward the door.

"Jonathan, I need you here," Houston called out. "We've got a ragged bunch of men that have to be whipped into an army."

Jonathan paused at the door. "Sam, when we were in Washington-on-the-Brazos, listening to all those politicians, I wanted to get back home, but you asked me to stay. Then you asked me to stay on with you and scout against the Comanches."

"We fought them and won, didn't we?"

"Yes, but bigger things were happening here, things that might have turned out different if we'd been around to help. Sam, my family is out there somewhere. I've got to find out what's happened to them. If that doesn't suit you, you can have my commission back." Without another word, Jonathan left the room.

Houston knew better than to stop him.

Jonathan rode hard for his ranch, trying not to let his desperate fears overwhelm him. In the late afternoon he spotted a wagon rolling through the prairie grass. As it came closer, he recognized the Kelleys' team of horses, and galloped toward them.

Suzannah saw him approaching and stood up in the buckboard seat, waving frantically. Then she was in his arms, feeling the beat of his heart against hers, giving her renewed strength. Becky and Zeb clutched at his legs.

"Where's Matty?" Jonathan asked.

When Suzannah told him what had happened, his face drained of color. He strode to the back of the wagon where Rebecca sat in a vague, disoriented state, holding Matty in her lap. He tried to take the boy from her, but she pulled back reflexively.

"Mrs. Brand, it's me, Jonathan," he said softly.

She stared at him, recognition coming in slow waves. When he reached for his son again, she didn't resist. "It's my fault," she said dully. "Devroe Connaught did this because of me."

Jonathan cradled his unconscious son and pressed his face to his. "Matty, it's your Papa," he murmured. "I'm with you now, and everything's going to be all right, hear?"

Matty's eyelids flickered and he opened his eyes briefly. His face lit and he mumbled, "We got that dumb old steer, Papa, we didn't lose him."

"I know you did, son. And you're my good right arm on our ranch. So you've got to get better as soon as you can, because I couldn't run it without you."

"I'll try, Papa," Matty whispered. "I'll really—" A flicker of pain contorted his face and he slipped back into darkness.

Jonathan returned the boy to Rebecca. "Sam Houston's got a doctor with him in Gonzales. We'll get him there right away." He mounted his horse and lifted Suzannah into the saddle in front of him. They rode in silence, savoring each other's presence.

"Devroe Connaught," he said softly. "I thought we'd left him far behind."

"I did, too," Suzannah murmured. "But that this innocent child should be made to suffer because he hates us . . . I can't believe anybody could be that cruel."

"He's no better than a mad dog," he said. "And that's the way he should be treated. If ever I see him, I'll kill him on sight."

They reached Gonzales the following evening. Jonathan immediately reported to Sam Houston, and learned that Deaf Smith had just arrived with Mrs. Dickinson, her daughter Angelina, and the black slave Joe. Deaf Smith had found them while on his scouting expedition.

Then Jonathan took Matty to see Dr. Sutherland, and Rebecca and Suzannah accompanied him. The doctor examined Matty and said tersely, "Skull fracture. See this depression here? The bone is pressing in on his brain, and that's what's making him drift in and out of consciousness."

"Can you do anything about it?" Jonathan asked.

He shook his head. "Wish I could, but it'll take a better doctor than me. Tell you the truth, I don't know if such an operation's ever been done successfully."

"But there is hope, isn't there?" Suzannah asked.

The doctor turned away. "I can't tell you about things I don't know. Wouldn't be fair. I can only tell you that your boy isn't going to get better unless something's done to relieve the pressure on his brain. But where you can find a doctor who knows how to do that—" He shrugged helplessly.

"Wingate Grange," Rebecca whispered. "He saved Gunning's life."

But Wingate was thousands of miles away in Washington, D.C., and neither Suzannah nor Jonathan paid much attention to her.

Jonathan saw that Suzannah and the children were bedded down, then he said to Rebecca, "If you're not too tired, Sam Houston wants very much to talk to you."

Rebecca shrugged listlessly, and Jonathan led her to headquarters. When she entered the room, Houston rose to his feet and embraced her. "My God, Rebecca, Jonathan's told me what happened. I wish I could tell you how grieved I am." He offered her a chair and a snifter of brandy, which she drank. She made a face and almost gave the brandy back, but it did help revive her.

"Mrs. Dickinson told me what happened inside the Alamo," Houston said to her. "It would help if you could add anything, especially about Santa Anna."

Rebecca haltingly recounted all she knew. When Houston heard her describe the red flag, the *degüello*, and Santa Anna's order of "No quarter!" he began to weep.

"Why didn't you send help, Sam?" she asked softly. "We might have been able to beat them if Fannin had come with his men."

Houston hung his head in his hands. "When I learned that Jim Bowie had disregarded my order to blow up the Alamo, I did order Fannin to go to his relief. By God, Fannin's got four hundred men with rifles and ammunition! He started out, but then he turned back, claiming that he couldn't jeopardize Goliad for someplace as indefensible as the Alamo. The damned fool! But what good are recriminations? I'm the commander of the army, and the blame rests with me. This will be on my conscience for the rest of my life."

Rebecca looked at Houston through swimming eyes. "Sam, we've failed Andrew Jackson. I know you're here on his behalf, and so am I. But his dream of one day annexing Texas, Sam— that's gone."

Houston clenched and unclenched his fists. "There's only one thing worse than the murder Santa Anna committed at the Alamo, and that's if those men died in vain." Houston was weeping unashamedly now. "I swear that monster will answer for his crime."

Rebecca shook her head slowly. "Sam, you don't understand his strength. I saw it with my own eyes. He has over five thousand men, hundreds of the finest cavalrymen, huge supply trains of food and munitions. How many men do you have here? Three hundred at the most? From what I see, your army is made up of farmers and ranchers, who'd rather be working the land than fighting. Sam, *think*. You mustn't risk any more lives. If you try to fight him, he'll kill every last one of you."

Houston pondered what she was saying. Then roused into action, he sent for half a dozen couriers. "You're to ride to Fannin tonight. Tell him to abandon Goliad. He's to join us at the Colorado River." He sent the same message to Captain

Johnson at Aqua Dolce, Captain Grant at San Patricio, and Captain King at Refugio.

"Are we going to make a stand at the Colorado River?" Jonathan asked.

"I'll know better once Fannin and the others join us. But even then, we may not be strong enough to hold off Santa Anna's total force." He went to a map of Texas lying on the table. "Our scouts tell us that Santa Anna's sent General Urrea up along the coast. General Gaona will cut inland to Washington-on-the-Brazos, hoping to capture our government there. And then there's Santa Anna's large force at San Antonio."

He turned to Rebecca. "This is important. You said that Santa Anna has lost a lot of men, but how would you assess his ability to field his army?"

"I believe he's on his way here right now," Rebecca said. "That's what he told me—to kill every Texan he could find, and I believe him."

"Then we've got to abandon Gonzales," Houston said. "To-night."

The order to abandon Gonzales swept through the town like a prairie fire. The settlers loaded all their possessions into the wagons that Houston gave them from his army. Jonathan managed to get a separate wagon for his family, since the Kelleys' horses were being overtaxed with all the extra weight. Grumblings were heard from those who wanted to stay and fight, but the majority were anxious to avoid the fate of those who'd fallen at the Alamo.

"Santa Anna's done his job well," Rebecca whispered to Suzannah as their wagon rolled through the darkness.

"Mother, don't say such things," Suzannah chided her. "We're sure to lose everything if people think that way."

"But we have lost everything," she whispered, feeling the weight of Matty in her arms.

"I don't believe that," Suzannah said. "You mustn't believe it either. Where's the woman I know who went to fight at Baltimore? Where's the woman who used her pen as a mighty weapon? Mother, if ever there was a time when you were needed, this is it. Not your pessimism, but your conviction that we'll win because we're in the right. That's what I want to hear from my mother, or I don't want to hear anything at all."

Rebecca closed her eyes, trying to fight off the waves of anguish that engulfed her. She tried to hear what Suzannah was saying, but hardly recognized the woman her daughter was talking about. Had she really done all those things? Perhaps, but she could never do them again.

"The good Lord gave you certain gifts," Suzannah was saying. "If you don't use them in the causes you feel are just, then you aren't fulfilling your function as a human being. How many times have you told me that about my own life? The way you're acting now, you might just as well give up, retire to a rocking chair, and talk about your memories. But if you're the woman I know, the woman capable of reaching out and rousing men, then I say it's time you did just that. The child you're holding in your arms . . . you know how much I love him. But I'd say that you love him less if you don't work for his future. And his future is Texas. He was born on this soil, his blood has been spilled on this earth. This land is his. You can either sit there and bemoan your fate, or you can help him realize his."

The long line of wagons continued to roll out of town. The night air hung hot and oppressive, and complaints were heard all along the line. Houston's force of three hundred men brought up the rear, making sure that everybody was safely out of Gonzales.

Then, inexplicably, the sky in the west began to grow lighter, faint at first, but then glowing into a red glare.

"They're firing the town," Suzannah said, the firelight reflected on her face.

All the houses, stables, barns, stores—everything was being put to the torch to keep Santa Anna from using anything.

Jonathan rode up alongside the wagon. "How's Matty? Any change?"

Rebecca shook her head. "But his breathing is regular, and he doesn't seem to be in any pain."

Jonathan turned in his saddle and looked back at the burning town. "Houston's doing the right thing. Some people are saying we should stand and fight, but that's the mistake they made at the Alamo. Santa Anna outnumbers us by about twenty to one. Our only hope is to draw him deeper and deeper into Texas, away from his supply lines. Then we attack."

"I hope you're right," Suzannah murmured.

"We've got no other choice."

As Gonzales burned, the wagon train rolled east, carrying a message on the wind: Head east. That was the only place of safety, east, across the Louisiana border.

The new government at Washington-on-the-Brazos issued a proclamation saying, "There's no cause for panic," then immediately abandoned the town and headed east to the new capital of Harrisburg. All over the coastal plain of Texas, settlers pulled up stakes and joined the exodus, to get away from the wrath of Santa Anna.

CONCLUSION

Chapter 48

ON MARCH 17, the wagon train of settlers from Gonzales reached the Colorado River. Jonathan, who'd been out on a scouting foray, rode up to the wagon where his family huddled against the driving rain. "Everything's clear up ahead," he told them.

The wagons lined up along the riverbank to be ferried across by flatboats, keelboats, and rowboats. Many families didn't wait, but took their chances by plunging right into the river and floating their wagons across.

Jonathan hitched his horse to the side of the wagon and then climbed into the driver's seat beside Suzannah. "You're going to take us across, but then you're not coming with us, are you?" she said softly.

He shook his head. "We're going to wait at the Colorado for Fannin to join us with his four hundred men. That way, the odds will be a little better for us. We need to train our men, make a fighting unit out of them. Otherwise, they'll never be able to stand up to the Mexicans."

He flicked the reins and the horse moved forward, down the steep embankment into the swirling river. Becky and Zeb called out simultaneously, "The water's coming in, Papa."

"Move everything that can get ruined onto the shelf," Suzannah called to them. "Mother, are you all right?"

Rebecca answered that she was and made sure that the water didn't touch Matty.

When they finally reached the far side, the horse couldn't pull the wagon up over the muddy bank, and Jonathan got out and put his shoulder to the wheel. At last the wheels rolled free of the mud, and they moved beneath the protective cover of a stand of cottonwood trees.

"There's enough time for a meal before you push on," Jonathan said, and began to build a fire. Zeb and Becky gathered

wood without having to be told. Suzannah heated up some
refried beans and cubed meat, and they ate in silence. Matty
managed to swallow a few spoonfuls, but Rebecca thought it
was barely enough to keep him alive.

"Where will the wagon train be going?" Suzannah asked.

"Harrisburg," Jonathan told her. "If Santa Anna does come
that far, then the wagon master will take you on to Galveston.
I'll meet you there."

After their hasty meal, Suzannah said to her mother, "Do
you think you could take care of the children for a bit? Jonathan
and I . . ." She flushed with embarrassment.

"Of course," Rebecca said.

Jonathan and Suzannah rode off to a heavily wooded area
about a half mile away. The rain had stopped, and leaves and
pine needles shone a brilliant, washed green.

"That's the way it will be with us," Jonathan said. "A new
start, a new life."

He put his arms around her, and she lifted her mouth to his,
tasting the joy that had been denied her these many, many
weeks, feeling his strength and goodness, experiencing all the
things that had given her a happiness beyond her wildest hopes.

"I love you," she murmured. "I didn't know what living
was like until I met you, and without you . . . You must come
back to me."

"I will, I swear it."

She slipped out of her clothes, and he stripped off his. He
spread his saddle blanket and they lay down on it, feeling
tentative and tender, as if they were lying together for the first
time. Their lovemaking was edged with desperation, for death
lay all about them, and this was the surest way to reaffirm life.
They both moved to an unendurable peak and then crested.
They remained coupled, and then, reveling in the feel of each
other's flesh, they made love again, slowly this time, knowing
that if such a thing was possible, their spirits were in communion.

Afterwards, she dressed hurriedly and tried to smooth back
her hair. Without warning, great tears began to fall from her
eyes. Gently, he brushed them away from her face.

"Matty?" he asked.

She hung her head and nodded imperceptibly.

"We'll get him the best doctors there are. If I have to work
for the rest of my life to pay the bills, he'll have the best." He
held her until she cried herself out.

When they had returned to camp, Jonathan had a word with Zeb and Becky. "Now I've got to go away again, so you mind your Ma. Do whatever she says. Understand?"

Both Zeb and Becky nodded vigorously. Then Zeb blurted, "Papa, I didn't mean to lasso that dumb steer, honest."

Jonathan glanced at Matty, who'd fallen into a deep sleep, and then put his large bony hand on his son's shoulder. "I know that, Zeb. But you've got a devil in you that needs holding back. So take heed, boy. I don't want to hear that you've caused any trouble. Not even for one little moment. Do I have your word on that?"

Zeb toed the ground and nodded.

Then Jonathan took Matty from Rebecca's arms and tried to waken him, but the boy remained unresponsive. He held him close. "Matty, this is your Papa. I know you can hear me, I know it. You're just too scared to come back into the daylight. But it's all right. You're safe now. And you're going to get well." He kissed the boy and gave him to Suzannah. Then he took Rebecca's arm. "If I could have a word with you . . ." he said, and led her away from the wagon.

He studied his hands, not knowing where to begin, his difficulty patently obvious in his face. "You and I have had a lot of troubles in the past."

Rebecca started to interrupt, but Jonathan said, "Wait, let me finish. What's in the past is done, and there's nothing we can do to change it, or to make it any different. Now we've got to look forward to the future. A future for all of us. This land is a good land, and our life here has been a good life. It's worth fighting for. You understand that, don't you?"

"Yes."

"In the time you've been here, I've watched you with Suzannah and the children. I know you love them, maybe as much as I do. Maybe I was a little jealous of that. But I've come to understand that there's a lot of different kinds of love, and if my family can be warmed by your kind, then that's only going to enrich them. So, if I've caused you any pain, I apologize."

Caught completely off balance, Rebecca could only mumble some inanity.

Jonathan went on. "Now nothing's going to happen to me, because I'm indestructible. But then the good Lord might not realize that and have other plans for me," he finished with a slow grin. "I know I can count on you to give Suzannah whatever help she needs."

She reached for his arm and gripped it. "You must come back. Nobody can take your place here. I'm the one who should apologize, for being a blind, stupid old fool. Please, please, don't take any unnecessary chances. They all love you so much, and for such good reason."

He took her hand from his arm, held it for a moment, and then brought it to his lips and kissed it. "Goodbye, Mother."

With a running stride, Jonathan vaulted into his saddle. Suzannah came to stand with Rebecca, and put her arm around her. They watched Jonathan spur his horse and plunge back into the river. The swift current carried him downstream. Once a sawyer threatened to entangle him in its branches, but finally, he emerged on the west bank.

"Mount up!" came the call of the wagon master. "Moving out!" and the wagon train headed east again.

As they bumped along, Rebecca began to think; her thoughts continued to crowd in on her when she relieved Suzannah at the reins; when they stopped to make camp that night, she still couldn't free her mind.

Patrick Donohoe killed, the confrontation with Santa Anna, his ultimatum, the thunder of the cannon, and the deadly sinuous trumpet call of the *degüello* . . . "Death, no quarter," she whispered.

She had seen men tossed on the bayonets of Mexicans mad with bloodlust. All this she remembered. But most of all she heard Suzannah saying about Matty, "This is his land. He was born here, his blood was spilled on this earth. You can either sit there and bemoan your fate, or you can help him achieve his."

With a cry, Rebecca roused herself and went to the wagon. She rummaged in the back, found her portmanteau, took out her writing case and went back to the light of the fire. The flames flickered across the blank page as her pen screamed across the paper.

"Texas Needs Men!"

"Oh foul murder and rape of a land! What mine eyes have seen they shall relive in nightmares for the rest of my life. I shall always remember the Alamo. A vain pompous little general has taken it upon himself to be judge, jury, and executioner of every man, woman, and child in Texas. Is this some creature from our barbaric past? Some hunnish plunderer of Rome? Worse! This man claims to be the Napoleon of the West, and is none other than General Antonio López de Santa Anna, known to some as the President of Mexico, but who shall hereafter be known to all as the murderer of the gallant men at the Alamo.

"With mine own ears I heard him say that every American left in Texas would be mercilessly slaughtered. That these people who'd settled the country were now considered nothing less than traitors and would be put to the sword. Run away, he laughs at us, that's all that is left for us, to run away.

"A madman is loose on our continent. With mine own ears I heard him say that with five hundred seasoned troops he could march on Washington, D.C., and take it! Is this a leader we can tolerate at our very borders? Oh my fellow Americans, murder is like a contagion: unless it's stopped, it will spread where it can, and we will no longer live by the rule of law and order, which is surely the foundation of any democracy. It's up to each and every one of us to stop it. Again I say, Texas needs men!

"Santa Anna dreams of a Mexican empire stretching from the Mississippi River to the Pacific Ocean. To achieve this, he's prepared to slaughter anybody who stands in his way. I don't know if he's being supported by any foreign country in this despotic grab for power; I can only report that at the Alamo, I saw British arms and munitions everywhere. The rifles that killed Jim Bowie and Davy Crockett and William Travis were all made in England!

"I cannot believe that you, my fellow Texans, will submit to this terror. I cannot believe you will allow yourselves to be hounded from a land made green by your own labors. Now that you've made it flower, the dictator wants it back. Oh Santa Anna, if there is a just God in heaven, then surely he will call down the lightning, and as you have lived by the sword, so your downfall shall come by the sword, the sword of justice, of decency, of democracy.

"Texas needs men. Remember the Alamo. Join Sam Houston for Texas and liberty!"

When the wagon train reached San Felipe, Rebecca hurried to the offices of the *Telegraph and Texas Register*. But the editor had abandoned the offices, taking all his presses with him save an ancient, near-derelict one.

Rebecca went from wagon to wagon, shouting, "Does anybody here know how to work a printing press?" An hour later, she found an old man who'd had some typesetting experience in Natchez. He, Suzannah, and Rebecca spent all night printing up two thousand circulars. The ink was smudged on many of the sheets, and on others, the columns were awry, but the passions of Rebel Thorne burned on every page. Everybody in the wagon train and in San Felipe snatched them up.

A rider took copies to the provisional government in Harrisburg. There they were reprinted and other copies sent to Galveston and New Orleans, and from there they found their way all over America. A groundswell of outrage grew, and men, munitions, and money began to pour into Texas.

Chapter 49

At the Colorado River, Sam Houston, aided by his division commanders, drilled the men until they became something of a fighting force. Jonathan, acting as Houston's righthand man, seemed to be everywhere, out on scouting expeditions with Deaf Smith, helping Colonel Hockley reconnoiter for food, then spending long nights with Houston going over contingency plans.

To Jonathan's amazement, new recruits kept arriving every day; a few of them carried a pamphlet written by Rebel Thorne. But Houston's big hope, Fannin's force of four hundred men, hadn't yet arrived.

"When Fannin does get here, you'd do well to relieve him of his command," Jonathan said to Houston. "I warned you long ago about that man's indecision. That's about the best that I can call it."

Two more days passed, then four, and still Fannin didn't arrive. Then on March 25, a soldier straggled into Houston's camp, dead on his feet.

"Fannin's been captured," he blurted. Jonathan caught him as he collapsed.

They forced a couple of stiff swigs of bourbon down his throat, followed by a mug of hot coffee. When he revived, the soldier said, "Colonel Fannin got your orders, but delayed moving out because he said he wanted to help some ranchers. I think the real reason was that he felt safe in Goliad."

Jonathan bit back a comment.

"Fannin waited almost a week before he finally gave the order to march. We got a few miles out of Goliad, and then before we knew it, we were surrounded by General Urrea's cavalry."

Houston punched his forehead with his fist, swearing and cursing.

"Urrea sent Fannin a message saying that on February twenty-seventh, he'd surprised Captain Johnson at Agua Dolce, and killed or captured his entire force of a hundred men; on March seventh, he'd killed Captain Grant and his men at San Patricio; and on March sixteenth, he'd trapped Captain King at Refugio and wiped out his entire detachment."

Houston ran his fingers through his long dark hair. "Good God—Johnson, Grant, King, all gone."

The soldier nodded. "Urrea said that now it was our turn, and unless we surrendered, all of us would be killed."

Jonathan jumped to his feet. "Don't tell me that Fannin took General Urrea at his word?"

"We put up a halfhearted fight," the soldier whispered, "but Fannin . . . well . . . about twenty of us managed to break through the Mexican cavalry line. But Fannin and about four hundred men surrendered."

"By God, when I get my hands on Fannin, I'll have him courtmartialed!" Houston swore.

"Fannin's got a whole lot more to worry about than a court-martial," Jonathan said. "You heard Santa Anna's decree— Kill every American in Texas."

"Urrea wouldn't dare!" Houston exclaimed. "Those men are prisoners of war, and are entitled to be treated as such." He began to pace the confines of the tent. "Without Fannin's men, we can't make a stand here at the Colorado. Jonathan, pass the word. We're moving on."

On the evening of March 26, Houston's small force retreated again. They crossed the Colorado River, then made sure to destroy every rowboat, flatboat, and canoe they could find.

Houston kept them at a forced march, and on March 31, they reached Groce's, on the Brazos River. "We'll rest here," Houston said. "We can regroup, and wait for any new recruits to join us."

The Brazos River was about three hundred feet wide at this point, the landscape a gently rolling plain, the waters of the river a muddy red. Cottonwood and cedar trees lined the steep banks, along with purple sage and mesquite.

For ten days the men rested and drilled. Here they received horrifying news. On March 27, Palm Sunday, General Urrea had divided Fannin's captured men into groups of fifty, and then marched them out of camp. They thought they were going to be freed, and one of the men played "Home Sweet Home" on his flute. But when they got out into the plain, the men found themselves looking down the barrels of Mexican guns. Realizing they were about to be shot, some broke from the ranks and tried to attack their captors with bare hands; others stood with arms folded, and received the mortal gunshots with stoic calm. All were killed.

Santa Anna immediately circulated news of the massacre, hoping to further intimidate the Texans remaining in the territory. It worked, for there wasn't one of the eighteen thousand settlers who didn't believe that it was time to leave. Santa Anna was a madman, and invincible.

Only Houston remained firm. "We'll beat him," he said to Jonathan. "Though the odds be twenty to one against us, or even fifty to one, we'll beat him."

"General, we've got to make some battle plans," Jonathan said.

But Houston shook his head. "No, not tonight. I need to be alone, to think." Then he retired to his tent to spend the dark hours poring over Caesar's *Commentaries*.

Daily, Houston's scouts brought messages of Santa Anna's movements. On April 2, he'd reached Gonzales, and found nothing in the burned out town to nourish himself or his army. Pressing on, he'd crossed the Colorado on April 5, and captured the abandoned town of San Felipe on April 7.

When news reached Houston's camp that Santa Anna was at San Felipe and making plans to cross the Brazos River, Houston ordered his force to break camp and move on. The steamer *Yellow Stone* chugged down from Washington-on-the-Brazos and spent all of April 12, and 13, ferrying Houston's men across the river. The *Yellow Stone* also brought Houston the gift from the people of Cincinnati—two six-pound cannon.

Houston was delighted with the cannon and took Jonathan aside. "You and I are the only ones who've had any experience with these things. Do you think you can put together an artillery unit?"

"Probably. Only trouble is, we're so low on ammunition that we won't be able to practice," Jonathan said. "But I'll do the best I can. And say a little prayer besides."

On April 14, Santa Anna's army marched south from San Felipe to Thompson's Ferry. There they captured a flatboat and managed to establish a foothold on the east bank of the Brazos. For Santa Anna was now determined to administer the coup de grâce. All the officials of the new Texas government

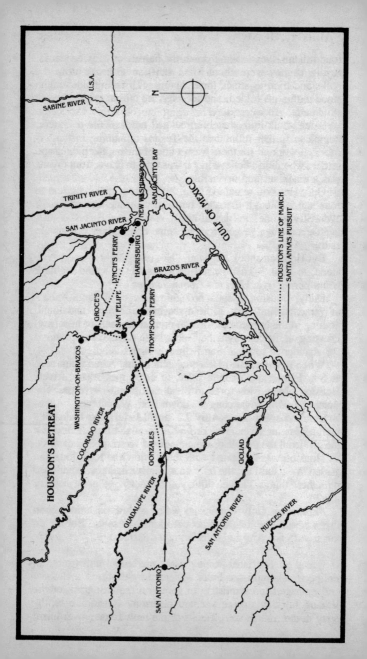

were at Harrisburg, less than thirty miles away. If he could surprise them, he could crush the rebellion with one blow.

Santa Anna began the mad dash to Harrisburg; under his command he had a thousand infantrymen, fifty cavalry, and a six-pound cannon. Just before midnight on April 15, Santa Anna invaded Harrisburg, but with the exception of a few Mexicans, he found the town deserted.

He cursed and swore in his disappointment. He picked up one of Rebel Thorne's leaflets, which were all over the town, and Devroe Connaught read it to him. Santa Anna's face turned an apoplectic red.

"I warned you to execute her when you had the chance," Devroe said. He touched his right eye gingerly. It was just beginning to heal, and mercifully, he was getting the vision back in it. But for the past month, he had feared he was going to lose it.

"If ever I catch that woman again, she will pay dearly," Santa Anna muttered.

The following day, informers paid by Devroe Connaught brought him news that Houston was upriver, at Groce's, and was heading east for Lynch's Ferry at San Jacinto.

"Houston is an even more valuable prize than the silly little officials of Texas," Devroe told Santa Anna. "Crush him and his army, and you'll snuff out every last bit of organized resistance. All you need to do is reach San Jacinto first, then let Houston fall into your trap."

Santa Anna studied the map and nodded. He told an aide, "Send word to General Cos to join us at the San Jacinto as quickly as possible. He has five hundred men, and along with my thousand troops, that will insure our victory. This time, we'll wipe them out totally. The same rules apply as before, no quarter!"

While out on a scouting expedition, Jonathan and Deaf Smith captured two Mexicans. They were couriers for Santa Anna, and when they were brought to Houston, they quite freely told him everything they knew. They were positive that he would be overwhelmed by what was about to happen to him, that he would surrender without a fight.

Houston called a meeting of his top aides. "Santa Anna is heading this way, hoping to cut us off before we reach Lynch's Ferry at the San Jacinto. He's got a thousand men with him.

Well, hell, with our new recruits, we've now got seven hundred men. I'd say that was pretty fair odds. If we can engage Santa Anna before he's joined by General Cos and his force, then I'd say we had a pretty fair chance of dealing him a crushing blow."

That night, camped just to the northwest of Buffalo Bayou and Vince's Bridge, Houston dictated a manifesto to his army. The men had been waiting for this since they'd started this retreat in mid-March.

"This morning, we are in preparation to meet Santa Anna. It is the only chance of saving Texas. From time to time I have looked for reinforcements in vain. We have only about seven hundred men to march with, besides the camp guard. We go to conquer. It is wisdom growing out of necessity to meet the enemy now; every consideration enforces it. No previous occasion would justify it . . . I leave the results in the hands of a wise God, I rely on his Providence. My country will do justice to those who serve her. The rights for which we fight will be secured, and Texas freed."

When Houston read it to Jonathan for his comments Jonathan broke into a wide grin. "Sam, I believe with all my heart that you're making the right decision."

Houston managed a smile also. "Santa Anna has a thousand men; his General Sesma at Thompson's Ferry has another thousand; Filasola has eighteen hundred more, and Gaona, who's near Batrop, has two whole battalions. If we allow them to join forces, then we have no chance at all. We've got to strike while we have Santa Anna isolated from the rest of his generals, hit him even before General Cos can reach him."

"Do you know what this will mean to our men, to be able to fight at last?" Jonathan said. "For the past month we've done nothing but run away. In fact, the men are calling this the Runaway Scrape. We've been running and hiding with our tails between our legs, but now, suddenly, we've become the pursuers."

Houston nodded soberly. "When Santa Anna decided to take Harrisburg, that was his fatal mistake. In his greed, he's put himself *east* of us, cutting himself off from his main force. Now we must capitalize on that. This may be the piece of luck we've been praying for."

Chapter 50

ON APRIL 18, Houston's force reached Buffalo Bayou and made camp. Just about nightfall, Jonathan and Deaf Smith returned from a scouting foray and burst into Houston's tent. "Santa Anna and about a thousand of his troops are less than eight miles ahead of us!" Jonathan exclaimed. "They've just crossed Vince's Bridge. Do you realize what that means? We do have him cut off from the other units in his army!"

All night long, Houston planned his attack. Just before dawn, he himself rapped out reveille on the big bass drum. "Men, Jonathan Albright and Deaf Smith have brought us news I think you'll want to hear."

The news electrified the men in the battalion. One of the men shouted, "This is our chance to avenge Travis, Bowie, and Crockett!"

Houston raised his hands to still them. "You'd best know something about what we plan to do. I know I've kept my own counsel up to now, and I know that many of you have resented it. But if I erred, then it was my fault, and nobody else's. Well, now Santa Anna is cut off. If he wants to rejoin the main force of the Mexican army, he's got to come back either by Lynch's Ferry or by the bridge over Vince's Bayou. From where we are now, we can get to either of those points before he can."

The enormity of the change in their fortune swept over the men as Houston shouted, "Victory is certain! Trust in God and fear not. And remember the Alamo!"

The men repeated it among themselves, and the call erupted into a wild shout as they broke ranks to get ready. The sick and the wounded, and all the superfluous baggage would stay behind to keep from hindering the army's mobility. The two six-pound cannon that had come on the *Yellow Stone* were hitched to horses. Everybody who was able grabbed his rifle

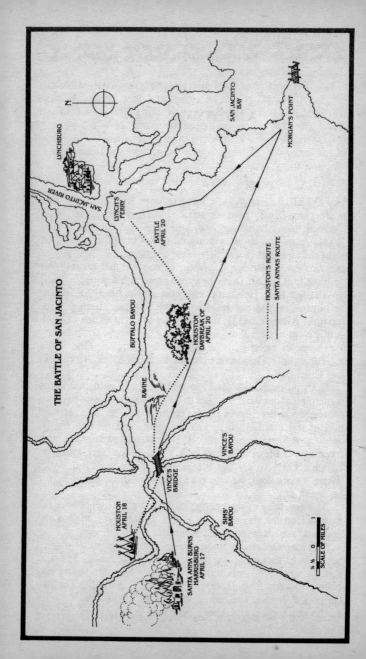

THE BATTLE OF SAN JACINTO

and haversack, and began the double-time march east, now chasing Santa Anna.

All day long Houston's men marched; they crossed Buffalo Bayou, then continued east again until they crossed Vince's Bridge late that night. Once over the bridge they saw evidence of the Mexican camp, including dead fires.

"I wish the moon weren't so bright," Jonathan said to Houston. "True, we can see where we're going, but Santa Anna's scouts can see us too."

At two a.m. Houston ordered the men to fall out and catch some sleep. "It won't help if we're too tired to fight when we finally do reach Santa Anna."

At dawn they were on their way again. They stopped at seven in the morning to eat, but just then they were spotted by a Mexican patrol, who galloped off.

"Damn!" Houston swore. "They'll be off now to warn Santa Anna. We've lost the element of surprise."

"I say go after him anyway," Jonathan said. "You'll never have a moment like this again. Our men are so ready to take the bastard on, they'll fight like ten. But if we backtrack again, we'll lose our momentum."

Houston nodded. "Forward, men!"

When the Mexican patrol brought the news of Houston's presence to Santa Anna, he immediately understood the implications of what was happening and gave orders to march for Lynch's Ferry. Now it was a race to see who would get to the San Jacinto first, who would be first to pick the most strategic position for the upcoming battle.

Houston's men were bone-weary and gasping for breath, but they reached Lynch's Ferry just bare hours before Santa Anna's army. Houston and Jonathan went out and reconnoitered the land. An old Indian fighter, Houston wasn't bound by the European battle strategies Santa Anna espoused, and he set up his force at the edge of a heavily wooded area at the confluence of the San Jacinto River and Buffalo Bayou. The trees would shade them from the heat of the sun, and also give them some protection should the Mexican cavalry come charging.

The men were given the order to fall out and eat; cattle were slaughtered, but before the meat could be cooked, the advance guard of the Mexican army came into view. Everybody scrambled to his position, taking shelter behind the trees.

Jonathan held up his spyglass. "They're not wasting any time—their cavalry's deploying for battle." He knew this would be the moment of truth for the Texans; would the ragged bunch be able to withstand the power of the Mexican army, or would they break and run?

Lieutenant Joe Neill, whom Jonathan had put in command of the two cannon—affectionately dubbed the Twin Sisters—aimed them at the advancing Mexican line. The cannon had never been fired, ammunition was far too scarce and far too valuable to waste. Would they work? everybody wondered. The six-pounders were loaded with scrap iron, cut mainly from old horseshoes and nails.

Across the prairie the Mexican infantry came, hip-deep in the prairie grass. Supporting them rode the cavalry, their lances held at the ready, the sun glistening off the burnished armor of their helmets and breastplates.

Jonathan looked around at his own ragtag men. If a battle were to be decided on looks, the Mexicans would win this one hands down. But there was something more important than appearance, the knowledge that unless they won today, there would never be a free Texas.

When the Mexicans reached a point about three hundred yards from the American line, they halted. The infantry deployed to the right, the cavalry to the left, and both prepared to charge.

"First battery, fire!" Jonathan shouted, and Neill complied.

The deadly shot whistled across the plain and sliced through the Mexican lines. Houston's men sent up a great cheer.

"Half a dozen of their men are down," Jonathan said. "And wait—I think we've hit their gun carriage!"

The Mexicans fired their cannon anyway, but with the carriage disabled, the shot whistled harmlessly overhead. A salvo from the second of the Twin Sisters ripped into the Mexican ranks. Then the Texas marksmen opened fire and their fusillade cut through the Mexican infantry.

Seeing that his troops were vulnerable in this exposed position, Santa Anna ordered a retreat. He gathered up his dead and wounded, and he pitched camp close to the banks of the San Jacinto River, less than a mile away from where Houston was camped.

Santa Anna chose his spot with care: a hillside with water at the rear, heavy woods on his right as far as the banks of the river, open plains to the left so that any attack from that quarter could be detected, and most important, a clear open front, across which he built a barricade of brambles. He'd followed every rule of military strategy. He felt content.

Houston, greatly relieved that the Twin Sisters had fired and that his men had aquitted themselves so well, pulled his forces back into the shelter of the woods. He set up a strong advance guard around his camp, then gave his men leave to eat. It was the first meal they'd had in more than twenty-four hours, and they attacked it ravenously.

That night, both the Texan and the Mexican camps settled down to sleep, each knowing that the fate of Texas would be decided that next day. But Santa Anna knew something that Houston didn't.

Devroe Connaught had just informed him that General Cos and his five hundred men were on their way to join them.

"I expect Cos to arrive by morning," Devroe said.

"Excellent! With a force double that of the Texans, I will crush these perfidious rebels once and for all," Santa Anna exclaimed. "I swear, not one of them will be left alive!"

Chapter 51

AT FOUR in the morning of April 21, Jonathan wakened to hear the drum roll of reveille. Sam Houston stood at the drum, beating the slow call.

Jonathan, Deaf Smith, and Colonel Hockley joined Houston for breakfast, a skimpy meal of beef, biscuits gone stale, and coffee that was more hot water than anything else.

"Bad news," Deaf Smith said. "My scouts just came in; they report that General Cos is on his way from Harrisburg. He should be joining Santa Anna sometime before the morning is over."

"Well, at least they'll be exhausted from their all-night march," Jonathan said.

Houston punched his palm slowly. "Cos or not, today Texas will either truly become a nation, or we'll all suffer the fate of the men at the Alamo."

After a silence Jonathan said, "I think we ought to chop down the bridge at Vince's Landing. That way, when we do rout them, none of the Mexicans will be able to escape."

"Good thinking," Houston said. "Deaf, take a couple of men and chop down that bridge. Let me know when it's done."

Deaf nodded and slipped away. Now the issue was joined; if the Mexicans couldn't escape, neither could the Texans.

In the predawn darkness, Houston checked his positions. On his left, the riverbank of the San Jacinto teemed with the men of the Second Regiment under Lieutenant Colonel Sherman. Next to them were the New Orleans Grays, the only company with any semblance of a uniform. Supporting these regiments were the reserves of Colonel Rusk, the secretary of war of the new Texas nation. In the woods, hidden and protected, stood the Twin Sisters, affectionately patted by every man in the army for luck. Neill had been wounded the day before, and Jonathan put Colonel Hockley in charge of the fieldpieces, along with a contingent of ten hand-picked men.

"What's the latest count on the number of men we can field?" Houston asked Jonathan.

"Seven hundred and eighty-three," he said. "From what we can estimate, when General Cos joins Santa Anna, he'll have more than fifteen hundred men."

"Then they outnumber us two to one," Houston said, then added with a grim smile, "I'd say those odds were just about right."

Satisfied that for the moment he could do no more, Houston went back to sleep and didn't waken until the sun had fully risen. The dew lay on the grass, the sun shone with increasing brightness. It looked as though it was going to be an unseasonably warm day.

Houston put on his fringed buckskin jacket, then his face all but disappeared as he donned his wide-brimmed hat with its jaunty feather.

Suddenly they heard a great shout from the Mexican camp. Jonathan peered through his spyglass. "It's what we feared, General Cos just joined Santa Anna. They're dancing a jig in that camp."

"Never mind," Houston said. "We'll have them dancing a different jig by the end of the day."

The sun climbed higher in the sky, and still Houston didn't move.

"What's he waiting for?" one of the cavalry officers demanded, and that question quickly made the rounds of the men.

At noontime, Houston gave the order to feed the men. They sat in the shade of the wood and ate. Some wondered whether or not this might be their last meal, but nobody said anything; it was bad luck even to think such a thing.

Houston barked another order: "Fill the canteens!" It would be a long, hard, hot fight, and the army more fully prepared stood the better chance of winning.

By two o'clock the sun stood at its zenith and the prairie baked under its rays; insects and animals sought the shade to escape the burning rays.

In the Mexican camp, optimism over the upcoming battle ran high. There being no movement at all from the enemy, Santa Anna agreed to let his cavalry rest, and feed and water their horses. By three o'clock, a torpor lay over the Mexican camp; the sentries, used to a midday siesta, lolled in the grass, or faced away from the Texans' camp, since it lay directly in the sun. Sam Houston had chosen his campsite with great care.

At three-thirty, Houston mounted his white stallion and called to an aide, "Pass the order to form for parade. But no noise!"

Officers went silently from company to company, giving the order. The Twin Sisters were jammed full of scrap iron and powder. The fifty-three men of the cavalry company mounted, and since he had a horse, Jonathan joined that group.

By four o'clock the men were ready, primed for the hair-trigger call to charge. Jonathan looked down the ranks, feeling the pride huge in his chest. Men from more than twenty states in America were represented in this army, men bound by a common cause, the cause of freedom. He remembered Rebecca's admonition, "Be careful, don't take any chances." And he would be careful. More than anything, he wanted to live in this wondrous country, and with Suzannah at his side, carve out a future for themselves and the children. But before that could happen . . .

Under the cover of the wood, Houston's entire force moved forward until they were at the fringe of the forest. Ahead of them, just to the south, lay the Mexican camp.

"Don't fire until the general gives the word," Jonathan told the cavalry. "He wants to take them by surprise."

All eyes were on Houston as he sat on his white horse. Then he shouted, "Men, forward! And remember the Alamo!"

The shout went up as the advancing line started to run across the prairie, the men's hearts beating in cadence to the call, "Remember the Alamo!" It reverberated in the beat of their feet against the earth, it hardened their resolve until they were more than just men running, they were avenging angels.

The American cry roused the few dozing Mexican sentries; they sounded the alarm frantically, but everybody was still at siesta.

Jonathan and the galloping cavalry swung wide to the right to outflank the Mexican camp. To their amazement, no enemy cavalry answered their challenge. "Can they all be asleep?" Jonathan shouted to the wind. Then he caught sight of the Mexican horses, grazing and unsaddled.

About two hundred yards from the flimsy barricade erected by the Mexicans to protect their frontal approach, Houston ordered the artillery to halt. With a mighty roar, the Twin Sisters fired, and the grape shot and shrapnel tore gaping holes in the barricade. Quickly the cannons were reloaded and fired again, and then again.

Now the American infantry came running through the tall prairie grass, faster, faster, but still holding their fire so as not to waste a shot. Some Mexican sentries took cover behind the barricades and began shooting, but fear and surprise made their shots go wide of the mark.

"Hold your fire, men!" Houston shouted as he led the charge. Suddenly his horse took a bullet in the chest, reared, and fell over, and Houston barely managed to scramble away.

Seeing him fall, Jonathan wheeled his own horse. He extended his arm and Houston vaulted into the saddle, still shouting, "Hold your fire until I command!"

The men raced forward, so close now that they could make out the faces of the Mexicans who were stumbling out of their tents, pulling up their pants. At about fifty yards from the barricade, Houston slid off Jonathan's horse and ran forward, a pistol in one hand, a knife in the other.

"Fire!" he shouted. "Fire—and remember the Alamo!"

Jonathan went leaping over the barricade, while other Americans swarmed through the breaches made by the Twin Sisters. Jonathan searched every face, looking to find Devroe Connaught. But he was nowhere in sight.

Mexican officers were shouting, and soldiers were shouting back, as they were inundated by the charging Texans. Most of General Cos's men, exhausted from their all-night march, were too befuddled to fight effectively. Not a bullet was wasted as the Texans fired, reloaded on the run, and fired again, all the time screaming, "Remember the Alamo!"

The battle turned into a rout, as the Mexicans gave way before the great scythe. The Texans fired their pistols at point-blank range, then went after the fleeing Mexicans with their rifles, clubbing them down.

Even if Santa Anna's army hadn't been caught asleep, there would have been no stopping these Texans, for they fought with more than guns and munition, they fought to avenge a frightful wrong to humanity itself, and justice fought alongside them.

Overwhelmed by the fury of the charge, many Mexicans fell to their knees and pleaded, *"Me no Alamo! Me no Alamo!"*

In less than eighteen minutes, it was all over.

As the firing died away, Houston limped slowly to where Jonathan was standing with Colonel Hockley. Jonathan noticed that blood was running from a hole in Houston's boot. During the heat of the battle he'd been shot, but had paid no attention to his wound.

Just as he reached Jonathan, Houston pitched forward. Jonathan and Hockley carried him into Santa Anna's tent and laid him on a pallet covered with fresh clean linen. Jonathan cut away the boot and inspected the wound. "The bullet's passed clear through the flesh just above the ankle," he said. "Don't worry, Sam, you'll be dancing in no time at all."

The rest of that afternoon and far into the night, the hunt for the remains of Santa Anna's force went on. Jonathan continued to search for Devroe, but if he had been with Santa Anna, he was nowhere to be found now. Santa Anna himself had vanished.

Houston recovered sufficiently for Jonathan to give him a report. "I've checked with the division commanders. In all, we suffered eight killed and twenty-five wounded."

"And the Mexicans?" Houston asked.

"Six hundred and thirty-two killed, including one general, four colonels, two lieutenant colonels, five captains, and twelve lieutenants. In addition they suffered two hundred and eight wounded."

"How many prisoners?" Houston asked.

"The count is over five hundred now," Jonathan said. "Very few escaped."

"Santa Anna?"

Jonathan shook his head.

"Damn," Houston muttered. "That would have made the victory complete."

"We also captured a fine supply of arms," Jonathan said. "Over nine hundred muskets. Incidentally, my mother-in-law was right—they're all English-made."

"That should tell us something about England's plans for this territory," Houston said.

"There are also three hundred sabers, two hundred pistols, four hundred mules and horses, along with tents and provisions. We've captured enough to outfit an entire army for Texas. Santa Anna was also carrying twenty-four thousand silver pesos with him, probably to pay off his troops after they won this battle."

"I'd say it was a good day's work," Houston said, grinning.

Jonathan's smile was tempered by the fact that both Devroe Connaught and Santa Anna had eluded him.

• • •

That night, hardly any of the Texans slept as they told and retold the battle of San Jacinto. For here along the river named after Saint Hyacinthe, the holy man martyred by fire, they knew that they'd avenged the shame of the Alamo, and had won the war for Texas.

The following morning, a Texan soldier brought in a prisoner wearing a faded blue cotton jacket and red worsted slippers. "I found him near Vince's Bridge. He had a mighty fine-looking black horse with him. He couldn't get across the bayou because we'd chopped down the bridge. The man claims he's just an ordinary soldier."

"Wearing red worsted slippers?" Jonathan asked. Recalling Rebecca's description of her first meeting with Santa Anna, Jonathan played a hunch, and walked the man past the ranks of the Mexican prisoners.

Several of them jumped to their feet and called out, "El Presidente, el Presidente!"

Jonathan felt a surge of rage so strong that it was all he could do to keep from killing the man right there. "Take him to Houston!" he barked.

Santa Anna was brought into the tent which had been his but was now occupied by Houston. The Mexican general immediately assumed an imperial manner, stating that Houston was very lucky to have captured the Napoleon of the West. He demanded adequate accommodations, demanded—

Houston's bellow of anger almost knocked Santa Anna over. "You're nothing but a common murderer, and you'll be treated as such!" Santa Anna was led away and put under guard.

"What are you going to do with him?" Jonathan asked. "Try him?"

Houston shook his head. "No, we're still too young a country to risk another confrontation with Mexico. Maybe I'll send him to Washington as a prisoner of war, but that depends on Andrew Jackson. Mostly I'm thinking that if we can get him to acknowledge Texas as a free and independent nation, it will buy us enough time to pull this country together."

Then Houston raised himself on the pallet and extended his hand to Jonathan. "We did it, Jonathan. We won."

Chapter 52

WHEN THE city of Harrisburg had fallen to Santa Anna, and it appeared that the Mexican general would conquer all of Texas, Suzannah, Rebecca, Enoch, and the children, along with hundreds of other settlers, had pushed on to Galveston.

They were in that crowded port when news of Houston's tremendous victory reached them. For days, a wild celebration erupted in the city, spilling from the taverns and houses into the streets. Texas was free! Texas was theirs!

Suzannah's joy was tempered by the fact that she'd taken Matty to every reputable doctor in Galveston, and they'd all confirmed what Doctor Sutherland had told her. An operation might be possible, but it would require such knowledge and expertise that none of them were equipped to handle it.

At the end of April, Jonathan rode into Galveston and searched out his family in the teeming city. When he saw Matty, his heart dropped. The boy had lost a great deal of weight and seemed far more fragile than he had a month before.

"We're losing him," he murmured to Suzannah. "He's just drifting away from us."

Then Rebecca spoke up, giving voice to a plan she'd been formulating for weeks. "You must let me take him to Washington with me. I tell you, Wingate's a genius." She went on to describe the operation he'd performed to save Gunning's life. "If we leave Matty as he is, he's just going to pine away. Oh, please, at least give him a chance at life."

They talked about it long into the night, and finally, Rebecca persuaded them that they had no other recourse.

"I should go with you," Suzannah said to her mother.

"But you have so much to do here," Rebecca said. "Taking care of Jonathan and Zeb and Becky, rebuilding the ranch, and your life. And Matty's recuperation may take a long time. You mustn't be away that long."

"She's right," Jonathan said to Suzannah. Then he turned to Rebecca. "But I don't like you traveling alone. Suppose you took Enoch with you?"

"That's a wonderful idea," Rebecca said. "I trust him, and I know he cares for Matty."

The following day, Rebecca booked passage on a steamboat sailing to New York via Baltimore. "In two weeks I'll be back in Washington," she told Suzannah. "I'll have Wingate examine him at once. Oh, you don't know the wonderful advances they're making in medicine. I'll write to you as soon as I know anything."

When Rebecca said goodbye to Zeb and Becky she thought her heart would break. "I want to go too," Zeb said.

"Of course you'll come visit me, and soon," Rebecca said, kissing him. "You've got two homes now, one in Texas and one in Washington."

Becky looked at her grandmother with her clear, large eyes. "I'm not going to forget anything you told me. Not even when you're gone."

"Good girl," Rebecca said.

"You make sure to send Matty back," Becky said.

"I will."

Enoch carried Matty up the gangplank. Rebecca kissed Suzannah goodbye, hugged Jonathan fiercely, and then boarded the boat. The whistle rent the air, the paddlewheels turned, and the boat carefully made its way through the sandbars and out to sea.

For Rebecca, the trip seemed interminable, her mind racing with so many things she had to do once back in Washington. See Wingate first, of course, but after that, go to Andrew Jackson and give him her firsthand account. And certainly expose Devroe Connaught. That would give her the greatest of pleasure.

Two weeks later, the boat docked in Baltimore. Rather than take the stage to Washington, a bumpy and tedious journey, Rebecca decided to book passage on a small packet boat that still ran between Baltimore and Georgetown.

"It will take a day or two longer than the stage," she told Enoch, "but I think that Matty fares better when he isn't jostled around so much." Giving Enoch detailed directions, Rebecca sent him ahead to Washington by stage coach with a message for Bravo. He was to meet her at Georgetown when the packet boat arrived.

When she transferred boats, she didn't notice Sisley Urquhart, Devroe Connaught's man, prowling the docks, watching her every move. Devroe, who'd carefully checked the boat schedule for arrivals from Galveston and New Orleans, had stationed him there for just this possibility.

Sisley Urquhart rode hard for the Connaught plantation.

Devroe was sitting with Véronique, playing with his new son, Carleton Connaught. During the months he'd been in Texas, Véronique had produced another male heir; the child looked so much like Devroe that it was uncanny.

When Sisley arrived and told Devroe the news, he turned pale. "Confound it! This is going to make things deucedly embarrassing for me. And that boy is still alive too? I can't believe it."

"What is the worst that could happen?" Véronique asked, thrown into a state of agitation herself.

"She could report me to Jackson. Other than her, nobody knows of my activities in Texas."

"Without question, she will say something," Véronique said. "But even if she does, you've committed no crime against the United States. Texas is an independent nation."

"True enough," he said, taking some small comfort in that legal technicality. "But once she exposes me, my entire operation here will be defunct. All these years of working—ruined because of that meddlesome old bitch." He thought for a moment, "Then, of course, there's the boy."

"Can she prove you had anything to do with his condition?"

He pondered that. "Technically, no, because we were alone. So it would be my word against hers. But she does have powerful friends here in Washington. It's entirely conceivable that our position could be ruined."

"*Tiens!*" Véronique exclaimed, now really alarmed. "Well, it seems to me that you have only one recourse. An old woman who's well past her prime? How can her life compare to all that we have to lose?"

"I see we're of a mind. But there must be absolutely no hint of my complicity in whatever happens. Suspicion would automatically fall on me."

"To be sure. But there are ways."

"You have an idea then?"

She tossed back her hair, and her wide dark eyes seemed to grow even larger. "Yes. It will be difficult, but if done well, it will be foolproof. Listen."

As she outlined her plan, Devroe's face creased into a smile. "I knew I made the right decision when I married you! What you propose means that the boy will die also, of course."

"From what Sisley said, he's half-dead already."

"That's right."

"The death of somebody who's already half-vegetable will be of little consequence to the world. We must protect the fortunes of our own children."

In a rare display of affection, he kissed her on the cheek. "When do you propose to leave?"

"Immediately," she said. "You have the name of the packet boat she's on and the time it docks?"

"Yes."

"Excellent. I think I can safely say that Rebecca Breech Brand will not reach Washington alive."

Selected Bibliography

For a more complete bibliography on Washington, D.C., the White House, and the earlier Presidents, please see the listings in Book 1 of this series, *Bless This House*.

The Presidents

Borden, Morton. *America's Ten Greatest Presidents*. Chicago: Rand McNally, 1961.

Frank, Sid, and Arden Davis Melick. *The Presidents: Tidbits and Trivia*. Maplewood, N. J.: Hammond, 1982.

Jackson

Boardman, Fon W., Jr. *America and the Jacksonian Era, 1825–1850*. New York: Henry Z. Walck, 1975.

Coke, Fletch. *Andrew Jackson's Hermitage*. Hermitage, Tenn.: The Ladies' Hermitage Assoc., 1979.

Davis, Burke. *Old Hickory*. New York: Dial, 1977.

Remini, Robert V. *Andrew Jackson and the Course of American Empire, 1767–1821*. New York: Harper and Row, 1977.

Remini, Robert V. *Andrew Jackson and the Course of American Freedom, 1822–1832*. New York: Harper and Row, 1981.

Washington, D. C.

Applewhite, E. J. *Washington Itself*. New York: Knopf, 1981.

Babb, Laura Longley. *The Washington Post Guide to Washington*. New York: McGraw-Hill, 1978.

Davis, Deering; Stephen P. Dorsey; and Ralph Cole Hall. *Georgetown Houses, 1780–1830*. New York: Bonanza Books, 1944.

Delany, Kevin: *A Walk through Georgetown*. Washington, D.C.: Kevin Delany, 1971.

Froncek, Thomas. *The City of Washington*. New York: Knopf, 1981.

Texas

Armstrong, O.K. *The Fifteen Decisive Battles of the United States*. New York: David McKay, 1961.

Coleman, Ann Raney. *Victorian Lady on the Texas Frontier*. Norman, Okla.: University of Oklahoma Press, 1971.

Lord, Walter. *A Time to Stand*. New York: Pocketbooks, 1963.

Phelan, Richard. *Texas Wild*. McGregor, Tex.: Excalibur, 1976.

Tinkle, Lon. *The Alamo*. New York: Signet, 1958.

Welch, June Rayfield. *Historic Sites of Texas*. Dallas: G.L.A. Press, 1972.

Miscellaneous

Adams, James T. *Album of American History*, vols. 1–5. New York: Scribner's, 1949.

Brierly, J. Ernest. *The Streets of Old New York*. New York: Hastings House, 1953.

Jessup, John E., and Robert W. Coakley. *A Guide to the Study and Use of Military History*. Washington, D.C.: U.S. Government Printing Office, 1979.

Nye, Russel Blaine. *The Cultural Life of the New Nation, 1776–1830*. New York: Harper and Row, 1960.

Phillips, Leon. *That Eaton Woman*. Barre, Mass.: Barre Publishing, 1974.

THE AMERICAN PALACE

As rich, as proud and fully as passionate as the
magnificent history on which it is based

VALIANT HEARTS

by

Evan H. Rhodes

is the third in a monumental new series from
the pen of a major American novelist, telling
the story of our country's beginnings.

Watch for the fourth book in
The American Palace series,

coming next spring...

I love this country. I love its people, and I cherish its political form of government. When I began to work on *The American Palace* series, I naturally expected to be fascinated by Washington and its political intrigues, fascinated by the Presidents and their families who had occupied the White House—our American Palace. But what I discovered beggared any of my expectations.

Along with my research in Washington, I also set out across America and traveled more than ten thousand miles gathering material. In one such journey I followed the Lewis and Clark Expedition, by car, horseback, canoe, and foot. What I learned in my travels reaffirmed my belief in the basic goodness of our people.

My hope for this series is that it will effectively portray some of the magnificence of our heritage, and perhaps indicate an even greater magnificence in our future. I believe it can be ours if we but remain true to the dreams and aspirations of our forefathers.